BERING

BERING

Edward John Crockett

POLYGON
EDINBURGH

First published in Great Britain in 2004 by
Polygon, an imprint of Birlinn Ltd
West Newington House
10 Newington Road
Edinburgh
EH9 1QS

www.birlinn.co.uk

ISBN 1 90459811 0

British Library Cataloguing-in-Production Data
A catalogue record for this book is available on request from the
British Library

Typeset by Palimpsest Book Production Limited,
Polmont, Stirlingshire
Printed and Bound by Creative Print and Design,
Ebbw Vale, Wales

FOR SHEILA

CONTENTS

Bering Sea and Strait

Russian: *Beringovo More* and *Proliv Beringa*
Northernmost part of the Pacific Ocean, separating the continents of Asia and North America. To the north the Bering Sea connects with the Arctic Ocean through the Bering Strait, at the narrowest point of which the two continents are about fifty-three miles (eighty-five kilometres) apart. The boundary between the United States and Russia passes through the sea and the strait.

The Bering Sea roughly resembles a triangle with its apex to the north and its three sides formed by the 1,100-mile long arc of the Alaska Peninsula in the east; the Aleutian Islands, which constitute part of the US state of Alaska, in the south; and the Komander (Commander) Islands in the west.

The Bering Strait is a relatively shallow passage averaging 100 to 165 feet (30 to 50 metres) in depth. During the Ice Age the sea level fell by several hundred feet, making the strait into a land bridge between the continents of Asia and North America, over which a considerable migration of plants and animals occurred.

The Imperial Great Northern Expedition (1733–42)

The continuation of an enterprise initially conceived by Emperor Peter the Great to map the northern sea route to the East. The earlier expedition mapped a large section of the Arctic coast of Siberia and stimulated Siberian merchants to develop fur trading on islands near Alaska. It was sponsored by the admiralty college in St Petersburg.

The planner of the expedition, Captain Vitus Jonassen Bering, a Dane serving in the Russian Navy, crossed the North Pacific and landed on the coast of Alaska (1741). Captain A. I. Chirikov, commanding another ship in the expedition, reached some islands off the Alaskan coast. Lieutenant S. I. Chelyuskin reached the cape named after him, the northernmost point of the Siberian mainland, and the cousins Khariton and Dmitry Laptev charted the Siberian coast from the Taymyr Peninsula to the Kolyma River.

PROLOGUE

Dark, impenetrable grey gradually lightens and tinges with blue. The dense fog clears slowly, then whips away to reveal a wall of stark, dazzling whiteness. The spectacular contours of Mt Elias.

The year is 1741. Russia's Imperial Great Northern Expedition under Captain-Commander Vitus Jonassen Bering has discovered the North American continent.

The officers and crew of the *St Peter* crowd the deck, exhausted but jubilant. Their relief is palpable. This is the climax of a gruelling eight-year expedition.

The First Officer goes below deck to report.

Bering lies on the bunk in his cramped quarters. He is sixty and looks twenty years older. His eyes are closed. The First Officer reports that their mission has finally been accomplished. They have sighted the North American continent. From the East. From Siberia. There is no land bridge between Russia and the Americas.

Bering's eyes flicker open. He stares unblinking at the bulkhead above his bunk. He says nothing, gives no sign of acknowledging the First Officer's presence.

The First Officer waits, shrugs his shoulders and leaves.

Bering continues to stare at the bulkhead, motionless.

There is no need to go on deck.

He has lived and relived the scene in his mind's eye for nearly a quarter of a century.

BOOK ONE

POINTS OF DEPARTURE

Chapter One

ST PETERSBURG

Kotka, Finland
November 18, 1732

He sat alone on the wooden terrace, an unlit clay pipe cantilevered from the corner of his mouth. He stared out over the remote expanse of snow-clad pine forest.

Over the brow of a distant hill came a solitary horseman, plunging and sideslipping down through the deep drifts. As he approached, Bering could make out his features: a heavily-bearded, fur-clad figure astride a sturdy quarterhorse. The rider reached the bottom of the hill and urged his mount up the other side towards the cabin.

Bering got to his feet. A muscular but gaunt figure in his late forties. He watched as the rider reined in below him and dismounted.

The bearded figure saluted Bering by name and rank.

'I bring greetings from the Csarina Anna Ivanovna. Captain-Commander Vitus Bering is required to present himself at court in St Petersburg. Without delay.'

'To what purpose?'

'I am charged to bring only this command.'

'Then I charge you to take this answer back. Captain-Commander Vitus Bering will not attend the court.'

'You defy the will of the Csarina?'

'I do.'

'On what grounds?'

'On the grounds that I am a free citizen of the Kingdom of Denmark and no vassal of the Russian court. I owe respect but no allegiance to the Empress of All the Russias.'

'This I cannot do.'

The two men stood their ground. Bering was the first to break the silence.

'I forget myself. You are welcome to enter and take refreshment.'

The bearded figure hesitated, then swept the snow from his furs, stamping his feet to dislodge the ice on his knee-high boots. He climbed the few steps to the cabin. Bering moved aside to allow him to enter.

The cabin was modest but impeccably clean. Pine logs crackled and spat in a cast-iron stove. A rough-hewn wooden table dominated the room, on it neatly-arranged tools of the seafarer's trade – sextant, dividers, charts and logbooks. On the far wall hung a telescope and a hand-coloured map of Russia.

The visitor pulled off thick leather gauntlets and set them by the stove to dry out. Bering motioned him to a chair.

Osa Bering emerged from the other room carrying a stone jug and two wooden cups. She set these down on the table.

'I am Osa Bering. I welcome you to our home.'

The unexpected guest rose and bowed.

'Imperial Guard Captain Vassilij Ivanovich Shaliakov. I am honoured by your hospitality and grateful for it.'

Osa Bering was unusually tall and full-breasted. She wore a coarse ankle-length skirt and a plain white blouse under an embroidered shawl. Her ash-blonde hair was swept back off her forehead and gathered loosely behind her neck. Her face radiated health.

Shaliakov looked at her admiringly. Bering smiled. He had witnessed this reaction many times before. Osa filled the two cups with a mixture of warm milk and honey. She placed the jug back on the table.

'The honour is ours, Captain Shaliakov. Our accommodation is modest but it is at your disposal should you wish to rest until tomorrow.'

'I would gladly do so, but I am expected back at the court.' He glanced over at Bering. 'Without delay.'

Osa smiled and left the room. The two men now sat facing each other across the table.

'I drink to your health, Captain-Commander, but not to your decision.'

'And I drink to *your* health and remain firm in my decision.'

'That is regrettable.'

Shaliakov tried another tack.

'You are not curious as to why the Empress commands – forgive me – requests your presence?'

'I am not.'

'Then perhaps you will permit me to observe that it is strange that a mariner of your experience and reputation should live in this landlocked wilderness in the depths of Finlandia. What is a sailor without the sea?'

'I am no longer a sailor.'

'But you are a man in his best years. I cannot – '

Bering interrupted him.

'I intend no discourtesy, but my calling is my own affair.'

'Nor do I wish to give offence. I submit only that your skills are wasted.'

'There are some who might disagree.'

Shaliakov detected a certain petulance in Bering's reply.

'I know of no-one who does not hold your skills in the highest regard.'

Bering waved a dismissive hand. The two men were silent. After a full two minutes, Bering stood up abruptly from the table.

'If you will permit, I must talk with my wife.'

From the other room Osa Bering had heard every word but given no indication that she had listened to the conversation. Bering sat down beside her on the quilted bedspread and took her hand.

'Osa, my dear, there is a decision that must be taken.'

'Then you must take it.'

'I cannot be certain, but I believe the Empress Anna wishes me to complete what her predecessor had me start.'

'This is what you have been waiting for, Vitus. I understand. You must go.'

'I shall go only if you will go with me.'

'To St Petersburg?'

'Yes. To St Petersburg.'

Osa Bering had difficulty in suppressing her excitement. Her eyes sparkled. She took Bering's other hand in hers.

'Of course I shall come.'

Bering nodded. He embraced her briefly, stood up and walked back into the main room.

'Captain Shaliakov, we leave at dawn.'

'A wise decision, Captain-Commander. And a welcome one.'

'That, sir, remains to be seen.'

St Petersburg
February 7, 1733

'You are a man of few words and little patience, Captain-Commander.'

'In some, that is a virtue.'

Bering had been in St Petersburg for over two months now. On arrival, he and Osa had been assigned lodgings in one of the new townhouses that had recently sprung up on the shores of the Gulf of Finland. He had reported to the Imperial Palace on a daily basis, only to be informed that his audience with the Csarina was not on the day's roster.

Bering knew he had to choose his next words with care. The man seated across from him in the ornate antechamber was reputed to be the most powerful – and the most corrupt – in the Csarina's administration.

Ernst Johann Reichsgraf von Biron was in his early forties. On the accession of Anna Ivanovna to the Russian throne in 1730, von Biron had become her chief adviser. It was an open secret that he had been Anna's lover since 1727. Von Biron held no formal position within the administration, but his influence on the Empress was such that a new and pejorative term had been coined for Anna's court: *bironovshchina*. Von Biron and the predominantly German circle grouped around him were ruthless in their suppression of the interests of the Russian nobility and unrelenting in their pursuit of personal gain.

Bering knew that von Biron's influence on Anna had been a key factor in her decision to abolish the Supreme Privy Council, the

Senate-like body conceived by Csar Peter I to replace the labyrinthine system of *prikazy* administrative departments and impose some semblance of bureaucratic order on the haphazard Russian state. He also knew that von Biron's extensive personal network of security agents – a legacy of Peter's *preobrazhensky* guards – had become the most feared organ of the Russian state.

'I sense that much has changed in St Petersburg.'

Von Biron's fingers drummed lightly on the desktop. Was this merely an observation or was it a criticism?

'Changed? Changed in what way, may I ask?'

'In a positive sense, of course. You will understand that it is some years since I was last here.'

'Quite.'

'The city has become more' – Bering groped for the appropriate word – 'European.'

This was certainly true, he thought. Peter the Great's legacy was in full evidence. St Petersburg had opened to the West. The extended court played host to architects, engineers, scholars and poets from as far afield as England, France, Italy, Spain and the Low Countries. Dress styles had changed under the influence of foreign visitors. And in the taverns and coffee houses of the city, Russian socialites were drinking coffee rather than the traditional tea.

Von Biron smiled, his eyes still cold.

'But we *are* European now,' he said. 'And we have much to thank the Csarina's uncle for.'

Bering knew he was on thin ice. Peter the Great had built a new Russia that was now a genuinely European power to rival that of Holland and England. But the revamped political, military and bureaucratic infrastructure needed to underpin this new status had uncovered major fault lines in Russian society. By inaugurating a Senate and the subsequent Supreme Privy Council, Peter had sought to build a new institutional structure which diluted the autocracy of the sovereign by substituting an oligarchy broadly in line with mainstream European political tradition. Authoritarian as he had certainly been, Peter had seen his role as that of a servant of the state rather than as its master.

What von Biron stood for ran counter to everything Bering had admired about Peter the Great. Sadly, von Biron held the key to Bering's dream.

'You have news for me?'

'Straight to the point as ever, Captain-Commander. Yes, I *do* have news for you. You are to appear before a council of experts two days from now to present your plan for a large expedition that will build on your earlier voyages of exploration.'

Bering found it difficult to hide his elation.

'Detailed plans and schedules of requisition are already in place, Your Excellency. I can assure you that – '

Von Biron wagged a forefinger in admonition.

'Let us not pre-judge the situation. You are to appear on the morning of Thursday at the Collegium of Naval Sciences. I shall also be present at that gathering.'

Bering stood up.

'I thank you, Your Excellency.'

He inclined his head, turned and left the antechamber.

Once outside, he could scarcely contain himself. It was true. He, a Dane, was to lead what was surely the most ambitious voyage of exploration in history. The bitterness he had nurtured over the years had dissipated. The opportunity was there for him to grasp, to prove once and for all that he had been right. That he had *always* been right.

Bering lathered his horse along the shorefront, anxious to tell Osa Bering the great news. His wife was sitting by the open fire when he arrived. Flinging the door wide open, Bering shouted from the hallway.

'Osa, I have news, great news.'

He climbed the stairway two steps at a time, his heart pounding. Osa Bering was already at the top of the stairs. She registered the delight on his face.

'Is it true?'

'Yes, yes, it's true. At last. I have an audience at the Naval Academy of Sciences in two days to present my credentials and provide details of the expedition.'

She clung to him as he swept her off her feet, swinging her round and round, hugging her close.

'Vitus, put me down this instant. And tell me all there is to tell.'

'It has come full circle, my dear wife. I am to mount the expedition of a lifetime. To Siberia and beyond. To the Americas, even. Yes, yes, it's all true.'

Osa Bering was overjoyed.

'I knew it would turn out well,' she said over and over again. 'Vitus, they need you. I knew they would.'

That night, for the first time in many weeks, they made love. Slowly and with great tenderness.

Academy of Naval Sciences
St Petersburg
February 9, 1733

Dressed in black breeches and a plain white silk shirt under a doublet of black velvet, Bering passed through a series of antechambers, each more imposing than its predecessor. Elegantly-uniformed naval officers stared at the long-limbed bearded stranger whose single-minded purpose was communicated by his decisive stride. Courtesans clustering in the public rooms eyed him and clearly liked what they saw.

He arrived at the brass-studded doors of the Imperial Chart Room to be greeted by a young lieutenant who ushered him into a vaulted chamber with an impossibly ornate gold ceiling. The walls were festooned with parchment and tapestry maps.

At the head of an immense table sat the Empress Anna Ivanovna, flanked by what would prove to be an assortment of admirals and generals, naval academicians, natural scientists and cartographers. Ernst Johann von Biron was seated immediately to the right of the Empress.

'Captain-Commander Bering,' said the Csarina, as Bering bowed in respect, 'it is our wish that you return.'

Bering said nothing. He bowed a second time. His mouth was dry, his mind in turmoil, as von Biron rose and came to the front of the table.

'The Empress Anna Ivanovna has formally decreed that Captain-Commander Vitus Jonassen Bering is to continue an enterprise originally conceived by her illustrious uncle, Emperor Peter the Great. He is to chart a northern sea route to the east and to prove or disprove once and for all the existence of the new continent of Gama Land that lies between Russia and the Americas. It shall be the task of this Imperial Great Northern Expedition to secure that new continent for the glory of the Russian Empire.'

Bering was stunned. The existence of this new continent was a cartographer's fantasy, of that he was certain. He made to reply, but von Biron had not finished.

'It shall also be the task of the Imperial Great Northern Expedition to explore northwards from the eastern shores of the Kamchatka and Chukchi peninsulas in order to ascertain the full extent and dimensions of the Imperial Russian territory of Siberia and to chart and document the resources of that region. This is an undertaking on the grandest scale. An undertaking, moreover, that will assert Russia's status as a world power in the fullest sense of the term – physically, geographically and politically. An undertaking that will redraw the map of the civilised world.'

Bering was in a quandary. If he voiced his misgivings or objected to the strategic basis of the proposed expedition, his involvement would immediately be at an end. If he accepted the specific terms of his appointment, failure was a certainty. The latter course, while unpalatable, at least had the advantage of ensuring his participation in what would most certainly be a benchmark voyage of discovery.

He decided to accept as graciously as he could.

'Your Majesty, Excellencies, this is indeed an honour. It has long been my ambition to lead such an expedition and I shall endeavour to discharge my duty to the fullest extent.'

There was an uncomfortable silence. The Empress Anna looked puzzled. Once again, it was von Biron who spoke.

'Captain-Commander, the precise details of this great undertaking remain to be decided. What we require of you at present is merely your assent.'

'That you have, Your Excellency.'

'And for that, we thank you.'

It was clear to Bering that the audience was over. He hesitated, uncertain whether to leave. Von Biron motioned him to stay.

'We have assembled experts who shall counsel and confer with you,' said von Biron. 'I would ask that you remain to consult with them on the structure and import of the expedition.'

With that, von Biron bowed low to the Empress, who nodded in cursory acknowledgment of this obligatory mark of respect. Bering bowed once more as the Empress rose and swept from the room. Von Biron followed.

Bering looked around the table at those who remained.

The assembled experts.

The air of hostility was palpable.

St Petersburg
February 14, 1733

Vitus Jonassen Bering was not a happy man.

In the days following his audience with the Empress Anna, he had worked long hours assembling maps and charts, drafting a command structure and elaborating requisition lists of equipment, supplies and personnel he regarded as essential to the success of the Imperial Great Northern Expedition.

'There is much to do,' he told his wife Osa, 'and they leave me so little time.'

Osa Bering was anxious for her husband. It was clear to her that a heavy mantle of responsibility had fallen on his shoulders. She knew that Vitus was a professional mariner in every sense: adventurous yet prudent, daring yet never foolhardy, resolute yet flexible, skilled yet never over-confident. To lead an expedition of discovery such as he had committed to, however, was an immense task in terms of logistics alone.

She constantly responded to his need for support and encouragement. Time and again, she reminded him that he was more than up to the task, that this was what he had always wanted, that obstacles were there to be overcome.

But Vitus Bering was *not* a happy man. He looked forward with trepidation to this morning's meeting with the Grand Council, uncertain how to approach it and them.

Shortly after sunrise, he was again admitted to the Imperial Chart Room of the Naval Academy of Sciences. As he had hoped, the members of the Grand Council were already assembled.

The meeting started badly.

Bering instinctively opened the proceedings by welcoming those present.

'Your Excellencies, gentlemen, I am honoured that you have consented to serve with me and to share your knowledge and counsel. As leader of this undertaking, I am aware that you are all – '

Inevitably, it was von Biron who interrupted.

'Captain-Commander, I must inform you that you will not *lead* the expedition. You will be the senior naval officer in command, but the expedition will be led by a representative of the Court whose appointment is to be determined in due course by the present Grand Council.'

'I fail to understand,' countered Bering. 'I had assumed I was to be in sole charge.'

'Not so,' said von Biron. 'You have been retained in your capacity as an experienced navigator and as a skilled mariner with first-hand knowledge of the region that is to be one object of this great voyage of exploration. That, sir, is a signal honour in and of itself. That you should lead this expedition is, of course, out of the question.'

'Of course?'

'Clearly. You are a Dane. You are not a Russian citizen. It is unthinkable that a non-Russian should be entrusted with the sole command of a project of such immense political and economic import. The expedition we envisage extends far beyond a simple voyage of exploration.'

Admiral Grigori Alexi Solchnov, the ranking naval officer in the room, intervened. A rough-and-ready sailor who had come up from the ranks, Solchnov was known for his directness. And for his earthy language.

'Captain-Commander, I must also inform you that there was not universal support in this Grand Council for your recall from self-imposed exile in Finlandia. Far from it. You have been tried and found wanting before now. I am one of several in this room who do not believe you have the qualities required by such an undertaking.'

Bering's jaw clenched. He had anticipated some opposition but nothing as blunt as this.

'May I ask in what way my qualities fall short of your high expectations?'

'You have failed us once already, Captain-Commander. You were entrusted with the leadership of an expedition once before. In 1724. An expedition, I submit, that concluded unsuccessfully.'

'I beg to disagree. That mission to the outer edges of Russia's territories in Siberia was successfully accomplished.'

'I think not. You found no new continent. You sailed through no *new* strait.'

'With the greatest respect, Admiral, that is unjust. As you well know, the *Syatoi Gavriil* under my command sailed on August 13, 1728 through the Arctic Ocean with East Cape receding astern. We helmed the *St Gabriel* north of the strait and found only open sea to port and to starboard for a full day at sea.'

'But you found no Gama Land. You saw no coast to the east.'

'We sailed in dense fog. Detailed observation was not possible. But – '

Solchnov snorted his derision.

'Fog? Detailed observation impossible? Horseshit. Excuses. Nothing but excuses. There is no excuse. You claim to have sailed to the end of Asia but you adduce no proof of this. Worse, you had the impertinence to name after yourself the waters you sailed through. I ask you, gentlemen, the *Bering* Strait? To be frank, such arrogance is totally unacceptable.'

'Gentlemen, gentlemen,' admonished von Biron, 'let us be civil. I am persuaded that Captain-Commander Bering acted for the best in the course of the First Kamchatka Expedition. After all, that is why he is with us here today. He has knowledge and skills that are of great use to us. If he now insists that the continents of Asia and North America are not joined, then so be it. For the present at least. May I remind you all that we are here to remove that uncertainty, not compound it?'

'Horseshit, I say again,' countered Solchnov. 'I say he returned with his mission unaccomplished.'

'That allegation is unjust and without foundation,' retorted Bering, angered to the point of indiscretion. 'Coming from one who sails on dry land, such criticism is intolerable.'

He knew at once that he had gone too far. Solchnov heaved his massive frame to its full height and roared back.

'You impertinent bastard! How dare you address a superior officer in that tone?'

'I acknowledge you as my superior officer,' Bering fired back, 'but I address you as one who knows nothing of the seas of Siberia. You can talk of Gama Land until hell freezes over but, I tell you, there is no such continent. It is a figment of the imagination. I have sailed those waters. I *know*.'

The two men glared at each other. Bering sensed he had made an implacable enemy.

'As a non-military man,' put in Yevgeny Kallinin, a senior scientist whose credentials were held to be impeccable, 'I am in favour of plain speech unfettered by rank or reputation. While I agree with Admiral Solchnov that Captain-Commander Bering did not adduce substantive proof that there is no land bridge between Russia and the Americas, I must add that neither do we have substantive proof to the contrary. Nor, for that matter, that there is a continent interposed between the two land masses.'

Kallinin paused.

'Of greater import, however, must be the fact that a non-Russian is incapable of appreciating the political and military significance of discovering another continent and colonising it in the name of the Motherland.'

Von Biron, a non-Russian, took no apparent offence at this remark.

'There is merit in that observation. There are fundamental

political, military and trade implications to be taken into account. The English, Dutch and Spaniards are unremitting in their quest to find a trade route to China and Japan. It is imperative that we consolidate our position to the east of Siberia.'

'This is true,' put in Count Gavriil Ivanovich Golovkin, the ageing senator who had served initially as State Chancellor under Peter the Great.

Bering was surprised to see the old man in the room. Although a favourite of the Empress Anna and a member of her cabinet, Senator Golovkin was known to have taken next to no part in government affairs for a number of years. A frail figure, it had been rumoured on several occasions that he had actually died. That he had insisted on participating in the Grand Council was further evidence, concluded Bering, that the Expedition was regarded as a matter of the very highest priority.

The Council waited for Golovkin to continue. When he did not, Field-Marshal Graf Burkhard Christoph von Münnich, an erstwhile commander-in-chief of the Russian Army under Peter II and, since 1732, President of the Imperial War Council, claimed the floor.

'I concur. We are already the greatest naval power in the Baltic, but it is essential that we expand to the east and secure our outposts in Siberia and beyond. This is a matter of utmost long-term importance to the Empire. Our armies and our navy are currently at full strength. We must use them and we must use them wisely.'

Sensing that he must reassert his potential role in the Expedition, Bering decided to restate his own position.

'While the political, military and trade implications are clearly not of direct concern to me, I fully appreciate their relevance. For my part, however, I am anxious only to coordinate the exploration phase from the sea. To accomplish this, I must have a measure of authority in assembling the expeditionary force and delivering it intact to our point of departure from Siberia.'

'There is some merit in that,' said von Münnich, much to Bering's surprise.

The last to speak was Count Andrey Ivanovich Ostermann, the German-born diplomat who had served as a negotiator under the successive administrations of Peter the Great, Catherine I and Peter II, and whose sustained support for the Empress Anna had been rewarded by his appointment in 1731 to the post of First Minister entrusted with the conduct of Russia's commerce and foreign affairs. Like von Biron, Ostermann was dedicated to elevating Russia to the status of a European and, by extension, global power. It was said, however, that no love was lost between the two men.

For Bering, it was essential that Ostermann speak favourably on his behalf.

'The importance of this expedition cannot be overstated,' said Ostermann. 'That is all too evident. What is also self-evident is that we must not undermine unduly the authority of Captain-Commander Bering. His knowledge of the region and the waters beyond it are a key to the Expedition's ultimate success.'

'You propose then?' asked von Biron.

'I propose that Captain-Commander Bering be accorded the fullest authority with regard to the logistics of the Expedition. This would include full rights of consultation as to the composition of the expeditionary force and sole responsibility for its delivery to the Siberian coast. I further propose that he assume full command of the subsequent naval exploration.'

'I object.' This from Admiral Solchnov.

'Your objection is noted, Admiral,' said Ostermann dismissively. 'I also propose that the powers and the authority thus ceded to the Captain-Commander be conditional upon standing review by this Grand Council. Moreover, that said authority and powers should vest in Captain-Commander Bering for such time only as this Grand Council adjudges him to have performed his duties to its satisfaction. Not least, I propose that the Supreme Commander of the Imperial Great Northern Expedition be none other than Her Majesty the Empress Anna Ivanovna.'

Spoken like a true diplomat, thought Bering. To oppose Count Ostermann's proposals was scarcely an option – for himself or, for that matter, for the members of the Grand Council.

'I submit these proposals to a vote of the Grand Council,' said von Biron.

The vote was unanimous.

Von Biron turned to Bering.

'Captain-Commander, do you accept these terms and conditions and are you willing to serve in accordance with them?'

Bering had no choice.

'I do and I am.'

'Then these matters are at an end. Members of the Grand Council have drafted a list of personnel to accompany the expedition. I urge you to review that list, to amend and extend it as you deem appropriate, and to present your recommendations to the Grand Council within fourteen days. I would remind you that time is of the essence. Additionally, you will convene with the College of Cartographers in the interim and report your conclusions based on their advice and counsel.'

The meeting of the Grand Council was over.

Bering felt drained yet relieved. Thanks to Ostermann's intervention and the alacrity with which von Biron had moved the Council to a vote, Bering had acquired a degree of autonomy and authority which, if not absolute, was at least acceptable. That ultimate authority would continue to reside with the Empress herself did not, on the face of it, seem unreasonable.

Unreasonable or not, the outcome of the Grand Council session had proved satisfactory beyond his initial expectations. If he proved capable of leading the expedition to a successful conclusion, the triumph would be his. And his alone. Should he fail, the onus and the retribution would fall, at least in part, on the Grand Council.

All things considered, he decided, his position had been secured.

Stockholm, Kingdom of Sweden
February 1733

From the journal of Lieutenant-at-Sea Sven Waxell

February 16, 1733

All Stockholm is rife with rumour that Captain-Commander Vitus Bering has been commissioned by the Empress Anna Ivanovna to lead a great expedition to search for the Northeast Passage and to chart the coastal waters to the north of Kamchatka. This is an endeavour of great import and one in which I must play a part.

I know the Captain as well as any man. He is a master mariner who inspires loyalty in all who do his bidding and do not shirk their duties. I was privileged to serve under him aboard the St. Gabriel, as fine a vessel and crew as have sailed those northern waters. In the year of Our Lord 1727 we drove due north into waters where few have sailed before, through that neck of ocean that lies between Russia and the Americas and now bears the name of the Bering Strait. We sailed far into the Arktis and saw only pack and drift ice with no trace of land.

On that voyage I discharged well my modest duties. I earned the respect of my Captain and that I cherish. It is my fervent wish to sail with him again.

February 17, 1733

My resolve is final. I travel this day to St. Petersburg. I leave behind the wife and son I hold so dear and I leave behind my native land, more precious to me than the air I breathe. I surrender this all in one great cause, to go forth once more into uncharted waters. I do so gladly, secure in the faith I place in one whose skill I admire and to whom my loyalty is unswerving.

To my wife and my son Laurentij I say only this: that the day will come when the name of Waxell shall be on the lips of all. He sailed with Bering, men shall say, and my pride in that endeavour shall be hers and theirs.

College of Cartographers
St Petersburg
February 24, 1733

'Gentlemen, I put my trust in charts that I myself have drawn and in soundings I myself have taken.'

Vitus Jonassen Bering was in his element.

There were nine in all, five of them mere copyists whose task was to transpose to parchment the conclusions and extrapolations of the senior cartographers. Of the latter, only two had ever sailed the eastern waters – and then only off the now-familiar White Sea coast. Of the two others Bering knew next to nothing, only that Ivan Stadukhin was the great-nephew of the celebrated Mikhail Stadukhin who had explored the Arctic coast of Siberia in the latter half of the 17th century.

To a man they paid lip-service to the absurd notion of a fabled Gama Land interposed somewhere between the Siberian Coast and the Americas.

At this juncture, Bering was not disposed to argue the point.

'It is alleged that Alekseyev Popov and Semyon Dezhnev circumnavigated the Chukchi Peninsula in the middle of the last century,' continued Bering.

'That is so,' replied Yevgeni Yerastov, the most senior of the cartographers.

'Then where, pray, are the records of that voyage? Their charts and logs?'

Bering held his breath. If earlier explorers had penetrated almost three-quarters of a century previously so far into the strait that now bore his own name, much of the glory to which he aspired would be dissipated.

'We cannot verify that account. Those records are lost or at best misplaced in the archives,' said Yerastov.

Bering had difficulty suppressing a smile.

'Then let us turn our minds to facts rather than hearsay.'

The charts spread out on the trestle table told him little he did not already know. These records of Arctic exploration went back over seven centuries to the first bold if tentative excursions of Uleb of Norgod in the 11th century. The real pioneers were arguably the coastal Cossacks of the White Sea coast, the *pomors*, who had ventured as far afield as Novaya Zemlya in the 11th and 12th centuries. They were followed by Russian pelt traders who pushed north to what would later come to be known as Cheluyskin Cape.

As Russia's modern navy came of age under the aegis and hands-on direction of Peter the Great, the need to establish with certainty the limits of the Empire was seen as a matter not only of national pride but of national security. Meanwhile, a new generation of mariners had emerged, proudly obsessed with detail and precision. The most accurate charts of the Arctic coastline extending from the White Sea towards the Bering Strait were the work of a new breed of explorer underpinned by revolutionary navigational aids such as the sextant and improved hull and rig design: Stadukhin, Beketov, Rebrov, Yerastov . . .

Bering glanced up at Yevgeni Yerastov. Was he a descendant of that same Yerastov? He elected not to ask.

'Bring me the Fyodorov logs,' said Bering.

Here he was on more recent ground. Ivan Fyodorov had set out in 1727 to navigate across the Bering Strait and approach the American land mass from the east. Bering knew that Fyodorov had not yet returned.

'But there are no such logs,' replied Yerastov. 'The Captain-Commander is surely aware that Ivan Ivanovich Fyodorov has not yet returned.'

Bering gave a grunt which those present interpreted as one of disappointment.

The reverse was true. He was relieved that Fyodorov was still at sea, the outcome of his mission as yet unknown.

Bering glanced down at the charts a final time, noting with some satisfaction how minute detail gradually tapered off into progressively vague extrapolation before petering out to the east into fantasy and nothingness.

'My decision is made. I shall sail from Nizhne-Kamchatsk and head due east then north. The bulk of the expeditionary force will remain close inshore to chart the Arctic coast. I propose four areas of responsibility – from Arkhangelsk to the estuary of the Ob River, from the mouth of the Ob to the mouth of the Yenisey, from the Yenisey to the Lena River and, finally, from the Lena to Chukchi and Kamchatka.'

Yerastov nodded. Bering's motives were transparent: the Imperial Great Northern Expedition would routinely fulfil its mandate, while one Vitus Jonassen Bering would reap the glory of discovery.

'The plan is excellent, Captain-Commander.'

Bering smiled.

'That will be for the Grand Council to decide.'

The Spaniard's Inn
St Petersburg
February 24, 1733

Martin Petrovich Spanberg raised his tankard yet again to toast the health of the mistress of the house. She smiled coyly back at him, her rosy cheeks dimpling.

By Christ, he is a fine specimen of a man, she thought. Taller than average, broad-shouldered, narrow-waisted, deeply-tanned.

And drunk.

Spanberg had spent the earlier part of the evening at a tedious reception at the Spanish Embassy where he had tried – unsuccessfully, as he himself had anticipated – to seduce the ambassador's daughter. He had taken his leave well before midnight and headed straight for the St Petersburg docklands, a labyrinthine tangle of ale houses and bordellos that reeked of tobacco, urine and vomit.

Spanberg loved the place.

These were surroundings familiar to him from ports of call across the globe, from Hamburg to Valparaiso, from Lisbon to Cathay. And these were his people, sea-goers all, their hands calloused and their skin leathered by tropical suns and winter gales.

Spanberg signalled to the landlady that his tankard was again empty.

Overweight and over-ripe, she minced over to him, her ample cleavage glistening with droplets of perspiration. Instinctively, she licked her lips.

'Does the gentleman want something?'

Spanberg smiled a dazzling smile, his white teeth glinting in the semi-darkness. He ran his fingers casually through his mane of blond hair.

'If something is on offer.'

The punch came from the right, a roundhouse swing that caught him high on the temple and spreadeagled him across a nearby table. Spanberg shook his head to clear it, then looked up, quickly assessing his assailant. A bear of a man, bearded, with a scar that zigzagged across his left cheek. He stood over Spanberg, daring him to get up.

'*Arschloch*!'

Martin Spanberg took stock. Getting back to his feet was not an option. The bear towered over him, his right fist clenched in anticipation.

Spanberg held both hands high, palms outstretched as if in submission. The bear hesitated, his clenched fist dropping to his waist. Spanberg quickly rolled to the right, dropped to the grime-encrusted floor and sprang back to his feet.

'Oh-ho, the arsehole wants some more, does he?' thundered the bear.

'At your pleasure.'

The onlookers howled in delight. It had been the better part of an hour since the previous brawl, a short-lived affair that had served only to whet their appetite for more of the same.

Sadly, this promised to be an uneven contest. On one side, the Russian bear with forearms the span of a man's thigh and, on the other, this blond fellow little more than half his size.

The contest *was* uneven.

Spanberg feinted with his left, ducked to allow the Russian's crude swing to whistle harmlessly over his shoulder, then drove in a straight right to the larger man's breastbone. The bear gasped in pain, stopped in his tracks. Spanberg's left cross rocked the Russian, causing him to drop his head. A right hand from seemingly nowhere caught the bear on the point of the chin. The Russian's head snapped back. His eyes rolled and his hands dropped to his sides. Spanberg had not finished. His right boot crunched into the bear's kneecap, causing him to yelp in agony. His head dropped once again. Spanberg clenched both hands together and brought them down in a sweeping arc on the back of the Russian's neck. The bear pitched forward onto his face, splitting his nose on the stone floor. He lay there, motionless.

Spanberg tucked his shirt back into his breeches.

Stepping carefully over the prostrate Russian, he repositioned himself at the counter.

'A tankard, my good lady. To drink the health of all those who sail the seas.'

A roar of appreciation broke the numbed silence.

There was a groan from the floor as the Russian came to his senses. He heaved himself to his knees, thought better of it, and sat back down with a thump.

'As Jesus is my witness,' he said at length, 'that was a blow to end all blows.'

Spanberg reached down and extended a hand.

'Come, my good man, drink with the *Arschloch*.'

The Russian clasped him by the wrist and pulled himself slowly to his feet.

'Nay, you shall drink with me, Master Navigator Khitrov.'

'And I, my friend, am Lieutenant First Officer Martin Spanberg, late of the *St Gabriel*.'

Academy of Naval Sciences
St Petersburg
February 26, 1733

The Grand Council convened at noon and a confident Vitus Bering presented his expedition plan, stressing its simplicity.

'Six ships, each with a complement of between forty-five and sixty hands. Four to explore and chart the inshore Arctic coast from Arkhangelsk to the Ob River, from the Ob to the Yenisey, from the Yenisey to the Lena and, finally, from the Lena to Chukchi and Kamchatka. The other two, under my direct command, to strike east and north from Kamchatka into the Bering Strait. The whole to be accomplished in three full years, taking account of the long overland journey by the body of the expedition to the Kamchatka Peninsula where it will rendezvous with an advance party detailed to build the six vessels. This also takes account of the need to over-winter twice in Kamchatka.'

The plan was rejected out of hand.

Of the members of the Grand Council, only Admiral Solchnov appeared to find some merit in Bering's proposals. To Bering's renewed surprise, Solchnov was again supportive, even conciliatory.

'You speak well as a mariner, Captain-Commander, and, as such, I applaud the straightforward lines of your argument. Yet I cannot endorse your recommendations for they take no note of the scale of this great undertaking.'

Count von Biron, seated as usual at the head of the table, was more forthright.

'You must understand, Captain-Commander Bering, that this is no ordinary expedition, but one which reflects the express will of the Empress of All the Russias and the fundamental aspirations of the Motherland. As Admiral Solchnov has said, this is indeed a great undertaking and it must – I repeat, must – be conceived, executed and, above all, *perceived* as such. This is no mere voyage of exploration, this is a statement of Russia's greatness in the eyes of the world.'

'I fail to take your meaning,' said Bering.

'In faith, my meaning is surely all too plain. The Imperial Great Northern Expedition must position Russia as a major power. Accordingly – and on this point the Grand Council brooks no discussion – it will be measured in terms not only of ambition but of scale.'

'Overseeing a flotilla of six craft is no mean undertaking,' objected Bering.

Von Biron sighed.

'My dear Captain-Commander, you still fail to appreciate our position. As you yourself so rightly say, to accomplish *your* mission you need an able and experienced crew. Your mission is however but one small part of the whole. And for the Expedition as a whole to succeed, we too need able and experienced men drawn from the widest possible spectrum of the arts and sciences – linguists for purposes of interpretation, botanists to study new species of plant life, ornithologists, physicians, geologists, evangelists to spread the Gospel to the heathen, illustrators to document the progress of the Expedition, and so on.'

'What is more,' put in the scientist Yevgeny Kallinin, 'the expedition must be self-sustaining. This implies grooms to tend the horses and pack animals, servants to look after the needs of the officers and scientists and their wives and children, cooks to feed them, musicians to provide entertainment and, not least, a substantial military presence to deter marauding tribes and protect the Expedition from attack. Convicts will be conscripted from Siberia to perform menial tasks.'

Servants? Musicians? Wives and children? Convicts? What nonsense was this? thought Bering.

'And just how many are to take part in this Great Expedition?'

'At the outset no more than two thousand,' said von Biron smoothly. 'You have seen the list. Our selection has been made.'

The list in question had been hand-delivered to Bering some days before. He had assumed it to contain recommendations for his consideration. Not so, it seemed. The Grand Council had already decided that the list was definitive.

'May I ask how you propose to feed this multitude?' asked Bering. 'Do you suggest they live off the land?'

'We do not. Provision will be made for food, drinking water, fuel and clothing to be transported by the main column. The advance party you propose – and the Grand Council compliments you on that proposal – will assume responsibility for the conveyance of all the materials and tools necessary for the construction of the expedition ships. To the extent, naturally, that such materials and tools are not available locally at our garrison outposts on the Kamchatka Peninsula.'

Bering nodded.

'When do we leave?' he asked.

'Such an expedition cannot be mounted overnight,' replied von Biron. 'We are aware of this. We are also aware that the journey to the coast is a long and arduous one through inhospitable and at times hostile terrain. This being so, an advance party will be readied to leave this spring, no later than three months from today. The main body will follow in the spring of 1734. In other words, Captain-Commander, you have three months to equip and ready the advance party and a further twelve months to prepare for the departure of the Expedition proper.'

'My understanding was that time is of the essence,' said Bering.

'Indeed it is,' answered von Biron, ignoring the sarcasm. 'And I trust you will use your time well.'

'A final question, if your Excellencies permit?'

'Certainly, Captain-Commander.'

'Which members of the Grand Council intend to accompany the Expedition?'

Von Biron glanced round the table.

'At this point, there are no plans for any of those present to join the Expedition, at least not in the initial stages. The second vessel, by which I mean that which will sail alongside you northwards into the Strait, will be commanded by Acting Captain Third Class Aleksey Chirikov. I am given to understand that you and he have sailed together in the past. Captain Chirikov will be the eyes and ears of this Grand Council and, as its plenipotentiary, will be consulted on all strategic and operational decisions taken by yourself.'

Von Biron looked Bering straight in the eye.

'The Grand Council assumes you entertain no objection in that regard?'

'None whatsoever,' said Bering.

It was the first real compromise of many that were to follow.

Gulf of Finland
February 26, 1733

The sky was overcast, the waters a dirty grey-brown. A pallid sun leaked through the cloud base and cast faint intermittent shadows on the shingle beach.

Osa Bering, a thick cloak wrapped around her to shut out the chill wind, walked along the beach. Today was, she felt sure, a red letter day for her husband. He had worked all hours to hone his strategic plan for the Imperial Great Northern Expedition, adding details here and pruning non-essentials there. By now, her Vitus would be standing in triumph before the Grand Council.

She smiled. After all these years, after all the humiliation and vilification, Vitus now had this singular opportunity to set the record straight once and for all. He had returned in 1728 from his initial voyage to Kamchatka, justly proud of what he had accomplished. And she had witnessed at first hand his utter dismay at finding Peter the Great no longer at the helm of the Empire. Peter's sudden demise at the comparatively early age of fifty-two years had spawned a round of backbiting and infighting at the Court as would-be successors jockeyed for position and traded favours in the struggle for power. The power brokers had had a field day, foremost among them Aleksandr Menshikov and the infamous Dolgoruky family.

And Vitus had suffered, caught up in the intrigues of the Court, his achievements derided and even his personal courage called in question.

That Vitus had taken this badly was understandable. The man she had married had been an imposing figure, confident and self-assured. As well he might be, given his service record.

His career had been remarkable, she thought to herself. The husband of whom she was so proud had come from a family of Danish clerics and priests with virtually no knowledge of the sea. Yet, from a very early age, her Vitus had been determined to sail the oceans of the known world – and he had done so.

He had also been fortunate. On his return to Amsterdam after a lengthy voyage to India, he had found favour with the Norwegian-born mariner Cornelius Cruys, by this time a vice-admiral of the Russian fleet. Cruys played a central role in persuading Vitus that his destiny lay in the service of the Russian navy which Peter the Great had in the interim built into a major military force, with upwards of thirty ships of the line.

Vitus had not hesitated. He enlisted at the age of twenty-two and, although a Dane, rose rapidly through the ranks. By 1707, he was a lieutenant and, by 1710, a lieutenant-commander. The year 1714 saw him promoted to the rank of captain second grade. From her parents, Osa Bering had learned that her husband had served with distinction in the Great Northern War which finally came to an end in 1721. He had then been promoted to the rank of captain – in 1724 – an appointment that coincided with Peter the Great's declared intention to chart the far-flung frontiers of the vast Russian Empire.

Who was better qualified to lead such an expedition than Captain Vitus Jonassen Bering?

Who indeed?

What her husband had accomplished during that epic 5,000-mile transcontinental journey overland from the Baltic to the Sea of Okhotsk on the Pacific Ocean had since become the stuff of legend. As little more than a child, Osa had been captivated by Bering's achievements. She pictured in her mind's eye the rigours of the journey by horse-drawn sled across inhospitable marsh and tundra; the trek alongside the watercourses of European Russia into and through the desolate plains of Western Siberia as far as Tobolsk; the inconceivable hardships and discomforts endured during a Siberian winter; the onwards struggle to reach the Ob River and beyond; crossing the central Siberian plateau and overwintering yet again in Yakutsk in the east; and, finally, the last leg of the journey to the Sea of Okhotsk.

And that, thought Osa, was only the beginning.

To this day, she wondered at her husband's determination and strength of will. After an expedition lasting the better part of three years, his real mission still lay ahead: to sail in search of where Siberia converged with the Americas. Then and only then, Vitus had been back in his element – as a mariner at sea in the *St Gabriel*.

Osa picked a round white pebble from the beach and threw it into the waters of the Gulf. Then, she reflected, was when it had all gone wrong.

By the afternoon of August 27, 1728, Captain Vitus Bering had sailed the *St Gabriel* through the Strait to latitude sixty-seven degrees and fifteen minutes north. He was now satisfied that Asia and North America were not connected. There was no land bridge. Dense fog had reduced visibility to a matter of metres. By Bering's estimations, the Alaskan coast must lie off somewhere to the east – how far he could only guess. The sea was icing up and there was little else for it: Bering turned south.

His mission had been accomplished. He had determined the

easternmost limits of the Empire. And he had established that it would one day prove possible to sail from Kamchatka to Japan, China and the East Indies.

He could return home in triumph.

Another white pebble plopped gently into the Gulf of Finland. Osa Bering shook her head in bewilderment as she had done so often in recent years. She could not comprehend why her husband's achievements had been so belittled, why the authorities in St Petersburg had not acclaimed his success, why the Academy of Sciences had refused to endorse his findings. What more could they have expected of him, these petty officials and self-seeking hangers-on at the Russian Court? What Vitus had achieved, what he had endured, had been lost in a web of intrigue and petty jealousies. They were fools, all of them.

They did not know Vitus as she did.

Another pebble.

And yet, if she were to be honest with herself, she had to admit there was so much about her husband she did not know. She had married him when she was barely sixteen and had lived long stretches alone, when he was at sea. Osa repeatedly told herself she loved her husband, but she knew in her heart that her immediate infatuation those many years ago had been rooted in unqualified admiration and respect.

As Vitus had grown older, his mood swings and despondency had become – she realised to her surprise and dismay – a source of increasing irritation. He was no longer the man she had met and married. His large frame had tended towards the corpulent, with only the hardships of his many years at sea helping keep his weight under control. In the four years since his return, she had watched anxiously as his features had become progressively gaunt. Vitus had not aged well. Osa, his junior by a good number of years, had looked on as her husband gradually withdrew from active life, developing mannerisms that bordered on petulance and self-pity, lapsing into sombre moods of self-doubt.

Nor, for that matter, was she the young woman who had worshipped at his feet.

The move to St Petersburg had changed him for the better. Although Vitus was by no stretch of the imagination a favourite at the Court, Osa had taken pleasure in his new-found acceptance. He had regained a measure of his self-respect. His walk had grown more confident, his eyes burned with a renewed intensity and his whole demeanour betrayed a fresher and more positive outlook.

Yes, she thought, things are changing for the better. St Petersburg, even during the long winter, was a far cry from their wooden cabin in the remoteness of the hinterland beyond the Finno-Russian border. More to the point, the move to the capital had afforded her an opportunity to be reunited with their only daughter Benthe, whom they had reluctantly left behind in St Petersburg three years previously to finish her schooling.

In the interim, Benthe had matured. The earlier vivacity was still there, but she had acquired a poise and budding sophistication that would not have been possible had she moved with her parents to the isolated confines of Kotka.

For Osa, the relationship between Vitus and Benthe was still a matter for some concern. There could be little doubt that Vitus cherished his only child, yet any outward sign of warmth in their relationship stemmed from Benthe, who positively adored her father. Still, thought Osa, Vitus has never been given to outward shows of affection. This much I know from my own experience.

To the extent that Vitus played no part in the social life of the Court, Osa's exposure to St Petersburg society was at best circumscribed. She had made some friends among neighbouring wives, who encouraged her to be more active in society. St Petersburg was not a drab northern outpost, they insisted. Far from it: new fashions had been imported from Paris and the Court receptions were festive occasions – despite the invariable presence of the Empress Anna Ivanovna, whom most of Osa's new acquaintances agreed was unattractively overweight and deficient in both beauty and charm.

Osa cared little for such gossip. She was content to walk on the beach, the wind whipping her fair hair about her face, and to spend quiet evenings reading after Benthe had taken herself off to bed and Vitus had retired to his study.

Today was the beginning of a new life, she told herself. Things *were* changing and could change only for the better.

St Petersburg
March 1, 1733

The interviews were going well and Vitus Bering was glad of it. The list of candidates he had received from the Grand Council included many people he knew either personally or by name or reputation. On perusing it, he immediately recognised that nepotism had played a substantive part in its compilation. He also suspected – although he had no way of proving as much – that many who featured on the list had hastened to purchase themselves a place in the Expedition, desperate to be associated with the event of the century. How much money had changed hands in that regard and between whom did not concern him personally, nor did he give it much thought. His instincts told him that scores of these hangers-on would fall by the wayside, unable to cope with the inevitable hardships of the overland journey. The two-thousand-strong Expedition would shrink to potentially manageable proportions before the first year was out. Of that he was certain.

In an unexpectedly frank exchange outside the Grand Council chamber, von Biron had virtually said as much.

'If it be some consolation, Captain-Commander, I predict that the ranks of the Expedition will thin in large measure before you even reach the Kamchatka Peninsula. I am, above all, a realist. The Grand Council has been at pains to accommodate many who will soon miss the creature comforts of the Court and who will turn tail and run at the first signs of danger or when their caviar stock is depleted.'

'This is my expectation also,' Bering had replied. 'There is no place for those who have no stomach for discomfort.'

Bering's initial task had been to effect a *triage*, separating out from the list those who could realistically be expected to stay the course. For this, he could devise no hard-and-fast criteria, although age, civil rank, and number of dependants and entourage offered some indication of those who, in von Biron's words, would 'turn tail and run'. He whittled the list down further by eliminating many non-essential personnel, including musicians and entertainers, together with dozens of porters, cooks and handymen who would be superfluous to requirements once the ranks of the main expedition party had been reduced.

He knew also that an expedition of this magnitude would attract in its wake a massive army of camp-followers. He resolved from the outset that these should be treated as non-essential. They would billet apart from the main body. Moreover, they too would gradually fall away as the expedition distanced itself from St Petersburg.

This exercise completed, Bering turned to the essence of the voyage of discovery. He knew now that his ship's complement would inevitably exceed the forty-five to sixty hands he had initially envisaged. Provision had to be made on board not only for the scientific contingent that would make the overland journey but also for those scientists who were scheduled to travel in smaller groups to join the Expedition's operational phase at its base on the Kamchatka Peninsula.

Time did not permit face-to-face interviews with each and every one of those on the original Grand Council list. In an attempt to be fair, however, Bering made a valiant effort to speak directly with as many as he could. In most instances, their special area of expertise held little interest for him. Some he found to be mildly entertaining and informative, others professed a passion for arcane subjects that he found frankly tedious. In every instance, however, he was at pains to appear open-minded and receptive – although his mind was invariably elsewhere.

His principal preoccupation was with his crew. Bering knew he had to assemble a ship's complement of officers and hands on whom he could rely. He was accustomed to running a tight ship, and known and respected for his ability to delegate responsibility to those around him. The most important task now was to ensure that his crew had the requisite experience and fortitude for the task that lay ahead.

That morning, Bering was scheduled to meet, among others, an engineer whose knowledge of metals and metalworking was reputed to be encyclopaedic. He was looking forward to a productive discussion and was anxious to establish whether or not this – he glanced down at the dossier before him – this Yuri Borodin could be of practical use to the Expedition.

There was a peremptory knock on the door and, before Bering could call out 'Enter!' it opened a crack to reveal unkempt blond hair and a dazzling smile.

'Martin!'

'Captain-Commander.'

'By all that's wonderful, it's good to see you again! What brings you to St Petersburg?'

Martin Spanberg entered the room, crossed to the desk and shook Bering's hand.

'It is said that a certain Captain-Commander I used to serve under has need of expert counsel if he is to find his way through the strait that bears his name.'

'Enough of your impertinence, you whippersnapper. The Captain-Commander of whom you speak can sail those seas blindfold without the help of a cabin boy such as yourself.'

'Then, sir, I shall take my leave. My only concern was to come to your assistance in your time of need.'

The two men embraced. Bering was beside himself with pleasure. Martin Spanberg was the son he had always wanted but never had. Yet the two men could scarcely have been more unlike in temperament. Where Bering was serious to the point of appearing slow-witted, Martin Spanberg was irrepressibly quick and devil-may-care. Spanberg had an easy social grace that Bering so obviously lacked. A notorious – and notoriously successful – womaniser, Spanberg had a charm and a lightness of touch that bordered on the frivolous. But, as Bering knew only too well, Spanberg was all steel underneath.

A skilled seaman and a born leader of men, Spanberg was a good man in any crisis.

Spanberg looked Bering over appraisingly. The Captain-

Commander has aged, he thought, and he does not wear his age lightly. He has lost weight during his years away from St Petersburg and his aura of authority has dimmed.

'You look well, Captain-Commander.'

'As do you, First Officer Spanberg.'

They faced each other across the desk, secure and comfortable in each other's presence. Spanberg was the first to speak.

'It is rumoured that this expedition of yours promises to empty St Petersburg of all its noble families, including their most eligible daughters. If, by this intemperate and ill-considered action, you elect to deprive me of my favourite sport, then I can see no option other than to follow my prey wherever it leads.'

'It has never been my wish to deprive you of anything, First Officer, least of all to remove the objects of your desire. But my mission is a serious one and I, too, have little option other than to follow where it may lead.'

Spanberg ran a hand through his hair, and leaned forward, his hands clasping the edge of the table.

'It is also said that you are to strike out with two vessels into the Bering Strait and beyond. That you will command one of those vessels. And that the captaincy of the second is shortly to be decided.'

Bering heaved a sigh.

'Nothing would give me greater pleasure than to have you command the second vessel. Alas, that decision is not in my hands. The command has already been allocated by a higher authority. It is to be Chirikov.'

'Aleksey Chirikov? An able mariner in all truth, but one for whom I have no great affection.'

'Affection is a luxury I am ill-placed to afford,' replied Bering. 'His nomination does not please me, although I can find little fault with his seamanship. We are men of the sea, you and I, with little knowledge of, nor liking for, the machinations of those who seek political advancement. I regret to say that Chirikov is among the latter.'

Spanberg fell silent. It was clear that he was weighing his options. Across the table from him sat a man who had once saved his life and that of his men. A man whose commitment and sense of loyalty were uncompromising.

'Then, if I cannot command, I shall offer my humble services once more as your First Officer.'

It was the reply Bering had expected but which he found difficult to accept.

'That is a sacrifice I cannot request of you. You are but months away from your *brevet* as Captain of your own ship. To sail as my First Officer would retard the promotion you have most certainly earned. I propose rather that you assume command of one of the other vessels in the flotilla. If I so recommend, such an appointment should pose no great difficulty.'

Spanberg smiled to mask his disappointment.

'Captain-Commander, you are and have always been my model and my inspiration. Promotion be hanged. I would rather sail to glory as your second-in-command than trawl my arse up and down the shallows off the Kamchatka coast playing nursemaid to a gaggle of academics.'

'Then let it be so.'

The two men rose and shook hands.

'I thank you, sir. And now I must take my leave.'

'Nonsense,' said Bering. 'I have earned a day's respite. Come, let us return to my home. My wife and daughter are here and I would have them meet you.'

'That is an honour I have no hesitation in accepting, Captain-Commander.'

The two men swept out of Bering's chamber past an astonished Yuri Borodin whose ground-breaking *Thesaurus of Known Metals and their Naval Applications* had earmarked him as one of the leading scientists of the age.

Borodin was not amused.

Gulf of Finland
March 1, 1733

Dinner was a simple affair: boiled salted cod, greens, delicious coarse brown bread and goat cheese. Osa Bering would have preferred prior warning that Vitus was bringing a guest. For all that, she was delighted to welcome a visitor to their home. She was equally delighted that, all through dinner, Vitus had displayed an enthusiasm and fire she had not witnessed for months, not to say years.

Martin Spanberg was the perfect guest. Within minutes, he was flirting openly with the nineteen-year-old Benthe. Osa he treated with almost exaggerated courtesy, complimenting her repeatedly on her home and her hospitality.

After dinner, the two men went outside to smoke a pipe. Osa and Benthe busied themselves in the kitchen before joining them.

Inevitably, talk had turned to the Imperial Great Northern Expedition. Vitus and Spanberg were discussing plots and channels. Osa was astonished at how vividly and precisely they appeared to recollect even the most minute detail without recourse to any chart or log. Benthe listened, understanding little but captivated by Martin Spanberg and hanging on every word he uttered.

'This will be a great adventure, Captain-Commander.'

'That it will, Martin. Yet I am troubled by the beginnings of it, what with all these landlubbers and hangers-on.'

'Aye, there is truth in that.'

To her surprise, Osa Bering found herself interrupting them.

'But it is a price that must be paid if Vitus is to pursue his dream.'

The two men looked up in surprise at what was, in essence, a breach of etiquette.

Osa blushed but ploughed ahead.

'You must understand, First Officer Spanberg, that my husband has endured all manner of ill treatment at the hands of those who have rarely strayed beyond the walls of the St Petersburg Court.'

'That,' said Bering, 'is no longer a matter for concern.'

'But it is,' insisted Osa. 'And this mission is a chance to put the record to rights.'

Vitus Bering was clearly embarrassed by his wife's blunt intervention but nonetheless proud of it. He looked at her fondly.

'My dear, you are right. And it is a chance that I will take.'

'I do not doubt it, Captain-Commander,' put in Spanberg. He was about to continue but Osa Bering had not finished.

It was now or never, she thought to herself. Her mind was made up. She took a deep breath.

'It is a chance we shall take together.'

'Of course, my dear.'

'You fail to understand, Vitus. I shall be coming with you, as will Benthe.'

Bering's jaw dropped. He was at a loss for words.

Spanberg sprang to his rescue.

'The journey is too hazardous for a lady such as yourself', he said. 'Besides, it is no place for such a delicate flower as your charming daughter.'

Osa Bering's eyes flashed.

'Do you imply, First Officer, that I am less of a wife than the ladies of the Court who will voyage with their husbands and their families?'

'I imply nothing of the sort,' said Spanberg. 'I find only that the presence of your good self and of your daughter might prove something of a –', he cast about for the tactful word.

'– something of a distraction?' said Osa. 'First Officer, let me assure you. Nothing and no-one has ever proved capable of distracting my husband once he has charted his course and embarked upon it.'

'Your wife is a lady of uncommon resolve, Captain-Commander,' said Spanberg once the two men were alone together again.

'That she is,' answered Bering. 'Yet I confess that her resolve is not unwelcome.'

Spanberg smiled.

He could not have agreed more.

Imperial Court of St Petersburg
March 27, 1733

Count Ernst Johann von Biron had been careful to allow Bering free rein in his conduct of the interviews. He perceived no threat from that quarter. Bering, he knew, was duty-bound to accept the directives of the Grand Council, and his endorsement of those on the master list was a mere formality.

In all, close on 200 names had been screened and approved. Together with their families and retinue, these represented over 1,200 persons, among them many that von Biron knew would not stay the course.

Von Biron had also been content to allow Bering his head when it came to selecting the crews and allocating their responsibilities. In that respect, he admitted to himself, Bering was without a doubt the best judge.

Designating the leader of the advance party was another matter entirely. To Bering's unconcealed distaste, Chirikov had been confirmed as the envoy of the Grand Council and, effectively, the joint leader of the Expedition. He would travel with the main body. What remained to be done was to determine who should command the advance party.

Von Biron's choice had fallen on Grigor Pisarov, a 33-year-old lieutenant who had his detractors but whose loyalty to von Biron was beyond question. Bering knew of Pisarov and vice-versa but the two had never met.

Their first meeting was not auspicious.

Bering took an instinctive dislike to Pisarov, whom he found disrespectful and truculent. The dislike was mutual: Pisarov thought Bering arrogant and dismissive.

'Lieutenant Pisarov, the specifics of your mission are clear. You are to proceed overland to Okhotsk on the sea of that name. You and your men will transport materials and tools as necessary to construct six vessels according to these specifications. You will do this with the aid of labour recruited from the convict settlement in the region.'

Bering handed across a sheaf of detailed drawings.

'The vessels are to be readied by late autumn. You shall over-winter on board and ensure that the flotilla is at our immediate disposal to start operations next spring.'

'At your orders, Captain-Commander.'

'That is all.'

Pisarov hesitated.

'Yes?'

'Captain-Commander, may I ask what my role is to be in the Expedition itself?'

'Your role, sir, is explicit. You will command and administer the onshore garrison.'

'I had hoped –'

'You have your orders, Lieutenant.'

Pisarov had envisaged for himself a major role in the voyage of exploration. The son and nephew of influential figures at Court, he found himself relegated to a role he considered to be below his dignity and incommensurate with his service record.

'Who does he think he is, this Danish upstart?' he later complained to von Biron.

'He is the choice of the Empress,' replied von Biron. 'And my own.'

Von Biron thought it superfluous to remind Pisarov that he was by no stretch of the imagination a darling of the Court. Pisarov had already spent some years in Siberia, exiled there as a dissident given to intemperate outbursts which had appeared to question the absolute authority of the Empress. This was Pisarov's opportunity to redeem himself, and both he and von Biron knew as much.

Bering cared little whether Pisarov resented both the mission with which he had been entrusted and the man under whom he was to serve. In truth, Bering would have been indifferent to Pisarov's resentment even had he recognised it.

Pisarov was, after all, only a minor cog in the wheel of Bering's destiny.

St Petersburg
April 1733

From the journal of Lieutenant-at-Sea Sven Waxell

April 2, 1733

On the prevailings of my sweet wife I have travelled with our son Laurentij to St. Petersburg. He is very young and both spirited in mind and healthy in body, yet I am uncertain of the prudence of it. He begs to be with us on the overland journey to Siberia, however, and I am loathe to dash his hopes.

In truth, I have been here some weeks and have yet to present myself to the Captain-Commander. It is known that he has recruited widely for the Expedition and I fear that my candidacy may come too late if I am to secure a position on his vessel. St. Petersburg teems with seafarers who seek to serve on the Expedition. It is said that wages are to be doubled for those fortunates who are accepted.

I have taken the liberty of sending another note to the attention of the Captain-Commander, requesting – nay, begging – him to review my petition to serve. I am without response, which saddens me greatly.

April 3, 1733

The Captain-Commander has responded to my note, bidding me to present myself this day.

His reply is most civil and my hopes are high.

April 4, 1733

I am to sail with Bering!

The Captain-Commander received me most graciously and spoke well of my ability. He is much preoccupied with readying the advance party which leaves here in one week's time. I am to leave next year a month ahead of the main body of the Expedition and will travel overland in command of hand-picked crews. I shall meet with the Captain-Commander in Okhotsk, by all accounts a most inhospitable place.

My mission calls for me to rendezvous with one Lieutenant Pisarov who leads the advance party and who is charged with readying six vessels for the Expedition. The Captain-Commander wishes me to inspect those craft for seaworthiness and to report to him on his arrival. The responsibility that falls on my shoulders is great but I shall discharge my duties to the best of my abilities.

The Captain-Commander is much as I remember him, yet

changed in some small respects that I find difficult to describe. He tells me that Martin Spanberg is to serve as his First Officer – an excellent choice to be sure. The Captain-Commander was most taken with Laurentij and has encouraged me to bring the lad. It will be the experience of a lifetime, he said.

I believe this to be so.

Gulf of Finland
April 26, 1733

The days grew longer, longer still now that the wait had begun.

The advance party had left on April 14. If all went to plan, it would reach the Kamchatka Peninsula by early October. If it encountered difficulties, it would overwinter in Yakutsk and continue on to Okhotsk in the spring of the following year.

Vitus Bering took long walks on the beach with his wife. Nothing further had been said of her decision to join the main expedition the following year. Bering was very much against it but did not say so: there was time enough to talk some sense into her.

There had been an inevitable lull in the preparations following the departure of Pisarov. Had Bering had his say, the entire Expedition would already be under way. But the Grand Council had decreed otherwise and Bering had no alternative but to comply.

The prospect of waiting a further full year weighed heavily on him. True, there were many preparations still to be made and many meetings to be attended, but it irked Bering that the Expedition had, to all intents and purposes, started without him. He was also irritated by the prospect of a caravan of courtiers and scientists.

Martin Spanberg was a frequent guest at dinner and it was to Spanberg that Bering habitually confided his misgivings.

'There are too many unknowns, First Officer. I cannot bring myself to have faith in this Pisarov and I suspect I may be about to place too heavy a burden on the shoulders of young Waxell.'

Spanberg, by now accustomed to these bouts of self-doubt, could offer only platitudes in response.

'You worry too much, Captain-Commander. Pisarov is a shit but he is a capable shit. And Waxell, for all his youth, is an officer of substance.'

And Bering would shake his head again and again.

'You don't understand, Martin. I should be there, I should be leading from the front not from behind a desk in St Petersburg.'

'Your time at the helm will come soon enough, Captain-Commander.'

Osa Bering looked on as the two men went through this ritual. Like Martin Spanberg, she sympathised with her husband and was understanding of his impatience. But she knew that the twelve months would pass more quickly than he believed possible.

Spanberg was right. Their time would come.

Chapter Two

OVERLAND

St Petersburg
April 13, 1734
They came in their thousands, lining the banks of the Neva and the grandiose avenues that led to the Imperial Palace. An early spring sun glinted dully off the water.

The Imperial Great Northern Expedition was leaving the next day and all St Petersburg had turned out to watch it depart. Many had come from the outlying regions of the capital – on foot, by horse and by bullock-drawn peasant cart – others still from much further afield, most of them experiencing for the first time the splendour that was St Petersburg.

They marvelled at the marble palaces and granite-block quays of the Baltic port Peter the Great had transformed into Russia's first great European city. They walked to the Peterhof on the outskirts, taking in the magnificent fountains and gardens of this Baltic Versailles. They strolled along the broad tree-lined avenues to applaud the grandeur of the spectacular Winter Palace built at the wish of Peter's daughter and successor, the Empress Elizabeth I.

The citizens of St Petersburg were inordinately proud of their city, prouder still that it was the point of departure for the greatest expedition in history.

At the prompting of Count von Biron, the Empress Anna Ivanovna had chosen the Amber Room in the Andrea Palladio-inspired Ekaterininsky Palace in Tsarskoye Selo as the setting in which to confer her formal blessing on the Imperial Great Northern Expedition. The room, gifted to Peter the Great by the Prussian King Friedrich Wilhelm I in 1716 to commemorate the Battle of

Poltava and the victory of the Russian Army over Sweden, was a swirling plethora of Florentine mosaics set in ornately engraved *bas-relief* panels laboriously crafted out of massive amber nuggets.

To a man of simple tastes like Vitus Bering, the Amber Room was outrageously extravagant. To his wife, standing straight and proud by his side, it was a thing of wonder, a tribute to patrician taste and neo-Renaissance craftsmanship.

The Empress Anna Ivanovna perched squat and ungainly on her throne, flanked by von Biron and the members of the Grand Council. She was bored by the ceremony, as well she might be. A recitation of all the noble families accompanying the Expedition was followed by a presentation of the scientists who were to join it, complete with lengthy profiles of their respective academic achievements.

Bering was growing increasingly uncomfortable – his feet hurt and his bladder was full – and he almost failed to hear his name being called. He stepped forward and bowed to the Empress.

'We expect much of you, Captain-Commander,' were her final words.

The presentations over, participants filed slowly from the room by order of noble rank or civic status. Among the last to leave were Bering and his wife. Osa clutched his arm as they emerged into the sunlight.

The waiting crowd had grown restless but they contrived to raise a cheer when they recognised Bering.

The leaving celebrations continued well into the night. Osa Bering, her face flushed with anticipation and two glasses of wine, prevailed upon her husband to dance with her – which he did with obvious reluctance – then gave her arm to Martin Spanberg, who betrayed no reluctance whatsoever.

For Benthe Bering, this was a night to cherish. They were leaving at first light and she had vowed to dance until then. She and her mother were to join the Expedition after all: Osa Bering had insisted and her father had finally relented. They would travel overland to the Siberian coast and spend the winter there, returning in late spring with a heavy military escort.

Who knew what adventures lay ahead, she thought, as she danced the night away.

St Petersburg
April 14, 1734
By Bering's estimation, the Imperial Great Northern Expedition had advanced less than eight miles over the first full day. By dusk, when they pulled in for the night, the column tapered back almost three miles.

Bering was beside himself. Furious at the sluggish pace, he rode back to the tail of the column to discover why the stragglers had failed to keep up with the main body. At this rate of progress, he reasoned, we shall be fortunate to reach Siberia before the end of the century, let alone the end of summer.

At the tail of the Expedition was the Dzerzinsky family – Count Dzerzinsky himself, together with a retinue which included his wife, two daughters, and eleven servants, along with a cook and, as Bering subsequently discovered to his amazement, the head gardener from the Dzerzinsky estates.

Bering's tone was conciliatory, almost deferential.

'My respects, Count Dzerzinsky. May I express the hope that the pace we set is to the convenience of yourself and those who accompany you?'

'The pace you set is quite admirable, Captain-Commander, yet I should remind you that the ladies must take their rest during the day. As for myself, I am no longer the youngster I once was.'

'We have an arduous journey before us, Count, yet we must sustain a steady pace. By my projection, the column must advance by forty miles or more each day if we are to reach our destination before the onset of the winter snows.'

'And, pray, what distance have we travelled today?'

Bering pointed to a small hill to the north.

'From the crest of that hill, Count Dzerzinsky, you can still see the spires of St Petersburg.'

'I take it you are dissatisfied with our progress, Captain-Commander?'

'I cannot say I am pleased, Your Excellency.'

Dzerzinsky sniffed.

'Then may I say that we are not an army and that this is not a forced march. You have my word that we shall endeavour to do better tomorrow.'

'I thank you, Your Excellency.'

Bering rode back to the head of the column. He dismounted and turned to Spanberg, who was unhitching the horses and rubbing them down.

'This is madness, First Officer. The Dzerzinskys travel at a snail's pace, as do others at the rear. This cannot continue.'

'True, Captain-Commander.'

Spanberg hesitated.

'And?'

'Might I suggest that your place is perhaps not at the head of the column, Captain-Commander, but towards the rear? From there, you can ensure that the Expedition keeps closer order.'

'It has always been my conviction that one leads from the front.'

'Then allow me to reposition myself towards the rear of the column where I can encourage the stragglers to keep up.'

'Let it be so.'

'I believe that, for their safety, it would also be advisable to reposition your wife and daughter.'

'For the moment they are safe where they are. But you are right, First Officer. When the terrain becomes more difficult, it would be for the best if they were to seek protection towards the rear.'

'At your orders, Captain-Commander.'

The Great Russian Plain
May 6, 1734

Bering was becoming increasingly resentful at what he regarded as a fundamental subversion of the chain of command. As nominal head of the Expedition and its ranking officer, he was under formal instruction to report to and consult with his Russian second-in-command, a man whose seafaring craftsmanship he respected but whose personality he disliked.

Aleksey Illich Chirikov sensed Bering's growing antipathy and was sufficiently shrewd to defer to his senior officer's judgment on most matters, particularly if Chirikov judged the issue in hand to be minor or inconsequential.

Chirikov was first and foremost a mariner – and a good one. He had served well under Bering during the voyage of 1724 to 1728 and knew that Bering could find little if any fault with his professional skills. Apart from anything else, he knew what lay behind Bering's frustration. True, as a non-Russian, the Captain-Commander's overall authority had been diluted to the point of humiliation. Of more import, however, was the fact that Bering – and, for that matter, Chirikov himself – was anxious to get on with the real business of the Expedition.

What the two men had in common was a constant awareness that they were thousands of land miles from their natural element, the sea, and months, if not years, away from their real mission. Chirikov was convinced that Bering was less capable than he of coping with the trials and frustrations of the overland journey and, in this belief, he was certainly justified.

All the more so, since Aleksey Illich Chirikov knew much that Bering had not been privileged to share.

It was increasingly evident that the Expedition would not reach the coast on schedule. Bering's calculations had already proved wildly optimistic, based as they were on the commitment and physical aptitude of a compact body of seasoned professionals who would travel light and hard. Chirikov knew that the Expedition would have to overwinter more than once *en route*. Back in St Petersburg, Ernst von Biron had predicted this eventuality and had even made light of it, taking what to Chirikov seemed almost a perverse pleasure at the prospect of several of Russia's noble families huddled together for warmth in some God-forsaken outpost of the Empire.

What Chirikov also knew was that the core mission to explore the upper reaches of the Bering Strait would be deferred for months, even years, until such time as the Expedition had completed what von Biron and the Grand Council considered to be the primary goal, namely charting and documenting Russia's Siberian coast-line.

As the Expedition moved slowly farther and farther away from the capital, communications with St Petersburg became increasingly tenuous and sporadic. Nonetheless, the lines of communications remained open thanks to a network of messengers mounted on strings of sturdy ponies who travelled to and fro between the Expedition and St Petersburg, carrying irregular despatches from Bering and, as Bering had every reason to suspect, from Chirikov.

That Bering was not privileged to view, comment on, or censure Chirikov's reports was a further thorn in the Captain-Commander's side.

An uneasy truce reigned. Both men were acutely aware of the paradox that was intrinsic to their respective roles within the Expedition and each contrived to avoid unnecessary confrontation by limiting their exchanges as far as possible to practical considerations of immediate rather than longer-term relevance.

For Bering, the prime consideration was and had always been the specifics of their ultimate mission. Night after night, he and Chirikov would pore over the composition of their respective crews, agonising over the sea routes to be followed and lamenting the presence of the scientific contingent they were obliged to accommodate on board.

In many matters, Bering respected and endorsed Chirikov's judgment. In all honesty, he admitted to himself, Chirikov had proved his worth during the months of preparation back in St Petersburg. In particular, Chirikov had been adept at justifying the exclusion of many would-be participants on the grounds of age, physical condition or rigorous scientific necessity. What was more, Chirikov had shown himself to be a good judge of men, not least by weeding out the inexperienced and the prospective troublemakers.

In one crucial respect, however, the two had been forced to agree to differ.

In the course of repeated visits to The Spaniard's Inn, Martin Spanberg had become increasingly intimate not only with the buxom landlady but also with Oleg Khitrov, the bearded Russian giant he had first encountered over two years previously. Spanberg had discovered to his surprise that Oleg was already in his early fifties.

'You carry yourself well for a man of your age,' he had said.

'Well enough, you Danish turd,' Oleg had replied. 'But these old bones are weary with age and salt water. My days at sea are at an end.'

Spanberg suppressed a smile. It was well known that he was to be Bering's First Officer and he had grown accustomed to approaches from all and sundry, urging him to use his influence to secure them a berth.

'And rightly so,' said Spanberg. 'You're too old and too ugly to helm any ship I'd care to sail in.'

'Too old, am I? Too old? Why, I've helmed in more seas than you can count, you arse-wipe. As for ugly, that's true enough, coming from a pretty boy such as yourself.'

They drank in silence.

Spanberg waited. He knew that Oleg had something on his mind.

'I have a son, you know, a good lad and a master helmsman.'

Shit, thought Spanberg, I know where this is leading.

'I didn't know.'

'Aye, he's a fine lad. And experienced with it.'

'How so?'

'He's sailed the White Sea and the waters off the Siberian coast.'

'As have many others. Where is he now?'

'He's here in St Petersburg. Doing duty at the Naval Academy.'

Spanberg emptied his glass and ordered a refill.

'His rank?'

'A lieutenant. And only twenty-six years old.'

Oleg waited expectantly.

'Then I should meet with him.'

Oleg Khitrov grinned broadly. He thumped Spanberg on the back, spilling his ale over the counter.

'That you shall, my Danish sweetmeat. That you shall, this very night.'

Spanberg had been backed into a corner, but he was unconcerned. There would be no harm in meeting the young lieutenant, he reasoned. And if he turned out to be as proficient as his proud father claimed, Spanberg would do what he could on his behalf, secure in the knowledge that the final decision on recruitment would be made not by himself but by his Captain-Commander.

Sofron Valery Khitrov was of medium height, as handsome as his father was ugly, and self-confident to the point of arrogance.

Vitus Bering took to him immediately.

Aleksey Chirikov disliked him on sight.

'This is a key post, Captain-Commander. It must not be entrusted to a fresh-faced youth.'

'His record speaks for itself.'

'His record is academic. He is a paper navigator. We need seasoned men at the helm, men that we can trust.'

Bering raised an eyebrow.

'And how seasoned were you, Acting Captain Chirikov, when we first set sail in 1724? Or does my memory play tricks with me? Was there not a certain youthful arrogance in your disposition when you and I first clapped eyes on each other? Do you not detect that same quality in Khitrov?'

Bering was on firm ground. Young Khitrov's arrogance would mellow into competence, of that he was convinced. Besides, Chirikov's reluctance to endorse the youngster's appointment could in all likelihood be attributed to the initial recommendation having come from Martin Spanberg, another non-Russian whose presence and assigned role in the Expedition clearly did not sit well with Chirikov.

'In all conscience, Captain-Commander, I cannot approve this.'

'And in all conscience, Captain, I can. We need young blood and youthful endeavour. That is the way of the sea.'

'Then, with respect, Captain-Commander, I propose that you take this fledgling under your wing.'

This was a direct challenge to Bering's authority and both men knew it.

'I shall do so gladly and with every confidence. Khitrov shall helm for me.'

'That is your decision, sir, and I respect your right to make it.'

Bering's fist slammed down on the table.

'That is correct, Captain Chirikov. I have at least that right. There are some decisions that I may take and this is one of them.'

'I pray it is not a decision you will live to regret.'

'Enough, Captain. You try my patience.'

'I am concerned only for the outcome of the Expedition, Captain-Commander.'

'Then concern yourself with this thought. This is a matter of judgment and in that, if nowhere else in this overblown undertaking, I remain your superior officer. You are dismissed.'

Aleksey Chirikov nodded, stood up, saluted and left.

A rider was due to leave next morning for St Petersburg. He would take with him a despatch recording Chirikov's misgivings on this and other disturbing aspects of Bering's behaviour.

Halle an der Saale
May 8, 1734

Georg Wilhelm Steller sat on a bench in the Universitätsbibliothek in Halle, a well-worn copy of the *De materia medica* of Penadios Dioscorides spread out on the wooden lectern in front of him. It was late and the university library was on the point of closing. Steller reluctantly gathered his notes together and returned the volume to the shelf.

Steller was scheduled to preach later that evening to a small gathering of Lutherans at a meeting house near the Dölauer Heide. Under normal circumstances, he would have looked forward to the cut and thrust of theological debate.

Tonight was somehow different.

For months now, Steller had felt uneasy about the lack of direction in his career, although he was convinced that opting for the University of Halle to continue his studies had been a wise move.

Halle University, founded less than half a century previously, already boasted a proud tradition of humanistic studies and was the hub of Lutheran scholarship. Like the University of Wittenberg before it, Halle had quickly established its reputation as a 'modern' university, not least in its espousal of objectivity and rationalism as an alternative to stolid religious orthodoxy. This was reflected in a liberal curriculum taught in the Saxon German of Martin Luther rather than in the arcane Latin of the Church.

Above all, Halle was recognised as the German seat of the Pietist movement that had developed in large measure under the influence of English and Dutch Puritanism. The Pietists stressed the virtues of personal improvement and upright conduct as twin pillars of the Christian faith.

Georg Wilhelm Steller was a committed Pietist. A career as a theologian beckoned, but Steller was pulled in another direction. He had other interests. Ever since childhood he had been fascinated by animals and plants and, of late, he had become more and more preoccupied with the natural world. He had read and reread *De varietate rerum*, fascinated by Girolamo Cardano's unprecedented grasp of natural evolution, and he found himself turning again and again to medicine and the natural sciences – and especially to biology and botany.

As he made his way across the heath, he was alarmed to find his thoughts drifting away from the immediate subject of that evening's *collegium* and towards his almost obsessive interest in the curative and restorative powers of plants and herbs.

Steller arrived at the meeting hall well before the meeting was scheduled to begin. The hall was still empty. He set his notes down on the lectern and tried in vain to focus his mind on the subject of that evening's debate. On a sudden impulse, he gathered up his notes again and left the hall.

He knew now what he had to do.

St Petersburg
May 30, 1734
Count Ernst von Biron read the Chirikov despatches with interest and disquiet.

If Chirikov was to be believed – and there was no reason to doubt him – Bering's conduct was becoming increasingly irrational and unpredictable. Earlier reports had described Bering's confrontation with Count Dzerzinsky and his entourage. Dzerzinsky himself had reappeared at court only days before, denouncing Bering as an impertinent upstart Dane with an uncivil tongue and no respect for rank and status.

Von Biron knew Dzerzinsky for the pompous ass he was, but he realised that the credibility of the Expedition could be jeopardised if Bering were not brought swiftly to heel.

He called for writing materials and settled down to compose a letter that Vitus Bering was not destined to receive until many weeks later.

Captain-Commander:
We send you greetings from the Court and from the Csarina Anna Ivanovna, Empress of All the Russias, and give thanks for your most recent and detailed report on the progress of our great undertaking which is the envy of the civilised world. It is a matter of grave concern to the undersigned that your progress has been frustrated by the numbers under your command and I am at pains to express my understanding of and my regret for the difficulties this has occasioned.

Allow me therefore to assure you of our unswerving commitment to take whatever steps lie within our powers to support your brave endeavours and to uphold the purpose of the Imperial Great Northern Expedition.

Allow me also to remind you of the specific responsibilities that are vested in you and of the express limits imposed on those selfsame responsibilities. If you are to reap the rewards of fame and fortune which will undoubtedly be your due, I urge you to heed the counsel of Lieutenant Chirikov who acts with the full authority and in accordance with the express wishes of the Grand Council.

I trust this letter finds you in good health and in good spirits. I append my respects to your lady wife.

Ernst Johann, Reichsgraf von Biron

Von Biron signed with a flourish. The tone of the letter was appropriate, he felt.

Friendly but firm.

The second despatch was for Chirikov's eyes only.

Captain:

Your most recent report was laid before the Grand Council
which has regard for the fears you express. You are
enjoined to continue to observe and report on the conduct
of Captain-Commander Bering.

You have in your possession a document by which the
Council formally empowers you to relieve the Captain-
Commander of his command when the time is right and as
circumstances permit. You are to implement this order with
prudence and discretion. It is however imperative that the
Expedition reach the Kamchatka Peninsula under Captain-
Commander Bering's command and that he assume responsibility for setting in motion the initial phases of
exploration. No deviation from this instruction will be
tolerated.

On execution of this order and not before, you shall
assume the rank of acting Captain-Commander.

Ernst Johann, Reichsgraf von Biron

Von Biron dribbled hot wax over the despatch and set his seal. He
stood up, walked over to the window and looked towards the east.

On balance, the Expedition was going according to plan.

The Great Russian Plain
June 24, 1734
The young girl screamed several times.

Two women bent over her, pinning her by the shoulders to the
coarse, straw-filled sack on which she lay. A third bathed her
forehead in cold water. She struggled to spit out the rag they had
wedged between her teeth. Her gums were bleeding. The pain in
her abdomen was excruciating.

The midwife worked feverishly to reposition the child in the womb. The baby lay badly. Both mother and child would certainly die if it could not be turned.

Osa Bering applied another cold compress to the girl's forehead as the girl howled again, her back arching convulsively.

'Hold her firm,' ordered the midwife, her hands thrusting deep into the pelvis, reaching for the baby's head. She tugged again and again, sweat running down her face. Suddenly, she felt the fleshy mass yield.

The girl screamed yet again and fainted. The midwife threw caution to the winds and pulled hard. The baby exited in a rush and with a sound strangely akin to that of a boot being extricated from seashore mud. Eyes clenched shut and its face and body an angry red, it lay on the silk shawl Osa Bering had spread beneath the girl's buttocks.

'It's a boy,' shouted the midwife triumphantly, holding the baby upside down by the feet and slapping it time and again. The new-born dangled from her hands like a raw, skinless salmon. The women stared at it, willing it to respond.

The midwife slapped the inert flesh one more time and suddenly there was a yelp which extended into a prolonged wail.

'He lives,' said the midwife, her broad peasant face creasing into a broken-toothed grin.

The girl opened her eyes. The pain had dulled. She heard the baby cry and she smiled in contentment. She felt an immediate urge to pass water.

The women took turns to fuss over the new-born, cleaning him and wrapping him in a blanket before returning him to his mother's arms. The young mother stared down at her offspring, taking in his features and counting his tiny fingers over and over as if to confirm they were all there.

'He is perfect,' she concluded. The women looked down at her and then, in turn, at one another.

'Does he have a name?' asked Osa.

The fourteen-year-old girl smiled up at them. She had given this some thought in the preceding weeks. The father could be one of several boys she had lain with.

'I shall call him Vitus,' she said, glancing up nervously at Osa Bering, seeking her approval.

'My husband will be honoured,' said Osa.

At his wife's insistence, Vitus Bering had halted the Expedition to allow the child to come into the world unhampered by the bumps and jolts of the rough terrain. Osa had also insisted that the baby be brought to the relative comfort of their own carriage.

Bering considered this a dangerous precedent – God only knew how many more of these wenches were with child and he could scarcely be expected to delay the column's progress every time one of them went into labour. On the other hand, he instinctively grasped the value to the Expedition of Osa's gesture and took pride in it – and in his wife.

The servant girl had been in labour for the better part of nine hours and there seemed little point in ordering the column back into motion now that evening was almost on them.

Bering was aware that the enforced stop had had the positive effect of enabling some of the stragglers to close up to the main body. By his reckoning, the Expedition now numbered some 1,100 souls, including the military escort. As many as six hundred or so had already returned to St Petersburg, disenchanted with the rigours and discomforts of the journey and the pace Bering had felt obliged to set. Behind the main body, the column of *colporteurs* had started to thin out within days of leaving the city. Among the artisans and hawkers still tagging along behind the column were a number of wheelwrights who continued to do good business and who showed no signs of turning back. He resolved to bring them into the protection of the main column where the need for their expertise was increasingly acute.

Bering identified the enforced halt as an ideal opportunity to instil a renewed *esprit de corps* into the Expedition. The word was passed back that there would be a feast that evening, ostensibly to mark the successful birth of the Expedition's first new recruit.

Orders were duly given: oxen were slaughtered, barrels of ale were tapped, and an *ad hoc* orchestra was assembled.

This would be a night to remember.

Lieutenant Valery Khitrov had so far acquitted himself well and had proved to be a valuable member of the Expedition. His primary responsibility was modest enough, namely to help Bering plot the overland route and to scout the terrain ahead to chart the least perilous course for the carriages, service wagons and pack animals. Progress across the Great Russian Plain was commendably brisk now, although Bering knew that the hardest part was yet to come.

Khitrov had contrived to make himself popular with all and sundry – with the notable exception of Aleksey Chirikov – and Bering was gratified that his first impressions had been confirmed. He could not fail to notice that Khitrov was anxious to attract the attentions of his daughter Benthe who, to the young Lieutenant's chagrin, seemed immune to his charms. Her gaze rarely wandered from Martin Spanberg, whose easy-going efficiency was not lost on the womenfolk of the Expedition.

As for Spanberg, he was disturbed to realise that *his* gaze rarely wandered from Osa Bering. He found her a remarkable creature, with a natural elegance offset by a simplicity that bordered on earthiness. As the weeks had gone by, he had begun to see in her an amalgam of the many women he had admired and bedded. His growing attachment to her was compounded by the fact that she seemed genuinely to like him and to enjoy his company.

Spanberg resolved to keep his distance. Vitus Bering was his superior officer, his friend and his surrogate father. To breach Bering's trust was unthinkable.

The festivities continued well into the night.

Benthe Bering danced – too often for her taste – with Lieutenant Khitrov. She looked on as her mother mingled with aristocrat and peasant alike.

Against his better judgment, Martin Spanberg found himself drawn to Osa's side. They danced and he could feel the warmth of her body against his. To his dismay, he found himself growing erect. Abruptly, he broke off and proposed they take refreshment. Osa agreed and, her hand resting loosely on his forearm, they made their way across to where a burly sailor was dispensing generous measures of a sweet but powerfully-fermented potato juice mixture from a huge metal vat.

Vitus Bering chose that moment to call for silence.

The dancers gradually slowed and stopped as the music faded.

All eyes were on Bering as he clambered up on the tailboard of one of the wagons.

Bering had judged the moment well.

'Excellencies and friends, we are gathered here to celebrate a new mouth in our midst. I hold it to be a singular honour that he has been named after myself and I see his birth as a positive omen for the continued success of our joint undertaking. I give you the health of young Vitus!'

The assembly roared its appreciation and enthusiastically joined in the toast. They fell silent again as Bering raised a hand.

'Today has been a benchmark day for us all. We have come many miles from the great city of St Petersburg, yet a long road lies ahead of us. In the course of a journey such as this there comes a point beyond which there is no return.'

The crowd shifted uneasily.

'Tomorrow I shall detach a small military escort to accompany those families who still wish to return to the capital. As of now, those who choose to remain with the Expedition must perforce continue with us at least as far as Okhotsk. In the days and weeks ahead, there will be others who may seek to turn back. They may do so, but they will do so on their own responsibility and at their own risk. I will not authorise on their behalf a further dilution of our military escort, nor will I assume responsibility for their safety.'

Bering paused.

'The military escort will be ready for departure by first light. Tonight, we have feasted and rejoiced in one another's company. To those who elect at dawn to return to St Petersburg, I wish God's speed. To those who remain, I pledge my word as Captain-Commander that the way ahead will be arduous but rewarding. God bless us all.'

There was silence.

Spanberg looked at the faces around him, gauging their uncertainty. He removed Osa Bering's hand from his arm and brought both hands together in deliberately loud and insistent applause. Slowly, those next to him joined in, the clamour building until the applause was general and sustained.

Bering was visibly moved. He nodded briefly and stepped down from the tailboard, turning briefly to stare out over the sea of faces.

Osa Bering watched as her husband disappeared into the crowd, making his way back to their quarters. She felt an acute pang of disappointment that she had not been standing beside him at what was clearly a turning point in the Expedition.

Spanberg whispered in her ear above the noise of the crowd.

'Your husband is a born leader of men.'

Osa nodded, her eyes moist with tears.

'I have known this for many years, Martin.'

Inadvertently, she squeezed his forearm.

Spanberg was at a loss what to do next. His first inclination was to detain Osa Bering in his company for as long as possible, but his innate sense of loyalty – and, for him, an atypical twinge of guilt – would not countenance this. He offered her his arm and volunteered to escort her back to her quarters. Osa Bering thanked him for the courtesy. Much as she wished to continue to enjoy what she anticipated might be the last such night of celebration, she knew where her duty lay.

They skirted the encampment, making their way in silence around the fringe of carriages and wagons. As they approached Bering's carriage, a sudden movement caught their eye. In the dim glow of the campfires, a seemingly disembodied pair of pale legs glinted pink and naked in the moonlight. The dull sound of flesh slapping against flesh was unmistakable, as were the grunts and moans of enthusiastic copulation.

Spanberg strode resolutely ahead, his gaze averted. Osa Bering gave no indication of what she had seen and heard.

The Confluence of the Ob and Vakh Rivers
July 1734

From the journal of Lieutenant-at-Sea Sven Waxell

July 9, 1734

This Russia is a land of great and savage beauty.

Today we reached the confluence of the Ob and Vakh Rivers

where the Great Plain extends towards the foothills of the central Siberian Plateau and the Plain of Yakut, many land miles distant. From there, we shall strike southeast as ordered, following the course of the Lena River in the distant shadow of the Verkhoyansk mountain range until we reach Yakutsk. And from there, we proceed to Okhotsk, where we shall await the main body of the Expedition which travels by the same route.

I have news of Captain-Commander Bering, whose progress is steady but slow. Riders have returned from the position of the expeditionary column which is now approaching Syktyvkar, a garrison outpost that lies below the Northern Hills on a tributary of the Sukhona River. They report that the Captain-Commander now leads a much-reduced force and that he is well but impatient, as those who have served under him will most certainly comprehend.

The news that the Captain-Commander has travelled without great incident is most welcome and I shall hasten to send despatches to him to report on our own advance. I shall inform him that we have made good progress and that the men under my command are in good spirit.

With little exception, discipline has been maintained. We have lost three good seamen, one to an ailment our surgeon-lieutenant could not determine and the others but three days ago at the fording of a treacherous river swollen by the late winter snows. I must hold myself accountable for their demise, yet console myself with the thought that they died in the line of duty and in a worthy cause, and that such losses are inevitable and acceptable.

Laurentij is a spirited lad who grows stronger and more adventurous by the day. His curiosity is without limit and I am as proud of him as any father can be. He looks well, as do we all, for our diet is rich and plentiful. The rivers here teem with fish and there is an abundance of game. A coarse corn grows wild all around us and we bake it to a nutritious dough.

Of the indigenous peoples we see little. There are small villages of no more than several rude huts which house stocky and well-muscled tillers of the soil. They speak of bands of horsemen whom *they fear greatly, but we have seen neither hide nor hair of these. It may be that a force such as ours holds them at a distance, if indeed they do exist. Be that as it may, we post a watch each night and guard the horses zealously. I shall report these rumours to the Captain-Commander.*

Converse with the villagers is difficult. They speak a thick dialect which our interpreters have great difficulty in understanding. Much of our intercourse with them is by way of sign language, but they are in the main friendly and curious as to our intentions, although they know little of the land to the east and care even less.

Laurentij misses his mother but is distracted by the great adventure of which he is part. I, too, miss my dear wife, but I find solace in the knowledge that I do her and our name great credit.

Our forward scouts report that the terrain ahead grows more difficult and that the weather is becoming less clement. I am conscious that our rate of progress may be slowed but am confident that our physical well-being will help harden our resolve and sustain our advance.

Syktyvkar Garrison on the Sukhona River
July 10, 1734

The Expedition reached Syktyvkar by late morning. Lieutenant Khitrov had scouted the terrain and reported back that the grassy plain on the far side of the river would afford a suitable encampment.

Bering and Aleksey Chirikov exchanged worried glances as they approached the garrison, a tiny collection of single-storeyed cabins clustered around a rudimentary fort which appeared to offer little protection against a hostile force or, for that matter, even against the seasonal elements.

Conventional military wisdom as set out in the official *Manuals of War* authored – some said plagiarised – in part by Peter the Great, decreed that a garrison fort was a place which afforded not only safety from attack but also served as a centre for active defence. A fort was defined as constituting the focal point of a position that was self-sufficient. Not only should it serve to deter potential aggressors, it should also be sustainable over time in terms of food storage and access to a continuous water supply. And, as a centre of active defence, it should boast a superior field of fire over a broad area in order to deny an attacking force easy access to its walls and, above all, to its vulnerable foundations.

The garrison fort at Syktyvkar met none of these conditions. It was a haphazard and hastily thrown together wooden building which had no apparent *raison d'être*. It was set in a low-lying water-meadow overlooked by a hill to the west and had neither a protected well supply nor direct access to the waters of the nearby river.

'An interesting defensive position,' observed Vitus Bering.

'Indeed,' said Aleksey Chirikov. 'One might ask what it is intended to defend or, for that matter, why it is even here.'

The garrison commander, a young but already world-weary army captain, was unable to enlighten them. Bering and Chirikov paid their respects and outlined their mission. The captain was at best only mildly interested. He had been detached to the garrison less than three months previously and was cheerfully unaware of why it had been built, where it was, or what conceivable strategic purpose it was intended to serve.

'Little of note happens here,' he explained. 'There are reports of savage tribes to the east but we have seen nothing of them. I have twenty-eight men under my command, and some have served here for the past four years. There has never been any trouble.'

Chirikov shook his head in disbelief.

'That may be because there is nothing here to defend,' he ventured.

'Perhaps not,' shrugged the Captain.

'And that may be because there has been nothing here of value,' said Bering. He looked across at Chirikov. 'Until now, that is.'

The attack came next morning, shortly after daybreak. Neither Bering nor Chirikov would ever learn the identity of the attackers or discover how, undetected, they had assembled in such force.

There were upwards of 200 of them, each mounted and protected by a light leather armour consisting of a breastplate and leggings. They wielded short curved swords and sturdy bows. Some carried iron-tipped lances, others brandished stubby axe-heads set into wooden handles bound to their wrists with leather thongs.

The attack was from the east, out of the morning sun. The Expedition had quartered, on Khitrov's recommendation, on the water-meadow to the east of the garrison. The outer pickets were taken by surprise and quickly overrun.

The attackers plunged into the heart of the encampment while the Expedition's military escort was still half asleep. Several of those who had roused themselves at the first sounds of the attack were cut down as they struggled to comprehend what was happening. Others scampered to retrieve their weapons.

The riders completed one pass through the encampment, leaving in their wake both military and civilian dead. They reined in just before the river, wheeled, and rode straight back towards the still largely undefended camp.

To their credit, Bering and Chirikov found themselves in the thin front line of defenders. Spanberg was at Bering's side, shouting instructions to the hastily-marshalled troops who had taken up position left and right of them.

The first wave of riders was met by a hail of musket-shot that stopped them in their tracks. The second wave plunged ahead, bearing down on the defenders who had crouched to reload their single-shot muskets.

'Down and reload,' yelled Spanberg, who had instinctively assumed command. The soldiers immediately responded, throwing themselves to the ground and rolling into position behind every available hummock as the riders swept up to and over them. A second line of soldiers had emerged from the bivouacs and now held formation some thirty yards beyond. They fired at will, each man choosing his target with care.

Riders catapulted from the saddle. The second wave had broken. The surviving riders checked, cut off from the main attacking force. They turned to retreat.

The army colonel in command of the Expedition's military escort was a seasoned veteran He understood immediately what Spanberg intended.

'Down and reload!' shouted the colonel.

The inner defensive line dropped to the ground in time to hear Spanberg call out a command to his men who had now turned inwards to face the attackers.

'Fire!'

Caught between the two lines of fire, the riders hesitated. They were cut down to a man.

'Advance!' came the voice of the colonel and the second line of defence ran forward to take up position between the front line and the main body of the attackers. Those under Spanberg's temporary command again dropped to their knees to reload.

The horsemen were trapped between the river behind them and the wall of defenders ahead of them. The wooden gates of the fort opened and the young garrison commander emerged at the head of his men. They plunged their horses into the shallow river and bore down on the attackers who, uncertain what to do next, were circling aimlessly.

Both lines of defenders opened fire this time, decimating the ranks of the remaining riders. The army colonel had reached Spanberg's side.

'Hold your position,' he rapped out.

Spanberg nodded.

'Second line advance!' shouted the colonel. His men promptly discarded their muskets and drew their swords, charging towards the depleted ranks of riders who broke in confusion and spurred their horses along the river bank to safety.

Bering and Chirikov had taken no real part in the action. Armed only with swords, they had done nothing other than stand their ground during the first wave of the attack. Dazed by what had happened, Bering gradually became aware that Spanberg was still at his side. Directly in front of them lay two horsemen, one dead with a ball lodged in his throat, the other groaning in agony. On the ground at Bering's feet lay a third attacker, his chest laid open to the bone and his lance-tip buried in the earth inches from where Bering had been standing.

Spanberg stepped forward and ran his sabre through the wounded horseman. He wiped his blade on the man's coarse vest and sheathed it. He was grinning from ear to ear.

'Now that, Captain-Commander, is what I would call a job well done.'

Bering could not share his First Officer's enthusiasm. He knew that there were dead and dying inside the encampment. His first and only thought was for Osa and Benthe. He ran back to their carriage and found them both unharmed.

Relieved, he turned to find the young garrison commander reining in alongside and dismounting.

'The field is ours, Captain-Commander.'

Enraged, Bering grasped him by the lapels of his cavalry officer's tunic.

'You incompetent young bastard!' he hissed. 'Where was your garrison?'

'We are here, Captain-Commander,' stammered the young captain. 'We came as soon as we could.'

It was Martin Spanberg who defused the situation.

'Better late than never, Captain. Your intervention was, shall we say, timely?'

Bering released his hold and pushed the captain away with a gesture of disgust. Benthe Bering worshipped Spanberg with her eyes.

And Osa Bering realised in that moment how much her husband loved her.

By the standards of the age, this had been a pitched battle rather than a skirmish. Khitrov reported the body count. Seventy-three of the horsemen had been killed and a further nine had been taken prisoner. The colonel had lost five soldiers with another seven wounded, two of them so seriously that they were not expected to survive. The garrison captain had no losses to report – not surprisingly, since his small force had not engaged the enemy.

Nine civilians had died, three of them lanced from behind. Four were women and two others were little more than children.

A burial detail was formed and the last rites administered.

The Expedition had been blooded and had survived almost

intact. The survivors crowded around Bering, one question on their lips:

'Will they come back?'

It was a question Vitus Bering could not answer with any certainty. He wished he could reassure them but, in all conscience, he could not. Martin Spanberg, confident as ever, believed that they were safe from further attack.

For the moment, at least.

The Expedition licked its wounds. A major issue to be confronted was what to do with the prisoners. Chirikov and Spanberg argued that they should be summarily executed. Bering spoke against this on the grounds that setting them free would be the act of civilised men.

The final decision fell to Bering, who ordered the captives to be shackled and driven from the encampment. A hail of insults and stones accompanied their departure.

Bering was never to know that a small detachment on horseback slipped out of the camp shortly afterwards. They quickly overtook the nine captives and executed them on the spot. The colonel had not taken kindly to the losses his command had suffered.

Berlin
July 14, 1734

That evening on the Dölauer Heide, Georg Wilhelm Steller had taken stock and found himself wanting.

Every instinct told him he was destined to go on to greater things. How he was to accomplish this was another matter entirely.

Steller was in his twenties and virtually penniless. He knew this was of little consequence at Halle University, where Pietist values held that impecuniosity constituted no impediment to scholarship, but Steller had vague ambitions which included a disinclination to live out his life as an impoverished academic.

Steller's scholastic record was excellent, marred only by a lack of direction. He had flitted backwards and forwards from one faculty to the next – in all fairness, as students at Halle were positively encouraged to do – dabbling in theology, philosophy, medicine and, at the feet of the great legal reformist Christian Thomasius, even in jurisprudence.

This indecisiveness, to which Steller was understandably reluctant to admit, had become particularly evident when he was exposed to the teachings of Professor Christian von Wolff, arguably Germany's foremost rationalist philosopher of the day, who argued among other things that the essentially European doctrine of Christian revelation was inadequate in that it failed to take account of the traditions, cultures, beliefs and ethics of other civilisations. What attracted the young Steller in particular was von Wolff's emphasis on the need to explore and assimilate other civilisations and cultures. To Steller, this seemed to flow naturally from the Pietist tradition.

Steller had come to recognise that the University of Halle was a potential conduit to the wider world beyond. Above all, it was a conduit to Russia and to the largely-unexplored cultures and civilisations of the Siberian wastelands. This was due in no small measure to the westernisation programme instituted by Emperor Peter the Great, who had invited to his capital of St Petersburg a number of prominent academicians from Halle University. Among them was the physician Daniel Gottlieb Messerschmidt to whom Peter, in the 1720s, had entrusted the broad brief of exploring and documenting Western and Central Siberia.

Identifying the Halle connection to Russia was one thing, exploiting it another. Fortunately, Steller was in the good graces of Friedrich Hoffmann, the doyen of the Medical Faculty in Halle.

Hoffmann had recently been seconded to Berlin as a *pro tempore* replacement for the recently-deceased court physician and College of Medicine President Georg Ernst Stahl. This was why Steller was in Berlin. He was determined to persuade Hoffmann to secure him a position on the Halle Medical Faculty as a specialist in the field of herbal science. If successful, he believed his credentials would ultimately take him to St Petersburg, the city a certain Captain-Commander Vitus Bering had recently left at the head of the widely-publicised Imperial Great Northern Expedition to Siberia and beyond.

Things had gone less than smoothly in Berlin. On arrival, Steller had been promptly and enthusiastically received by Hoffmann, who had assured him that he would be invited to present himself before the Medical Council in due course. That initial meeting with Hoffmann had taken place over a month ago and Steller had heard nothing since. He resolved to call on Hoffmann again and request that his appearance before the board be treated as a matter of urgency.

Time was running out and Siberia beckoned.

Syktyvkar Garrison on the Sukhona River
July 20, 1734

Valery Khitrov had acquired a taste for vodka during his early days as a student at the Naval Academy in St Petersburg.

As a proud and arrogant new generation Russian, Khitrov would have been appalled to discover that Russia's national tipple was not indigenous to that country. Historical records show that the pernicious spirit was in all probability first distilled in Mallorca in the 12th or 13th century and not introduced into Russia – by Genoese merchants – until the turn of the 15th century.

Khitrov was not privy to this information. Even had he been, it is extremely doubtful that his addiction to the 'little water of life' would have been any less severe.

A centuries-old Russian proverb held that there cannot be too much vodka, there can only be not enough. Vodka exemplified, in the literal and extended sense, the true spirit of Russia. By turns, it fuelled despondency and dissipated it, it excited the passions and dulled them. It warmed the body during the long winters and cooled the brain in the searing heat of summer. In its limpid purity, it was the ideal accompaniment to any food and the highlight of any festive occasion.

And, when all was said and done, real vodka *was* Russian. Vodka can be distilled from almost any organic matter, but every Russian worthy of the name agreed that it was only when filtered through *Russian* birch charcoal that it truly came into its own.

Khitrov was seriously drunk on double-strength *vino dvoynoe*, a potent and virtually flavourless spirit multiple-distilled from rye grain. He had been lying in his cramped quarters for three days. Unshaven, unkempt, uncaring.

Valery Khitrov lived a lie.

He had graduated from the Naval Academy under false pretences, having hired a fellow student to write his final thesis and subsequently bribing the examiner to 'adjust' his poor practical grades. His professed hands-on experience as a navigator was also negligible, based as it was on several months at the helm three summers previously in the comparatively benign waters of the White Sea. His claim to have sailed the ocean off the Siberian coast was as false as the papers which ostensibly attested to his qualifications.

It was only a matter of time before he was found out. As Vitus Bering's navigator, Khitrov would, as a matter of course, be promoted to the rank of Fleetmaster. The responsibilities that this position entailed were daunting and Khitrov knew that he was not capable of meeting them.

Worse, he suspected he had already failed the Expedition. He had scouted diligently ahead but detected no trace of the subsequent mounted threat from the east. Even worse perhaps, he had recommended an encampment that had proved highly vulnerable to attack.

In these latter respects, Khitrov's feelings of guilt and remorse were largely of his own making. No-one had blamed him for the surprise attack or questioned his judgment on the matter of site selection, least of all his Captain-Commander.

On the morning of the fourth day, Vitus Bering visited Khitrov in his quarters. He found the Lieutenant lying glassy-eyed on his rumpled cot, a gossamer thread of saliva trailing from his open mouth. Bering roused him with difficulty and manhandled him outside into the glare of the sun. Khitrov squinted up at Bering as if trying to place him.

The sudden realisation that the Captain-Commander in person had come in search of him jolted Khitrov into a semblance of sobriety.

'Captain-Commander, sir, you do me an honour –'

'And you do yourself none, Lieutenant,' said Bering. He propped Khitrov into a sitting position and looked him over. The young Lieutenant was a wreck. His linen was filthy, his hair matted, his breath that of a St Petersburg whore.

'May I inquire, Lieutenant, what this means?'

Khitrov was on the point of telling Bering everything, of pleading guilty to a long chapter of deceit and false pretences. He found he was unable to bring himself to do so. Over time, deceit and false pretences had become second nature to him. Instead, he looked Bering in the eye as best he could.

'Captain-Commander, I feel I was responsible.'

Bering had somehow anticipated as much.

'Responsible, Lieutenant? In what way, responsible?'

'For the attack, for the loss of life.'

Bering felt a surge of sympathy for his young protégé. He had taken a gamble on Khitrov, excusing his hands-on inexperience and insisting that the Lieutenant would mature into an able officer. He thought back to the confrontation with Chirikov. We need seasoned men at the helm, Chirikov had said, we need men we can trust. And he had answered that young blood and youthful endeavour were the way of the sea, and that he, Vitus Bering, would take this fledgling under his wing.

Bering was damned if he'd prove Chirikov right.

'Your sense of responsibility does you credit, Lieutenant, but I and others hold you in no way to blame for the events that transpired.'

'There is more, Captain-Commander.'

'Yes?'

'I am uncertain whether I am skilled enough to do my duty as Fleetmaster.'

Bering shook his head.

'That promotion has yet to be conferred,' he replied. 'But when it is, I have every confidence that you will discharge your duties admirably.'

To Bering's surprise, Khitrov broke into tears. The vodka has taken its toll, thought Bering. How many times have I witnessed this before?

'Lieutenant, hear this. There are many months ahead of us and many long nights when we can sit together. I shall instruct and you will listen and learn. There is much I can teach you. Be assured, I have faith in your abilities.'

Bering had thrown him a life-line and Khitrov was not slow to respond.

'If the Captain-Commander has faith in me I shall do everything in my power to live up to that faith.'

'I am persuaded that you will.'

Bering stood up, pleased at the outcome of the discussion yet suddenly embarrassed by its substance. It was not his habit to coddle subordinates as if they were children.

'Your first duty, Lieutenant, will be to pull yourself together. I shall expect you in my quarters one hour from now. Well-turned out and sober. That, sir, is an order.'

'Aye-aye, Captain-Commander.'

Bering turned and left.

He had much to do. The Expedition would strike camp the following day. They had lain over in Syktyvkar for a full ten days to reprovision, to effect repairs and to see to the wounded, two of whom had since died. More valuable time had been lost.

Of one thing, however, Bering was now certain: Lieutenant Khitrov would continue to prove an asset to the Expedition.

St Petersburg
July 22, 1734

'What news of Pisarov?' asked Ernst Johann von Biron.

His aide glanced up from a bundle of documents he was sifting through.

'Of Lieutenant Pisarov there is none,' he replied.

Von Biron paced the room.

'It is unthinkable that we should be uninformed as to his present whereabouts.'

'That is true, Excellency. But may I remind you that he left with but a small contingent of men. He will travel hard and is most certainly at many land miles' distance from the capital.'

'Yes, yes, I realise that. I'm not a fool. But I am concerned that no news has come from him in months. We cannot be left in such ignorance. The lines of communication must be improved. You will draft a despatch to Bering to that effect. He must maintain forward contact with that other Dane, what's his name . . . ?'

'Waxell, your Excellency. And he is a Swede.'

'No matter. Instruct Bering immediately that he is to establish permanent forward contact with Waxell and that this Waxell – or whatever his name is – must send riders forward to locate Pisarov and report back down the line.'

'At once, Your Excellency.'

'Intolerable,' muttered von Biron. 'Simply intolerable.'

He was irritated by the progress of the Imperial Great Northern Expedition, or the lack of it. To be more exact, he was irritated by his own failure to predict and make allowances for an inevitable waning of interest. The initial impact had been overwhelming, but time and distance had bred disenchantment. The Empress Anna Ivanovna herself had lost whatever enthusiasm she had been able to muster and von Biron was only too aware that his own reputation and, more significantly, his influence at Court, hinged in part on keeping interest in the Expedition alive.

That this was difficult went without saying. The vast distances covered by the Expedition had dissipated its immediacy and diluted its impact. Bering, Waxell, Pisarov and the rest were out of sight and, as a result, out of mind. This much von Biron regretted but could do nothing about.

Nothing, that is, except to report authoritatively and positively on the Expedition's progress whether or not he had accurate information to hand. There was considerable risk involved in this, but he had always been prepared to take risks to bolster his position. The alternative was simply to let the Expedition run its course in the hope that the eventual outcome would be positive. This, too, was not without risk: who knew what that upstart Dane might or might not achieve?

He was forced to admit to himself that the Expedition had been mismanaged in the sense that too much had been promised at the outset and too little delivered in the interim. It had been a mistake to whet the appetites of the academic and scientific communities only to have them wait God only knew how long before they became directly involved.

He called his aide back into the room.

'An addendum to the despatch to Bering,' he instructed. 'You are to inform him that he must collect and return for inspection here in St Petersburg typical examples of the flora and fauna in each region through which the Expedition passes. Moreover, he is to submit detailed descriptions of the terrain and of the living conditions of the inhabitants. These reports will be filed each week and will be sent by special courier back here to St Petersburg. The specimens collected by the Expedition will be transported under armed escort and with all due diligence.'

The aide scribbled furiously.

That is the key, thought von Biron. Continuity of information. What was needed was to sustain a flow of that information to the academics and scientists and to release regular bulletins on their subsequent speculations and conclusions. That, he was sure, would keep interest in the Expedition alive.

It would also keep himself at the centre of attention.

The West Siberian Plain
August 4, 1734

Martin Spanberg, his coarse breeches coiled about his ankles, squatted in the shade of a large bush and defecated with a vengeance. As God is my witness, he thought to himself, I'll be damned if I ever eat another fucking salmon. Or any other fucking fish, if the truth be known.

Spanberg, like the majority of those in the main body of the Expedition, had chronic diarrhoea. For the previous two weeks he had been taken short time and again. His bowel movements were spectacularly unpredictable and a constant source of embarrassment.

He decided to confront Bering one more time. The Captain-Commander, whose bowels appeared to be functioning with infuriating regularity, had been deaf to his complaints and adamant that the Expedition should not waste precious time hunting game to supplement their monotonous diet of boiled, stewed or roasted fish.

Spanberg knew that the Expedition could not afford to slaughter the limited number of oxen remaining to them, and he did not suggest as much. The oxen were needed as draught animals and had proved their worth time and again when axles became bogged down or gradients were too steep for the horses to handle alone.

'The game is plentiful here, Captain-Commander,' argued Spanberg. 'And it is as easy to shoot a cock pheasant or a hare as it is to catch a fish.'

Bering laughed outright.

'My dear Martin, you know that is not true. We set our nets and catch our fish at dusk when the column has already settled for the night. Fish are plentiful, too, and nutritious. And, tell me, how many cock pheasants and hares do you plan on shooting to feed this multitude?'

'I care not for the multitude, Captain-Commander. My principal concern is my own gut and the ring of fire that used to be my arse-hole.'

Bering laughed again.

'Well, Martin, set your ring of fire in that bucket over there. The cool water from the river should douse the flames.'

Spanberg was not amused. He had little medical knowledge, but he knew that a balanced diet was essential if the Expedition was to stay healthy and functional.

'I insist, Captain-Commander. By all that's holy, if I don't get my teeth into a rib of beef, my mind will turn to water as have my bowels. I am not alone in this.'

He has a point, thought Bering.

'Then you have my permission to take a detail of men ahead of the column and scavenge at will. When the column comes abreast of you, we shall feast on what you can provide.'

'I shall do as you command, sir. We will make camp ahead of you and prepare a feast the likes of which you will never see again.'

'Then go,' said Bering with a wave of the hand. 'And don't forget to save a rabbit for me.'

Spanberg and ten men known to be handy with a musket left the column early next day and headed east across the plain. They made good time and were soon several miles ahead of the main body. Late that afternoon, they came upon a meandering stream bordered by a rare stand of trees.

Spanberg dismounted to survey the location.

Hoofprints on the river bank confirmed that the river course was a natural animal draw and the shallow river bed a much-frequented waterhole. Satisfied, Spanberg signalled to his men to start setting traps and to dig a trench that would serve as a hide when covered with branches from the nearby trees and with the coarse grasses which grew on the banks of the stream.

Spanberg sought shelter in the trees, his breeches once more down around his ankles.

As before, the horsemen materialised from nowhere, surging round the fringe of stunted conifers and charging across the short distance between trees and stream. Within seconds, two of Spanberg's men lay face-down in the water. Another clutched the stump of a severed arm, blood spurting wildly in every direction.

Spanberg struggled to his feet, yanking his breeches back around his middle. He saw immediately that only two or three of his men had had the foresight to take their muskets with them. Most had left their weapons back where the horses were tethered.

He knew at once that this was a small raiding party rather than a main force. There were at most between fifteen and twenty mounted attackers. The fury of their first charge had swept them past Spanberg's small contingent.

'To the horses!' shouted Spanberg.

They reached the horses and unsheathed their muskets as the riders turned to charge again.

'Hold your fire! Hold!'

The riders were very close now. Spanberg's men knelt, muskets at the ready. They fired at a distance of less than ten paces and four of the riders arched back out of the saddle, one trailing by the stirrup as his mount shied and bolted. The remainder checked. Spanberg discharged his pistol directly into the face of what he took to be the leader. The man's features turned to pulp and he slid gracelessly from the saddle.

'Reload!'

Four of the musketeers dropped to their knees and started to reload while Spanberg and three others formed a crude defensive semi-circle to protect them. The horsemen came forward again, hacking and slashing with their stubby swords. Spanberg ducked low then brought his sabre up in a stabbing motion. The impact wrenched the sabre from his hand as it embedded itself in the rider's chest.

To his left, he saw a burly seaman reel back, his forehead split open by a sword. More shots rang out and two more riders fell from the saddle. Spanberg retrieved his sabre and made to finish off the man on the ground. He was too late: a short dagger had already pierced the man's throat.

The odds against them had shortened now and their attackers knew it. They promptly wheeled right and vanished back into the cover of the nearby stand of trees.

Spanberg took stock. Two men dead, certainly. Another – the one with the severed arm – bleeding to death. There was nothing they could do for him. Miraculously, the seaman with the head wound had got to his feet and was shaking his head furiously to clear the blood from his eyes.

The men had reloaded yet again. They took up position in the animal hide, their muskets trained on the trees.

But the horsemen had disappeared as swiftly as they had come.

Spanberg looked around at the survivors.

'It's always this way, is it not? Never a moment's peace to enjoy a decent shit.'

Sukhona River
August 6, 1734

It did not escape Bering's notice that the main body of the Expedition had maintained closer order since the incident at the garrison fort. The civilians in the party were particularly edgy, scouring the surrounding countryside for any sign of the hostile tribesmen who had attacked them so unexpectedly and ruthlessly.

The Expedition was moving forward with a new urgency, its progress facilitated by the flatness of the terrain and the sun-dried soil. For all that, the river courses criss-crossing the Western Siberian Plain continued to be formidable obstacles. Admittedly, some were shallow and readily fordable, but others gouged deep into the earth, with a swiftness and unpredictability of current that posed major problems to livestock and humans alike.

The region had been extensively mapped but Bering soon discovered to his annoyance that the charts were hit-and-miss affairs which distorted distances between such salient landmarks as existed and which yielded precious little practical information on the width or depth of rivers and streams, let alone any recommendation as to where they could best be forded.

The military escort was now deployed at regular intervals ahead, alongside and behind the column. Thinly-dispersed as they of necessity were, this tactical deployment was such that, at the first indication of trouble, they could immediately align themselves between the column and any perceived threat. The deployment was by no means optimal, but frequent drills conducted at the insistence of the regimental colonel suggested that it should prove effective.

Among the civilians still with the Expedition were some veterans of the Swedish War who had volunteered to swell the ranks of the military escort. Bering was not wholly in favour of this, although he acknowledged their good intentions. In the final analysis, they were still civilians under his protection; as such, he believed their primary obligation was to remain with their families and retinue. He conceded, however, that in the case of another attack upon the column, they should deploy as appropriate to reinforce the armed escort.

Overall, the mood in the column was anything but positive. The incident at Syktyvkar had brought home to all and sundry that this was indeed a hazardous undertaking. The death of several of their number had confirmed as much and their anxiety was plain for all to see.

Bering did what he could to maintain both discipline and morale – a prime consideration – and a sense of security. It was an uphill battle. Several families who had earlier indicated that they were prepared to brave the rigours of a return journey to St Petersburg even without military escort now resigned themselves to staying with the Expedition until it reached the comparative security of the coast, where a strong Russian military presence was ensured. Their truculent displeasure at having to continue with the Expedition was all too evident.

The nights were chill and the Expedition now huddled in loose family units around an assortment of campfires that were increasingly difficult to provision, given the growing scarcity of trees and bushes. Bering watched as some searched desperately through their once-precious belongings to find combustible material to stoke the fires.

This, too, did little to boost morale. On the other hand, Bering saw a positive side: as the fires inevitably flickered and died in the early light of morning, the civilians showed an unprecedented eagerness to snatch up their remaining possessions as quickly as possible and to move on, anxious to rid their bones of the aches and pains brought on by the cold night. As a result, each day not only seemed but actually *was* longer than the previous one, not least because loads were lightened as unnecessary items were discarded or burnt.

Despite the general atmosphere of gloom and anxiety, the Expedition was actually moving faster now than at any previous stage. Bering continued to be optimistic that the Expedition could reach the coast, if not on schedule then at worst with a delay of only some two to three weeks. His optimism was based on a number of factors, chief of which was that he had travelled, broadly, along this selfsame route once before – in 1724 – albeit at the head of a much smaller party that had been appreciably fitter and better-disciplined. In the Expedition's favour, he knew, was the fact that the going would be comparatively easy over the next few weeks, given the flatness of the terrain. Provided, of course, that no further unforeseen obstacles were encountered.

A matter of growing concern was the overall physical well-being of the Expedition. Nearly every member had intestinal disorders. Additionally, some civilians – granted, not many – had fallen foul of a condition that both the civilian doctors and the army surgeons proved incapable of diagnosing, let alone treating. Blisters and sores appeared round the mouth and in the armpits and groin, to be followed by successive bouts of fever and chills. Three civilians had died as a result of this condition and several others were in serious discomfort.

Also of concern was a heightening of tensions between the civilian members of the Expedition and their military counterparts. The latter had husbanded their food resources sufficiently well to stay the course, whereas the civilians had tended to exhaust their provisions by an early date. Bering discovered that the soldiers were doing a roaring trade selling off some of their rations to the civilians in exchange for cash and jewellery. He determined to put a stop to this practice and instructed the regimental colonel to introduce strict disciplinary measures. The colonel undertook to do so, but the practice continued, since both parties to the trade-off were careful to conceal transactions which each deemed to his or her own advantage.

Chirikov took a harder line: he proposed that the barter trade be stamped out by ordering the summary execution of any soldier found guilty of selling off rations for personal gain. Bering rejected this suggestion on grounds of morale and because he was unwilling to deplete the ranks of the military escort. Horseshit, said Chirikov: killing one or two would set an example and discourage the practice entirely.

Bering did not agree but he did pressure the colonel to flog any soldier caught in the act. To his consternation, he found that floggings were becoming increasingly frequent while the illicit trade continued to grow.

Living off the land was an option that Bering had first mooted back in St Petersburg, where the proposal had been summarily disregarded. He had taken Spanberg's point about the need for a more varied diet, however, and now considered the authorisation of hunting parties to be a valid option. If Spanberg's initial foray proved successful, he decided, a hunting party roster would be put in place. Moreover, the bounty would be put under lock and key and a system of rationing initiated. This could only be beneficial, he reasoned, to the extent that it would serve a double purpose: it would ensure on the one hand that the Expedition had sufficient stores of food and, on the other, it would go no small way towards stamping out the persistent and worrisome barter trade.

With these thoughts in mind, he looked forward to seeing how well Martin Spanberg had fared.

Okhotsk
August 6, 1734

Lieutenant Grigor Pisarov grunted loudly and ejaculated.

He immediately rolled off the young girl beneath him and stood up, stretching his limbs. He looked down at her, taking in her flattened features, her short, almost stumpy legs and the matted bush of coarse black pubic hair that now glistened moistly in the grey light of morning.

Pisarov leant over and slapped her roughly on the thigh. The girl's eyes opened and she stared up at him.

'Out!'

She continued to stare, uncomprehending.

'Out!' repeated Pisarov, pointing to the door.

The gesture was unmistakable. The girl gathered her thin over-garment from the floor and scurried out of the room. Pisarov aimed a desultory kick at her departing buttocks but missed. He slammed the door behind her.

Whore. Slant-eyed whore. Still, she had served her purpose well enough.

Pisarov pulled on his breeches and shirt and coaxed his feet into the tight black leather boots that stood beside the bed. He flung open the window on a distressingly familiar scene.

Under a leaden sky the sea churned grey and white, sending

flurries of spray against the half-finished pier. It was mid-morning but no-one was up and about. Crates littered the port area, some unopened, others splintered and empty.

This was the anus of the Empire, thought Pisarov. What in Christ's name am I doing here?

The question was rhetorical, because Lieutenant Grigor Pisarov knew only too well what he was doing there in Okhotsk or, rather, what he was supposed to be doing.

Pisarov had arrived in Yakutsk late in the previous year after a long but, on balance, uneventful journey across the Siberian hinterland. He had over-wintered in Yakutsk and pushed on to Okhotsk in early spring. With him came a complement of shipwrights, carpenters, riveters, sailmakers, riggers, blacksmiths and marine engineers.

The Expedition schedule had called for six vessels to be readied for immediate use by that smug whoreson Dane and his motherfucking Expedition.

Fuck him, thought Pisarov. Fuck them all.

A start had been made on two of the vessels and the hull of a third rested on blocks in the rudimentary dry-dock. Pisarov had been assured that there were adequate port facilities in Okhotsk. Adequate? What in fuck's name was that supposed to mean, adequate? There was a bay where ships could anchor and a rickety wooden pier where they could discharge their cargo. No derricks, no workshops, no smithies, no chandler's yards.

How in Christ's name did they expect him to build six vessels under these conditions? And what had he done to draw an assignment such as this?

Pisarov knew only too well that the vessels could not be outfitted before the end of the year at best. He would be blamed for the delay, of course, but he had his excuses at the ready.

He had been promised 300 convicts from Siberia's penal settlements, a mix of out-and-out criminals and political exiles, whose main task would be to cut and haul timbers to the port. He had been given no more than 200 of them. Of these, some sixty or so were political exiles who stubbornly refused to work under his direction, asserting their right – right? what shagging right? thought

Pisarov – to be treated with the dignity commensurate with their status. Pisarov, who had himself spent some time in exile in Siberia, was reluctant to force them: who knew which of them would subsequently be reinstated in the favours of the Empress? And who knew what revenge they might take on him once they were back in the good graces of the Court?

Of the others who had been conscripted, the majority were old or under-nourished. A few, doubtless fearful of additional punishment, seemed willing enough to follow orders but turned out to be incapable of implementing them in practice, being either too weak or too inept. Others still, of a much tougher disposition, had at first refused flat-out to cooperate. After a few judicious floggings, they now went through the motions, but they worked as slowly as they could and, in some cases, they were (as Pisarov suspected but could not as yet prove) guilty of outright sabotage.

Pisarov reasoned that Bering would be hard-pressed to reach the coast within anything approaching the ambitious deadline he had set himself. The Lieutenant knew that his own group had progressed fast and hard over the route to Yakutsk but had been forced to remain there once the bad weather had set in. Bering, in his estimation, could do no better, what with the complement of self-indulgent, flabby civilians that trailed in his wake.

He'll be fortunate to get here this year, he concluded. And he can set about building his own fucking vessels.

Pisarov knew that he was playing a dangerous game. The orders from von Biron were plain enough and he would be in trouble if he failed to respect them. But what did von Biron know about conditions here in Okhotsk? Damned little, he suspected. Accordingly, within days of reaching Okhotsk and evaluating the hopelessness of the schedule set him, he had sent a despatch to St Petersburg outlining his situation and undertaking to do his level best in the circumstances.

He had no way of knowing whether or not the despatch had been received. When all was said and done, it didn't matter, since his situation seemed without remedy. The best would be to press on as far as possible with construction of the hulls. That way he could argue that, despite untenable local conditions, he had never-theless made a tangible effort to accomplish his mission.

Fuck Bering, he thought again. Fuck him and fuck them all.

With that, he closed the window and lay back down on the bed.

The Lena River
August 1734

From the journal of Lieutenant-at-Sea Sven Waxell

August 4, 1734

This day we reached the banks of what must surely be the Lena River or a major tributary thereof. We shall follow its course for three days and take bearings by the hour.

The men are weary but jubilant. I have informed them that we are within striking distance of our destination, which heartens them greatly. My adjutant reports that they are fit and well to a man, and that our cargo is secure and undamaged.

August 6, 1734

We know now that this is in truth the Lena River, for it can be none other. Yesterday I ordered the column to be halted for a day of celebration. There was much drinking and lighthearted sport, but no breaches of discipline were reported.

Laurentij joined in the festivities. Much fuss is made of him as he is well-liked by the men who look on him as a mascot.

Late this afternoon, we espied a troop of horsemen on the far horizon. They were considerable in number but not so as to represent a danger to us. My scouts reported that they held position behind us for an hour, then broke off and headed north. We shall remain vigilant.

August 7, 1734

My best estimate is that we shall attain Yakutsk after three weeks' hard travel over terrain that is inhospitable yet tolerably conducive to steady progress.

I note this morning that Laurentij complains of a thick head and a dull aching in his limbs. I can ascribe this only to one cause, namely that he has tasted the rough vodka which the men drink in mighty quantities to keep out the cold. I indulge them in this for they have performed well. As to Laurentij, I shall console him that his condition is but temporary and constitutes an important rite of passage. I doubt he will understand my meaning or that his dear mother would approve.

The West Siberian Plain
August 8, 1734

The forward scouts reported to Bering that Martin Spanberg and his men were camped by a stream some four miles to the east. From their expressions, Bering knew at once that all was not well.

'He is unharmed, Captain-Commander. But three of his men are dead and two others are wounded.'

'Continue.'

'The First Officer reports that they were attacked by a troop of riders, some fifteen to twenty in all. The First Officer counted eight dead among the enemy, who dispersed to the north.'

'The enemy?' asked Bering.

'Yes, Captain-Commander.'

Bering's point was lost on the scout who, understandably, assumed the attacker to have been from the same body of men who had struck at them at the Sukhona River. Bering was not convinced of this. They had inflicted severe losses on the horsemen and he found it hard to credit that they would be bold or foolhardy enough to attack again.

'I shall ride forward with you.'

'First Officer Spanberg feels that will be unnecessary, Captain-Commander.'

'I don't give a damn what the First Officer feels. I shall ride forward with you.'

Spanberg and his men were spaced out along the river bank, muskets by their sides. Bering noticed that there were three rough wooden crosses jutting out from the earth below a stand of trees.

A man lay still under a cover spread over him. His face was ashen and his breathing laboured. Another boasted a head swathed in bandages. Spanberg himself was unscathed, although his tunic had been slashed and one sleeve ripped away. Flecks of dried blood – his or that of an assailant – spattered his shirt.

Spanberg leapt to his feet at Bering's approach.

'I bid you good day, Captain-Commander, and regret to report that I have failed to capture a single rabbit.'

Bering was in no mood for such flippancy.

'Your report, First Officer, will set out in detail what has transpired here. And it will explain how these men met their deaths.'

Spanberg knew Bering well enough to read the signs. He wiped the grin from his face in an instant.

'I must report that three of the men under my command are dead as the result of a cowardly assault by mounted tribesmen who came from and departed to the north. Two others are wounded, one gravely, the other with a head wound from which he is recovering. The men fought well, Captain-Commander, and we accounted for half if not more of the attackers.'

'Let me inform you, First Officer, that you are not here to wage war. Our immediate mission is to protect the column.'

'My immediate mission was to protect myself and the men under my command.'

'First Officer!'

The rebuke was unequivocal.

'My apologies, Captain-Commander.'

'Your apologies are accepted. As indeed is the fact that this incident will not be repeated.'

Bering was immeasurably relieved that Spanberg had emerged unhurt. His long years at sea had inured him to sudden and violent death, but his affection for Spanberg was such that losing him would have been a major personal blow.

'I cannot afford to lose you at this time, First Officer.'

'I have nine lives,' answered Spanberg, grinning again.

'Then you should safeguard all of them,' said Bering gruffly.

He turned away, amazed as he always had been at Spanberg's

capacity to shrug off danger. The man *has* nine lives, he thought
to himself, and he lives each to the full.

Spanberg instructed his men to saddle up and rejoin the main
column. As they rode back, Bering turned to him.

'You know what this means, Martin?'

'Sir?'

'It means that your hunting days are over. From now on, the
Expedition keeps close order. Only the forward scouts will detach
and they – and they alone, mind you – may leave the column.'

Spanberg made to protest but Bering cut him off.

'No buts, Martin. Our security lies in numbers and the
Expedition is better served by staying alive and hungry than by
prospecting for food and courting death. We are the hunted not
the hunters. And there's an end to it.'

Spanberg elected not to reply.

The Captain-Commander's word was final.

Martin Spanberg would eat fish and like it.

The West Siberian Plain
August 26, 1734

Even before the Imperial Great Northern Expedition had set out
from St Petersburg, Osa Bering had resolved to keep a written
record of its progress and of her experiences *en route*. In many
ways, the Expedition was the high point of what had been a sheltered life and she was resolved to record as much of it as she
possibly could.

Osa Bering did not write well but she wrote copiously. Her private
journal recorded names and dates of places reached and passed,
exhaustive descriptions of the changing terrain, and details of daily
life within the column.

As the months went by, she was aware that this written record
had evolved into something more. In addition to reporting on the
day-to-day events which punctuated the Expedition's progress, she
had started – inadvertently, it seemed – to sketch profiles of the
people around her. Her remarks were perceptive rather than intimate, thumb-nail profiles rather than in-depth characterisations.

Of Spanberg she noted that he was 'happy-go-lucky yet serious, professional yet easy-going, responsive to command yet irreverent, courageous yet irresponsible, attentive yet distant'. Of Khitrov, that he was 'inexperienced yet anxious to learn, arrogant yet deferential, confident yet given to moments of self-doubt'. And of Chirikov, that he was 'polite but surly, given to action rather than words, and one whose undoubted professional qualities are tainted by political ambition'.

Of Vitus Bering she wrote little but thought a great deal. She could feel her husband slipping away from her as he grappled with a task that was alien to his natural calling, seeking refuge in prolonged soul-searching and introspection and becoming increasingly disenchanted with the *minutiae* of a mission that she was beginning to suspect would either crown his career or sully his name and reputation for ever. She could understand his frustration. He was a mariner after all, not an administrator.

In the early days of the Expedition, her husband had been with her and her daughter almost constantly, checking that they were comfortable and safe, bringing them abreast of the day-to-day details of the Expedition, sharing his thoughts and fears. As time went by, however, she gradually realised he was becoming more and more distant. As problems arose and escalated, he had become progressively withdrawn, lost in his thoughts and oblivious at times even to the presence of others.

She was thankful that he continued to interact with Martin Spanberg, the only person who appeared to hold and secure his attention, however sporadically. She was even grateful for the brooding background presence of Aleksey Chirikov, whose barely-concealed antagonism at least had the effect of shaking Vitus out of what she could only describe as lethargy. Not least, she welcomed her husband's patient commitment to young Khitrov, who stopped by most evenings for instruction in the arts and crafts of the sea.

She consigned none of this to paper, concerned that Vitus might stumble on this record of his journey into darkness and ashamed at her own limited ability to express her feelings as succinctly and clearly as she would have wished.

Osa Bering's inability with words was, however, largely offset by her meticulous approach to the task in hand. Her written journal was fleshed out with samples of flowers and grasses she had collected on the way and, not least, complemented by an exceptional skill: an ability to sketch swiftly and accurately any scene that drew her attention.

Martin Spanberg was the first to learn of this.

He came upon her early one evening as she sat, charcoal in hand, on the edge of a moss-covered slope on the fringe of the encampment. He walked up behind her quietly, not wishing to disturb her concentration. Sensing his presence, she quickly hid the sketch she was working on, but not before Spanberg had glimpsed how well she had captured from memory the graceful lines of a stag they had seen earlier that afternoon.

'But this is wonderful. Do you have more such drawings?' Spanberg asked.

Like many amateur artists, Osa Bering was reluctant to show her work, afraid that others would feel obliged to comment favourably whether they were impressed or not.

'Some,' she answered.

Spanberg was not to be put off.

'Some, you say? May I see them?'

'I couldn't −'

'Most certainly you could. And shall.'

From the loosely-bound cardboard folder at her feet Osa Bering carefully selected several examples of her work. Herons in flight, reindeer at the river bank, herds of bison grazing on the plain.

She gazed expectantly up at Spanberg, challenging him to be candid.

'Well, First Officer, do they meet with your approval?'

'My judgment is not that of an expert but, to my eye, these are magnificent. Your husband must value them greatly.'

'My husband has not seen them. I would not care to trouble him with such trivia.'

Spanberg could scarcely believe his ears.

'Nonsense. These are magnificent, I tell you. They bring the whole Expedition to life.'

Osa smiled.

'But surely, First Officer, the Expedition *is* life and these girlish sketches no more than a poor attempt to recall some of what we have seen and what we have done.'

'You do yourself a grave injustice, Madame Bering. These are works of great beauty.'

As you are yourself, he wanted to add.

'Thank you for your kind words, First Officer – Martin,' replied Osa, tucking the sketches neatly back into their folder. 'I am glad my diversion finds favour in someone's eyes.'

'These are such as would find favour in anyone's eyes,' Spanberg pressed on. 'And I shall insist they be displayed to every –'

'You will do no such thing,' said Osa, cutting him off with a tartness that was uncharacteristic. 'These are private matters and I would thank you not to betray my confidence.'

'I would not dream of it,' answered Spanberg.

But dream of it he did. Betrayal of confidence or no, the word soon spread that Osa Bering was compiling a pictographic record of the Expedition. Reluctantly, then with greater self-confidence, she showed her pictures to a growing circle of admirers.

'You betrayed my confidence, Martin,' she chided Spanberg.

'That is true, dear lady. And I do not for one moment regret that I have committed such an unspeakable act.'

In time, it seemed that the only person in the Expedition who had not glimpsed Osa Bering's work was her husband. Vitus Bering had other things on his mind.

Berlin
August 28, 1734

Things were beginning to fall into place for Georg Wilhelm Steller.

Friedrich Hoffmann had arranged for him to be interviewed in mid-August by the Berlin *Medizinerrat*. Steller had presented well and it came as no great surprise when, only days later, a communication from the Medical Council confirmed as much.

An appointment in Halle would be conditional upon further certification, however, this time by none other than Michael

Matthias Ludolf, the celebrated botanist and member of the *Königliche Akademie*. Steller had looked forward to meeting Ludolf but was daunted by the prospect of being examined by him. As it turned out, his fears were groundless. Not only did Ludolf take to him almost immediately, he also seemed suitably impressed by Steller's command of the subject matter at hand and by the young man's ability to think across various natural science disciplines.

The *viva voce* examination had been conducted in the third week of August and Steller had already received notification that he had passed with a *cum laude* distinction. Steller was justifiably elated. He now had formal certification in both medicine and natural history. The faculty appointment to the University of Halle would follow in due course, of that he was certain. In the interim, he decided to visit St Petersburg.

Confluence of the Ob and Vakh Rivers
September 26, 1734

The main body of the Expedition had arrived at the confluence of the Ob and Vakh Rivers. Bering knew this to be a substantial achievement given that he had routinely scheduled – and adhered to – one rest day in every ten.

Bering calculated that, since leaving the garrison fort at Syktyvkar on July 20, they had covered over 1,700 land miles, albeit across terrain that had in the main been as flat as it was desolate. For the last 200 land miles or so, however, they had been in an area where clusters of broad-leafed trees had gradually become more frequent and finally thickened into a forest which boasted all manner of wildlife. Further north, they had spotted only the occasional elk, brown bear, reindeer or alpine hare, whereas now the forest played host to wild pig, deer, marmots and mink and the skies above were replete with finches, orioles, larks, kestrels, owls, woodpeckers, cranes and eagles.

For some time they had been moving in a broadly southeasterly direction, following the course of the Ob River. Heading directly east up the Vakh River was not an option. This would take them into the foothills which climbed inexorably and steeply towards the mountainous Central Siberian Plateau, as hostile and unforgiving a terrain as any in Russia.

To the southeast, on the other hand, lay a clutch of settlements extending south towards the newly-discovered coal deposits around Kusnetsk on the Kondoma River. Well before Kusnetsk itself, the Expedition would again strike east, making for the mighty Lena River which rose in the uplands northeast of Lake Baikal and flowed through Yakutsk and across the Central Yakut Plain to discharge into the Arctic's Laptev Sea.

Yakutsk had been Bering's original goal but he had finally been forced to concede that his schedule had been over-optimistic, to say the least. Compounding this were the facts that the weather had taken a turn for the worse much earlier than anticipated and that the Expedition was in poor physical shape.

He saw little alternative. The Expedition would quarter for the winter at the garrison town of Tomsk on the Tom River above its confluence with the Ob. It would reassemble as early as possible the following spring.

He sat by candlelight late into the night, drafting and redrafting a lengthy despatch to St Petersburg. The following morning, he formally announced his plans to the members of the Expedition. He could not be certain, but he believed they welcomed his decision.

He wondered how well it would be received in St Petersburg.

Chapter Three

TOMSK

Tomsk

October 22, 1734

The shaman crouched low over the drum, striking it with the ritual *pogonyalka* baton to summon his spirit helpers. Crude representations of birds and beasts dangled from the shaman's apron, together with miscellaneous metal, leather, fur, bone and wood ornaments. His ankle-length kaftan was covered in flint arrowheads and obsidian knives which glinted dully in the glow from the banked fires.

He moved slowly around the watching circle, the small stones set into the hollow head of the *pogonyalka* rattling as he shook the baton first at one member of the Sel'kup tribe then at another.

'What is he doing?' whispered Benthe Bering.

Stepan Krasheninnikov was only too pleased to answer. A fresh-faced but already distinguished academician who had been with the Expedition from the start, Krasheninnikov was eager to please, betraying all the classic symptoms of puppy love. Benthe Bering was the most beautiful creature he had ever clapped eyes on and nothing she said or did escaped his notice – much to the irritation of Valery Khitrov, who also danced daily attendance on Benthe.

'This is a special ceremony,' he whispered back. 'The Sel'kups call it *kamlaniye*.'

'Yes, yes. But what is he *doing*?' repeated Benthe.

'You see the drum?' asked Krasheninnikov, pointing to the oval wooden hoop covered with reindeer skin.

'Of course,' answered Benthe impatiently.

'Well, that represents the Cosmos,' said Stepan. 'The Siberian tribes believe the universe is divided into three layers – the Upper World above the heavens, the Middle World – our Earth – and the

Lower World beneath. It is believed that once every member of the tribe could journey without difficulty from one world to the other, but that ability has since been lost. They believe only the shaman can now embark upon such a journey. The shaman has special powers of knowledge and healing and prophecy which he brings back from his expeditions to the other worlds.'

'What kind of powers?'

'That depends on the shaman. If the shaman is experienced, as this one certainly is . . .'

'How can you know that?'

Benthe was teasing him, but Stepan was so caught up in his explanations that he failed to notice it.

'Well, this one has an apron *and* a kaftan, which shows that he is a senior figure in the tribe. And, if you look at all the ornaments and decorations about his person, you can see that the tribe holds him in great respect. Those beasts and birds and other markings are his spirit helpers and protectors who accompany him on his travels.'

'And what is that rattle thing?'

'That is his talking stick. He uses it to tell the future and to heal the sick. If you watch closely, you'll see him throw the baton towards one of the members of the tribe. Depending on how it falls, he will predict what their future holds or how well the reindeer hunt will go.'

At that moment, the shaman paused, then hurled the *pogonyalka* to the ground.

He was chanting unintelligibly now, his head shaking gently from side to side, his cloth headdress flapping as he did so. The young man at whose feet the baton had fallen stood as if transfixed, his eyes bulging in what could have been fear or merely anticipation. He suddenly fell to his knees as the shaman approached him, retrieved the baton and rattled it furiously above the young man's head. The young man fell forward on his face and the watchers emitted a low growl of approval.

'What's happening now?' asked Benthe.

Crestfallen, Krasheninnikov had to admit he wasn't sure.

'Perhaps he hit him on the head,' said Valery Khitrov.

'Be quiet, Valery,' said Benthe. She watched, fascinated, as the shaman continued to work his way around the circle, singling out one member of the Sel'kup tribe after another. Anxious to redeem himself in her eyes, Krasheninnikov played his trump card.

'Of course, this is a *very* powerful shaman,' he announced. 'He's a woman.'

Stepan Krasheninnikov had Benthe's full attention again and he was intent on keeping it.

'You have to understand,' he said, 'that women have *very* special magic powers. Sometimes the shaman is a man dressed as a woman and sometimes a woman dressed as a man. But it is believed that it is always the woman who wields the greater power.'

This was not quite true and Krasheninnikov knew it. Transvestite shamans *were* held to be the most potent of all, but no distinction was made between male and female transvestites. Krasheninnikov had made up the last part, but he spoke with such authority that Benthe was impressed.

Osa Bering looked on, amused at Stepan Krasheninnikov's desperate attempts to impress her daughter – and doubly amused by the angry expression on Valery Khitrov's face.

Yes, thought Osa, Stepan may be right.

Perhaps women do have the greater power. She looked over again at the shaman who had by now completed his – or was it her? – round of the tribe.

An expedition to the Middle and Upper Worlds? How wonderful that must be. Perhaps that was really what the Imperial Great Northern Expedition was all about?

She folded away her sketching pad, dismissing the thought as too fanciful.

All the same, she wondered if she could somehow get her hands on a *pogonyalka*. It would make a splendid gift for Vitus.

Tomsk
October 22, 1734

Vitus Bering was in a black mood that evening.

Little had gone right since their arrival in Tomsk. That the

Expedition had failed in its initial objective of reaching Okhotsk before winter was not his fault, he reasoned, although the blame would undoubtedly be laid at his door.

Now that winter was beginning to set in, morale was at a low ebb. The prospect of five or even six months in Tomsk weighed as heavily on him as it did on all the others.

Conditions in Tomsk were deplorable, far more inhospitable than even he had anticipated.

The garrison commander was an army captain called Voznesensky, a scrawny individual with a sparse moustache grown – with great difficulty it seemed – in a vain attempt to conceal his youth and inexperience. From the onset, Voznesensky made it plain that he hated Tomsk, hated the Sel'kups, hated his dreary garrison posting, and hated the prospect of doing anything to make life easier for the thousand or so members remaining with the Expedition.

'We have no quarters for you,' he informed Bering at the first opportunity. 'And I have neither the men nor the materials to build any.'

Bering was tempted to reply that he expected no preferential treatment from the garrison commander. He had brought the Expedition this far across hostile terrain and without undue losses. The Expedition was weary but travel-hardened and it was perfectly capable of fending for itself.

'We shall have to fend for ourselves,' he said to Martin Spanberg.

'As we have done until now,' said Spanberg with characteristic optimism.

Looking around Tomsk, Bering did not share the First Officer's optimism. By the standards of the age, Tomsk was a large township huddled under the walls of an imposing fort built on the orders of Csar Boris Fyodorovich Gudonov shortly before his death by alleged suicide in 1605. Bering knew that incursions by groups of *zemleprokhodtsy* – 'land-travellers' – across the Urals into Siberia went back at least three centuries. The real conquest of Siberia had begun much later, however, and was generally agreed to have started after Csar Ivan IV Vasilevich – the legendary Ivan the Terrible –

had captured the Tatar khanate of Kazan. Cossacks in the pay of the powerful Stroganov family had crossed the middle Urals in the late 1500s to attack and capture the Tatar stronghold of Sibir – 'the sleeping land' – which had subsequently given its name to the whole region of Siberia.

At no financial outlay, Ivan IV had effectively annexed all of Siberia and secured a new and important source of revenue.

It had been those selfsame Cossacks and their descendants who had pushed on eastwards by land and by river portage until they finally reached the Bay of Okhotsk on the fringe of the Pacific Ocean, their principal legacy a string of garrison forts and a reputation for unprecedented cruelty towards the native tribes they encountered along the way.

The Stroganov family's willingness to underwrite the annexation of Siberia had been by no means altruistic. The glittering prize was the furs which they exacted in tribute from the indigenous populations, primarily on the Csar's behalf but always in exchange for a generous commission. Selling those furs, especially sable, throughout Western Europe had filled the coffers of the Russian Treasury in Moscow, the then capital, although it had done little to alleviate conditions for Russia's serfs during the infamous Time of Troubles that set in after Gudonov's death.

The Stroganovs were also shrewd enough to recognise another source of revenue and, with the Csar's willing connivance, had imposed a swingeing tax on all raw materials imported into Russia from its Siberian colony. This revenue had proved in time to be even more substantial than that from the fur trade; as fur stocks were gradually depleted, duties levied on imported Siberian lead and copper from the mines around Tomsk and elsewhere were a progressively welcome source of income.

Tomsk, although larger than most, was a typical garrison fort town. A strong military presence kept hostile tribes at bay while ensuring that increasingly harsh levels of taxation in kind were imposed to sustain the flow of furs. Bering found one practice particularly distasteful, namely the detention as hostages of women and young children to ensure that their menfolk returned with the prescribed quota of furs. He voiced this criticism to Voznesensky, but the garrison commander shrugged it off.

'You forget that these Ostyaks are lower than animals,' he said of the Sel'kups, 'and deserve no better treatment.'

Voznesensky's attitude to the growing convict population was broadly similar. Most of Russia's penal colonies lay farther to the east, but Tomsk had played host to an increasing number of political exiles since the beginning of the previous century.

Like the outbreaks of smallpox and venereal disease that plagued the garrison fort, corruption was endemic. It started with the garrison commander, whose duties included of necessity laying in winter supplies for his men and animals. This was a boring task but not unduly difficult: despite the exceedingly cold winters, the region was fertile, with maize, oats, flax, potatoes and beets grown in abundance and a still comparatively plentiful – if greatly depleted – supply of game.

'They say a dead fish starts stinking first from the head,' had been Spanberg's reaction when Bering told him that Voznesensky had volunteered to make available to the Expedition additional stocks of food to provision them through the winter months. Naturally, said Voznesensky, the food would have to be paid for. Bering had little option other than to agree, but promised himself that he would report the exorbitant cost of the transaction – and the garrison commander's role in it – in his next despatch to St Petersburg.

The immediate problem was how to house the Expedition. It was feasible to quarter some members inside the walls of the fort and Bering decided that it would be prudent to accord this privilege to the households of several of the noble families who were still with the main body.

For reasons of morale, he decided that he himself would live outside the fort. He regretted having to inflict this additional hardship on his wife and daughter, but found to his surprise that they were so fascinated by the native tribes – whom Voznesensky consistently and inaccurately referred to collectively as Ostyaks – that they were more than willing to move into one of the typical *chum* huts which dotted the landscape around the fort.

In this respect, Osa Bering had proved a tower of strength. She had supervised the furnishing of their primitive quarters, herding their horses and oxen into makeshift pens and filling the framework *chum* dwelling with a modicum of creature comforts.

The *chum* was a simple construction: fifty or more long thin poles had been cut from the branches of deciduous trees and arranged in a circle around a tripod of three thicker central poles sunk deep into the now-frozen earth. Knotted rope canopy beds were slung from the centre poles and the whole was covered by layers of deer hide and birch bark. The *chum* subsequently proved remarkably warm and comfortable even on the coldest day.

Vitus was amused to see that both Osa and Benthe had taken to wearing a variant of native dress: loose-fitting tunics of reindeer skin set off by decorative strips of fur from smaller animals, garnished with beads and embroidered with multi-coloured threads. Others in the Expedition had followed suit, and the resultant miscellany of apparel had the unexpected effect of boosting morale, however briefly. Gone was the finery with which the barons and counts and their respective entourages had decked themselves in the first weeks after leaving St Petersburg. By now, it was difficult to distinguish nobleman from commoner or soldier from servant.

Predictably, Aleksey Chirikov gave vent to his wholehearted disapproval of this new pattern of behaviour. He dressed as always in his mariner's boots and breeches, his only concession to the harsh climate being a fur cape slung around his shoulders. Chirikov was careful not to voice such criticisms in Bering's presence – after all, Osa and Benthe had pioneered the new fashion – but he remarked to Spanberg that it was not conducive to discipline. Besides, it was an affront to Russian manners and tradition.

'Balls,' said Spanberg, who thought Benthe looked delightful. As for her mother, he could scarcely find the words to describe his growing admiration and respect.

Bering's mood was sombre as he reread the despatch that had reached him that day from St Petersburg. It was dated some months

before and had clearly been written without knowledge of his precise
location or of the current status of the Expedition as a whole. The
chain of communication had by this time been stretched to breaking
point and it was evident that few, if any, of his own despatches had
been received, let alone read and acted upon.

'Read this,' he commanded Spanberg, thrusting the paper under
the First Officer's nose. 'Just read this. I ask you, what do those
bastards in St Petersburg think we are doing out here in this God-
forsaken backwater of the Empire?'

Spanberg took the despatch and read it through carefully.

Captain-Commander:
We send you greetings from the Court and from the
Csarina Anna Ivanovna, Empress of All the Russias, and
give thanks for your most recent and most detailed report
on the progress of our great undertaking which is the envy
of the civilised world. It is a matter of grave concern to the
undersigned that your progress has been frustrated by the
numbers under your command and I am at pains to express
my understanding of and my regret for the difficulties this
has occasioned.

Allow me therefore to assure you of our unswerving
commitment to take whatever steps lie within our powers
to support your brave endeavours and to uphold the
purpose of the Imperial Great Northern Expedition.

Allow me also to remind you of the specific responsibilities that are vested in you and of the express limits
imposed on those selfsame responsibilities. If you are to
reap the rewards of fame and fortune which are undoubtedly your due, I urge you to heed the counsel of Lieutenant
Chirikov who acts with the full authority and in accordance with the express wishes of the Grand Council.

I trust this letter finds you in good health and in good
spirits. I append my respects to your lady wife.
Ernst Johann, Reichsgraf von Biron

Spanberg looked up.

'Hot air, Captain-Commander. Words, words, words. Think no more of it.'

'There is an addendum,' said Bering, handing a second page to Spanberg.

You are instructed by the Grand Council to collect and return for inspection here in St Petersburg typical examples of the flora and fauna in each region through which the Expedition passes. Moreover, you are to submit detailed descriptions of the terrain and of the living conditions of the inhabitants. These reports will be completed each week and will be sent by special courier to St Petersburg. The specimens collected by the Expedition will be transported under armed escort and with all due diligence.

Bering waited for Spanberg's reaction to what he himself had already concluded was a singularly unreasonable command.

'This appears quite reasonable, Captain-Commander. I can well understand that the Grand Council must seek to sustain interest in the Expedition and its progress by disclosing news of our experiences and of the land and peoples we have encountered.'

Bering's jaw dropped. This was a far cry from the snort of derision he had expected.

'Have you taken leave of your senses, First Officer? There is no way I can or will comply with an order that is as unreasoned as it is unreasonable.'

'With respect, Captain-Commander. I beg to differ. There *is* a way.'

Bering listened as Spanberg explained.

He was thoroughly ashamed that he seemed to be the only one in the Expedition who had no knowledge of – and, worse, had shown no interest in – what Osa Bering had been doing every single day since they left St Petersburg.

Grand Council, St Petersburg
January 10, 1735
'Tomsk!'

Ernst Johann von Biron looked up and smiled. He had expected that the first reaction to news of Bering's winter quarters would be hostile and that it would inevitably be voiced by none other than Admiral Grigori Solchnov.

'Tomsk!' bellowed the Admiral again. 'What in fuck's name is Bering doing in fucking Tomsk?'

The veins stood out at his temples as he glared round at the other members of the Grand Council.

'As I have just said, my dear Admiral, Captain-Commander Bering has been forced to take to winter quarters at the garrison town of Tomsk on the Tom River, a tributary of the Ob.'

'I know where the fucking Tom River is,' said Solchnov, crashing a huge fist down on the polished birchwood table. 'And don't tell *me* where fucking Tomsk is, I've *been* there.'

He was beside himself with rage. Von Biron knew he could turn this to his advantage.

'The Captain-Commander has set out compelling reasons for the Expedition's delay, Admiral, and I believe that those reasons are, in part at least, acceptable.'

'Acceptable my hairy arse,' shouted Solchnov. 'What do you mean, "acceptable"? That son of a Danish whore was to have been in Okhotsk by now instead of running for cover at the first sign of winter snow.'

'In his defence, let me say he reports that he has of necessity taken the condition and the needs of the Expedition into consideration.'

'We have only his word for that,' bellowed Solchnov again. 'Why defend him or take the word of a whoreson Danish turd? I told this Grand Council he would fail us again, just as he did before.'

'Come, come, Admiral,' said Yevgeny Kallinin in an attempt to defuse the situation. 'At this distance we cannot judge what difficulties the Captain-Commander may have encountered or what reasons warrant this enforced delay. It may be that his decision to overwinter in Tomsk is both prudent and justified. As I say, at this distance, how can we tell?'

Solchnov was not to be placated.

'How can we tell? How can we tell, you ask? I'll *tell* you how we can tell. It was Bering's calculations that were wrong from the very start. You cannot force-march an undisciplined column of civilians over such terrain in the few short months he proposed. By God, I should know. The man is a dreamer. A dreamer, I say. No more, no less.'

Kallinin stuck to his guns.

'That may be so. I fully concur that the Captain-Commander may have miscalculated,' he began.

'Miscalculated? How can you say that? He was fucking wrong. And if he was wrong, then how wrong are we to continue to entrust him with this vital mission?'

This was what von Biron had been waiting to hear.

'I should inform the Grand Council,' said von Biron, 'that I have given a specific order to Acting Captain Chirikov to remove Bering from his command as and when the moment is opportune. That moment will no doubt come in due course, but on no account before the Captain-Commander has fulfilled the first part of his mission.'

The Grand Council was silent. They all understood the implications. Bering was to secure the first stage of the Expedition and orchestrate its initial exploration phase. As soon as the time came to move into the Bering Strait, however, Chirikov would invoke the Grand Council's authority to assume command. In this way, the credit and the glory would pass to a Russian.

Von Biron waited for further comment. When there was none, he spoke again.

'I have also received long despatches from Pisarov in Okhotsk and from this Swedish Lieutenant Waxell. In sum, Pisarov reports from the advance party that work is progressing well on the six vessels required by the Expedition. Waxell writes that he has reached and passed Yakutsk and is presently on course for Okhotsk. Indeed, he should have reached there by now. This, gentlemen, I take to be more welcome news.'

'That is true,' said Solchnov, calmer now. 'Granted, Pisarov is a bit of a hothead at times, but he's a fine officer. A fine *Russian* officer,' he added, hammering the point home. 'I wish we had many others like him.'

Field-Marshal von Münnich, known to be a man of few words, spoke for the first time.

'Count von Biron, I understand that your motives are well-intentioned, but I am disturbed that you appear to have arrogated the authority of this Grand Council to sanction what might later be construed as mutiny.'

Von Münnich allowed no opportunity to pass if there was the slightest chance of undermining von Biron's glib presumption of authority which, as von Münnich knew (but was always careful not to say), derived largely from his fellow German's frequent visits to the bedchamber of the Empress Anna Ivanovna.

'Mutiny is a harsh and ugly term, Field Marshal, and one that I would be hesitant to use in this instance. Much depends on whether Bering succeeds in what, I am forced to concede, is a delicate task.'

'Are you saying that the order to relieve him of his command can or will be rescinded?'

'I am saying that the order is conditional upon events.'

Von Münnich, clearly dissatisfied with the reply, was silent.

Kallinin spoke again.

'I fail to comprehend why Bering should not be allowed to continue in command,' he said. 'It is ultimately within our discretion in this Grand Council to allocate credit for the success of the Expedition to whomsoever we choose.'

'A point well taken,' said von Biron triumphantly, delighted that Kallinin had recognised what he himself had come to realise, namely that the ability to manipulate the outcome of the Expedition lay entirely within the remit of the Grand Council.

Von Biron chose his next words with care.

'Which brings me to the crux of the situation. The outcome of the Expedition as a whole must be measured not only by its successful completion but by the interim achievements we can attribute to it. Accordingly, I have instructed the Captain-Commander to send back to St Petersburg a detailed record of how the Expedition has fared to date, together with descriptions and specimens of the flora and fauna they have encountered along the way.'

Von Biron paused.

'That includes, let me add, details of the peoples they have seen and their language and customs.'

'I fail to see the immediate gain from this,' said von Münnich.

'The immediate gain is that we keep alive interest in the Expedition and start reaping tangible scientific benefit from it. What we gain in the longer, term, however, will be whatever we in this Grand Council choose to gain,' countered von Biron. 'As Count Kallinin has so rightly said, it is ultimately within the discretion of those in this room to allocate credit and, by the same token, to attribute blame to whomsoever we choose.'

Admiral Solchnov grunted his approval.

Von Münnich spoke again.

'I am not happy with this.'

'I see no reason to be unhappy, Field Marshal', said von Biron. 'We shall continue to act in what we discern to be the best interests of the Empire. That is our duty, is it not?'

Von Münnich had been out-manoeuvred. To question von Biron's motives further would be tantamount to treason. He nodded his agreement.

Von Biron gathered his papers together and stood up.

'Excellencies, I thank you for your attention.'

With that, he turned and swept from the room, his lips etched into a thin but distinct smile.

Okhotsk
January 1735

From the journal of Lieutenant-at-Sea Sven Waxell

January 8, 1735

It is two months to the day since we reached Okhotsk after a distressingly arduous journey from Yakutsk accomplished by dog-sled and to no small degree on foot. As I reflect on the rigours of our route, I accept that I may have pressed the men too hard in my anxiety to reach the coast. The decision to move on from Yakutsk rather than over-winter there was mine and mine alone, however, and I do not regret it. The men performed well and without great complaint, but all were much relieved when our months of hardship and endeavour were at last behind us.

On reaching Okhotsk, my first action was to declare a leave of two weeks to enable the troop to recover its strength. The men rejoiced at this and fell to revelry. There were several breaches of discipline and I pride myself that I punished firmly but fairly.

To my great regret, I must record that one able seaman was set upon by a horde of ruffians from the advance party and was stabbed fatally in the chest. I reported this to Lieutenant Pisarov and counselled that he take immediate action by placing those responsible in the stockade. This he refused to do on the grounds that the cowardly attack was merely occasioned by a surfeit of strong drink.

That he elected to take no action in this matter and attributed the incident to high spirits is a source of great concern. By punishing the offenders, justice would have been seen to be done and all would have been satisfied. By failing to do so, the Lieutenant has given great offence and there now exists a state of tension between those under my command and those of the advance party.

It grieves me to write these thoughts on the conduct of a fellow officer, but I am constrained to do so in this journal of record.

January 12, 1735

On our arrival here I was most taken aback to learn of the little progress in building the vessels that the Captain-Commander requires to pursue the course of the Expedition. I know now that I was too ready to excuse this failure on the part of the advance party, attributing it as I did to the severe winter conditions in this place and to the onerous journey which, from my own experience, they had to endure.

I am persuaded that I demonstrated a generosity of spirit that is now revealed to be inappropriate. This Pisarov does no credit to *his rank or to the service. That he is arrogant and dismissive in his demeanour I can perhaps excuse; that he is slothful, I cannot and will not.*

The hulls of only four vessels are built (but not caulked). No masts have been mounted and only a small amount of canvas has been sewn. Of the other two vessels the Lieutenant was charged to ready there is no sign. The convict details that are conscripted to aid the advance party in their task most regularly fail to report for work and, when they do, work slowly and with great indifference.

Lieutenant Pisarov asserts that he has too few men to complete his mission. I do not agree and have told him so, urging him to spur his own party to apply themselves with greater diligence. He replies that his men are weary of their task and the conditions in which they must perform it.

This is unacceptable.

I have endeavoured to lead by example and have set my men to readying the other two vessels. They have applied themselves with enthusiasm and have worked as best they can, yet they are mariners not labourers and so have none or too few of the necessary specialist skills. Progress is slight and continuing antagonism between my men and those of the advance party constitutes an ever-present impediment to cooperation.

I have sent a despatch to the Captain-Commander wherein I report on these matters. I did so with the utmost reluctance, wishing neither to criticise a fellow officer nor to alarm unduly the Captain-Commander. I have received word that he is over-wintering in Tomsk. His progress has also been slow, for I know his intention was to reach Yakutsk or even Okhotsk by the onset of winter.

In private, I draw some small consolation from the news that he has been delayed as this will most likely afford us more time in which to ready the vessels as ordered.

Lieutenant Pisarov professes to share this view and argues that there is time enough for all six vessels to be built by the time the Captain-Commander reaches Okhotsk. This may prove true, but it does not excuse that Lieutenant Pisarov now stands revealed as

*one who is derelict in his duty and as a man too ready with excuses
and self-justification.*

*I have left a small detachment of men (sixteen in all) in Yakutsk
to await the Captain-Commander's arrival, to report directly our
decision to press on to Okhotsk and to provide him with additional escort. I am reinforced in this judgment by the knowledge
that his assignment is by far more difficult than my own and that
his military escort may have been depleted by hostile attack – from
which we ourselves were mercifully spared.*

*Laurentij works with the men now and continues to be a great
favourite of all. They speak most well of him and treat him as one
of their own despite his years. His language has coarsened some-
what and I have chided him on this account. He continues to be
in robust good health, for which I give thanks to God.*

Aboard the Konstantin
January 22, 1735

Georg Wilhem Steller leant over the ship's rail and vomited for the
umpteenth time that day. He wiped the spittle from his lips and
stood facing the chill wind that blew off the Baltic, fervently
thanking the Good Lord that land was finally in sight and that the
Konstantin was less than two hours from docking at St Petersburg.

He dreaded the thought of the return voyage.

Steller had never been to sea before and had never experienced
such discomfort and distress. His head pounded, his ribs ached,
and every muscle in his abdomen was stretched in torment. Little
wonder: he had been seasick every day since the vessel cast off from
the north German port of Kiel. It was no consolation that other
passengers had been similarly afflicted or that several crewmen had
repeatedly (and, he felt, condescendingly) assured him and his co-
sufferers that the seas were anything but heavy. Like many before
him, he had made the fatal mistake of going on deck and fixing
his gaze resolutely on the horizon in the belief that this would take
his mind off the swell that rocked the small vessel up and down
and from side to side. The effect had been quite the opposite, as
he had learned to his cost.

Steller was not given to strong language but, inwardly, he roundly cursed the Berlin Medical Council, King Friedrich Wilhelm of Prussia, the University of Halle, the captain and crew of the *Konstantin* and anyone and anything else that came to mind.

His interview with the Medical Council in Berlin had taken place in the middle of the previous year. Confident that his appointment to the Halle Faculty of Medicine would be ratified within weeks, he had fully expected to take up his new post at the commencement of the winter semester. In the interim, he decided to travel to St Petersburg and make inquiries about the Imperial Great Northern Expedition and how he might later be seconded to it as a member of the scientific contingent.

Steller was not without means but his resources were limited and, as he knew, insufficient to underwrite a protracted stay in the Russian capital. The cost of passage to St Petersburg was modest enough, but nevertheless represented a drain on his meagre savings. Uncertain what to do, he sought advice from his mentors Friedrich Hoffmann and Michael Matthias Ludolf. Through their good offices and several of his own ecclesiastical contacts, he had finally acquired letters of introduction and accreditation as physician to the household of the Russian Orthodox theologian Feofan Prokopovich, Archibishop of Pskov. The letters were prudently wrapped in oilskin and safely stashed in his battered leather trunk in the cabin below.

The whole process had dragged on for several months and it was not until January 1735 that Steller was at last able to book and pay for his passage on the *Konstantin*, secure in the knowledge that he would be welcomed as a member of the Archbishop's household.

Steller was aware that his voyage to St Petersburg could well mark a turning point in his career. He knew the Archbishop to be a man of great influence, not only within the Church but beyond it. Feofan Prokopovich had come to prominence as a counsellor on ecclesiastical and theological affairs to Peter the Great and was credited with having made a major contribution to Peter's westernisation programme. Equally impressive had been both his liberalising influence on the Russian Orthodox Church, which he had radically reformed along Lutheran lines and, it was said, his shrewdly opportunistic interpretation and advocacy of the Church as a political arm of the State.

Of direct relevance to Steller's appointment, moreover, was the fact that Archbishop Prokopovich's ecclesiastical reforms were largely based on the model developed by the Lutheran faculty at the University of Halle. As a result, the recommendations Steller had been given by Hoffmann and Ludolf carried considerable weight.

Steller resolved to do whatever necessary to remain in the Archbishop's good graces. He had already read and digested Prokopovich's theological doctrine as set out in the Archbishop's seminal tracts *De Deo* and *De Trinitate,* and he had resolved to read the third and final tract in the trilogy – *De Creatione et Providentia* – during the voyage to St Petersburg. To his regret, the volume lay, still unread, in the cramped cabin below.

When the *Konstantin* docked at St Petersburg, Steller hurried to the far rail and vomited for what he hoped was the last time.

Tomsk
January 28, 1735

It was bound to happen sooner or later.

Lieutenant Valery Khitrov and Stepan Krasheninnikov competed almost daily for the attentions of Benthe Bering, who was cautioned on several occasions by her mother.

'Be careful, Benthe. This could end in tears.'

Benthe disregarded the warning and felt quite justified in doing so. She realised full well that the two men thoroughly disliked each other and that she was probably the root cause of their mutual antipathy. On the other hand, she considered that she treated them both with equal courtesy. She knew that she was flirting with them and toying with their affections but, in her defence, she made a consistent effort to treat neither more favourably than his rival.

She was understandably flattered by their devotion, however, and, as she confided to her mother, liked both young men equally, if for different reasons. Khitrov she admired for his blond good looks, his confident swagger and his frank and direct manner, which reminded her increasingly of her own father in better times. Krasheninnikov she admired on account of *his* good looks, his erudition and the unfailing patience he showed when explaining to her things about which, as she now admitted, she knew depressingly little.

What Benthe did not consciously grasp was that virtually all the best features of both were combined in the person of Martin Spanberg, whom she continued to adore but who had recently – for some reason she could not fathom – chosen to limit his direct contact with the Bering family to formal discussions with Vitus Bering.

It happened late one evening.

Valery Khitrov was ensconced in Bering's private *chum*, a secondary frame dwelling that the Captain-Commander had ordered built so as not to disturb his family when formal discussions with members of the Expedition were scheduled. It did not escape Osa Bering's notice that, in moving that short way from their principal dwelling, Bering had effectively distanced himself further from her and her daughter, not only physically but emotionally. He was spending more and more time on his own these days, poring over the charts that littered the makeshift table he had installed.

Bering had just finished explaining a fine point of navigation for Khitrov's benefit when Benthe quietly slipped into the room through the layers of reindeer skin that helped shield the entire structure from the elements. She came late every evening without fail around this time to bid goodnight to her father, staying only moments so as not to disturb him.

'I come to say goodnight, father,' she said.

Bering stood up at once and came over to embrace her. Khitrov leapt to his feet, in the process knocking one of Bering's precious charts from the table. As he scrambled to pick it up and return it to its rightful place, he noticed – to his consternation – that Stepan Krasheninnikov was with her.

'I also bid you goodnight, Captain-Commander,' said Krasheninnikov, extending a hand which Bering grasped and shook warmly.

'I bid you good night, sir, and I thank you for returning my daughter safely.'

'It has been an honour to escort her, Captain-Commander.'

Escort her? Escort her *where*? This was the first thought that sprang into Khitrov's mind. Other than those low-life taverns within the garrison walls there was nowhere to go in this shit-hole of a town.

Benthe Bering, her eyes shining with unalloyed pleasure, confirmed his worst fears.

'We visited a tavern in the garrison,' she said. 'It was exciting. There was a fight and one of the men – '

Bering raised a hand, cutting her off in mid-flow. He turned to Krasheninnikov.

'Sir, I do not wish my daughter to frequent such places. They are coarse and unseemly for a girl of her years.'

'But, Father,' put in Benthe, hurt at the injustice of Bering's sudden anger, 'we remained only a short time.'

'That is of no consequence,' snorted Bering. 'I forbid you to venture into the garrison taverns ever again. I absolutely forbid it and that is my final word on this matter.'

Bering turned away abruptly and sat down at his charts.

Krasheninnikov looked suitably crestfallen. Benthe was chastened and contrite, but her eyes flashed defiance.

'That is unjust, father.'

Bering did not look up.

'That is unjust, I said.'

Bering made no reply. Benthe turned on her heel and pushed her way out of the *chum*. Stepan Krasheninnikov left behind her. Seeing that Bering was in no mood for further conversation, Khitrov followed them out into the dark night.

Khitrov was uncertain why he acted as he did. Perhaps it was the strength of his affections for Benthe or the unmitigated resentment he felt for Krasheninnikov or the long months spent cooped up in Tomsk? Or perhaps it was all of these? That he acted out of unalloyed jealousy did not cross his mind.

Catching up with the pair walking ahead of him, he slammed his shoulder into Krasheninnikov, sending the young scientist sprawling into the soft snow. In the darkness, Khitrov could barely make out the other man's features, but he sensed that they were contorted into a mixture of indignation and embarrassment.

'Please forgive me. I did not see you there in the dark.'

Krasheninnikov struggled to his feet, brushing the loose snow from his topcoat.

'You did that on purpose.'.

'Nonsense,' replied Khitrov.

'You know that is not true.'

'You dare call me a liar?'

'I do.'

To Benthe Bering's horror, Khitrov slapped Krasheninnikov across the face. The gesture was unequivocal.

Krasheninnikov responded in kind.

'Stop it!' shouted Benthe, alarmed. 'Stop it this instant, both of you!'

It was too late.

'Have your seconds call on me early tomorrow morning,' said Khitrov.

'At your pleasure.'

Khitrov bowed formally to Benthe and walked off into the night.

'This is madness, Stepan,' said Benthe.

'This is my affair,' replied the young scientist. 'And I shall see it through.'

The formalities were duly observed the following morning. Khitrov's seconds – a junior lieutenant and an army surgeon – presented their compliments and offered to convey Krasheninnikov's apology to their principal. As ritual demanded, Krasheninnikov refused to apologise. His seconds – two fellow scientists who were clearly bewildered by the turn of events – learned that the duel was scheduled for eleven o'clock that morning when the light would be adequate. In a departure from traditional etiquette, Khitrov, nominally the offended party, had conceded to Krasheninnikov the right to choose which weapons were to be used.

Stepan Krasheninnikov was secretly grateful for this gesture although he knew that it was intended to humiliate him even further.

Since he professed no intimacy whatsoever with the sword, he opted for pistols with which he had a passing familiarity.

It remained only to appoint a referee.

The seconds approached Martin Spanberg, who seemed remarkably willing to act in that capacity.

They met at eleven. As protocol required, Khitrov again invited Krasheninnikov to apologise and, as ritual and etiquette also required, Krasheninnikov again refused.

Benthe Bering was terrified at the prospect of a duel between her two admirers and had done her best to prevent it. She had appealed to her mother to intervene with Bering, but her mother refused. This was a matter of honour, Osa had explained, however silly it might seem. Benthe had then turned to Martin Spanberg, only to be shocked and disgusted to learn that not only was he reluctant to stop the duel, he had even agreed to stand as referee.

The duel was to be held at fourteen paces. The duellists would position themselves back-to-back and walk forward seven paces at Spanberg's count, then turn on command, extend their forearms to bring their pistols to the line of fire, and fire simultaneously.

It was accepted practice that duels take place with only the principals, seconds and referee in attendance and at a secluded location away from prying eyes. This had proved impossible. Word of the uneven duel had spread throughout the Expedition and a huge crowd had congregated. This was, when all was said and done, a major event which would leaven the tedium of a Tomsk winter.

Benthe Bering watched as Martin Spanberg approached the two men. It was his duty as referee to ensure that the rules of engagement were respected to the letter. It was also his duty to ensure that, in the event of a misfire, the luckless duellist would have an opportunity to reload and fire once more – always assuming he was still alive. If both should fire and miss, they would return to their original places and the sequence would recommence.

Spanberg rehearsed these rules for the benefit of Khitrov and Krasheninnikov and routinely offered them the honourable alternative of settling their grievance without violence. He knew that this final offer of conciliation would also be refused.

Until the very last moment, Benthe prayed that Spanberg would do something to stop the deadly charade. She knew that Krasheninnikov was no match for Khitrov, an officer skilled in the art of weaponry. She knew also that Krasheninnikov had blundered by electing for pistols. This meant that it would be a duel to the death, whereas crossing swords would have been a less serious affair, curtailed in all probability when first blood was drawn or when the first telling blow incapacitated one of the duellists.

The two stood back-to-back at the ready. Out of earshot of the crowd, Martin Spanberg spoke his final instructions.

'Either party who violates the ritual by firing prematurely or shooting his opponent in the back will be ostracised. Should either party die as the result of such a violation, the survivor shall not only be ostracised but shall also be held guilty of murder in cold blood and sentenced accordingly.'

Spanberg paused.

'There is one more rule which shall apply,' he continued. 'Should one or the other of you two idiots die as a result of this childish petulance, I shall immediately challenge the survivor to a duel. To the death, naturally. That is all. Gentlemen, you have been warned.'

The count started.

As he paced out to the firing point, Krasheninnikov could feel the sweat running down his back. His mouth was dry and his pistol hand was shaking. Stepan was no coward but he certainly regretted the incident of the previous evening. He knew that, in a few seconds, he would reap the consequences.

Valery Khitrov was also afraid. Not of this pathetic civilian but of Martin Spanberg. He knew Spanberg to be a man of his word.

'Seven and turn!'

They faced off at fourteen paces, dropped their pistols to shoulder level and fired within a split second of each other.

To his utter consternation, Khitrov realised that he had missed completely. As an accomplished marksman and the veteran of several duels, he was unable to explain why his hand had jerked involuntarily at the very last moment, sending the ball whistling harmlessly past Krasheninnikov's left ear and into the trees beyond.

Khitrov stood stock still, uncertain whether Krasheninnikov had already fired. His opponent's pistol still pointed in his direction and he was alarmed to see that Krasheninnikov's hand no longer trembled. In such a situation, a party who fired without riposte was entitled to turn his body side-on to present a more difficult target. This, to his credit, Khitrov refused to do. He stood full-on to his opponent and waited.

It was exceedingly cold that morning and Khitrov was surprised to find that his left cheek was burning. He edged out his tongue and explored the side of his mouth. The salt taste of blood – his blood, he realised to his astonishment – was unmistakable.

Krasheninnikov's ball had sliced open his cheek.

'Honour is satisfied, gentlemen,' declared Martin Spanberg, marching from the field.

He walked over to and past where a relieved Benthe Bering was still trying to come to terms with what had happened. As he passed her, she could not fail to notice that he was smiling broadly. He looked at her and winked.

In that instant, Benthe acknowledged the depth of her feelings for Martin Spanberg.

For a radiant Benthe Bering, the hapless Krasheninnikov and the swaggering Khitrov had vanished, both of them consigned to distant memory as losers in a pointless duel from which only a smiling non-combatant had emerged as the clear victor.

Okhotsk
February 17, 1735

The men of the advance party under Grigor Pisarov were artisans. As a matter of course, they took pride in their work and in their ability to deliver according to contract. An added inducement in this instance was that they were being paid double the normal rate for work which, although admittedly performed under near-impossible conditions of severe cold and driving snow, was essentially routine.

His men had watched with interest and, as time went by, irritation as the seamen under Lieutenant Sven Waxell made laboured but nonetheless discernible progress in shaping the hulls for the two additional vessels. At first, the advance party had made fun of the lack of expertise shown by Waxell's contingent. Gradually, this amusement had given way to grudging admiration for their efforts. In the end, professional pride had asserted itself: they were not to be outdone by a group of amateurs, however well-intentioned.

The advance party returned to work. Waxell's men noted this and redoubled their own efforts.

Pisarov's daily routine was unvarying. He rose late in the day, his head still thick after the excesses of the previous night. He ate a meal washed down by ale and vodka and, late every afternoon, made his way to one of the taverns that provided the only distraction for the garrison.

His favourite retreat was located down a dank alleyway close to the outer fortress wall. Here, native whores plied their trade in exchange for trinkets and the occasional glass of ale, and fights broke out with monotonous regularity as the women played one customer off against the next. Pisarov would sit alone, drinking steadily until late into the night before selecting one or more of the remaining whores to share his bed.

He sat that evening at a table close to the wall, a flagon of ale at one elbow and a bottle of low-grade vodka at the other. He watched through red-rimmed eyes as one of the political exiles fingered the buttocks of a sturdily-built whore with the Mongol features and spiky dark hair typical of the Sel'kups.

Those exiles are a curious bunch, he thought to himself. They volunteer next to no information about why they are here or about what they did or why they did it. They speak little among themselves and seem resigned to living out their term of exile until, for reasons that are rarely if ever disclosed, word comes from St Petersburg that they are no longer out of favour. The only real punishment they have to endure is excommunication from the Court and they see such banishment as punishment that is sufficient in and of itself. They are not without means, however, and live in constant fear of being attacked and robbed. Cowards to a man, they shrink away from any form of physical confrontation and cut and run when a soldier or sailor comes into the room let alone approaches their table.

Pisarov watched as the exile's hand kneaded the woman's fleshy buttocks. She sat passively, her dull eyes betraying no great interest in the grimy fingers that explored her intimate parts.

Looking round the smoke-filled room, Pisarov was surprised to see that, tonight, there were many more whores than there were customers. There were a number of officers and enlisted men in the room and almost as many political exiles, each surrounded by a group of women. It was odd, he thought: he recognised at most only three or four from his own advance party when, only a month previously, the tavern would have been packed with groups of tradesmen swilling ale and spoiling for a fight. He had noticed this increasingly over the past two to three weeks and he was puzzled by it.

Had they found a better place to spend their money and sow their wild oats? Pisarov did not know and, he told himself, it was no concern of his. What they did in their own free time – and Christ knows, they had plenty of it – was not his business. But curiosity got the better of him and he resolved to find out what was going on.

The next morning he rose comparatively early, dressed and made his way through the streets to the naval yards. To his surprise, they were a hive of activity.

He noticed that Waxell's men had almost finished readying the two hulls they had been working on. And, to his consternation and anger, he saw that several of his own men were looking on, pointing fingers and, he was certain of it, giving instructions and good-humoured advice.

A master carpenter whose face he recognised but whose name escaped him, was on his knees on the hard-packed snow, his finger tracing over a blueprint of a ship's hull. As Pisarov looked on, the carpenter jabbed his finger repeatedly at various points on the diagram and spoke animatedly to the small group of Waxell's men clustered around him. They were nodding intently and smiling.

Pisarov glanced up at the hull and saw another of his own men standing on the partially-timbered deck, supervising the cutting of a well which would take one of the masts. He saw yet another group of men sitting close by, sewing sails under the watchful eye of one of Pisarov's foremen.

Had Grigor Pisarov spent more time at the yards and less in the tavern, he would have realised that the earlier antipathy between his own men and Waxell's party had disappeared. The stabbing incident Waxell had reported to him (and which he had chosen to do nothing about) was clearly forgotten. Rivalries were a thing of the past as the two sets of men made common cause. Healthy competition had spawned cooperation. Skills were being shared.

And the vessels were being built.

Pisarov was in two minds. His first instinct was to reprimand his men and return them immediately to their own duties. But he thought better of it. In the long run, what did it matter as long as the vessels were being fitted out?

Waxell suddenly emerged from the other side of the hull, saw him and came over.

'Please accept my gratitude, Lieutenant Pisarov. Without your counsel and the help of your men we would have made little headway.'

The sarcasm was not lost on Pisarov.

'I hold it to be in the best interests of us all, Lieutenant.'

'Indeed.'

Pisarov knew now why the taverns were so deserted of an evening. His men were exhausted after a full day's work in the yards and needed their rest.

He turned to the carpenter who was briefing Waxell's men.

'Carry on, master carpenter.'

The man glanced up from the diagram. He looked Pisarov up and down. It was clear what he was thinking: who did this lazy shit of a lieutenant think he was?

'It is good to see you again after all these weeks, Lieutenant Pisarov,' said the man, carefully weighing how far he, as a civilian, could go. 'Now, if you'll excuse me, I have work to do.'

Pisarov gave a cursory nod as if the reply were to his satisfaction.

He noticed that his own men were watching him, gauging his reaction. That they held him in contempt was only too evident.

Pisarov had lost face. And he knew it.

'May I congratulate you on the progress you have made, Lieutenant Waxell?'

'That you may, Lieutenant Pisarov. And, on behalf of my men, may I say that we have been privileged to make a modest contribution to what you yourself have accomplished.'

Tomsk
March 4, 1735

A head count established that there were 917 persons still remaining with the Expedition. By Bering's reckoning, 613 had returned to St Petersburg at the first opportunity and a small number – forty-eight in all – had since left the main party on their own recognisance. Two hundred and six officers and enlisted men now comprised the military escort. One hundred and eighty-two seamen – deck officers and hands – were with Bering's own party. Their ranks would in due course be swollen by those who had set off under Waxell's command and by some of the master craftsmen from the advance party led by Lieutenant Pisarov who would travel aboard ship during the exploration phase proper.

In all, there had been twenty-three deaths and seventeen live births among the accompanying civilians, whose total now numbered five hundred and forty-eight. As anticipated, the bulk of the camp followers had returned to St Petersburg very early on; the eighty or so who remained – including the invaluable wheelwrights and carpenters – had long since closed up to and been assimilated into the main column.

As far as Bering could ascertain, these figures were accurate. They made allowance for some 160 civilians who had announced their intention to remain in Tomsk when the Expedition moved on to Yakutsk and Okhotsk in early spring; they would wait for an opportunity to return to St Petersburg as soon as an appropriate military escort became available. To his surprise, eighty or so persons in Tomsk had requested and had reluctantly been given his permission to join the Expedition when it left Tomsk. Of these, most were reckoned to be anxious to travel to Yakutsk or Okhotsk under the comparative protection of the expeditionary force and would play no part in the later proceedings.

Among the 548 civilians were 178 persons who could justifiably lay claim to being scientists and academics. For the most part, these were young men anxious to further their careers and/or were motivated by a spirit of adventure. Among them were, however, some older and more established academics who already boasted a distinguished career and whose willingness to submit themselves to the hardships of the Expedition could only be attributed to a genuine commitment to learning and a supreme indifference to their own discomfort.

Bering conceded that most of the academics and scientists – and especially the younger ones among their ranks – had given a good account of themselves on the journey to Tomsk. Some had sought refuge with the noble households travelling with the Expedition, but most had automatically formed themselves into small groups of kindred spirits who shared duties and chores and clearly enjoyed and profited by one another's company.

They were a mixed bunch, drawn from a wide spectrum of disciplines, and it was essentially to them that the Imperial Great Northern Expedition owed its international flavour. Scientists from Russia rubbed shoulders with their counterparts from Germany, Spain, Italy and England, and there was even a sprinkling of 'observers' from the New World.

On the whole, Bering had shown little concern for them in St Petersburg and he now showed equally little interest in their comings and goings, other than to assume overall responsibility for their general welfare and to ensure that they in no way impeded the Expedition's progress.

Meanwhile, Bering was grateful to Martin Spanberg for disclosing Osa Bering's journal of record, which Bering had now – finally – taken the trouble to inspect. Spanberg had been unusually forthright in his insistence that the demands made on Bering by the Grand Council could be met at least in part by adding Osa's compendium of drawings and artefacts to the collective observations of the scientific contingent.

Although Bering himself considered the scientific contingent to be no more than an inconsequential adjunct to his own mission, he was forced to concede that the plethora of research materials now being routinely transmitted back to St Petersburg could go some way towards bolstering his own standing as Expedition leader in the eyes of Ernst von Biron and the Grand Council at large. He looked on indulgently as the cartographers in the Expedition worked long hours charting the terrain, computing distances, calculating the height of distant mountain ranges and consigning their findings to paper. The naturalists appeared to be having a field day *every* day as new specimens were discovered. The botanists plucked and annotated each grass and flower along the way. Records of temperature and wind strength were assiduously maintained. The interpreters struggled gamely and despairingly with local dialects and the anthropologists monitored the physiognomies of indigent people encountered in the path of the Expedition.

Bering also conceded that this welter of scientific activity had a distinctly positive effect on morale and *esprit de corps*. For the first time in ages, the members of the Expedition seemed to have acquired a sense not only of what they were doing but of why. Nevertheless, he found it difficult to reveal these thoughts to others, including Martin Spanberg.

'You must realise, Captain-Commander, that your wife has compiled a personal and consistent record of almost all we have seen and done. Although no specialist myself, I venture to say her drawings are of a quality and accuracy commensurate with scientific rigour.'

'Continue.'

'If I may be so bold, Captain-Commander, may I also observe that many of the scientists and academicians who journey with us have not been idle. It would seem that they too have collected many specimens and dutifully recorded their observations. It would be but a small matter to collate their findings and illustrate them by reference to the splendid sketches executed by your lady wife.'

'That is an unnecessary distraction from our mission. We have no time for such trivia.'

'With great respect, Captain-Commander, we must make time.'

'Then let me say, First Officer, that *I* have no time for this. If *you* can find time and if such a futile exercise does not conflict with your other duties, I propose that you assume responsibility in the matter, at least until our departure from Tomsk.'

Osa Bering had been aware of Spanberg's proposal and she welcomed it. Above all, she felt that contributing in such a material way to the Expedition would bring her closer to her husband, if only to the extent that she would be on hand to help him prepare his regular despatches to St Petersburg. She relished the prospect of acting as an intermediary between the scientists and academics on the one hand and her husband on the other.

To her dismay, she discovered that her new duties as a chronicler of the Expedition would ensure her less rather than more time at her husband's side. Vitus had formally delegated the task of coordinating reports to the Grand Council to his First Officer.

This was not to her liking and she made Vitus Bering aware of this in no uncertain fashion.

'I had hoped, Vitus, that this would bring us closer.'

'My dear wife, we are as close as we ever can be given the circumstances in which we find ourselves. My duties and responsibilities do not allow for such, shall we say, diversions?'

Diversions? The word angered Osa Bering more than she cared to admit. To her mind, Bering's preoccupation with the *minutiae* of his impending voyage was obsessive and surely premature at this stage of the Expedition. She had hoped that the time spent overwintering in Tomsk would bring them closer together, not prise them farther apart.

Martin Spanberg was also upset at the prospect of his newly-acquired role. Of late, he had studiously avoided Osa Bering other than when to do so would have seemed discourteous. He made up his mind that he would act as a liaison between Osa and the scientists but keep his distance from her whenever possible.

Osa was not alert to Spanberg's misgivings and was hurt by his curt manner.

'Have I offended you in some way, Martin?'

'Offended me? Of course not. But, like your husband, the Captain-Commander, I have many duties to perform.'

'If that is so, then I regret that this additional burden has been placed on your shoulders.'

'It is a burden that I shall endeavour to carry as lightly as possible.'

Osa leant forward and touched his hand.

'But I have this sense of hostility, as if something untoward has transpired between us.'

Spanberg could feel her fingers resting lightly on the back of his hand.

'My dear lady, I can assure you that nothing untoward has transpired. And never will.'

'I am glad of that, Martin, for I value your friendship and your company greatly.'

'As I yours.'

Spanberg slowly and deliberately turned his hand over, taking her hand in his outstretched palm. He raised his eyes to hers.

'This is such a delicate hand. It is difficult to believe the strength and fullness of character that it can express.'

Osa Bering laughed out loud. She withdrew her hand from his and brought both her hands together in merriment.

'But, my dear Martin, that is my right hand. I draw with my left!'

Spanberg was embarrassed but recovered his composure quickly.

'To me, Osa, both are equally precious.'

Colour suffused Osa Bering's cheeks. For a moment, Spanberg thought he had gone too far, that he had overstepped the bounds of propriety. Then he realised that Osa was still laughing.

'And *you*, First Officer Spanberg, are what my daughter Benthe has always said you are – an incorrigible tease.'

Spanberg bowed low in mock humility.

'I am what I am,' he replied. 'But I shall forever be at your service.'

'One day I may hold you to that promise,' said Osa, conscious that, for the first time ever, he had called her by her given name.

St Petersburg
March 28, 1735

'*J'adoube.*'

Reichsgraf Ernst von Biron's finger hovered over the black rook, indicating to his opponent that he had not yet committed to the move. From the outset, von Biron had played with aggression, shifting pieces around the ornate mother-of-pearl board with a speed and decisiveness he knew to be disconcerting to his opponent.

Von Biron chose his opponents with care.

He liked to win.

Feofan Prokopovich loved the game but was the first to concede that he was no match for von Biron. The Archbishop attributed von Biron's uncharacteristic hesitation to his belief that the next move was critical. For the life of him, Prokopovich could not see why. His own defence had been unusually sound that afternoon and he had countered von Biron's every move. Slowly, perhaps, but effectively.

He watched as von Biron removed his finger from above the rook and moved his knight, flicking a white pawn from the board.

'Check! And mate in three.'

Prokopovich stared hard at the remaining pieces. Von Biron's knight was completely exposed and could be removed easily and with apparent impunity by the Archbishop's queen.

Von Biron leant back in the brass-studded chair, placed his fingertips together, and nodded to himself in satisfaction. The Archbishop could see no immediate reason for this. If anything, he thought, von Biron had been careless. But he knew his opponent too well.

Mate in three, von Biron had concluded.

How on earth?

Long minutes passed without the Archbishop offering any

response. Von Biron sat patiently, studying his opponent. Prokopovich shifted uneasily in his chair. He was a good if all-too-frequent loser, but he preferred to understand exactly where he had gone wrong. After all, that was the only way to improve his game. Besides, the ultimate humiliation in chess – as, indeed, in life itself – is not to lose but to lose without knowing why.

He decided to remove von Biron's knight from the board, then thought better of it. He had missed something, of that much he was now convinced.

Fingertips still pressed together in front of his face, von Biron sat motionless, smiling.

The Archibishop was not about to give von Biron the satisfaction of admitting that he failed to see why the announced checkmate was imminent.

Feofan Prokopovich lowered his eyes to the board one last time. He sat forward in his chair and tipped the white king over on its side. He stood abruptly and held out his hand.

'An excellent move and one that I had not anticipated.'

Von Biron rose and clasped the Archbishop's hand.

'Thank you, Your Eminence. We must play again soon.'

When the Archbishop had taken his leave, von Biron surveyed the pieces scattered about the board. Mate in three? Never. He had been forced to bluff, a tactic that rarely succeeds unless an opponent's level of skill is substantially inferior to one's own. The Archbishop had played a better game than usual and a draw would have been inevitable.

And *that* would have been unthinkable.

He tapped the elegant gold paperknife on the leather-topped desk, lost in thought.

His pieces were still intact. Bering was in Tomsk and would leave for Yakutsk and Okhotsk any day now. Pisarov and Waxell had readied the vessels in Okhotsk for the voyage to the Kamchatka Peninsula. Chirikov had proved a reliable informant. The Grand Council continued to recognise von Biron's authority. And, here in St Petersburg, the scientific community had been alerted to exciting discoveries soon to be reported from the east. Of late, even the

Empress Anna Ivanovna had shown a modicum of interest in the progress of her Imperial Great Northern Expedition.

He had played himself into a winning position and would continue to press home his advantage.

Ernst von Biron *liked* to win.

Tomsk
April 9, 1735
It was still bitterly cold, but the sun had shone the previous day and again this morning. The Tom River was running higher now as the first thaw began to set in.

Slowly, the Expedition roused itself from its enforced hibernation. Vitus Bering sniffed the air and was satisfied. He gave the order to strike camp. The Expedition would assemble on April 16 and leave for Yakutsk the following morning.

The long winter was at last behind them.

Chapter Four

OKHOTSK

Okhotskoye More
August 22, 1735
Vitus Bering stood on a rocky promontory which jutted out into the Okhotskoye More, shielding his eyes against the harsh glare of a morning sun that still hung low on the horizon.

The weather was clear and the Sea of Okhotsk was calm. Far off to the east lay the Kamchatka Peninsula. To the southeast lay the Kurilskiye Ostrova, the 750-mile-long Kuril Island archipelago that separated the Sea of Okhotsk from the Pacific Ocean beyond, extending almost as far as Hokkaido, the northernmost island of Japan.

The Expedition had made good time along the Yenisey River to Yakutsk and had quartered there for the better part of a week before striking out due east again for the garrison town of Okhotsk. A number of scientists in the party had expressed the wish to remain in Yakutsk and to return to St Petersburg the following spring – among them the celebrated German professor of botany Johann Georg Gmelin, one of the few scientists for whom Bering had developed any great respect.

Bering was saddened by Gmelin's decision but took considerable comfort in the fact that Gmelin and his companions would not only report favourably on the scientific discoveries they had made, but would also applaud the diligence of his own leadership of the Expedition.

The detail left behind in Yakutsk by Sven Waxell had been detached to escort Gmelin and his party back to St Petersburg. Most were more than willing to return home, although three of them had petitioned Bering to be allowed to travel with the main body to

Okhotsk. Bering found their commitment to the Expedition highly commendable and resolved to reward their loyalty as and when he could.

The overland trek from Yakutsk had not been without incident but the Expedition had suffered no significant human or material losses. Inevitably, however, progress had been much slower than Bering would have wished. Throughout the final weeks before reaching Okhotsk he had found it difficult to conceal his rising impatience. He was anxious to regain his own element: the sea. The hardest part, he had told himself, was over, and the real purpose of the Expedition was now at hand.

They had reached Okhotsk five days ago, to a warm welcome from Waxell and a lukewarm welcome from Lieutenant Pisarov. Bering had been briefed by both men. On the whole, their reports were not encouraging. Pisarov complained incessantly of the problems he had encountered, whereas Waxell took a more positive view, acknowledging the difficult conditions but stressing what had been accomplished.

In the final analysis, however, the situation was far from that which Bering had hoped to find. Four vessels were, as Waxell reported, 'almost readied' and had been floated off and moored in the harbour. The two others were still in dry dock and would not be available to the Expedition for at best a further two months.

This was a major setback and Bering could not contain his disappointment. He knew instinctively that Grigor Pisarov had dragged his heels and was scarcely surprised when Waxell confided as much in private.

Bering knew the Sea of Okhotsk well – well enough to know that it is completely icebound from early November to April or early May. During the short period when it is free of ice, the Sea of Okhotsk is plagued by the thickest of fogs. These, he knew, constituted no great obstacle to navigation by a single vessel but could pose a major problem in the case of a six-vessel flotilla.

The prospect of another winter on land loomed large.

Okhotsk
August 1735

From the journal of Lieutenant-at-Sea Sven Waxell

August 17, 1735

The Captain-Commander arrived in Okhotsk today amid scenes of great rejoicing. Many in his party are close to exhaustion but the humour of the Expedition is positive and they express great relief that they have completed their long journey.

It fell to me to escort the Captain-Commander and his family to the quarters we have readied for them. These are in all truth rudimentary, but I can report that his lady wife and most charming daughter are most content at the efforts made on their behalf.

Save for the military escort, which has billeted north of the town, all the members of the Expedition have been housed. Some few express discontent at the quality of their quarters but most seem mightily pleased to have over their heads a roof which is not made of reindeer hide or birch bark.

The Captain-Commander has already called me and Lieutenant Pisarov to him to give account of our progress. He expressed his satisfaction at our efforts to quarter the Expedition but is greatly displeased that the six vessels have not been fully readied for sea. In private, I confided to him my misgivings about Lieutenant Pisarov. He made little comment, but I understand the Captain-Commander does not care greatly for the Lieutenant. I am content that he values the efforts of the men under my own command.

August 19, 1735

The Captain-Commander has ordered all hands to fall to in order that the vessels be readied without further delay. Although I did not say so, I find this order strange, for he knows full well that we are proceeding as best and fast as we can.

There is great consolation to be found in that the Expedition has within its ranks many who are skilled wheelwrights, carpenters and blacksmiths. The Captain-Commander has detailed these to be at our disposal to complete the timbering and masts. I estimate that all six vessels will be seaworthy in perhaps two months from now. The Captain-Commander did not receive my estimations with good grace.

August 22, 1735

The Captain-Commander has informed Lieutenant Pisarov and me that the Expedition is to overwinter in Okhotsk. This distresses him greatly, but it is clear that a flotilla squadron of six vessels cannot be sailed in safety to Kamchatka before the winter sets in. Already the nights are chill and the fogs are heavy. The days of ice will be upon us soon.

The Captain-Commander is much changed by the journey. He is withdrawn and quick to anger. He sees but little of his wife and daughter. This I find curious, yet I know it is not given to every man to be as attentive to his family as I myself am. I say this not in criticism – for the Captain-Commander is a man charged with great responsibilities – but he cuts a lonely figure now.

Laurentij is much captivated by the Captain-Commander's daughter, who is called Benthe. She is truly a delightful person but I feel Laurentij is too young for her. I have observed that she has eyes only for Lieutenant Spanberg, a man for whom all in the Expedition harbour the utmost respect. It is a respect which I most readily share. He is a man of great wit and ready good humour, but I know him to be most qualified in the ways of the sea. I have much to learn from him.

The Captain-Commander is closeted each day with a junior lieutenant called Khitrov, a man I cannot warm to, but who seems to be held in high esteem by the Captain-Commander. It is said that Khitrov will helm the Captain-Commander's vessel and I must surmise that he is well-equipped to do so. Khitrov is of a surly disposition and is greatly disliked by many. Time will tell if he is up to the tasks that lie ahead, but in that respect I bow as I do in all things to the judgment of the Captain-Commander.

Acting Captain Chirikov I see almost every day and find to be a man of few words yet most expert at his trade. He is always on

*hand with sound nautical counsel and will prove an asset to the
Expedition. He talks only seldom with the Captain-Commander
and there is respect but little affection of the one for the other. This,
too, I find strange for, as God is my judge, the two men are alike
in many ways.*

Okhotsk
October 19, 1735

The remaining two vessels were launched on October 16, 1735 –
marginally ahead of Waxell's predictions – but the Sea of Okhotsk
was beginning to ice up and full sea trials for the six ships were
postponed until the thaw set in the following late spring.

Vitus Bering was furious at the delay yet elated that all six vessels
had finally been built and fitted out. He relayed the news back down
the line to St Petersburg, conscious that the information would
probably not reach the Grand Council for some months.

Bering thought it appropriate to mark the occasion and, in some
small way, to reward all those in the advance party and in Waxell's
contingent who had worked so hard. He decided that a major
celebration would be scheduled for October 19 to coincide with the
birthday of the Empress Anna Ivanovna. That it was subsequently
discovered that Anna Ivanovna had been born in February did not
detract unduly from the festivities.

Martin Spanberg somehow found himself in charge of the
October 19 celebration and, as everyone expected, fulfilled to the
letter his obligations as master of ceremonies. Wrestling and marks-
manship tournaments were arranged, a bear-baiting pit was
constructed, jugglers and fire-eaters were found within the ranks of
the Expedition, musicians were co-opted to perform at a grand ball,
and tents and stalls were set up on every street corner, dispensing
vodka and assorted delicacies.

Bering took little part in the festivities other than to declare them
formally open. Spanberg and others had hoped that Bering would
address those assembled but in that they were disappointed. He
mumbled only a few indistinct words that were lost in the general
buzz of excitement, then immediately repaired to his quarters.

Osa Bering and her daughter had dressed for the occasion and were determined to celebrate until dawn. Benthe was quickly caught up in a circle of young admirers and whisked off to dance with first one, then the next.

Osa stood alone. She was happy for her daughter and for her husband who, in his own taciturn way, had communicated his respect for her signal contribution to the Expedition. She was proud that she had demonstrated her utility.

It was well into the night when Martin Spanberg came across to her. He has been drinking, she said to herself, but what of it? He deserves to enjoy tonight after all he has done to make it such a success.

'My dear lady,' said Spanberg, bowing extravagantly low. 'May I say how beautiful you look this fine evening?'

'Indeed you may,' replied Osa. 'And may *I* say that you have given us all a night to remember?'

'This night will remain in my memories forever,' said Spanberg. 'Provided, that is, that you will honour me with a dance.'

He took her arm and they made their way to the floor. The orchestra was playing a brisk Cossack medley and Spanberg whirled her around and around until her head began to spin. The music came abruptly to a stop and she fell forward into Spanberg's arms.

'No more, Martin, please!'

Spanberg's arm had gone about her waist and her hair was in his eyes and mouth. He looked down at her, noting the thin film of perspiration that had broken out across her brow. He lowered his head and ran his tongue across her forehead. Slowly and deliberately. He felt her shiver in his arms. He held her at arm's length for no more than a second or two, looking into her eyes.

She stared back.

Spanberg pulled her gently towards him, his other arm circling her waist. He kissed her once on the forehead, then on the nose and, finally, on the lips. His touch was firm but gentle. She felt herself responding to it. Her lips parted and she returned the kiss, her arms reaching round his broad shoulders, her hands clasped behind his head.

He whispered her name over and over again. His body arched into hers, pulling her against his erection. She gasped, suddenly aware that they were standing in full view of people she knew and people who certainly knew her.

Osa made a determined effort to disengage from Spanberg's embrace but found she could not. She clung to him as he eased her away from the pool of light cast by the oil lamps which circled the makeshift dance floor. As they moved into the shadows beyond, she knew that she had to stop this before it was too late.

'No, Martin, please, no!'

It *was* too late. Spanberg's hands stroked her back as his body pressed against her. She was whimpering softly now, kneading the corded muscle of his shoulders. Her head tilted back as she felt herself being lifted off her feet. Her legs wrapped themselves around his back as he entered her. She heard herself shout 'Yes!' as his buttocks clenched and unclenched with each thrust.

It was all over in seconds. She felt him jerk uncontrollably time and again as her legs clutched him tighter still. A strange and unfamiliar sensation flooded through her. From somewhere she had never been she heard her own voice calling out over and over again.

'Vitus! Vitus!'

Spanberg gave no sign that he had heard, but his grip relaxed as he eased her to the ground. Her legs uncoiled from his back and they stood, foreheads touching.

'My wonderful Osa,' said Spanberg.

He tucked a finger under her chin. Her eyes met his. He kissed her one last time. Lightly and tenderly.

Osa Bering did not know what to do next. She was stunned by what had happened, but she felt her heart continue to pound and she had no strength in legs that, moments before, had held him in a vice. Her voice shook.

'Martin, what have we done? How can we ever forgive ourselves?'

'Forgive? There is nothing – nothing – to forgive. I have loved you since I first saw you and I have wanted you all these many months. There is truly nothing to forgive.'

Forgiveness was the last thing on Benthe Bering's mind.

Benthe had looked on as her mother and Spanberg danced together. She had seen them fall into each other's arms. She had seen them walk off together into the darkness. She had followed them and watched as they coupled frenetically.

There is truly nothing to forgive?

Benthe felt the tears course down her cheeks. Two of the three most important people in her life had betrayed her.

And themselves.

St Petersburg
November 4, 1735

Steller's day-to-day duties as physician to the household of Archbishop Feofan Prokopovich did not tax him unduly. One house-maid miscarried, another broke an arm, and the coachman complained of a racking cough that Steller treated with a chest poultice of garlic, vinegar and eucalyptus gum. The mixture stank to high heaven but appeared to alleviate the man's condition, if only temporarily. The practice of medicine, when all is said and done, has never been an exact science.

Steller's most constant source of worry proved to be the health of the Archbishop himself. Prokopovich was advanced in years and routinely complained of minor aches and pains which, Steller believed, were attributable to his age rather than to any life-threatening condition.

Keeping the Archbishop healthy was an overriding priority. Should anything happen to him, Steller's employment would terminate forthwith. This possibility preyed on Georg Wilhelm Steller's mind. The Archbishop was the key to the door which would admit Steller to the Imperial Great Northern Expedition.

Steller was aware by now that the Archbishop was in regular contact with Ernst von Biron both in a formal capacity – as a member of the inner circle of advisors to the Empress Anna Ivanovna – and, in a private capacity, as a chess partner. He noted with some amusement that Prokopovich always returned in a foul mood from his weekly games with von Biron and surmised that, once again, his employer had been bested.

Steller was well-attuned to the Archbishop's moods and knew that any reference to von Biron would fall on deaf ears in the day or two following yet another ignominious defeat. Accordingly, he planned his intervention with care.

His timing was impeccable.

'It would be of great personal advantage to me, Your Eminence, if I were to be introduced to the Reichsgraf von Biron. I would be most indebted were you to intercede with him on my behalf.'

Feofan Prokopovich was immediately intrigued.

'Such an introduction can be effected without great difficulty, Herr Doktor,' said the Archbishop, out of habit according Steller the courtesy of an academic qualification to which he was not entitled.

Steller merely nodded expectantly.

'Might I ask to what purpose?' continued Prokopovich.

'As you may be aware, Your Eminence, my interests are wide-ranging. It is my fervent wish to pursue my studies in one particular direction.'

'And that direction would be?'

'That direction, Your Eminence, would be in the discipline of taxonomy.'

'Which, if I am rightly informed, relates to the classification of living and extinct organisms?'

'That is correct, Your Eminence.'

Prokopovich was amused but took care to keep a straight face. He liked Steller immensely. He admired this delicate, almost effeminate young German on account of his inquiring mind. But he also knew Steller to be intensely ambitious and self-seeking.

'I venture to say that the Reichsgraf may be insufficiently schooled in that discipline to contribute to your already considerable fund of knowledge.'

Steller plunged ahead, impervious to the Archbishop's gentle sarcasm.

'I seek no knowledge from the Count, merely greater access to those who share my scientific curiosity and from whom I might learn.'

Prokopovich nodded. He was an old man and he knew he had not much longer to live. In his daily ministrations, Steller dutifully addressed the symptoms of his deteriorating condition without suspecting the underlying cause. The Archbishop had not disclosed to his personal physician that he coughed up thick phlegm each morning and that his urine habitually ran dark with blood.

'I shall see what can be done.'

'Thank you, Your Eminence.'

Prokopovich was as good as his word. Within hours, he had arranged for Steller to be received by Ernst von Biron.

'What does this young man wish of me, my dear Archbishop?' von Biron had asked.

'He is a young man of some ambition and of uncommon ability. I would regard it as a personal favour if you were to find a place for him when I am – when I am no longer.'

'A *place*?'

'I sense that young Dr Steller has no greater wish than to participate in the Imperial Great Northern Expedition.'

Von Biron laughed.

'If that is truly his wish and your request, then it shall be so. But I trust that Your Eminence will be with us for many years to come.'

'Would it were so. But I am as ready now to meet my Maker as I have been these many years.'

Steller's subsequent interview with von Biron was brief but pleasant. Von Biron informed him that, for the moment, he would be welcome to take part in regular *colloquia* convened at the Academy of Sciences and that his subsequent participation in the Expedition was assured. Steller was overjoyed.

There was only one fly in the ointment. The Archbishop was old but seemed in comparatively good health. He could live for years. Steller's joy was tempered by that knowledge, but he consoled himself that the most recent news from the Expedition was that it had fallen seriously behind schedule.

Okhotsk
November 19, 1735
'We are seriously behind schedule,' said Bering for the third time that morning.

Martin Spanberg knew this to be true but felt there was next to nothing to be done about it. Inevitably, they would wait out the winter in Okhotsk, run sea trials as soon as conditions were relatively clement, then sail the six-vessel flotilla to Kamchatka the following spring. For the present, it remained only to take every reasonable precaution to maintain discipline and sustain morale.

Spanberg was growing increasingly irritated by Bering's constant litany of complaints. While he had sympathy with Bering's frustration, he had little time for the Captain-Commander's obsessive behaviour and was annoyed at Bering's implicit assumption that he and he alone was anxious to press on with the principal business of the Expedition.

We are *all* bored shitless, Spanberg told himself, but we have little option other than to wait things out.

He stared over the pack ice, cursing the elements, cursing Siberia and cursing all and sundry who were behind this exercise in self-aggrandisement. Most of all, he cursed the situation in which he found himself.

Since the festivities on the night of the Empress Anna Ivanovna's 'birthday', Spanberg had seen next to nothing of Osa Bering. No reference had been made to that night or to their frantic copulation. It was as if nothing had occurred between them. He also noticed that Benthe Bering, who had been constantly under his feet since the Expedition had left St Petersburg, now gave him a wide berth. He could discern no reason for this except that – and surely the possibility was remote – her mother had confided in her.

As First Officer under Bering, Spanberg assumed direct responsibility for the crew of the Captain-Commander's own vessel, the *St Peter*, and acted as liaison with Acting Captain Chirikov, who was to command the *St Paul*. For the time being, however, Spanberg's responsibilities were virtually in abeyance. The crew rosters had been provisionally established for both vessels and there was scant need for daily liaison between them.

The *St Peter* would, God willing, have a ship's complement of seventy-six, including Bering as Captain-Commander, Spanberg himself as First Officer, and Valery Khitrov as Fleetmaster. As it happened, the *St Paul* would also have a complement of seventy-six, with Acting Captain Aleksey Chirikov seconded by two lieutenants (one senior, one junior) and by Fleetmaster Dementiev. The complement of each vessel was further comprised of first and second mates, boatswains and assistant navigators, supported by able seamen and augmented by ship's surgeons, surveyors, soldiers, interpreters, Cossack guards, and assorted military riflemen. Each vessel would carry a small contingent of scientists from a range of disciplines.

Spanberg found himself with time on his hands and next to no-one to share it with. To his shame, he now found Vitus Bering repetitive and tedious and spent only such time in his company as his duties dictated. That he felt so uncomfortable in the Captain-Commander's presence was, of course, due in no small measure to what had occurred between Bering's wife and himself. Osa Bering and her daughter now avoided him studiously, and he had little interest in any form of personal contact with Aleksey Chirikov or Valery Khitrov.

Chirikov was as truculent as ever, thought Spanberg, and Valery Khitrov was now beginning to show his true colours. His already considerable ego had been inflated further in the wake of the attention paid to him by the Captain-Commander and his upgrading to the rank of Fleetmaster, and his burgeoning arrogance was a thorn in the flesh of the seamen under his command, whom he treated with ill-concealed disdain.

In the circumstances, Spanberg found himself keeping regular company with Sven Waxell, a hardworking and decent mariner with a strong sense of duty and an unflagging devotion to Vitus Bering, and with Waxell's son Laurentij, who was provisionally scheduled to sail with them on the *St Peter*.

Waxell *père*, to his chagrin, had not been assigned a berth on the *St Peter* and repeatedly urged Spanberg to find him a place on board rather than in command of one of the other four vessels, which were destined for the more mundane task of housing the horde of assorted scientists and academicians who would investigate the flora and fauna of the Siberian coast region and the waters immediately offshore. Spanberg felt there was little he could do on Waxell's behalf but volunteered to bring up the matter with the Captain-Commander.

Waxell *fils*, meanwhile, proved to be a splendid young man who had filled out nicely and whose passionate interest in all things nautical was a pleasure to behold. Young Laurentij was understandably upset that he might enjoy the privilege of sailing aboard the *St Peter* which was denied to his father. Spanberg was at pains to reassure the youngster that final dispositions in this respect had not been made.

Spanberg was more than happy to instruct Laurentij in the ways of the sea. The young Waxell exhibited a particular interest in the two vessels which were to spearhead the Expedition's voyage of exploration. To Spanberg's astonishment – and to Sven Waxell's unmitigated delight – Laurentij quickly and accurately assimilated any information they passed to him.

Within days, it seemed, Laurentij was totally familiar with how the *St Peter* and the *St Paul* were rigged. They tested him on a daily basis until his knowledge of sprits, arrows, jibs, stays, tops, gallants, halliards, shrouds, pennants, foresails and mains was exhaustive. He could tell at a glance whether a vessel's plan of sails was square, fore-aft or lateen-rigged and knew how each and every vessel was best rigged in proportion to the length of its masts and yards.

Clews, bunts, leech and bow lines, bolts, braces, ties, tacks, jeers, burtons, garnets and cross-jacks – all were part and parcel of Laurentij's expanding vocabulary – and Spanberg and Waxell would laugh uncontrollably as Laurentij spoke increasingly in seafaring terms of which he could have no conceivable practical knowledge.

As time went by, Laurentij could sarve a rope, bend a cable, thwart a hawse, parcel a seam or French the ballast with the best of them. On entering a room, he would sing out 'How cheer ye fore and aft?'; on leaving, he would announce it was time to 'tack about'.

'In faith, Laurentij, we'll make a master mariner of you yet,' promised Spanberg.

'Aye,' said Sven Waxell, his face flushed with pride, ' we'll do that and more, my lad. All that lacks you now is your first day at sea.'

That day seemed interminably far off. But Laurentij would be ready, of that Spanberg and Waxell were surer by the day.

As to his own future, Spanberg harboured considerably more doubt. He was guilty of what he freely acknowledged to have been an unpardonable breach of friendship and trust. He found it difficult to look Vitus Bering square in the eye and flinched every time the Captain-Commander made mention of his wife and daughter. Fortunately for Spanberg, Bering rarely spoke of them and seemed largely indifferent to their well-being.

Spanberg no longer lusted after Osa Bering: that lust had been sated, to be replaced with what he could only describe as a passion that was intrinsically alien to his habitual dealings with the opposite sex. It was said of Spanberg, on occasion even to his face, that he had bedded more women than an albatross had feathers. He had always taken this as a compliment, but now he felt strangely ashamed of his past conquests. And of one conquest in particular.

He had no way of knowing how Osa Bering felt about what had happened between them and he needed desperately to find out. Several opportunities had already presented themselves, but her cool detachment – and the alarming prospect of being within earshot of others – had precluded any prospect of intimate conversation.

But Spanberg simply had to *know*.

In the end, he had done what, he now admitted to himself, he should have done several weeks earlier. He had gone directly to her quarters and insisted on speaking with her.

Osa Bering was alone. She greeted him coolly and by rank rather than first name. Taking his cue from her greeting, he responded formally.

'Madame Bering, I present my compliments and wish to express my deepest regrets for my unspeakable behaviour on the last occasion we met in private.'

'I return the compliments, First Officer, but I cannot accept your regrets.'

This was worse than Spanberg had feared.

'But, Madame Bering . . .,' he began.

'I cannot accept your regrets for what you deem unspeakable

behaviour. You imply that my behaviour was also unspeakable and that you regret what transpired. I have given this a great deal of thought and I have concluded that what we did was deeply wrong. I do not consider, however, that my behaviour was unspeakable, only that it was unforgivable. Your expression of regret does little to assuage my conscience, which is deeply troubled. But you ask me to accept regrets for something I do not regret, merely cannot condone.'

It was evident from her considered reply that Osa Bering *had* given the incident a great deal of thought.

Spanberg was uncertain what to say next.

'The circumstances were such that I could not control . . .'

'The circumstances were such that neither of us could control ourselves,' interrupted Osa. 'Let us say no more about forgiveness and regrets. Except perhaps this, First Officer. You have done my husband a great wrong and I, too, have done my husband a great wrong. But, in the doing, you afforded me immeasurable pleasure which my husband has long since chosen to deny me.'

Osa Bering turned away from him and spoke over her shoulder.

'I would be grateful, First Officer, if we can in future refrain from meeting like this.'

Spanberg waited. She said nothing more.

'As you wish, Madame Bering.'

Spanberg left the room, closing the door gently.

Osa Bering stood at the window and watched as he walked away. The tears ran down her cheeks and she wiped them away angrily.

Okhotsk
November 28, 1735

Grigor Pisarov was dismayed to discover that Aleksey Chirikov was unreceptive to his complaint at having been relegated by Bering to what he claimed was the lowly task of commanding onshore operations. Pisarov moaned that he had discharged his duty by bringing the advance party safely to the coast and readying the six vessels for the Expedition. It was his understanding that Chirikov had great influence in St Petersburg: couldn't Aleksey bring this influence to bear to ensure him command of one of the vessels in the Expedition flotilla?

Chirikov had disliked Pisarov on sight. He was fully apprised of Pisarov's contribution – or, to be more exact, lack of it – and he was firmly opposed to any steps that would improve Pisarov's standing in St Petersburg or, for that matter, redeem him in the eyes of those he had originally commanded here in Okhotsk.

Like Vitus Bering, Aleksey Chirikov was certain, or as certain as any could be, that the fabled Gama Land was a figment of the cartographers' imagination. There was no 'lost continent' out there in the North Pacific, no more than there was, he suspected, a land bridge between Russia and the Americas. Chirikov believed that Vitus Bering had many faults, not the least of which were his impatience and an undeniable self-opinionated arrogance, but he could find little wrong with the man's judgment both as a mariner and, to date, as leader of the Expedition.

The most recent secret communication he had received from St Petersburg effectively gave him *carte blanche* to remove Bering from command of the Expedition as and when the moment was opportune. Chirikov sensed a growing reluctance on his own part to do any such thing. He had sailed with Bering on the first voyage of exploration mandated by Peter I and had been mercifully spared the abuse that he knew was unjustly heaped on Bering's head for failing to deliver conclusive 'proof' of the Northeast Passage. What is more, he had believed then, as now, not only that Bering was right in his conclusions but also that the Captain-Commander had acted prudently and in the best interests of his crew in deciding that the harsh weather and persistent fog had made further reconnaissance impossible.

What, he asked himself, exactly *what* do those bastard politicians in St Petersburg know of conditions out here in this desolate region? What do they know of the sea and its perils? What do they know of the mariner's craft?

But Aleksey Chirikov was a realist. Advancement in the Imperial Russian Navy did not happen overnight and was never purely a matter of seniority. On the contrary, as Chirikov already knew to his cost, having been passed over twice for no discernible reason prior to being promoted to the rank of Acting Captain. To safeguard any claim to his full captaincy, Chirikov knew he would have to play the political game.

This he was ultimately prepared to do, but only in his own good time. *He* would decide when the moment was opportune *and* justified.

The dangerous part of the Expedition lay far ahead. Who knew what might happen in the uncharted wastes beyond the Bering Strait?

Okhotsk
December 1735

From the journal of Lieutenant-at-Sea Sven Waxell

December 2, 1735

I have no knowledge as yet as to whether the Captain-Commander will assign me to the post of Second Officer aboard the St. Peter or oblige me to serve the Expedition as the commander of one of the inshore vessels. Such latter assignment would present a hardship greater than I can imagine, greater by far than sailing into the uncharted waters of the Bering Strait.

I have expressed my misgivings to First Officer Spanberg, who has volunteered to speak with the Captain-Commander on my behalf. It is known that the counsel of the First Officer is held in great esteem by the Captain-Commander and I cherish some hope that a heartfelt plea entered on my account will not go unheard.

I fear there is another difficulty that needs to be surmounted and it is indeed a delicate affair. Laurentij has applied for and has been granted leave to travel on the St. Peter and will do so subject to my agreement. This I cannot grant, for he is as yet still a boy and has no practical experience of the rigours of a voyage such as lies before the Captain-Commander. I shall be constrained to withhold my approval if I am not assigned to sail also with the St. Peter. This is only prudent, as it would accord me every possibility to care for

Laurentij and his welfare, showing, let me add, no undue favour to the lad.

It was planned only that Laurentij accompany me on the journey to the coast. I feel I cannot deny him this great opportunity to voyage further, given that he has developed into a strapping young man with an unbridled passion for the sea. Yet I know I cannot in all conscience release him alone on such a venture. My responsibility is not only to him but to his dear mother, whose forgiveness I should never regain were I to be the instrument of his loss.

First Officer Spanberg has now reported that the Captain-Commander will weigh my request carefully. It is clear that he thought to do me an honour by taking Laurentij under his wing but I pray he will prove receptive to my fears.

December 4, 1735

I have word from the Captain-Commander that I am to join his complement as Second Officer.

The news has filled me with pride and I am heartened to see that Laurentij has welcomed it with much enthusiasm. I know that he was greatly troubled that I would find no berth on the St. Peter. That we are now to voyage together is a great comfort to us both. I fear only that his dear mother will not thank me for acceding to Laurentij's wish to undertake the voyage, yet I know that she will learn of it only many months from now and, God willing, perhaps approve.

I have thanked First Officer Spanberg for his kind intercession on my behalf. I look forward to sailing with him, although I concede that he appears much distraught of late for reasons that I cannot fathom. This may be due to his concern for the Captain-Commander, who grows more morose and withdrawn each passing day. Whatever the reason, the First Officer shows little enthusiasm for our great undertaking and I am anxious that further delays do not weaken his resolve to serve.

Laurentij is now the most proficient of dry-land sailors and I am most proud of him. His easy way has found great favour with all, although the crews tease him without mercy.

I had thought the St. Peter a stout vessel in which to sail but too small to accommodate the full complement of crew and scientists. I must of necessity withdraw this objection now that I am granted leave to swell the ranks of those destined to sail in her.

Sea of Okhotsk
March 26, 1736

The *St Peter* ran at a full seven knots before a brisk southeasterly, her full plan of canvas stretched and billowed. Laurentij Waxell stood forward by the bowsprit, his long blond hair blown horizontal in the cutting sea air. His lips were chapped, his cheeks were raw and his fingers numb from the biting cold of morning.

He had never been so happy.

The *St Peter* was coursing through a lead, a clearwater channel close on a full sea mile across that had opened through the pack ice. Salt spray streamed off the bows and lashed his face, but Laurentij's gaze never wavered. His was an awesome burden – to call out warning of rogue ice drifting in the channel ahead – although he knew full well it was a responsibility shared with others who clung to the cross-trees securing the top gallants high above the deck. No more than two hundred yards behind them and a point to windward, the *St Paul* plunged through their wake.

Valery Khitrov was at the helm of the *St Peter*. Vitus Bering stood by Khitrov's shoulder, feet splayed and hands clasped behind his back. The vessel sailed fast and true before the wind and Khitrov laughed at the sheer joy of it.

They had been at sea for a full week and Bering was satisfied that the *St Peter* was as fine a vessel as he had ever captained. True, she rode a touch too high, but Bering knew that she was under-provisioned: when her cargo holds were full and the ballast divided, she would sit four-square.

The teething troubles were behind them now.

The sheets had been furled and cut several times over without serious incident, and bonnets – additional sails – had been laced on and shaken off repeatedly. Two days out from Okhotsk, the vessel had bilged, striking off some timber and springing a small leak.

Bering had looked on approvingly as the ship's carpenter and hands deftly paid the seam, laying on hot pitch and tar to caulk it, then parcelling the mend with a strip of canvas that was again pitched over.

Valery Khitrov had performed admirably, adapting quickly to the touch of the helm. Bering had occasion to criticise only once when he observed that Khitrov tended to helm the *St Peter* too far to windward, causing the vessel to gripe. Khitrov had corrected the oversteer immediately and, to give the helmsman his due, had subsequently held the *St Peter* on a true course.

The sea trials were at end. It was time to leave for Kamchatka.

Chapter Five

KAMCHATKA

South of Awatska Bay, Kamchatka Peninsula
August 11, 1736

The Koryak chieftain stood at the cliff edge overlooking Awatska Bay and watched dispassionately as the six vessels rounded the point in tight formation. He continued to watch as they made their way slowly into the bay and until they slowed and stopped.

The Koryak was a long way from his ancestral home in the northern part of the Kamchatka Peninsula. His tribe had been *chavchu* – nomadic reindeer herders – before coming south to settle in the central valley of the Peninsula. He was of pure Mongol stock: squat, thick-set and dark-skinned, with a wide, flat face and nose, prominent cheekbones and coarse dark brown hair.

The Koryak hated the Russians. Even more than he hated the Chukchis, Itelmen and Evens. Those other tribes were at least men like himself, who fought bravely and died well. The Rus were different. They fought with firesticks, slaughtering the menfolk among his people and carrying off their women.

Each year more and more of them came, plundering the land, stealing Koryak livestock and killing reindeer, sea otter and walrus. The Rus were without honour: they lied and cheated, trading trinkets and tobacco for the furs they prized but never wore. And their shamans were impotent creatures who spoke of some single God and knew nothing of the Great Spirits from the Other Worlds.

The Koryak turned away, anxious to be about his own business.

The brown bear tracks led down the grassy hillside towards the lake below. Spear at the ready, he walked slowly down the slope.

Bolcheretsk Garrison, Kamchatka Peninsula
August 19, 1736

The flotilla lay at anchor with a skeleton crew in Awatska Bay, a natural harbour close on eight fathoms deep and bounded to the south by a narrow isthmus of sand.

The Russian presence on the Kamchatka Peninsula was secured by a garrison stationed at Bolcheretsk, some 140 land miles up the Awatska River. Its principal task was to protect the *promyshlenniki*, the loose community of trappers and fur traders lured to Kamchatka by the prospect of easy pickings of sable pelts for sale in the lucrative Chinese market.

Bering and several of his senior officers had travelled upriver to Bolcheretsk to pay their respects to the garrison commander and to secure fresh provisions for the Expedition. As they travelled inland, they marvelled at the innumerable hot springs along the way and at the towering volcanoes that loomed in the distance. The vegetation was surprisingly lush, with few trees but an abundance of low shrubs and grassland sprinkled with dark lily-like flowers that gave off a curiously disagreeable odour redolent, according to Martin Spanberg, of horse manure.

The garrison commander welcomed them with unexpected courtesy and warmth, in sharp contrast to the treatment they had received at the hands of his counterpart in Tomsk.

Despite the warm reception, Bering was apprehensive. The list of provisions compiled by his commissary would, he felt, represent too great a demand on the garrison's resources.

Conventional wisdom held that provisions for a crew of one hundred for a full year should include thirty-six vats of beef, eleven of bacon, twelve of smoked meat and sixteen of boiled and salted tongue, together with sixteen whole cured hams, 11,000 pounds of hard bread, seventy-five sacks of peas and beans, 3,000 pounds of dried cod, 300 pounds of cheese, four vats of butter, nine hogsheads of pickling vinegar and four of oil. To swill this down, Admiralty experts counselled that eighteen barrels of wine and six of vodka be carried, together with eighty-two 100-litre vats of watered beer and 150 butts of fresh water.

Bering needed no reminding that, on top of everything else, he had six vessels lying offshore, each with a complement of around seventy men.

Garrison commander Igor Yossonovich skimmed through the long list, nodding his head as he turned each page.

'Your list can be filled, Captain-Commander.'

'All of it?'

'No. But much of what you require can be substituted by what is freely available to us.'

In the days that followed, Bering, Martin Spanberg, Sven Waxell and Commissary Lagunov were closeted with the garrison commander and his quartermaster, poring over the list, cutting an item here, adding one there, and substituting local produce where Admiralty specifications proved impractical.

It was evident that there was a plentiful supply of beef, salt, flour, fresh water and – inevitably – fish. Certain luxuries had to be eliminated, among them cheese, which Spanberg airily dismissed as presenting no great hardship since the crews were not Nederlanders. Besides, other delicacies could be readied: ox tongues could be smoked over wood fires and sides of bacon from wild pigs could be cured.

A principal concern was the dearth of alcohol. Whereas the garrison had a seemingly limitless store of plug tobacco to be smoked or chewed, there appeared to be a dearth of alcohol of any kind – most notably vodka. Bering and Spanberg suspected that Yossonovich was perhaps holding out on them in this respect, but they did not press the point.

'No beer? No vodka? The men will not take kindly to this, Captain-Commander.'

'You are right, First Officer.'

'If I may make so bold,' put in Yossonovich, 'the tribes of the region drink a fermentation from a root vegetable . . .'

'Of course,' cut in Spanberg. 'Show me a Russian who cannot distil vodka or brew beer from anything that grows!'

Bering nodded, uncertain at the prospect of authorising the construction of vodka stills and brewing vats.

This was part of a larger problem, namely where to quarter the Expedition. Yossonovich promptly offered the hospitality of the garrison, arguing that he would be honoured to house the Expedition and glad of its company. Bering was forced to decline on the grounds that Bolcheretsk lay too far inland and too distant from the ships. The garrison fort would represent a safe haven should the need arise, but the Expedition would make camp close by the ocean.

One question remained to be resolved. How much time would be necessary to lay in all the necessary provisions? Two weeks? Three?

'Two months more like,' said Yossonovich, sucking on his unlit pipe. 'I am confident that this can be achieved within eight weeks at the outside.'

Bering and Spanberg exchanged glances. It was already late in the year, although the weather was still tolerably warm. That the Expedition would again have to lay up over the winter months was regrettably all too clear. The best they could hope for was to make themselves as comfortable as possible.

'I will detach under escort those civilians who wish to overwinter in Bolcheretsk,' said Bering. 'My crews and outfitters will remain under canvas at the Bay of Awatska.'

Spanberg made as if to interrupt but kept his own counsel.

'As you wish, Captain-Commander,' said Yossonovich, clearly disappointed. 'But I must warn you that the winters in this place are long and cold.'

'No longer and no colder than we have already encountered,' said Bering gruffly.

Christ, he thought, how will I break the news to the Expedition? How much more of this will they stand for? For that matter, how many more delays can I myself sustain?

He had no ready answer to any of these questions. What he did know, on the other hand, was that he would not countenance subjecting his wife and daughter to another winter of hardship.

He would send them to Bolcheretsk under the supervision of his First Officer.

Awatska Bay
September 19, 1736

The onshore encampment quickly took shape as an embryonic *ostrog*, a settlement of crude huts built of wood and lined with pelts which was fortified by a simple birchwood palisade. Latrines had been dug and several wooden structures had been cobbled together to house the first of the vodka stills.

The crews were rotated each week and opinion was divided as to whether life on board was more or less uncomfortable than in the camp. Many preferred to remain in their bunks and hammocks on board, but there was a general consensus that the food onshore was better and more varied. Besides, onshore was where the vodka was, not to mention the native women, who showed an instant readiness to spread their legs in exchange for a cup of the clear spirit or a piece of broken mirror. Several seamen had already found themselves regular bedmates and one, more adventurous than the rest, had risked a visit to the neighbouring tribal village. He had not been heard of since.

Little was seen of the male members of the Koryak and other tribes. They kept a very respectful distance, tacitly acknowledging that they were as unwelcome as their women were welcome.

Grigor Pisarov was nominally in command of the onshore settlement. Junior officers drew shore detail every other week and those unfortunate enough to be aboard the *St Peter* when Valery Khitrov returned had every reason to dread his arrival.

Khitrov had that streak of vicious cruelty that so often partners arrogance. On several occasions, invariably for minor offences, he had ordered men lashed until the skin split off their backs. His treatment of the native women went beyond contempt. One he had flogged for daring to resist his advances, another because she stole a scrap of food.

Ever since the aborted duel with Krasheninnikov that day in Tomsk, Khitrov had sought to reassert himself in the eyes of the Expedition. It had never dawned on him that he was going about things the wrong way if he was to regain respect.

His lack of judgment had been demonstrated most forcibly that morning when he ordered a detail of musketeers to enter the tribal lands west of the encampment to kill and bring back a number of the reindeer that grazed freely on the tundra. They had obeyed unquestioningly, returning at noon with two dog-sleds piled high with reindeer carcasses.

The Koryak chieftain tracked them unobserved until they reached the outskirts of the camp where they deposited the animals next to a pit that had been gouged out of the hard ground. He waited until they had disappeared behind the palisade before signalling to his men.

The Koryaks crept forward to the chief's vantage point. There were eighteen of them, no match for the two hundred or so Russians in the camp. But the Koryaks had the advantage of stealth. And they were bent on revenge. Stealing their womenfolk was one thing, stealing their reindeer something else entirely.

They inched closer to the pit, hugging the cold earth. The first Koryak to reach the reindeer edged past the carcasses and dropped into the pit. The second and third followed suit. The others formed a human chain, dragging the reindeer back across the open ground and towards the shelter of the low shrubs that fringed the area.

What the Koryak intended by this manoeuvre was not immediately apparent. There was no conceivable way they could drag the animals all the way back to their own village. But the Koryaks were a proud people whose resistance to Russian colonisation had initially been fierce and protracted. Their spears and arrows had proved totally inadequate against the Russian firesticks, but they had given a good account of themselves. They had lost the battle but not their dignity. What they intended now was merely to register their anger by displacing the carcasses from where they had been deposited. By this gesture, they would demonstrate that they were not afraid of the despicable Rus.

It was a midshipman who saw them first. Preoccupied with unbuckling his belt as he made his way out to the latrine, he finally glanced up in time to see a reindeer carcass move slowly away from the pit. His first thought was that one of the animals was only wounded.

It was then that he saw another carcass move. Then another.

He raised the alarm and Russians piled out of the fort, Valery Khitrov at their head. Swords drawn and muskets in hand, they charged in the direction of the pit. The Koryaks hurried to their feet and ran off. Khitrov and the others were about to give chase but realised that the Koryaks were faster over familiar terrain than they could ever hope to be. Khitrov called his men to a halt and they surveyed the scene.

He did not know how many reindeer had been killed but he saw at once that none appeared to have been stolen. The Koryaks had been content to move the carcasses away from the pit in a simple but effective gesture of defiance.

The musketeer to his immediate left did not see the spear which entered his throat and exited at the back of his neck. His body shuddered at the impact, then toppled slowly backwards. He was dead before he hit the ground.

The Koryak who had thrown the spear leapt from the pit and raced away before any of the musketeers could draw a bead on him. The two remaining Koryaks also leapt from the pit, brandishing their spears as Khitrov and his men closed in around them.

'Take them alive! Alive, I say,' shouted Khitrov.

His men moved in closer, wary of the spears jabbed in their faces. One of the Koryaks suddenly leapt forward, thrusting his spear deep into a musketeer's chest and jerking the stone tip up under the man's rib cage, rotating the handle of the spear as he did so.

Khitrov shot the Koryak through the temple.

The remaining Koryak hesitated, then struck out at a seaman who jumped backwards in the nick of time. Khitrov's sword was in his hand and he slashed it down across the Koryak's neck, slicing the jugular.

He sheathed his sword, confident that he had done his duty.

The Koryak chieftain watched as the Rus started dragging the reindeer carcasses back towards the pit. They have been warned, he thought.

With that, he turned away and loped off into the brush beyond.

St Petersburg
September 22, 1736

His Eminence Archbishop Feofan Prokopovich passed away peacefully in his sleep on the late evening of September 18 and was found by a manservant the following morning. As a matter of course, resident house physician Georg Wilhelm Steller was called from his quarters to attest to the Archbishop's death.

The death of an archbishop was a major event, all the more so in the case of Prokopovich, given his standing as a theologian and politician. The funeral mass had been celebrated that noon, with all the appropriate solemnity and trappings.

Steller was in attendance. His mood was a discordant mixture of grief and excitement. He mourned the Archbishop's passing, of course: he had genuinely liked and admired Prokopovich and had learned much from him. At the same time, Steller admitted to a sense of relief bordering on elation. Inasmuch as his term in the Archbishop's service was *de facto* at an end, his earlier overtures to Ernst von Biron were now revealed as both prudent and opportune.

Steller felt a twinge of anxiety as he waited in the antechamber to be called into von Biron's presence. Would the man keep his word? Or were the rumours that circulated constantly about von Biron's duplicity justified after all?

His guilt at greeting the Archbishop's death with a sense of release was compounded by the knowledge – imparted to him that morning – that the Archbishop had made unexpectedly generous provision for Steller in his will, bequeathing to the young scientist some personal jewellery, a number of his precious books and manuscripts and, not least, a modest annual stipend to be granted in perpetuity from the Prokopovich estate. Steller would by no means be rich, but the Archbishop's generosity of spirit had ensured that his financial situation was no longer precarious.

In a letter left by the Archbishop, Steller was enjoined to pursue his taxonomy studies. To that end, a document under the Archbishop's seal was enclosed. It was addressed to Ernst von Biron and carried a gentle reminder of the latter's commitment to offer Steller a position within the Imperial Great Northern Expedition.

Steller presented his compliments to von Biron and handed over the letter. Von Biron glanced at it, looked up and nodded curtly.

'It shall be as the Archbishop wished. My secretary will draw up the necessary papers and have them sent round to you. I wish you well in your endeavours.'

The audience had lasted no more than thirty seconds. Steller mumbled his thanks, but von Biron was already hunched over his desk, sifting through a mound of correspondence. He did not look up as Steller took his leave.

Kamchatka Peninusla
November 12, 1736

A broad swathe of cirrus cloud brought heavy rain and hail which swept across Awatska Bay and pummelled the vessels moored offshore.

At the encampment, the men huddled together in silent groups around meagre fires, their eyes red and watery, their bodies wrapped in improvised blankets of reindeer pelt and strips of canvas yet chilled to the bone through innumerable layers of pullover, reefer jacket and oilskin.

Vitus Bering breathed the air and knew that worse was at hand. He had experienced tropical cyclones in the China Sea, off the coast of Arabia and in the North Atlantic. He knew what to expect.

The cirri dispersed as quickly as they had formed. The sky cleared momentarily and the sleeting hail gave way to a light drizzle which soon stopped. Relieved, the men concluded that the storm had passed.

Bering knew it had not yet hit.

A wall of dark grey cumulo-nimbus filled the horizon. The wind freshened once more and it started to hail again. The wind intensified, whistling through the encampment and tearing at the flimsy dwellings.

Out in the bay, the vessels strained at their moorings. Rain and hail lashed the decks, slanting towards the horizontal. Rigging creaked, masts groaned and anchor chains drew taut. Out to sea, the spray had built to a solid wall of water which churned and foamed as it rushed towards the frail flotilla.

Bering ordered his vessel to be turned as far as possible to head the oncoming wall of water. The crew complied, then braced themselves for impact. The sea surged forward, catching the furthermost vessel by the bows and sending it spinning madly. Its main mast snapped and rigging crashed to the deck. Crewmen struggled to cut it free, hacking at the tangle of ropes with axes and knives. For a second, it seemed that the vessel would overturn. Instead, it was lifted high and hurled shorewards, smashing into the ship berthed closest to it, stoving in its timbers and snapping the bowsprit.

Aboard the *St Peter* closer inshore, Bering watched as the dark sea thundered towards them. The vessel shuddered at the impact, then was driven back towards the shore. The anchor tore loose and, for a moment, Bering thought the vessel would beach.

The mighty wave broke on the isthmus and swept through the encampment, snapping tent poles and demolishing the vodka stills.

The anchor flukes of the *St Peter* dug deep into the soft sand of the foreshore, slewing the vessel back round into the teeth of the cyclone. Bering saw that one ship – he could not make out which – had beached. Another two had lost masts and most of their top rigging. The *St Paul*, lying close to windward, seemed intact. It was too early to tell.

As the wind dropped and the sky cleared, Bering's first thought was for his ships and crews. But the encampment had to take precedence. He ordered longboats launched.

The scene that confronted the shore party was one of total devastation. Most of the huts had been swept away. Bodies were strewn about the shoreline and higher up on the tundra. Some were moving, others lay ominously still.

He saw Valery Khitrov wandering aimlessly across the sand, picking his way through the pathetic remains of the camp. Khitrov's right arm hung at a curious angle and there was blood on his face.

The ship's surgeon from the *St Peter* rushed towards him but Khitrov, his eyes dulled with pain – and vodka – waved him away.

'Attend to the others,' he shouted.

The final toll was not as great as Bering had at first feared. One vessel was damaged almost beyond repair, while three others had lost their masts and rigging. Amazingly, the *St Paul* had emerged virtually intact and the *St Peter* had survived with comparatively minor damage. Barrels of provisions floated to and fro on the tide or had been thrown up on the foreshore. Some had held, others had been dashed to pieces. Seventeen men were pronounced dead, fifteen of them among those quartered ashore. Only two seamen had died on board, although dozens of others had sustained injuries ranging from minor cuts and bruises to broken limbs. Among the dead were four scientists and three soldiers from the escort. Khitrov's shoulder had been dislocated but was quickly snapped back into place. Pisarov had only severe bruising. A junior lieutenant from the *St Paul* had a serious head injury and was not expected to survive the night.

Bering barked out orders. The men responded, searching out what remained of their possessions and salvaging what they could of the provisions that had been scattered to the winds.

There was much work ahead.

Kamchatka Peninsula
November 1736

From the journal of Lieutenant-at-Sea Sven Waxell

November 12, 1736

This day saw a storm the like of which I have nowhere witnessed in my years at sea. A great wall of water came at us from the east and left great devastation in its wake. Those aboard when it struck must count themselves fortunate to be alive. Those onshore fared less well. Many good men perished – as many as fifteen at the first count.

We recovered the bodies of two seamen who died aboard one

of the vessels, and we have learnt since that three others were carried off on the heavy seas. Junior Lieutenant Leoninov of the St. Paul has a broken head and we can do little for him save pray that his suffering will soon be at an end. Many are injured.

For my part, I make no complaint, being as I am only bruised about the ribs. Laurentij was aboard the St. Peter and is unhurt but sore shaken, for he has learnt now that the sea is a hard taskmaster. That we escaped with our lives is to the credit of the Captain-Commander who led by example, turning our vessel head on into the teeth of the great wave and riding it out. The other vessels followed his lead, all save one – the St. Anna – which was dashed upon the shore.

Lieutenant Khitrov put a shoulder out. He complains loudly and without cease and is excused duty on account of the pain, while others worse off than he go quietly about their tasks. He is not a man to whom I can take kindly and I have scant respect for his navigation skills. Yet he is still favoured by the Captain-Commander.

November 15, 1736

Junior Lieutenant Leoninov passed away this morning and was buried with the others. Of the seamen carried off by the wave there is no trace.

The men work from first light each day to restore order to the encampment. It is in truth a sorry sight, but broken poles have been recovered and mended and the huts are for the most part repaired. The men fear that another wave may strike and I, for one, share their trepidation. The Captain-Commander believes the great wave to be one of a kind and untypical of these waters, but there is great unease in the encampment.

It will be the work of many weeks to rebuild the St. Anna and some, among them myself, think it a thankless task. The two survey vessels which were unmasted are more readily repaired, although a severe lack of timber in this region of the coast means that more trees must perforce be felled far inland and dragged to the coast. Such timbers as were on hand have already been exhausted to build cradles for the vessels that the Captain-

Commander has ordered to be drawn up on the beach before the drift ice sets solid.

To the satisfaction of myself and others, Lieutenant Khitrov has been severely and publicly censured by the Captain-Commander for his part in an action that caused the death of two musketeers and two Koryak tribesmen. It was thought that the incident had passed unnoticed by the Captain-Commander, but not so. He is a man of great vision.

First Officer Spanberg arrived here today from Bolcheretsk, where there was much concern for the safety of the Expedition and our well-being. The garrison caught the back end of the storm but is unscathed, for which thanks must be given. The First Officer at once volunteered to remain among us, but the Captain-Commander has ordered him back to the garrison where he is to report on our condition and set minds to rest.

November 19, 1736

The wind blows hard and cold, but the sea is still now that the ice has fully set. Our five vessels are safely cradled and timbers from the unfortunate St. Anna are being applied to effect repairs on them.

The men are in better heart on learning of the Captain-Commander's decision to move the encampment a good land mile inland. Some eighty men are set to work repairing the damaged vessels while the remainder, myself among them, are detailed to effect a more robust construction for the camp.

Some now say that the first camp had better been constructed at a greater distance from the shore. While, in hindsight, this is true, I find fault not with the Captain-Commander but with the men themselves who, in their haste to find shelter, built makeshift huts that were inadequate to withstand the elements.

Lieutenant Khitrov has done himself no credit in the Captain-Commander's eyes by his formal request to be transferred to the garrison at Bolcheretsk in order to nurse his injury. The request was denied.

Laurentij works with the repair party and is of good cheer.

Bolcheretsk Garrison, Kamchatka Peninsula
November 23, 1736

Martin Spanberg sat low in the front of the sled, swathed in furs. He wiggled his toes to confirm they were still attached to his feet.

Jesus, it was cold.

Behind him, the musher urged on the nine-strong team of Siberian huskies, shouting encouragement to the lone lead dog which set the pace for the other eight hitched side-by-side and in double file behind it.

This was a far cry from St Petersburg and those leisurely winter sleigh rides through the woods that Spanberg's assorted female companions had found so romantic. The sled rocked fiercely from side to side, its birch frame hissing over the ice, bucking and jolting at each obstacle and bruising Spanberg's buttocks as he was lifted from, then thumped back down again on the thin transverse spars.

The worst thing, Spanberg had long since concluded, was being stuck behind these fucking dogs.

The huskies, which feasted at every opportunity on a copious diet of fresh salmon, farted enthusiastically but with monotonous regularity, polluting the otherwise pristine Siberian air with fishy exhalations which, somehow, seemed to waft inexorably in Spanberg's direction. The musher, from his vantage point at the rear of the sled, was either habituated to these collective emissions and impervious to them, or sufficiently distant from them that their impact was diluted to the point of acceptability.

Spanberg adjusted the muffler around his face, shielding his nostrils against the stench. They were now perhaps no more than an hour from Bolcheretsk. He gritted his teeth as the sled ran precipitously down a long slope and leapt high in the air over a hummock before crunching down again on the unyielding ice.

Give me the sea any day, thought Spanberg.

The journey from Bolcheretsk to the coast had taken little over nine hours spread across two days. The return journey would inevitably take longer since it was predominantly uphill, although the musher tracked as best he could alongside the frozen river.

What Spanberg had seen at the coast had depressed him even

more than he had anticipated. The vessels, mercifully with the exceptions of the *St Peter* and, notably, the *St Paul*, were in dire need of major repair. One – the *St Anna*, he recalled – was, in his view at least, beyond salvage.

That so many had died as a result of the freak wave was regrettable, all the more so since he was persuaded that Bering had failed to exert his full authority over the initial choice of the encampment site and had acquiesced in its makeshift construction. In private, Valery Khitrov had come out and said as much and, although Spanberg disliked the Lieutenant, he was forced to agree that the Captain-Commander's judgment on this occasion appeared to have been flawed. Naturally, Spanberg declined to express this conviction to Khitrov – agreeing with that pompous little shit was out of the question – but he believed that Bering's subsequent order to move the encampment further inland was a tacit admission of his earlier mistake.

What troubled Spanberg was not so much the fact that the Captain-Commander had shown poor judgment but that Bering seemed indifferent to anyone and anything that did not directly impact on his ultimate voyage of discovery. Spanberg had listened to Waxell's glowing report on Bering's seamanship but told himself that, after all, one should have expected little less of the Captain-Commander.

Seamanship was not the issue.

Leadership was.

Spanberg's thoughts turned – as they so often did – to Osa Bering. He suspected that she had been alarmed to learn that her husband had elected his First Officer to escort the civilian families to the Bolcheretsk garrison. Spanberg himself had accepted the assignment with the greatest reluctance, concerned that he would be thrown together with Osa on an almost daily basis.

As it turned out, this was emphatically not the case. They were quartered at some distance from each other, and Spanberg had seen her only once – and then only a glimpse – since they arrived at the garrison several weeks previously.

As the sled slid to a halt in Bolcheretsk, Spanberg realised that a face-to-face meeting with Osa Bering was imminent. She would be anxious to learn first-hand of developments at the coast and concerned for the safety and well-being of her husband.

Spanberg eased himself out of the sled and stood up, stretching his limbs and stamping his feet. Military protocol required that he report at once to the garrison commander. He went to his quarters, intending to spruce up and change into his dress uniform then thought better of it. Fuck it. Why *should* he wash off the grime and sweat of the week? Why not let the garrison commander see what he had been put through?

The same, he thought, went for Osa Bering.

Osa was alone in her quarters when he knocked respectfully on the door. She hurried to open it, certain that it was someone bringing news of the Expedition. She clearly did not expect that someone to be Spanberg. Her hand flew to her face in surprise and then, to Spanberg's amusement, to her hair, which she smoothed carefully back into place.

'First Officer Spanberg?'

'Yes, Madame Bering. I call to inform you of my return from the Expedition encampment and to report that your husband is well.'

'Thank you.'

Osa was visibly relieved. Spanberg turned to go.

'And what of the others?'

'The others?'

'The Expedition. Was there much damage?'

'I regret to say, yes. Our vessels have suffered considerable damage, one of them to my mind irreparably. And there have been casualties.'

'Casualties?'

'Among the crews, five are dead that we know of. Six, counting young Lieutenant Leoninov, with whom I believe you were acquainted. The greatest number – fifteen souls – perished on land when the sea broke in over the encampment. Among them four scientists.'

'Was young Professor Krasheninnikov among them?'

'No, he was not.'

'This is grave news, First Officer.'

'I am aware of that, Madame Bering. And I shall hasten to return to do whatever I can to help relieve the situation.'

He paused, then continued.

'The Captain-Commander was greatly concerned for your safety. And that of your daughter.'

'On your return, you may inform him that we are well. And that I appreciate his great concern which he will no doubt one day express in person.'

From her tone, Spanberg was uncertain whether she had guessed that Bering had expressed no specific concern for his family but merely for the civilian contingent as a whole. To tell her as much would be unnecessarily hurtful. He decided against it.

Osa Bering looked him over. This was so unlike the immaculately turned-out Spanberg she was accustomed to. His hair was lank and greasy, his uniform creased and filthy, his face etched with weariness.

She had never loved him more.

'Thank you, First Officer.'

'At your service, Madame Bering.'

She gave the merest hint of a smile and closed the door.

Spanberg could hear her footsteps inside the room as she walked across the timbered floor. He waited for a full minute, but there was no further sound. Spanberg shrugged and walked down the stone steps. What he needed most was a drink.

Or several.

St Petersburg
January 22, 1737

The Grand Council met only sporadically now.

The chain of communication between the Council and the Expedition had effectively been broken once Bering and the Expedition had left Okhotsk for the Kamchatka Peninsula, and no fresh intelligence would be forthcoming until well after the spring thaws. By then, thought Ernst von Biron, the final members of the

Expedition – a several-thousand-strong motley group of academics and scientists – would already be *en route* under heavy military escort to link up with Bering in Kamchatka. As von Biron knew, the Expedition Plan called for Bering – or, by that time, more likely Aleksey Chirikov – to despatch two vessels back across the Sea of Okhotsk to ferry the final contingent to Kamchatka.

On paper, he thought, it all looked so feasible. In reality, there appeared to have been many more obstacles than anyone, except possibly Bering himself, had bargained for.

Von Biron neither wished nor sought a specific mandate from the Grand Council to cut fresh orders for Bering and Chirikov. Whichever one of them was in command would be informed that the overarching priority was to initiate the scientific phase of the Expedition and see it through to completion. At their discretion, Bering and/or Chirikov could sail in quest of the fabled Gama Land, but on no account were they to venture north into the Bering Strait. That was to be the last phase of the Imperial Great Northern Expedition and its crowning glory. Orders to this effect had already been drafted, far in advance of their despatch.

On von Biron's specific instructions, two copies were made. The original would be sent via the normal chain of despatch riders. One copy would be entrusted to the officer in charge of the scientific contingent. And the other would be carried by that young doctor – what was his name again? – Steller, that was it. Georg Wilhelm Steller.

He seemed reliable enough. He was a fellow German, after all.

Von Biron returned to his desk. Among the routine chores earmarked for that day was to affix Empress Anna Ivanovna's official seal to promotions within the Imperial Russian Navy. The Table of Ranks drawn up years previously by Peter the Great provided that advancement to the rank of captain and above required confirmation by the Emperor himself. The Empress Anna Ivanovna found this task tedious and had decreed von Biron to be in this, as in many other matters, her plenipotentiary.

He scanned the list carefully, deleting two names which particularly displeased him, and placing a question mark against a third. He paused when he came to the name of Martin Petrovich Spanberg, whose captain's *brevet* was submitted for approval.

Spanberg? That name rang a bell.

Of course. Spanberg was Bering's First Officer.

Without further ado, von Biron placed a neat tick against Spanberg's name and continued on down the list.

Awatska Bay, Kamchatka Peninsula
March 9, 1737

Aleksey Chirikov's respect for Captain-Commander Vitus Bering had grown considerably since that dark November day when the sea had reared up against and nearly destroyed the Expedition. Like others, Chirikov had at first questioned Bering's judgment in the matter of site deployment. He had even, however briefly, weighed the possibility of exercising his formal authority to relieve Bering of his command.

As time passed, however, and no other natural disaster struck at the Expedition, he came to realise that the Captain-Commander had been vindicated to a degree. Chirikov knew in his own heart that he himself would not have anticipated the freak weather conditions that had hit the vessels at anchor and flooded the encampment. Bering had perhaps been less cautious than he might but, Chirikov concluded, he had also been extremely unlucky.

Chirikov had watched in admiration as Bering took a firm hold on the repair operations and directed the relocation of the camp. Bering appeared to have shrugged off the lethargy which Chirikov had found so disturbing. The Captain-Commander appeared each day at first light and shuttled back and forth between the beach and the new encampment, rapping out instructions, giving encouragement where it was most needed and, on occasion, lending an expert hand to set a rigging or replace a shattered timber.

This was the Bering of old, whose reputation for cool strength in any emergency was well-founded.

Chirikov was not blind to the fact that Bering's sudden burst of energy had come about in part because of his feelings of guilt at having placed the Expedition in jeopardy. Of greater relevance, however, was the fact that Bering was clearly motivated by the prospect of his final chance to vindicate himself.

As the Expedition's second-in-command, Chirikov continued to support Bering to the hilt, relaying Bering's orders and supervising their execution. Never should it be said that Aleksey Chirikov shirked his responsibilities.

The same could not be said of Valery Khitrov, whom Chirikov continued to keep at arm's length. Nothing Khitrov had said or done convinced Chirokov that the man had the experience or the commitment to helm the voyage into the Strait. To the extent that Bering insisted on thinking otherwise, Chirikov vowed not to bring up the issue again, sensing how Bering would react.

Despite the atrociously difficult conditions, the ships had been rebuilt. Five vessels stood in their respective cradles waiting impatiently for the blocks to be knocked away to allow them to float off again into Awatska Bay. Further proof of Bering's determination to keep the flotilla intact was the gradual progress made on building a new *St Anna*. At this rate, all six vessels would again be fully seaworthy by late spring.

Bering was indefatigable in another respect, travelling repeatedly from Awatska to Bolcheretsk to chivvy the garrison commander into the provision of additional stores to alleviate the shortfall caused by the many barrels that had been lost. During his visits to Bolcheretsk, Bering saw as much as possible of his daughter Benthe, but precious little of his wife. Bering remarked that Benthe had grown into a beautiful young woman. He noticed also that she was often pensive and withdrawn, but attributed this to her age and to the tedium of a journey that had promised much and delivered little. She misses her friends in St Petersburg, he concluded, resolving that, come late autumn, when the final batch of scientists had been delivered safely to Kamchatka, she and her mother would return with the military escort as planned.

That Osa Bering was also pensive and withdrawn did not preoccupy Bering greatly. His wife had always been self-possessed and self-contained. Besides, in retrospect, Bering had never really forgiven her for insisting on accompanying the Expedition. This was no place for her, he thought, although he admitted that her skills had made an unexpected but telling contribution.

Bering confided, as usual, in Martin Spanberg.

'I feel my duties have caused me to neglect my wife and daughter.'

Spanberg swallowed hard.

'In what respect, Captain-Commander?'

'Osa seems most distant and in some way even angry,' explained Bering.

'But surely, Captain-Commander, she has endured many months of hardship. Your absences have been hard on her.'

'I have been absent many times before, Martin. As every mariner knows only too well, leaving our loved ones for months and years on end is a cross all of us must bear.'

Bering paused. Spanberg was intensely uncomfortable by now.

'It gives me no pleasure to assign you to this nursemaid detail, Martin, especially when I have great need of you by my side. Yet I would ask you to remain a while longer here in Bolcheretsk. And I would ask one more thing of you.'

Bering paused again and it was clear to Spanberg that the Captain-Commander had great difficulty in continuing. Spanberg waited, dreading what Bering might say next.

'I would ask you to talk with my wife. Talk to her and hear also what she has to say. I am anxious to have some explanation of her mood.'

'But, Captain-Commander, with respect, that is scarcely my place.'

'That I know, Martin, but it may well be that she will confide in you. She has great affection for you, as you may have surmised. I feel she will perhaps express to you what she appears determined to withhold from me.'

The pain of betrayal twisted like a sabre-thrust in Spanberg's gut. He answered out of desperation rather than logic.

'Have you talked with your daughter on this matter?'

'Indeed I have. She professes not to know what ails her mother. Perhaps she, too, might confide in you.'

'I think not, Captain-Commander. I see next to nothing of either your wife or daughter.'

'Then you must seek out their company more often. I ask this of you as a friend, not as your senior officer.'

The knot in Spanberg's gut grew ever tighter.

'I shall do what I can, Captain-Commander.'

'I could not ask for more,' replied Bering, clapping him affectionately on the shoulder. 'You are so expert in such matters. And I, it would seem, am but a mere novice.'

Sea of Okhotsk
April 22, 1737

The *St Peter* ploughed through a choppy sea, her gunwales awash as the bows dipped deep into and reared sharply back out of steel-grey waters still flecked with ice.

Valery Khitrov was at the helm and Martin Spanberg watched with grudging approval as the young Russian held a steady course, holding the wind tight in the sheets and correcting course only as and when absolutely necessary. The Captain-Commander has taught him well, thought Spanberg.

Bering was below in his cramped cabin. They were eleven days out of Kamchatka and the crossing to Okhotsk was as yet without incident. Somewhere astern lay the *St Anna*, fully refurbished and refitted now. Bering had decided to kill two birds with one stone, ordering that the *St Anna* accompany them to Okhotsk to shake her down. He had also decided that one more vessel – the *St Luke* – would make the crossing to Okhotsk. Who knew how many passengers he would be expected to take aboard and quarter for the voyage back to the Peninsula?

Bering was in a better mood than for many months.

He was at sea again and that was good. Better still was the knowledge that this was the last stage of the Expedition's journey to Kamchatka. Once the final contingent had been transported to the far coast, the Expedition could begin its real work. Finally. The long waiting had weighed heavily on him. Worst of all, it had estranged him from his wife and daughter, the two persons he held most dear. Osa and Benthe were also aboard the *St Peter*, sharing a tiny cabin on the afterdeck and speaking rarely to him or to each other. They

were returning to Okhotsk and would travel back as and when practical
to St Petersburg. His earlier decision to take them on to Kamchatka
had been wrong, he knew that now, but he could not bring himself
to apologise at any great length. After all, it had been Osa who had
insisted on their accompanying the Expedition in the first place.
Perhaps now she would understand that her insistence had been inappropriate and her presence an unwarranted distraction.

Bering was also aware that there had been some subtle shift in
his relationship with Martin Spanberg. The First Officer was not
his normal ebullient self. Their conversations long into the night
were a thing of the past. Spanberg performed his duties to the letter
and Bering could find no fault with him on that account. But the
First Officer was taciturn where he had been talkative, withdrawn
where he had habitually been outgoing.

He had questioned Spanberg repeatedly to ascertain why Osa
Bering seemed so distant. The First Officer's answers were at best
evasive. Osa was exhausted, he had reported. The rigours of the
journey had sapped her strength. She would be herself again when
she regained St Petersburg. As would Benthe. This had been a trial
for all of us, Spanberg had added, himself included.

The journey *has* sapped our strength, Bering had agreed, but
not our resolve. And now we are about the business we know best.

Leaving Chirikov in Kamchatka had been a logical decision. The
Acting Captain would use the time well, bringing the vessels and
crew to full readiness and initiating the first phases of exploration
northwards along the Peninsula and up the Siberian coast. If
Chirikov was unhappy at this prospect, he had not shown it. Besides,
Chirikov had proved to be the one person to whose authority Grigor
Pisarov responded with any degree of enthusiasm. It was imperative that the commander of onshore operations be reliable. If Bering
had had his way, Pisarov would have been removed from his post
long since, but that decision was not in his hands: Pisarov was the
onshore commander designate at the express wish of Ernst von
Biron and the St Petersburg Grand Council.

Perhaps the most positive development in recent months had
been the support shown by Lieutenant Waxell, who had backed to

the hilt each and every decision Bering had made. Waxell was a good man and a fine sailor, thought Bering. He would make an excellent first officer when the time came. Bering had had occasion to record in the ship's log that Waxell was efficient and loyal to his captain and unusually adept at managing the crew. Bering had also recorded that Waxell's son Laurentij was as likable and decent a young man as one could hope to encounter.

Waxell had stood down from his watch two hours previously. He lay on his bunk, unable to sleep, his mind turning over the dilemma he now faced. Laurentij had more than demonstrated his love for the sea and its ways, but Sven Waxell was in two minds whether to petition the Captain-Commander to take the lad along on the final stages of the voyage through the Strait. Waxell knew that, if something should happen to Laurentij, his mother would be distraught. Even now, after such a long time without news of her boy, she would be consumed with concern.

On the other hand, Waxell could not bring himself to deprive Laurentij of the opportunity of a lifetime. The decision was Sven Waxell's and his alone. He knew he must take it before the *St Peter* docked in Okhotsk.

Port of Okhotsk
May 18, 1737

The *St Peter* had docked late the previous evening. Bering and his full complement remained on board until first light, scanning the dawn horizon for a glimpse of the *St Anna* and the *St Luke*.

The two vessels arrived within an hour of each other, heaving to and anchoring inshore. Only then did Bering give the signal to launch longboats and make for the harbour. Spanberg and Waxell were in the longboat with him. Valery Khitrov was at the rudder.

It was not until they came alongside the pitted timbers of the harbour wall and scaled the crude steps hewn into it that Bering fully appreciated how many people were standing on the wall above them. To his astonishment, they were cheering wildly, almost as if the Expedition had reached its successful conclusion rather than being only at its real beginning.

On reflection, he understood and appreciated their pleasure at his arrival. They, too, had made the terrible journey from St Petersburg and they, too, must have endured many hardships along the way. What was more, they were mere men of letters and men of science, not seafarers or soldiers. His arrival was a sign that they had not travelled in vain. Bering's presence in Okhotsk confirmed to them that the Expedition had become reality.

Bering shook hands with all and sundry as he and his men passed along the quayside. Eager hands slapped him on the shoulders and back and there was a smile of relief and expectation on every face. Bering knew he had to respond.

'Gentlemen, I bid you a belated welcome to Okhotsk and trust that your journey has not been too eventful. My officers and men salute your courage and your resolve. May I take this occasion to inform you that full provision has been made to receive you in Kamchatka. For my part, I have duties to attend to here in Okhotsk. We shall embark for Kamchatka on the late tide three days from today.'

There was a renewed round of cheering as Bering and his men left the quayside and made their way to the quarters of the garrison commander.

Despatches from St Petersburg had accumulated in Okhotsk.

Impatiently, Bering tore them open.

Much of what was written had been superseded by events. Von Biron had written of his disappointment that the Expedition had seen the necessity of overwintering in Tomsk and had transmitted the wishes of the Grand Council that he proceed without delay to rendezvous with Pisarov in Okhotsk and sail immediately for Kamchatka.

Bering thrust the despatch to one side.

The following despatch recorded news of Pisarov's sterling work in Okhotsk and urged Bering to make all haste to bring the body of the Expedition to that port of departure.

That, too, he pushed to one side.

The next despatch from von Biron, dated many months before, congratulated Bering and the Expedition on the excellent flow of information routed to St Petersburg for scientific investigation, specifically complimenting the Captain-Commander on the quality of the sketches made by his wife. Bering smiled to himself before laying this one on top of the pile.

The most recent despatch was, he felt, the only one of any real relevance. And it made for unpleasant reading.

Von Biron ordered on the authority of the Grand Council that Bering was to 'observe as an overriding priority the need to initiate forthwith the scientific phase of the Expedition and see it through to completion'. At his discretion, he and Chirikov could in the interim sail in quest of the fabled Gama Land, but on no account – and this was stressed more than once – were they to venture north into the Bering Strait. That, he read, was to be the final phase of the Imperial Great Northern Expedition and its crowning glory.

Bering crumpled the despatch up into a ball and hurled it across the room.

Bastards, he thought. Bastards.

He would, of course, comply. He had not come this far for nothing.

Among other despatches in the pouch was one addressed to *Captain* Martin Spanberg, informing him of his promotion to that rank and ordering him to return to St Petersburg immediately to assume command of his own vessel.

Spanberg read the despatch with mixed feelings. The seemingly interminable journey to Kamchatka had dampened his enthusiasm but he still wished fervently to be a part of the voyage of exploration. On the other hand, the increasingly precarious nature of his relationship with Bering was a constant source of worry and guilt. The opportunity to captain his own vessel was a substantial inducement and, at the same time, presented a means of escaping from a situation he found intolerable.

His mind made up, he visited Bering in his quarters in the garrison.

'I have news from St Petersburg, Captain-Commander. I have been advanced to the rank of captain and am enjoined to proceed at once to the capital to take command of my own vessel.'

'May I be the first to offer congratulations, First Officer.'

Bering paused, then smiled.

'Forgive me. Congratulations, *Captain* Spanberg. I would add that your promotion is long overdue and greatly merited.'

Spanberg expected Bering to continue. He did not.

'I have made my decision to accept the posting, Captain-Commander.'

'That is a wise decision, Martin, and one in which I can only concur.'

'It grieves me greatly to abandon the Expedition at this late date. All the more so, after what we have been through together.'

Bering was silent. Spanberg could see that he was struggling with his emotions. Finally, he spoke.

'You have your career, Captain, and this is a most important step in that career. It grieves *me* that you will not be with us, but I would counsel you to accept this new challenge. Your time will come. I know you will go on to greater things.'

'I know of nothing greater than your present mission, Captain-Commander.'

Bering's eyes drifted to the corner of the room where von Biron's despatch lay crumpled.

'By all accounts, that mission may lie even farther in the future than you can possibly know. If it is time to part company, Captain, then let it be in the proper spirit.'

Bering came across the room to Spanberg and embraced him.

'I wish you God's speed, Captain. And I shall miss you, Martin.'

'And I you, sir.'

There was little left to say. Spanberg was relieved that the Captain-Commander had accepted his news gracefully. He was also proud that Bering continued to hold him in such high regard. By leaving the Expedition now, Spanberg knew he could extricate himself from any further involvement with Osa Bering and, over time, perhaps expiate his guilt.

Bering would never – need never – know what had transpired.

'One more thing, Captain Spanberg. My wife and daughter will be leaving for St Petersburg under military escort. I ask you as a friend to travel with them and to look to their welfare. I know they mean almost as much to you as they do to myself.'

Spanberg paused in the doorway. This was too much.

'My orders are to leave for St Petersburg without delay, Captain-Commander —'

'And my order is that they shall leave in your care. There is no-one to whom I would rather entrust a cargo so precious.'

'Aye-aye, Captain-Commander.'

Spanberg saluted one final time and left the room.

Bering walked to the far corner and retrieved the crumpled despatch. He read it again, more carefully this time. He would compose a diplomatic answer to the Grand Council. He smiled at the thought.

Before any reply could reach him, he would be at sea.

Interlude

ST PETERSBURG

St Petersburg
November 10, 1740
Reichsgraf Ernst Johann von Biron, Duke of Courtland, Count of the Holy Roman Empire and erstwhile lover of the late Csarina Anna Ivanovna, lay fully-clothed on the quilted brocade cover and stared up at the ornately-coffered ceiling in his private quarters.

Bastards.

Conniving bastards, every single one.

And none worse than his own fellow countrymen.

Ernst von Biron was the first to admit that he had connived and intrigued with the best of them. But that was the way of politics. Surely everyone knew as much and accepted it?

Von Biron wondered how history would judge him. Less than kindly, he imagined.

He felt strongly that the charges commonly laid at his door – corruption, tyranny, oppression, not to mention self-serving arrogance and administrative inflexibility – were largely unjustified. Or, at worst, greatly exaggerated. He had never been popular – he realised that and could understand it – but he knew in his heart he had done much that was in the best interests of his adopted country.

Granted, he had capitalised on his physical liaison with the Empress to advance his own interests and consolidate his position. Now that the fat bitch was dead and buried, his power base was in imminent danger of being eroded.

He lay there, turning the day's events over in his mind, wondering whether the country's best interests would continue to be served by those who were in the process of casting him aside in a frantic scramble to remain in power.

Where did I go wrong, he asked himself.

Initially, it had all looked so promising.

Von Biron had prevailed on the childless Anna to name her successor and had been delighted when, at his suggestion, she had opted for her newly-born nephew Ivan Antonovich, who would rule as Ivan VI under the co-regency of his mother – Anna's great-niece Anna Leopoldovna – and von Biron himself.

Ivan VI had duly acceded to the throne on the death of the Empress Anna Ivanovna in October 1740. During the coronation ceremony, Ernst von Biron's hand had rested lightly but firmly on the infant's gold-encrusted cradle.

Circumstances dictated that the Grand Council convene in emergency session immediately following the death of the Empress Anna. Von Biron had routinely assumed the presidency. Among the various matters of state on the agenda was the continuing progress of the Imperial Great Northern Expedition.

'There are some here who may have questioned the wisdom of committing to this protracted undertaking. Others still have been critical of how it was designed and led.'

Von Biron paused and looked around the table before continuing.

'Those critics are now silenced. The Expedition has been a triumph in terms of the scientific and political prestige it has conferred upon this great nation.'

On the basis of despatches and word-of-mouth reports, von Biron had gone on to present a glowing report. The Expedition had succeeded beyond every expectation. The scientific contingent had amassed and was continuing to amass an inordinate amount of invaluable material; the Orthodox Church had made new converts; the geography of the Siberian coast had been established beyond question, among other things with the news that Lieutenant Chelyuskin had successfully sailed to the northernmost cape of the Siberian mainland and Lieutenants Khariton and Laptev had charted the Siberian coastline from the Taymyr Peninsula to the Kolyma River.

What was more, von Biron had added, the most recent intelligence had confirmed that Captain-Commander Vitus Bering and

Acting Captain Aleksey Chirikov had long since readied for sea to complete the final leg of the Expedition, their specific mission being to search for Gama Land and, crucially, for the Northeast Passage from the North Pacific to the Russian Arctic and, in the longer term, to secure Russian access to Japan, China and the Indies.

'In all,' said von Biron in conclusion, 'close on 10,000 persons have participated directly or indirectly in the Expedition since it was first mooted over seven years ago. Many have already returned to St Petersburg or are on their way back from Kamchatka.'

He paused. Then:

'Our Expedition has been more, so much more than a simple voyage of discovery. It has demonstrated to the world at large and to those who may one day seek to oppose us, that the Russian Empire is a power to be reckoned with, both militarily and economically. It has uncovered new resources, it has annexed new territories, it has stamped the name of Russia indelibly on the map of the modern world. It has served notice on the English, French, Nederlanders, Spaniards and others that Mother Russia is a force to be reckoned with and, as Peter the Great envisaged, a nation among nations.

'Gentlemen, I thank you for your years of service on this Grand Council and for your loyal commitment and dedication. Our reward shall be this: a proud and forward-looking Russia that fears none and has no equal.'

Von Biron looked at each member of the Grand Council in turn. He smiled and took his seat with studied humility.

The applause was muted.

Before the close of the Grand Council session, Count Ostermann rose to pay a carefully-worded tribute to von Biron and his accomplishments.

'The Grand Council formally congratulates Ernst Count von Biron on his endeavours. He has rendered this country remarkable service as adviser to the late Empress and his contribution to the success of the Expedition has been incalculable. I would ask that the Grand Council commend Count von Biron in anticipation of

the Expedition's successful conclusion. This Grand Council nour-
ishes the hope that Count von Biron will continue to be on hand
to serve the Empire in whatever capacity proves appropriate.'

Bastard, thought von Biron.

He should have seen it coming.

During Anna Ivanovna's reign, German-born Heinrich Johann
Friedrich Ostermann had prudently metamorphosed into Count
Andrey Ivanovich Ostermann. As Anna's First Minister, Ostermann
had always been von Biron's principal rival as the power behind
the throne. Where von Biron had been manipulative and devious,
however, Ostermann had been straightforward and direct. Whereas
von Biron had opted to pull the strings from behind the scenes,
Ostermann's every move had been calculatingly out in the open.

Ostermann had long enjoyed a positive public image. During
Anna's reign, he had brokered and sustained a contentious alliance
with Austria. He had shepherded Russia through the costly War of
the Polish Succession which placed a pro-Russian king, Augustus
III, on the Polish throne. He had advocated the invasion of Turkey,
sparking the Russo-Turkish War that substantially extended Russia's
interests to the east. He had negotiated a vital commercial treaty
with England. And, by no means least, he had served on a Grand
Council which had masterminded the Imperial Great Northern
Expedition and orchestrated Russia's determined thrust into Central
Asia and Siberia.

More perhaps than any other since Peter the Great, Ostermann
had publicly contrived to raise Russia's profile as a European power.

Ernst von Biron also recognised that Ostermann had an influential ally in Graf Burkhard Christoph von Münnich. In his own
prudent Russian reincarnation as Count Burkhard Kristof Minikh,
Field-Marshal von Münnich had captured Gdansk – and the admiration of Russians everywhere – and inspired the country's armies
to victory in the War of the Polish Succession. His reputation as
an outstanding military strategist had subsequently been confirmed
by his brilliant campaigns during the Russo-Turkish War, which
had resulted in territorial gains for the Empire following the
conquest of Perekhop, Ocharov, Azov and northern Bessarabia.

Ostermann and von Münnich were powerful and highly visible players in every sense of the term. Von Biron was also aware that, throughout Anna's ten-year reign, his two fellow countrymen had struggled to contain and conceal their resentment at the influence he wielded over an empress whose interest in affairs of state was at best desultory. With Anna Ivanovna dead and these two ranged against him, he knew his own position was now at best precarious.

Von Biron swung his legs over the side of the bed and stood up. He walked slowly across to the generously-proportioned window which opened out over the Neva. I love this city, he thought to himself. And I love this country which I have always tried to serve to the best of my ability.

'Bastards,' he muttered under his breath.

He recalled how that son-of-a-whore Ostermann had extended his hand to him as the Grand Council left the chamber. Ostermann had looked von Biron squarely in the eye, holding his gaze. Smiling.

That smile had said it all. A new chapter of Russian history was being written and von Biron was being informed, politely but unmistakably, that he was to have no part in it.

As a political animal, von Biron was astute enough to acknowledge that the issue went far beyond thinly-disguised personal animosity. To Ostermann and von Münnich, Ernst von Biron posed a subtle yet genuine longer-term threat. All three were in one way or another leading figures in the German clique whose influence on Russian affairs of state was anathema to Russia's rank-and-file nobility and senior civil servants alike. As non-Russians, all three were widely perceived as interlopers who blocked access to the throne and to the highest echelons of power, savagely crushing all and sundry who dared oppose them. Of the three, however, two – Ostermann and von Münnich – were grudgingly accepted as public figures with a long record of achievement, whereas Ernst von Biron was universally perceived as a sinister, manipulative, *private* figure with no formal position in the imperial administration.

As a result, it was von Biron who aroused the greatest resentment.

It happens time and again throughout history, thought von Biron.

A price must be paid for political advancement. He, Ernst von Biron, was earmarked as the sacrificial lamb, that much was now certain.

He turned away from the window, shaking his head sadly. Ostermann and von Münnich had taken stock of the situation and had bowed to the inevitable. Both knew that Peter the Great's daughter Elizabeth basked in the reputation of her illustrious father. She was attractive, popular and Russian to the core. And she made no secret of her ambition to take what she considered her rightful place on the imperial throne. She had the support of the guard regiments and several foreign powers – predictably the French, who were solidly opposed to Russia's continuing alliance with Austria. With this in mind, Ostermann and von Münnich knew it was only a matter of time before Elizabeth made her move. She would depose the infant Ivan VI and accede to the throne. To ensure their own political survival, Ostermann and von Münnich would be required to rally to her cause and offer their unequivocal support. Von Biron, meanwhile, could only hope to retain a semblance of authority if he could somehow thwart Elizabeth's inevitable bid for power. This he would be unable to do.

Ernst von Biron's fate was as conveniently sealed as his fall from grace was neatly orchestrated.

They came to the door just after midnight.

An equerry presented his compliments and handed over a letter from Count Ostermann. It was with the greatest regret, von Biron read, that it had been decided that the continuing presence on Russian soil of Reichsgraf Ernst von Biron was no longer desirable. As befitted his rank and station, he was accorded a grace period of one month to put his affairs in order before leaving St Petersburg.

For exile in Siberia.

Ernst von Biron read the letter a second time.

Siberia?

He thought back to what Vitus Bering had asked years before: which members of the Grand Council intended to accompany the Expedition? And he had replied that there were no immediate plans in that regard. At least not in the initial stages.

To give credit where credit is due, Reichsgraf Ernst Johann von Biron, Duke of Courtland, Count of the Holy Roman Empire and erstwhile lover of the late Csarina Anna Ivanovna, laughed out loud at the quintessential irony of it all.

BOOK TWO

THE VOYAGE

Chapter One

GAMA LAND

Awatska Bay
June 4, 1741

First Officer Lieutenant-at-Sea Sven Waxell stood on the afterdeck of the *St Peter*, his arms draped loosely about the broad shoulders of his son Laurentij. Together, they peered through the salt drizzle and drifting fog.

The *St Paul* lay at sea anchor no more than a hundred metres to windward, turning sluggishly on an ebb tide, its fore and main masts barely visible. To the west, they could make out the vague contours of the hastily thrown-together settlement of Petropavlovsk, as unprepossessing a township as Waxell had ever had the misfortune to live in.

'Mark my words, we'll soon see the back of that hell-hole,' said Waxell. 'The wind is freshening from the southwest and we'll sail on this next tide.'

Laurentij Waxell smiled and nodded.

He was unconvinced. The *St Peter* and the *St Paul* had lain at anchor in the bay for almost a full week now, waiting for a favourable wind. And, each day around this time, he had stood beside his father on the afterdeck, gazing back towards Petropavlovsk and hearing his father utter the same confident prediction.

Laurentij Waxell was consumed with impatience.

He was in his twentieth year and had grown to full adulthood since first joining the Imperial Great Northern Expedition those many years ago in St Petersburg. He recalled his initial excitement at having been permitted to travel with his father to the Russian capital. He recalled his anxiety that he might not be allowed to travel onwards with the Expedition to Kamchatka. He recalled his relief at his father's decision to accede to his boyish entreaties. He recalled the rigours of the overland journey – the long days on foot and by sled, the biting cold, the endless winter nights, the monotonous diet, the permanent threat of attack, the uncertainty of it all. And he recalled his desperate disappointment as, winter after winter, the Expedition had quartered in one desolate garrison town after another before limping into Okhotsk for the crossing to Kamchatka.

Most of all, however, he recalled Benthe Bering, as vivid to him now as those many months before when she and her mother had left Kamchatka to travel back to St Petersburg in the company of Martin Spanberg and that arrogant pig Grigor Pisarov. He could picture her at court, a slender figure resplendent in virginal white, her golden hair piled high, dancing a sprightly *mazurka* on the arm of some fresh-faced army cadet, smiling that inimitable smile, laughing that inimitable laugh . . .

Laurentij shrugged. What did it matter now? She was there and he was here. He doubted he would ever see her again.

'Make sail for'ard!'

Laurentij was suddenly aware that something was happening. He looked around to see hands scurrying to their posts. He felt the sea anchor wrench free, heard its chain rasp across the anchor plate. Sails unfurled, ropes grew taught, and the *St Peter* lurched into motion.

The Captain-Commander was on deck now, rapping out commands.

The voyage of discovery was finally under way.

St Petersburg
June 7, 1741

Count Ostermann stood up and came from behind his desk as Martin Spanberg entered the room.

'Captain Spanberg. I bid you welcome and regret that I have prevailed upon you to make your report so soon after the end of your long journey. Which, I am given to understand, was arduous but without great mishap?'

'That is mercifully true.'

'And how fares our undertaking?'

'The Expedition is in the most capable of hands,' replied Spanberg.

'Of that I have no doubt.'

Ostermann waited, but Spanberg did not continue.

'And the Captain-Commander is well?' asked Ostermann.

'He is well but greatly distressed at the years that have elapsed since the Expedition first left St Petersburg. The way has been long and hard. For the Expedition. But also for the Captain-Commander.'

'That is precisely why we entrusted the Expedition to his seasoned care and leadership. He is a man of considerable resolve.'

'That he is. And I venture that the *St Peter* and the *St Paul* are as seaworthy as any craft in the Imperial Navy. What is more, Your Excellency, much credit in that regard must go to Lieutenant Waxell and his men, who were most diligent.'

'Quite. Waxell, you say?' said Ostermann, scribbling a note to himself. He pressed his fingertips together and looked again at Spanberg.

'You await new orders, Captain Spanberg?'

'I have a new command, sir, but as yet no new orders.'

'That is a situation we can remedy.'

'I would be most grateful.'

Ostermann looked down at the papers on his desk, fingered them briefly and extracted a single sheet.

'I have your orders here. You are to proceed with all due speed with your new command to Cathay. The purpose of your mission is set out in this document.'

'As Your Excellency wishes.'

Spanberg was relieved and disappointed at one and the same time. Relieved that his orders had come through so quickly, yet disappointed that he was to leave St Petersburg immediately.

The circumstances of the overland journey back to St Petersburg had afforded him little opportunity to speak with Osa Bering. They had met frequently but always in the presence of others. On the solitary occasion they had found themselves alone together, he had been careful to avoid any remarks that might offend her. Osa had responded in kind. The exchange had been stilted and unsatisfying. Spanberg wondered if he would have an opportunity to pay his respects to her before leaving.

'In accordance with tradition, Captain Spanberg, you may, if you so wish, rename the vessel of which you now take command,' said Osterman. 'Have you chosen a name?'

'I have, Your Excellency.'

'And?'

'I shall name her *The Bering*.'

'Most commendable, Captain. I am certain the Captain-Commander will be flattered and most honoured.'

Aboard the St Paul
June 12, 1741

Captain Alexsey Chirikov had instructed his helmsman – Fleet-master Dementiev – to hold station aft of the *St Peter* and to close on Bering's vessel only as and when weather conditions dictated. For a full week, a favourable wind had blown strongly from south-by-southwest, driving the two vessels on a swift southeasterly course.

Spread out on a table in Chirikov's cramped quarters were Russian Admiralty charts, duplicates of those being used by Bering aboard the *St Peter*.

Like Bering himself, Chirikov placed little store by the charts. And, like Bering, Chirikov deeply resented what he saw as a point-less excursion to the southeast when the real challenge lay to the north, in the potential discovery of the elusive sea route between the North Pacific and Russia's Arctic Ocean.

Chirikov was in no doubt that the charts were flawed. The originals had been drawn in 1722 on the express orders of Peter the Great by the celebrated Nuremberg mapmaker Johann Baptist Homan. Chirikov had little quarrel with Homan's work. As far as it went, it deserved to be applauded as an honest attempt to map what was then known of the Kamchatka coast. What irritated him – and never failed to infuriate Vitus Bering – was not so much that the charts had been revised but that they now showed a large land mass purporting to be Gama Land, which an obscure Portuguese navigator called Juan de Gama claimed to have seen during a voyage from China to New Spain almost a century previously. De Gama's dubious account had been transposed by the Portuguese geographer Texeira in 1649 but had never been substantiated.

None of this would have mattered except that the charts had been specifically revised for the benefit of the Imperial Great Northern Expedition by the influential French astronomer Joseph-Nicolas Delisle, who directed the Imperial Institute of Astronomy in St Petersburg. Delisle was a powerful figure in the Russian scientific and political establishment and his conclusions had been accepted at face value by the Grand Council.

Worse still, standing next to Chirikov and Fleetmaster Dementiev, was none other than Professor of Astronomy Louis Delisle de la Croyère, whose secondment to the Expedition was clearly intended to ensure that his half-brother's theories were fully tested and, he hoped, confirmed.

Both Chirikov and Bering knew that it was out of the question to disregard the revised charts and dismiss the notion of Gama Land out of hand. They had their orders from St Petersburg and those orders had to be followed to the letter.

Chirikov silently applauded Bering's shrewd judgment in assigning Delisle de la Croyère to the *St Paul* rather than quartering him aboard the *St Peter*. De la Croyère's presence was a permanent thorn in Chirikov's side.

Fleetmaster Dementiev jabbed a gnarled finger at the coordinates.

'By my reckoning, we are too far to the southeast. We must bring her round to tack full east, then bear north until we sight land.'

Chirikov was tempted to agree, but de la Croyère would have none of it.

'It is too soon, Fleetmaster Dementiev. We must pursue our course and hold our heading for some days yet, as the chart clearly shows.'

'The chart may be flawed,' ventured Chirikov.

'The chart is drawn on the basis of precise astronomical computations,' retorted de la Croyère. 'I insist it be followed.'

Chirikov disregarded this challenge to his own authority. When all was said and done, he had his own career to consider.

'Then let it be so,' he instructed Dementiev.

The Fleetmaster acknowledged the order, clearly displeased.

'The Captain should know that the wind has dropped and that the fog is closing in,' he replied.

'Your conclusion, Fleetmaster?'

'That we draw a closer bead on the *St Peter*, Captain, lest we lose her.'

'It is so ordered.'

A mile or more ahead of them on the *St Peter*, Valery Khitrov held course towards a bank of fog that ballooned out of the slate-grey sea and closed in over the vessel like a shroud.

St Petersburg
June 14, 1741

Osa Bering walked along the banks of the Neva, warmed by a welcome sun.

She walked alone, content to admire the late spring blossoms and the early tints of summer. She walked as far as her favourite stone bench and sat down to watch the crowds thronging by the river. Looking out towards the islands in the Neva and to the open sea beyond, she noticed a clutch of vessels moored in the leads, their sails fluttering in a light breeze.

It already seemed a lifetime since she had returned from Kamchatka, that beautiful and dangerous land she had instinctively loved and hated. Sitting here, surrounded by the imperial magnificence of St Petersburg, her thoughts turned to the shabby wooden cabins and dirt roads of Petropavlovsk, the town that Vitus Bering had ordered built to house the Expedition which had changed her life.

Vitus.

He was gone now. Gone in every sense.

He had left her and his only daughter in order to pursue a dream that he would never share, to make his mark on a century of discovery, to write his name into the pages of history.

Or die in the attempt.

She felt no great sadness. Her respect for her husband had not diminished and her admiration for his single-mindedness had not waned. Instead, there was only a sense of hollowness. Her useful life, it seemed, was over.

On her return to St Petersburg, she had been welcomed – even fêted – as the wife of the Expedition's nominal leader. She had modestly accepted the compliments showered on her by members of the Grand Council and others, gracefully acknowledging their admiration for what, to her, still seemed a trivial contribution to the success of the Expedition. Not so, they had all hastened to reassure her: the journal she had kept and illustrated had been welcomed as an invaluable record of the Expedition's progress. The late Empress Anna herself had requested a copy to be made and had wished to grant Osa an audience. Osa had been presented at court, reluctant to attend but secretly pleased to discover that she had gained respect in many quarters, not only as an artist but also as a loyal wife.

But then it was over. The brief flame of celebrity flickered and died.

She had not seen Martin Spanberg since their return from Siberia. During the journey, they had met only occasionally and as circumstances required and there had been no further suggestion on his part that what they had shared had been more than a casual encounter. She knew, of course – St Petersburg was a hotbed of informed and misinformed gossip – that Spanberg had taken command of his own vessel – *The Bering* – and that he would leave soon for Cathay.

She wondered whether he would seek her out before he departed. She concluded he would not.

She was wrong.

That very morning, Martin Spanberg had ridden out to Bering's house on the Gulf of Finland. Benthe Bering opened the door and politely but curtly informed him that her mother was not there. Spanberg thanked her for the information. As he turned to leave, Benthe grasped him by the arm.

'I know.'

Spanberg looked at her and waited.

'I know about you and my mother.'

'And just *what* do you know, Benthe?'

'I know that you and she – that you and she were intimate. I saw you. I saw you that night.'

Her voice broke.

'Then, Benthe, you should also know that I hold your mother in the deepest affection.'

'And what of my father? What of him? Do you nurse the same affection for him?'

'I have always cherished your father's friendship and continue to do so. You must know that.'

'Then how could you?'

'How could I? How could we? To my discredit, I can find no excuse for our actions. But I can offer an explanation.'

'There is nothing to explain. You have wronged me and you have wronged my father.'

'Your father, most certainly, although he knows nothing of this. But you? In what way have I wronged you?'

'You must know how I felt for you.'

'In all honesty, I had no knowledge of your feelings. What transpired was between your mother and myself.'

'You must have known I was in love with you.'

Spanberg hesitated. He had no wish to hurt this young woman more than he had already. Her infatuation had been obvious to him and, as he now admitted to himself, he had taken modest pleasure in it. But this had to end.

'Let me ask you, my dear Benthe,' he said gently. 'Would I have wronged your father less had I taken advantage of his only daughter?'

Benthe's eyes widened.

'But that is not the same,' she replied uncertainly.

'True, but had I done so I should have lost the respect of a man I look upon as a father and of a woman I love deeply and unashamedly.'

Benthe was in tears now. He reached out to her and she came

into his arms. He held her close as a father would. As her own father had not done for a long time. When finally she pulled back, her eyes sought his. Spanberg held her gaze. She wiped her eyes and smiled.

'My mother walks each day alone on the banks of the Neva.'

'Thank you.'

Benthe smiled again and closed the door.

It was as if he had been granted absolution.

He rode back into the city, skirting the river at the earliest opportunity. He found her, as Benthe had predicted, sitting alone by the Neva.

Osa's eyes rose to meet his as he dismounted. He knelt before her, taking both her hands in his.

'Osa.'

'Martin.'

They stood and embraced. He held her hand tightly as they walked back together to his quarters.

Next morning, he rose quietly and dressed. Osa was still asleep. He walked over to the bed and kissed her tenderly on the forehead. She stirred and looked up at him.

'I am leaving now, Osa. But I shall return.'

'I know, Martin. I know. And I shall be waiting.'

Aboard the St Paul
June 17, 1741

'Fuck and double fuck!' shouted Aleksey Chirikov, slamming his outstretched palm against the bulkhead.

Fleetmaster Dementiev shrugged his shoulders.

'We have lost them, Captain. They are nowhere to be seen.'

For five days, the St Paul had held course, running silently through dense sea fog. The ship's trumpeter had blown signals until his lips split but each note had died away with no echoing response.

'That son-of-a-bitch Khitrov,' said Dementiev. 'That shagging son-of-a-bitch. All he had to do was hold his bearing or heave to. Where is the bastard?'

Chirikov did not reply. The fog had lifted, the skies were clear and the sea was unusually calm. There was no sign of the *St Peter*.

Chirikov knew it was not his fault nor that of his helmsman. They had tracked and backtracked along precisely the same heading for five whole days and nights without sighting or hearing the *St Peter*.

He had said all along that Valery Khitrov was incompetent. He had felt it in his bones and recent events had proved him right. Only a few months before, in broad daylight, Khitrov had helmed the *St Peter* off course into a rocky outcrop, striking off several timbers and losing precious supplies in the process.

And now this.

Chirikov slammed his palm into the bulkhead once again. Fuck Khitrov. And curse Vitus Bering for his stubbornness. And to hell with Gama Land.

'Bring her about, Fleetmaster, and set us a course due east then north. As I know the Captain-Commander, he will act likewise. No doubt our paths will cross again soon enough.'

Aboard the St Peter
June 17, 1741
Sven Waxell was acutely conscious of how infrequently Vitus Bering was seen on deck these days. It seemed the Captain-Commander preferred to remain below in the company of that strange German scientist who had been billeted in Bering's quarters.

Waxell understood Bering's absence and excused it. It was clear to him that the Captain-Commander saw little need to come topside to direct the futile quest for a new continent, this preposterous Gama Land they all knew in their hearts to be a myth.

In the event, First Officer Waxell and his junior officers were flattered by Bering's faith in their ability to crew the vessel efficiently. As a result, they troubled the Captain-Commander as little as possible.

Today was different.

They had sailed through dense fog for five days, emerging into the glare of the sun only hours previously. There was no sign of the *St Paul* and Waxell was worried.

The lookout had seen nothing during the midnight watch but had reported sounds to windward that might have been those of a trumpet. Waxell had ordered complete silence on deck and commanded the *St Peter*'s trumpeter to respond. His high notes were muffled in the dense fog. When he paused, there was silence. Then a faint sound that was perhaps no more than a distant echo. The hands crowded the ship's rail, ears straining to catch any sound that might suggest the *St Paul* lay close by. Still nothing. Only the slap and hiss of the *St Peter*'s bow wave.

'Your report, First Officer?'

Vitus Bering was clearly annoyed at having been summoned to the afterdeck. His eyes were rimmed with fatigue and he had visibly lost weight. His hair was matted and he was unshaven. He glared at Waxell.

'I beg to report, Captain-Commander, that the *St Paul* has not been sighted these five days.'

'And?'

'And that I await your orders, Captain-Commander.'

'My orders are unchanged, First Officer. You are to hold course.'

'Shall I take off sail, Captain-Commander?'

'Indeed you will not, First Officer. It is merely that we have made better headway than the *St Paul*. She will come alongside us in due course. That is all.'

Bering turned to go below but paused. He was too experienced a mariner to dismiss the possibility that the *St Peter* had veered off course. He looked across at Valery Khitrov, who stood at the helm, his eyes staring directly ahead.

'You have nothing to report, Fleetmaster Khitrov?'

'Nothing, Captain-Commander.'

Bering shrugged. He turned back to Waxell.

'Post extra lookouts, First Officer. And report to me in four hours.'

'Aye-aye, sir.'

Waxell watched as Bering went below. He brought his spy-glass to his eye and scanned the horizon.

Nothing.

Waxell shivered.

Suddenly, he felt very alone.

Aboard the St Peter
June 1741

From the journal of Lieutenant-at-Sea Sven Waxell

June 18, 1741

It is my sad duty to record that we have searched in vain for the St. Paul, our sister vessel which sails under the command of Acting Captain Chirikov. The insufferable sea fogs that plague this coast separated our two vessels these six days ago and we have seen nought since of the St. Paul.

The Captain-Commander is untroubled by this unwelcome circumstance and bids me hold course in firm expectation that the St. Paul will do likewise. It is his belief that our two vessels shall perforce meet in better times.

As the Captain-Commander's First Officer, I do his bidding, yet I do so with a heavy heart, for I am not persuaded that we shall see the St. Paul again. It is my own belief that the St. Peter had best have laid off sail to let the St. Paul close on us. My orders were however to run before the wind and in this, as ever, I bow to the sound knowledge and experience of the Captain-Commander.

We run south by southeast. The noon watch reports a calm sea whose surface holds many traces of leaves and plants. The German scientist who quarters with the Captain-Commander says the varieties of birds that circle our vessel betoken land close by, but he is no sailor and knows little of the ways of the sea. More lookouts have been posted but they signal no land to the north or east.

It also grieves me to record that the men grow restless and fearful. Many say the St. Paul has foundered on the shores of Gama Land, of which we ourselves saw no trace and which I know the Captain-Commander believes not to exist. Yet among the men are many who are superstitious, as is the wont of seafarers. They say our voyage is ill-fated. In all truth, I cannot share this superstition, for I have seen little to bear it out.

I attribute no blame for the disappearance of the St. Paul to Acting Captain Chirikov or to Fleetmaster Dementiev, as steadfast a helmsman as any I have yet come to know. Yet no blame for what has transpired is laid at the door of our own Fleetmaster, Lieutenant Khitrov, who gives assurances that he has helmed the St. Peter as ordered. The Lieutenant is as surly as any man can be and is most disliked by the crew, who recall with great bitterness the unwarranted harshness of their treatment at his hands on Kamchatka. Yet he performs credibly and remains moreover in the good graces of the Captain-Commander.

The St. Paul is lost to us and we trust in God and His Mercy that the vessel's officers and hands are safe.

At noon this day the Captain-Commander came topside. His looks are drawn but he was of good cheer. He let his decision be known that we shall change course forthwith and bear due north. We have reset our course and sail north now into the near unknown.

I was most pleased to see the Captain-Commander again at his post. His absence has troubled the men and his presence must greatly hearten them. The German Steller was with him and seems most put out we did not sail another day to the east. To my mind, the Captain-Commander indulges him and his strange ways – for, indeed, he is a most curious fellow – and I am concerned that his constant chatter may distract the Captain-Commander from his task.

Laurentij sits forward and does his duty without complaint. I have confided most often to this journal the pride I take in him. I do so again without apology, thanking Our Lord for his most pleasant disposition and demeanour, yet taking every care to praise him infrequently to his face. Laurentij is born to the sea and does our family name much credit.

I am thankful that the myth of Gama Land has been laid to rest and that our every effort is now given to our central mission.

Chapter Two

LANDFALL

Aboard the St Peter
June 24, 1741

The pain was excruciating.

Mercifully, it was not constant.

Vitus Bering lay on his bunk, his right fist pressed tightly against a distended lower abdomen, his face contorting in agony as the pain stabbed through him again and again. It had been like this since only a day or so out of Awatska Bay. He had given little thought to it at the time. A chronic diarrhoea, he had diagnosed, brought on no doubt by a rudimentary diet and compounded by the anxieties of command.

The pain came again, knifing through his belly. He drew his left hand up to his face and thrust the knuckles into his mouth, biting down hard. Sweat trickled down his cheek and into the stubble on his chin, drying cold against his skin in the chill air that whistled through his cramped quarters.

He had downed a mixture of laudanum, quinine and arsenic, diluted and made palatable by the addition of honey-sweetened water. The dose was larger than usual and more concentrated than he normally permitted himself. It was having the desired effect – not of eliminating the pain but of changing his perception of it. The pain still racked his body but he felt his mind gradually drift into euphoria as images flitted across his inner eye.

The dominant image was that of Osa.

Osa of the knowing smile. Of the purposeful gait. Osa laughing. Osa self-contained. Osa wilful. Osa gentle.

Osa alone.

Osa. Osa. Osa.

Gradually, his daughter's features superimposed themselves. Benthe, his pride and joy. Benthe of the white skin. The burnished gold of long hair. Eyes that darted this way and that. A smile that melted hearts.

Now Spanberg.

His son, his only son.

Martin. Martin the impetuous. Martin the breaker of hearts. Captain Spanberg. A leader of men.

Martin and Benthe now, then Martin at the helm of the *St Peter*.

No, not Martin. Khitrov. His protégé. His creation. At Khitrov's shoulder, Aleksey Chirikov. Dour Aleksey, peering at him through the fog.

And there was Sven Waxell, the loyal Swede. With Laurentij, ever innocent, always happy.

Then Steller, impassioned and argumentative. A poor sailor.

And, in the far distance, the knowing smile of Ernst von Biron.

The images pressed in on him, their faces taut and anxious.

But he was sailing alone now, standing ramrod straight and proud on the afterdeck. His dark hair streamed in the wind. 1728. Alone on the *St Gabriel*. A stout vessel rearing and plunging through a heavy swell. The *St Gabriel*. Ice and fog and the strait that bore his name.

And now the *St Peter*. 1741.

Tomsk. Yakutsk. Okhotsk. Kamchatka. Petropavlovsk. Awatska. St Petersburg again. St Petersburg and Osa. Osa with Benthe at her side. Martin. His son Martin. His family. His legacy. His.

He felt no pain now. He smiled and turned to face the bulkhead.

He was at sea again.

At sea at last.

What could be more beautiful?

More cruel?

His sea, his beautiful, cruel sea.

It would not be long now. He could feel it in his bones. No, it would not be long. Not long. He was coming home.

Home.

His eyelids grew heavy.

He closed his eyes and slept.

Aboard the St Paul
June 24, 1741

Aleksey Chirikov was a man of few words. His careful entry in the ship's log that day was uncharacteristically detailed:

> June 24, 1741. At Sea. Ten days have elapsed since the *St Peter* was last sighted. To anticipate that such a fine vessel and her crew are lost without trace is most premature and we do not abandon hope.
>
> It is surmised that Captain-Commander Bering has broken off our common search for Gama Land and has helmed the *St Peter* due north by northeast in search of the North American land mass. We pray that our course may cross hers as the strait narrows, as narrow it must.
>
> As this log records for June 17, the *St Paul*, at my command, has also abandoned the fruitless quest for Gama Land and has struck out due north.
>
> We are most watchful and unstinting in our efforts to espy the *St Peter* and make common cause with her under the leadership of a mariner for whom the undersigned has the most profound respect.

Chirikov set down his quill and poured salt on the page to blot the entry.

He closed the leather-bound log and pushed it to one side. He reached into a compartment in the desk and took out a buff-coloured sheet which bore the signature and seal of Reichsgraf Ernst Johann von Biron. The sealed order empowered him to depose Captain-Commander Vitus Bering and assume command of the Imperial Great Northern Expedition as and when the time was appropriate.

Chirikov did not hesitate.

To hell with von Biron and to hell with the Grand Council.

He held the document in his left hand and, grasping it between the thumb and forefinger of his right, ripped it from top to bottom in one swift movement. He put the two halves together and tore them across a second time. And again and again, until the document lay in an untidy pile of scraps.

Scooping up the scraps in his right hand, Chirikov went on deck. He held his fist over the side and slowly unclenched it. He watched as the tiny fragments of parchment were whisked away on the prevailing wind, fluttering like so many demented butterflies.

Aboard the St Peter
June 28, 1741

Georg Wilhelm Steller still hated the sea, but that hatred was now tempered by the exhilaration of discovery and the thrilling prospect of celebrity.

It had been over four years since Ernst von Biron had entrusted Steller with a copy of written orders to be transmitted directly to Captain-Commander Vitus Bering. Steller had finally delivered those orders to Bering in person. In Okhotsk – nearly two years later.

He recalled their first meeting vividly.

Bering had torn open the sealed orders and scanned them briefly before tossing them aside with what appeared to Steller to be a gesture of contempt. Steller could only assume – rightly, as it transpired – that Bering had already received a copy of the selfsame orders from another source.

'I thank you, Herr Steller.'

'I am privileged to be of service, Captain-Commander.'

Steller turned to leave but Bering spoke again.

'May I ask what brings you to this desolate corner of the Empire?'

'Curiosity, Captain-Commander. Scientific curiosity, to be more precise.'

'I understand. You are attached to the scientific contingent which has just arrived from St Petersburg?'

'I am.'

'And you are – well, *what* are you, precisely?'

'If you mean what discipline I espouse, Captain-Commander, then I would reply that I am proficient in the discipline of taxonomy.'

'And what, pray, is taxonomy?'

'It is most commonly defined, sir, as the scientific classification of living and extinct organisms.'

'Extinct organisms? You mean fossils?'

'The study of fossils is an important part of it, yes.'

'And otherwise?'

'Otherwise?'

Bering gestured with his hands.

'Forgive me, Herr Steller. I am not a man of science and perhaps I express myself badly. But I would be interested to learn of the practical uses of your field of endeavour.'

Steller hesitated, uncertain whether Bering was being sarcastic, was genuinely interested or merely feigning interest out of a natural desire to be polite.

'My discipline is of considerable practical application. Of that I can assure you.'

'In what respect, precisely?'

'The subject is a complex one, Captain-Commander.'

Bering's eyes narrowed.

'I have admitted, Herr Steller, that I am not a man of science. You must not take that to imply that I am incapable of understanding concepts. Lest you forget, I am also versed in a number of disciplines myself, not least in astronomy – a branch of the *exact* sciences which, to you, may seem of no practical import but which is an essential and invaluable component of my profession.'

'I did not wish to give offence, Captain-Commander.'

'Then none is taken. Please continue.'

Georg Wilhelm Steller then took a decision which was to shape the rest of his life. He sensed that this hulking figure sitting across from him was no man's fool. And he decided he must on no account treat him as one.

'As you will know, the study of living organisms is as old as time, but the discipline of taxonomy is more recent. In a nutshell, taxonomy is a branch of biology which seeks to advance our knowledge of the world around us by systematically identifying and classifying the most divergent groups of organisms in terms of their relationship one to the other. These groups are known as *TAXA – TAXON* in the singular form – which comes from the Greek *TAXIS*, which . . .'

'. . . which means order or arrangement,' Bering interjected. 'Or so I seem to recall.'

'That is correct,' said Steller, contriving to keep the surprise out of his voice.

'Go on.'

'The fundamental unit in taxonomy is the species. To determine how different *taxa* relate one to another, of course, it is essential to explore the distribution of measurable features or characteristics and to determine what is peculiar to each species and what marks one species off from the next.'

Steller paused at this point. He looked at Bering, wondering whether the Captain-Commander wished him to continue.

'Go on,' said Bering. 'This is most illuminating.'

This time, Steller detected no hint of sarcasm.

'Defining and sorting *taxa* is difficult, as you will understand, and much of what we in the field do is conjectural. It follows that, for practical purposes, we must assimilate as much data as possible. And that means amassing and analysing new species, typically by collecting evidence of new plant forms and living organisms.'

'This is the practical use of which you speak?'

'It is.'

'Then permit me to remark, sir, that I understand the term "practical" in another sense entirely.'

'I do not follow.'

'Come, come, Herr Steller, surely you must follow. You say that in the exercise of your chosen profession you collect evidence of new plant forms and living organisms. That is indeed practical and I concede the point. But I say to you that your practicality is circumscribed, restricted as it is to furthering the development of the discipline of taxonomy *per se* rather than yielding practical benefits which lie outwith that discipline. You work, sir, within a closed circle. I say this merely as an outside observer and imply no criticism.'

Steller's mouth hung open. Bering was right. This tired-looking mariner with deeply-etched worry lines and a skin like reindeer hide was right. Bering had identified him for what he was, a full-blown academic whose vision was limited to and, worse, limited *by* his own narrow field of study.

Steller struggled to find a reply.

'The field is extremely broad, Captain-Commander. It could not be broader. It encompasses all living things, past and present.'

'Quite so. Your field is broad but your vision is narrow.'

'I submit, sir, there are many practical implications. In your sense of the term.'

'And those might be?'

'By careful study of the species we collect we can acquire new insights into botany, into agriculture, into medicine.'

'Aha,' said Bering. 'Now that is what I would call practical. And, may I inquire, have *you* acquired those insights?'

'I am a graduate of the University of Halle, with distinctions in botany and in medicine.'

Bering stood up abruptly, as if recalling that he was late for an appointment.

'This has been a particularly revealing discussion, Herr Steller. And for that, I thank you.'

Bering held out his hand. Steller shook it.

The meeting was over.

Three days later, Steller received word that the Captain-Commander wished to see him. He hurried over to Bering's quarters and was admitted immediately.

'Herr Steller, I have formally requested your detachment to the *St Peter*. It is my belief that this secondment may prove of considerable utility to us both.'

This was precisely what Steller had hoped for.

'It would be an honour to serve in whatever capacity you feel me to be adequate, Captain-Commander. But I must inform you that my superiors in St Petersburg authorise me only to conduct my researches within the bounds of the Siberian Peninsula.'

'My dear young taxonomist, allow me to remind you that we are in the process of redrawing the map of Siberia. And to inform you that my request carries some authority. You should not be troubled on that account. It will take months, even years, for my request to be approved or denied. I repeat, you need have no fears on that score.'

'Then, Captain-Commander, I am yours to command.'

'Excellent, Herr Steller. You will not regret this and my hope is that neither shall I. It is also my fervent hope that you shall have ample opportunity aboard the *St Peter* to study at first hand a living organism that is shortly to become a fossil. I refer, of course, to myself.'

Bering smiled and Steller warmed to him.

'I am confident, Captain-Commander Bering, that we both have much to learn from each other.'

Aboard the St Peter
June 30, 1741

Sven Waxell had witnessed Fleetmaster Valery Khitrov's vodka-induced indiscretions at first hand and on a number of occasions. Waxell held the *St Peter*'s helmsman in no great regard but chose to remain civil at all times.

Today was the exception.

To a degree, Waxell understood Khitrov's black mood. The search for Gama Land had cost valuable time and had been an exercise in futility, compounded by the disappearance of the *St Paul*.

Day after day, Khitrov had helmed the *St Peter* to and fro between latitudes 46 and 50 degrees north as lookouts scanned the horizon in every direction for a sign of their sister vessel or any vestige of land.

'A word, First Officer?'

'I am listening, Fleetmaster Khitrov.'

'Has the Captain-Commander taken leave of his senses?'

'Have a care, Fleetmaster Khitrov. I caution you to choose your words with prudence.'

'Then, First Officer, permit me to say – in all prudence – that I regret the Captain-Commander's long absences from the deck. The men are fearful and I with them.'

'Your duty, sir, is to helm this vessel and to respect the chain of command.'

Waxell was seething. He was aware that his promotion to First Officer of the *St Peter* had provoked resentment. The men had been dismayed at the departure of Martin Spanberg, for whom they had unswerving respect and affection. It was no easy task for Waxell to fill Spanberg's shoes.

'I intend no disrespect, First Officer. And I know full well where my duty lies. But the Captain-Commander – '

' – the Captain-Commander has much on his mind, Fleetmaster Khitrov. More than you can know. I counsel you to say no more on this. That is an order.'

Waxell turned away.

But Khitrov was right.

Waxell was aware that the crew were surly. The loss of the *St Paul* had been a body blow and morale had never been at a lower ebb. Bering had appeared on deck only twice since the *St Paul* had disappeared. Once, to instruct his First Officer to hold course and, a second time, to order that *St Peter* bear due north. On both occasions, Bering had been distant and – much as it grieved Waxell to think this – even listless.

It was obvious to Waxell that Bering was in pain. The Captain-Commander had lost his usual aura of authority. He walked slowly now, his broad shoulders drooping and his body bent almost double as he clutched the rail in front of him with both hands.

'You are unwell, Captain-Commander?' Waxell had suggested. Only once.

'I am as well, First Officer, as I have need to be.'

Waxell had spoken with the ship's surgeon, who had diagnosed fatigue. Christ, thought Waxell, fatigue? What kind of diagnosis was that? We are all exhausted, that much is evident. But the surgeon, whose expertise was essentially limited to sawing off the occasional gangrenous limb, had been adamant. The Captain-Commander had all the symptoms of fatigue, he insisted. What he needed more than anything else was rest.

'The Captain-Commander is unwell, First Officer. We both know it and the men see it,' said Valery Khitrov.

'That is enough, Fleetmaster Khitrov. Stand down, sir. You are relieved.'

Waxell couldn't believe his ears. Would Khitrov never learn?

Of even more immediate concern to Waxell was that the crew were also showing what the surgeon passed off as symptoms of fatigue. Many complained of mouth ulcers and bleeding gums. Some had running sores on their hands and feet, others complained of dizziness and acute stomach cramps.

Waxell was no exception. Although he now spent eighteen hours or more on deck each day, he slept only fitfully when he finally went below. It was increasingly difficult to rouse himself from his bunk to go back on deck. His head ached, his limbs felt heavy, and his stomach churned.

Fatigue. That was it. The ship's surgeon was probably right after all.

Gulf of Finland
July 2, 1741

Osa Bering sat at the window and looked out over the Gulf.

She was deeply saddened at Martin Spanberg's departure and at the knowledge that he would not return for many months. She closed her eyes and felt his arms about her, remembering his insistent yet unexpectedly gentle lovemaking, the firmness of his body, the musky scent of him, the curve of his smile, his hair tousled on the pillow.

She was forty-four years old and she had found what she had looked for all her life. The memory of him was still strong and that was almost enough.

He would return to her, of that she was certain.

The letter lay before her, unsigned. She had written it many times in her mind, angered at her inability to express what she still felt for the man who had shared most of her adult life:

My Dear Husband:
I trust this letter finds you well and within sight of your

life's goal, which I have been privileged to share in part with you. My admiration for you knows no bounds and I am most proud and honoured to have been the wife of a man who has accorded me much decent and sincere affection.

It is not given to me to express in words the deep guilt I now feel at having traduced that essential bond between man and wife and I understand that you may not find it in your heart to forgive me. For there is now someone who stands between us and whom I hold in the highest affection. I shall not attempt to explain this, nor can I excuse it. I know only that I am more happy now than at any time in my life.

I have thought long about the consequences of this letter and the pain it will inflict upon you so far from home. I draw consolation from the knowledge that you serve perhaps a greater goal. Our life together has had its foundation in openness and honesty. I cannot bear to hurt you yet cannot bring myself to live a lie, for I know that you prize honesty and sincerity above all things.

I enclose a drawing which I hope you will cherish as a memory of what we both hold most dear. I wish you God's speed and assure you of my unreserved respect.

Osa read the letter through once again, crossing out 'traduced' and inserting 'betrayed'. She signed the letter and folded it carefully, enclosing a drawing of Benthe she had completed some days previously.

There was something else she had to do. She went into the small drawing room where Benthe sat reading. Without saying a word, she handed the folded letter to her daughter and left the room. Minutes passed. Then Benthe knocked and entered Osa's room. She crossed to her mother and embraced her.

They had been apart too long.

Aboard the St Peter
July 6, 1741

Steller had his sea legs now.

He spent most days on deck, savouring the cold wind on his face. The subtleties of seamanship continued to escape him, and he would watch in frank astonishment at how officers and crew instinctively reacted to each imperceptible shift in the prevailing winds and currents, hoisting and furling sail, scampering here and there about the tiny vessel as it beat against the elements. To him, the most remarkable thing was how the hands responded immediately and unquestioningly to each and every command. Did they ever think for themselves, he wondered, or were they content to let the officers do all their thinking for them?

The most frustrating thing of all was that they seemed to be in perpetual motion whereas he himself had nothing to do.

He might know next to nothing about the sea and the seafarer's art, he told himself, but he prided himself on being a student of human nature. And it had not been difficult to detect signs of a growing tension ever since they had lost sight of the *St Paul*.

Steller thought the officers an arrogant lot. On several occasions, he had volunteered an opinion on this or that, but whatever he said had been treated with derision or, at best, amusement. Waxell was a courteous enough fellow, it had to be said, but Khitrov was unacceptably rude to him at every turn and the junior officers simply ignored him.

He had complained to the Captain-Commander.

'I am no sailor, sir, but I am no fool.'

'Has anyone said otherwise?' asked Bering, smiling.

It was, Steller noted, one of Bering's better days. He had observed that the Captain-Commander was more often than not in severe pain. The small bottle which unmistakably held a laudanum-based mixture was never far from Bering's grasp. Today was different. The Captain-Commander had shaved and dressed in a clean white tunic. His eyes were clearer and his mood had perceptibly improved.

Steller resolved to speak his mind.

'I accept that my usefulness on board this vessel is greatly diminished, Captain-Commander, but I believe my observations should not be rejected out of hand.'

'Continue.'

'These last days there have been unmistakable signs of land.'

'Do you wish me to chastise the lookouts, Herr Steller?'

'I apportion no blame to them, sir, but to those who disregard my counsel.'

Bering chuckled.

'And the substance of your counsel would be?'

'That we are sailing close to land, no more than twenty sea miles to the east. And closer still, perhaps to the north.'

'And on what, pray, do you base this claim?'

'There is great evidence of this, Captain-Commander. The birds that circle our vessel are land birds which never venture far from shore. Gulls, terns, cormorants, harlequin ducks, puffins and guillemots. And your officers have seen the seaweed and grasses that float in the water all around us. These are species – '

'– *taxa*, I believe you are about to say?'

'Indeed. *Taxa*. Organic forms that typically grow on rocks close inshore. And there are other signs. The seals and sea otters I have observed these last few days and other aquatic species –'

'– are species which favour the sea *and* the land. I congratulate you on your powers of observation and deduction, Herr Steller. But less on your understanding of our mission. Neither I nor my officers harbour any doubt that there is land to the east or, possibly, even to the north. Our concern is not to establish where land is but to establish where it is not.'

'But if there is land –', protested Steller.

'– then we shall chance upon it in due course. And you shall have your day in the field, that I can promise you.'

Bering grimaced in pain.

'My officers enjoy my full confidence, Herr Steller,' said Bering, his tone suddenly abrupt. 'I would enjoin you to accord them the same courtesy.'

He turned and went below deck.

Steller was aware that Sven Waxell had been in earshot and had most likely heard the exchange between himself and the Captain-Commander.

'It seems you have misjudged us, Herr Steller,' said Waxell cheerfully. 'How say you now?'

'I say only that my intentions are honourable and my conclusions justified.'

'As you wish,' replied Waxell. 'But let us poor sailors continue about our business.'

Steller noticed that the First Officer's gums were bleeding badly and that an ugly rash had spread across the lower part of his face and down his neck. He recognised the signs.

Gums bleed. Teeth loosen. Joints stiffen. Bone and cartilage disintegrate. The lower extremities bloat until the skin splits and suppurates. Diarrhoea, nosebleeds and nausea set in. A general lassitude ensues as the body shuts down.

Scurvy had been the scourge of sailors and explorers since the beginning of time. By the middle of the eighteenth century, the symptoms were well established but the root causes of the disease were not fully known – some blamed lead poisoning, others the lack of personal hygiene aboard ship. Most certainly, no cure was yet in sight.

Georg Wilhelm Steller found this unacceptable. Unacceptable and illogical. The curative and restorative properties of many plants were long since beyond dispute and some plants had been shown in practice to have antiscorbutic properties.

From his reading, Steller recalled that the well-known English merchant and explorer Sir James Lancaster, who had captained the *Edward Bonaventure* under the admiralship of Sir Francis Drake in the rout of the Spanish Armada, had demonstrated almost a century and a half previously that small doses of lemon juice administered daily were effective. Lancaster had sailed to Batavia with four ships in 1601. Aboard his own *Red Dragon*, he had dispensed a daily ration of lemon juice, while the crews of the other three ships ate a normal sea diet. On the other three ships, almost half the crew had perished. Aboard the *Red Dragon*, however, there had been only a handful of cases of scurvy.

And what of Jacques Cartier, whose crew had fallen victim to

scurvy and had recovered almost to a man by drinking a concoction of cone needles and white cedar bark boiled in sugar water as
favoured by the local Eskimo population in Canada?

Steller had long since concluded that eating fresh fruit and vegetables and drinking infusions of certain plants must inevitably constitute some kind of antidote to scurvy. English and Dutch sailors in
the sixteenth century had recognised this, but the English Navy had
stopped feeding its crews fresh fruit and greens in the early seven-
teenth century – with disastrous consequences. The English had
since lost more men to the ravages of scurvy than to enemy action.

The *St Peter* carried neither fresh fruit nor vegetables, this much
Steller knew. But he had found scurvy grass, dock leaves, wild garlic
and cloudberries growing wild in Kamchatka and had collected
specimens of each. They promised to be more effective remedies
than the traditional and pointless practice of bloodletting.

He had already urged Bering and the officers of the *St Peter* to
eat and drink the plant remedies he had prepared. Predictably, they
had laughed at him.

Steller determined to follow his own regime, reasoning that
prevention should take precedence over cure.

Let them laugh, he decided.

Aboard the St Peter
July 16, 1741

The dawn breaks grey. A dark, impenetrable grey. Which gradually
lightens and takes on tinges of blue.

They watch as the dense fog slowly clears, then whips back to
reveal a wall of stark and dazzling whiteness.

The spectacular contours of Mt Elias.

The Imperial Great Northern Expedition has reached the North
American Continent.

From the East.

From Siberia.

The officers and crew of the *St Peter* crowd the deck, exhausted
but jubilant. For many, it is the climax to a gruelling eight-year
journey.

First Officer Sven Waxell hurries below deck to report.

Captain-Commander Vitus Jonassen Bering lies on his bunk in his cramped quarters, his eyes closed.

'We have done it, Captain-Commander. We have sighted land to the east. The Americas. If there *is* a Gama Land, then this is it. There is no land bridge between Russia and the Americas.'

Bering's eyes flicker open. He stares unblinking at the bulkhead. He says nothing, shows no acknowledgment of the First Officer's presence.

Waxell waits. Bering lies still.

Waxell shrugs his shoulders and leaves. Bering continues to stare at the bulkhead. There is no need to go on deck. He has lived and relived the scene in his mind's eye for nearly a quarter of a century.

He knows now.

As he has always known.

Chapter Three

AMERICA

Off Kayak Island
July 16, 1741

The officers and crew cheered long and wildly when Vitus Bering finally appeared on deck late that afternoon.

Bering, in dress uniform and seemingly in good spirits, nodded his appreciation of the crew's applause then motioned them to be silent. They crowded round, straining to hear the Captain-Commander's words.

'Gentlemen, we give thanks today that our task is at an end. We have travelled many a year together, you and I, and we have endured more than it is given to most men to endure. This is our reward. This is your reward. I thank you one and all. It has been a signal honour to have sailed with you.'

The cheers broke out again, then died away expectantly. There must be more, they felt.

Bering turned slowly away and looked out over the ship's rail towards the mainland. A massive mountain range spread out before him, extending down to jagged cliffs that fringed the shoreline. He stood silent for a moment then turned again to face the assembled hands.

'Now that we are here, gentlemen, we had best see what there is to see.'

The cheering broke out again and was sustained until Bering went below.

Georg Wilhelm Steller looked on.

He had expected more of the Captain-Commander. Much more. Especially now, at this culminating point in a life marked by hardship and self-denial. This was surely the occasion for Bering to reassert his authority, to reassume command. Now, at this moment of undiluted triumph.

Instead, Bering appeared to have abdicated hands-on leadership of the Expedition.

The man is an enigma, thought Steller, his whole life an odyssey of obsession. An obsession with discovery. An obsession with self-discovery. An obsession with a single challenge. And an obsession with the inner self, with a personal conviction more powerful and more enduring than external forces to which others – like myself, conceded Steller – all too readily capitulate.

Steller felt he had come to know the Captain-Commander as well as any man. They had quartered together these many months, huddling over a tallow candle late into the night. And, in his more lucid moments, Bering had spoken of many things – ambition, self-vindication, doubts.

His was a tale replete with contradictions.

The vast unexplored wastes of Siberia set against the clearly-defined constraints of his chosen profession. The spectacular kaleidoscope of the Expedition and the stark simplicity of his vision. The single-mindedness of a simple mariner and the small-mindedness of the establishment of the day which subordinated individual sensitivity to the cynicism of the collective.

If the Captain-Commander was a hero, concluded Steller, then he was a flawed hero, tainted by irreconcilable ambitions – to journey to the ends of the earth and to the innermost recesses of the soul. There could be no other explanation for the enigma that was Vitus Bering. A competent sailor who tolerated an incompetent navigator, a loving husband and father whose quest for self-vindication had estranged him from his wife and daughter, a born leader who failed to lead but, somehow, never failed to inspire.

Steller turned to Sven Waxell who stood beside him at the rail.

'The Captain-Commander is an enigma.'

'That may be,' answered Waxell, 'but he is *our* enigma. He has led us here and he will lead us home.'

Aboard the St Peter
July 20, 1741

Laurentij Waxell stood forward in the bow and watched as the *St Peter* tacked perilously close to shore. A light surf broke softly on a sand and shingle beach that curved elegantly to the north-west.

Laurentij was impatient for the *St Peter* to find a safe mooring, impatient to go ashore, impatient to feel land under his feet.

In this he was not alone. They had cautiously skirted the coastline for four whole days now, gazing out at the dense stands of trees extending back into the interior as far as the eye could see. The crew had grown impatient too, prepared to throw caution to the winds. They had come so far and the land beckoned. They were like seamen the world over – prepared to voyage for weeks, months, even years without great complaint, but insistent on going ashore at the first sight of land.

Laurentij was puzzled and not a little disappointed that his father had appeared so reluctant to anchor the *St Peter* at the first opportunity. He suspected, however, that the Captain-Commander had ordered his First Officer to proceed with due caution. In this he was right. The land was alien, Bering had warned, and must be treated with respect.

Laurentij called out a sounding of four fathoms as they rounded the headland and entered a sheltered bay sprinkled with tiny island outcrops of rock. The *St Peter* moved with agonising slowness under shortened sail, inching forward hesitantly and in permanent fear of breaching her hull.

Three fathoms and rocks below. Laurentij called out the sounding, peering down into the limpid waters to anticipate the contours beneath the belly of the vessel.

Two fathoms now and shelving.

Then three fathoms.

Then five.

The *St Peter* eased to a standstill and the order came to drop anchor. Laurentij looked around. As far as he could tell, the mainland lay some distance to the east, but he found it impossible to judge whether they had anchored off an island or merely off a spur of the mainland that jutted far out into the ocean.

It was of no consequence. They were here and they would soon be putting ashore.

First Officer Sven Waxell heaved a sigh of relief. He knew he had shepherded the *St Peter* through seemingly calm yet intrinsically treacherous waters. He was uncertain of their exact position and, like his son, could not say with any conviction whether they had anchored off the mainland shore.

He turned to Valery Khitrov.

'My compliments, Fleetmaster.'

'And mine,' said Vitus Bering, who had emerged on deck.

They watched as the hands scrambled to ready the longboats.

Fleetmaster Khitrov was to command the larger of the two yawls and would go ashore with a detachment of armed sailors and musketeers, together with an interpreter. The smaller boat was entrusted to First Mate Hesselberg and boatswain Jansen, whose task would be to ferry back to the *St Peter* barrels of fresh water, should any be found.

Bering was amused to see that Steller was frantic in his attempts to persuade Khitrov that he should be permitted to accompany him in the larger longboat. Khitrov appeared perfectly willing to take Steller along but could not resist poking fun at the young German.

'But, Herr Steller, who can tell what monsters lie in wait for us on shore?' asked Khitrov. 'Have a care, sir, for there are fiery dragons there and all manner of evil creatures.'

The deckhands laughed at this and Steller was furious. He rounded on the Captain-Commander, his eyes flashing indignation.

'Captain-Commander Bering, I insist you intercede. I insist that you allow me to go ashore. This is what I am trained to do. This is why I was sent here. I insist, Captain-Commander.'

Bering had every intention of sending Steller ashore with the landing party and fully appreciated that this made sound sense. But he, too, could not resist teasing the German.

'You insist, Herr Steller? In spite of all these unknown dangers? In total disregard of fiery dragons and other evil creatures?'

'This is no laughing matter, Captain-Commander. I shall not hesitate to report your behaviour at the highest levels.'

Bering pretended to be upset by this.

'At the highest levels, indeed? That is a threat I must take most seriously. Go then, Herr Steller, and may your God go with you and protect you from the perils of the land as He has protected you from the perils of the deep.'

They were all laughing now but Bering could see that Steller was not amused.

'And, lest you think I do not take this seriously, Herr Steller –,' added Bering, motioning to the ship's trumpeter who stood on the afterdeck, '– then let us part company with the pomp and circumstance that befits those such as yourself who have friends in high places.'

Steller clambered over the side. Instead of stepping into the yawl, he inadvertently climbed into the water boat. The Cossack guard assigned to protect Steller hesitated, then followed him into the smaller boat. The trumpeter placed his instrument to his lips and sounded a mock fanfare.

Bering immediately regretted his actions. He could see from Steller's flushed cheeks that the young man was embarrassed to the point of humiliation. As the small boat pulled away from the *St Peter*, Bering raised a conciliatory hand and waved. Steller looked away, his eyes fixed on the shore.

Sweet Christ, thought Bering, do these Germans *never* have a sense of humour?

Aboard the St Peter
July 1741

From the journal of Lieutenant-at-Sea Sven Waxell

July 16, 1741

Herr Steller seems to think that the Captain-Commander may have abdicated responsibility and command. I swiftly disabused him of this notion. As he is most ignorant of our ways and does not under-

stand the chain of command, he has perforce no comprehension of the duties and responsibilities that fall on the Captain-Commander's shoulders, nor yet any reasoned knowledge of how ably the Captain-Commander has discharged his duty.

Whereupon Herr Steller vouched safe that the Captain-Commander is no longer himself and that he is sick. As are we all, I replied with some tartness. And let it be at that.

July 20, 1741

On the orders of the Captain-Commander I have proceeded with due caution and diligence along the mainland coast. The wind is passing strong and we must helm carefully to avoid the rocks which stretch far out from the shore. The Captain-Commander instructs me to proceed with the utmost care to determine where best we should moor the St. Peter. I have resolved to hold position off the coast and to circumsail the islands which adjoin it.

Laurentij is at the bow and takes forward soundings most judiciously. I have complimented him on this. We tack constantly and his is a great responsibility.

The mainshore is at some distance now but we steer a wide berth of the islands that lie off it lest we run our good vessel aground. We have sailed now some four days since first sighting land and I am anxious to find a safe mooring.

This day on a northwest tack we espied a large outcrop of land, a sizeable cape let it be recorded, and this we shall round in search of a mooring beyond. The men clamour to go ashore and I have great understanding for their impatience.

We have closed on the large island and rounded what I shall henceforth call Cape St. Elias, this being the day of the saint of that name. We have come upon a large bay beyond and have moored there in readiness to put ashore the yawl. Fleetmaster Lieutenant Khitrov has helmed our vessel most skilfully and I expressly commended him for his conduct.

An incident of unaccustomed levity has relieved our day. Herr Steller, whose anxieties and insecurities are the cause of much amusement among the crew, was set ashore in the water boat to

the accompaniment of a blast on the trumpet given at the orders
of the Captain-Commander. Herr Steller was greatly discomfited
by this harmless jape, but the men laughed most heartily. Morale
is now high, although many of the crew complain of ulcers and
sickness. I am myself not unaffected by similar complaints, but I
trust my condition will benefit as we seek respite and rest onshore.

In truth, it is the German Steller who seems most healthy. I
attribute this to the simple fact that he has not suffered from the
rigours of duty with which I and my fellow officers have had to
contend.

We have great need of fresh water and I have detailed a second
boat to proceed to the shore and convey to the St. Peter as many
barrels as we can safely stow on board.

Cape St Elias
July 20, 1741

Steller's heart was in his mouth as he made his way eastwards along
the foreshore towards where he estimated the mainland to lie. He
glanced anxiously and often up the beach towards the stands of
spruce, persuaded that wild-eyed hostiles would emerge, and he
was immensely grateful for the presence of the Cossack Lepekhin,
who trudged dutifully alongside him, musket at the ready. Steller
himself was unarmed.

For all his nervousness, Steller was no coward. Even had he been,
the perceived humiliation on his departure from the *St Peter* would
have been enough to cement his resolve: he was more than ever
determined to prove his value to the Expedition. This was an opportunity he could not afford to let pass.

Steller had no notion of what he would find. Signs of habita-
tion, certainly. New flora and fauna, hopefully.

He was rewarded sooner than he anticipated.

Less than a mile along the beach they came upon a clearing
where spruce bark had recently been stripped and branches broken.
A section of tree lay on the ground, its innards hollowed out and
partially filled with stones. Shards of bone – fish bone and reindeer, he concluded, although he could not be certain about the

latter – nestled among the stones. Clam and mussel shells were scattered on the ground.

He knelt and placed his hand against the stones. They were still warm.

Next to the trunk he found a number of large shells filled with a liquid he at first took to be sea water. He dipped a finger and licked. Sweet. Fresh water perfumed by a coarse grass he had seen earlier on the Kamchatka Peninsula. A pile of the same grass stood nearby, next to it a flat strip of bleached driftwood with a hole punched in its centre. Littered nearby were what looked to be thin dry twigs but which proved on closer inspection to be sections of lichen, dried rock-hard and sharpened at one end to a charred point. This was how the fire had been lit. Friction.

Lepekhin showed little interest in Steller's investigation of the site. The Cossack's eyes scoured the trees beyond, alert to any sudden threat. He stooped, tapped Steller on the shoulder and pointed.

A path of sorts led from the clearing into and through the trees yet still broadly parallel to the shore.

Steller nodded agreement.

They walked along the path which soon petered out. A number of smaller paths trailed off into the forest. Steller hesitated. Which way? There was no telling.

For no particular reason, they elected to follow the tiny path to their right. Almost immediately, they came upon another clearing where the grass had been trampled down. In the centre of the clearing was an area where long blades of grass had been cut and laid cross-wise in the form of a rectangle.

Cautiously, Steller shifted the grass aside with his foot. Underneath were rocks laid out in a crude pattern and, beneath them, large pieces of bark arranged on top of long branches placed lengthwise over what was unmistakably a crude dwelling dug into the earth.

Steller could not believe his good fortune. He reached for his notebook and made a careful inventory of the items that lay in the underground cavern. Bowls fashioned from wood and bark held quantities of smoked fish and dried meat. Other bark receptacles stored a pungently-sweet fermented liquid. Some polished stone harpoons, bone needles and arrowheads. Nets fashioned from dried seaweed.

Conscious that he had invaded private property and that the residents would not take kindly to this, Steller quickly selected a few specimens and tried as best he could to replace the bark, rocks and the top layer of grass as he had found them.

They had been gone little more than an hour, thought Steller, and already they had stumbled on evidence of a primitive culture. He was ecstatic. He turned to Lepekhin and instructed him to hurry back to the *St Peter* with the samples he had collected.

This was only the beginning, he thought. He needed more time – and more men – to continue his exploration. He was confident that the Captain-Commander would grant him both.

The Cossack loped off.

Steller's excitement at uncovering the underground dwelling was immediately forgotten at the realisation he was alone and unprotected. His mouth was dry and his hands clammy. Should he stay where he was or should he seek the comparative safety of the beach? The latter course was preferable, he reasoned. Who knew when the inhabitants might return?

He made his way back to the shore. It would be at least a couple of hours before Lepekhin returned. It seemed pointless to spend that time sitting on some rock or other. He would press on.

He had walked some distance along the shore when he came to an *impasse*. A wall of rock loomed out of the sea and extended so far up the beach and into the trees beyond that it seemed impossible to go on. Curiosity got the better of him and, much to his own surprise, Steller decided to climb the cliff to gain a better impression of his surroundings.

Steller was by no means strong but he was fit and nimble. He climbed carefully, checking at every other step that there were footholds and handholds he could count on in order to descend without too much difficulty. Looking down at the beach below, he calculated that he had climbed well over 300 feet when the ground above him flattened out. He heaved himself up on a smooth slab of rock and got to his feet.

The island – and he could see now that this *was* an island and not, as he and others had assumed, part of the mainland – extended some miles to the east across dense forest. He scanned the scene below, looking for signs of life. A tiny plume of grey-white smoke pearled up from amidst the trees about a mile distant.

A village?

More than likely.

His first inclination was to make his way down the far side and towards the smoke. But common sense prevailed. There was no trace of a path. Even had there been, he concluded that Lepekhin would never find him if he ventured farther.

Disappointed, he made his way gingerly back down the cliff.

There was still no sign of Lepekhin and there was little else for it other than to head for the beach where he had first come ashore. He arrived without mishap and was just in time to see that the water boat was on the point of returning to the *St Peter*.

Steller waded into the surf and grabbed hold of the boat. First Mate Hesselberg and boatswain Jansen stared at him.

'You are to convey my respects to the Captain-Commander and request that I be given command of the water boat on your return, to row northwest around the point. You are to inform him that I have made some important discoveries and that I must be accorded the time and men I need to explore more thoroughly.'

'Aye-aye, sir,' said Hesselberg, suitably impressed by the urgency in Steller's voice.

Steller slumped on the beach, tired but elated. He watched as the water boat made its way to the *St Peter* where full barrels were offloaded and empty barrels taken on board the water boat for the return trip.

Steller leapt to his feet as the water boat approached the beach.

'The Captain-Commander sends his respects, Herr Steller, and orders you to return to the *St Peter* forthwith.'

Steller was aghast.

'I refuse to comply with such an order,' he spluttered.

'The Captain-Commander orders me to instruct you to return with us or remain here alone. The choice is yours.'

'Those were his *exact* words?'

'Aye, sir. His exact words.'

Aboard the St Peter
July 20, 1741

'Damn you, sir! Damn you to hell!'

Steller's fist crashed down with such vehemence that the inkpot recessed into the table top leapt from its well and crashed to the floor.

Bering looked up at Steller, taking in the contorted features and the vitriol in the German's eyes.

'And good-day to you, Herr Steller. How can I be of service?'

'Of service? Of *service*? What do you know of service? What do you know of *anything* other than the pathetic, narrow confines of this cabin?'

'I fail to take your meaning.'

'Then understand this, Captain-Commander Bering. By what authority do you dare refuse my request for men and time to conduct my scientific observations? By what authority, may I ask? You are here, sir, to lead this Expedition, but you are also here to serve it.'

Bering rose.

'By what authority, Herr Steller? Then I shall tell you. By the authority vested in me by the Empress of All the Russias and by the Supreme Grand Council of the Imperial Court of St Petersburg. And, let me remind you, by an even greater authority, the authority conferred upon me by my rank and status as Captain-Commander of this vessel.'

The two men glared at each other across the table.

'Then permit *me* to remind *you*, Captain-Commander, that I too act on the authority of the Empress as delegated by that self-same Council. I repeat, sir, that you have no right – '

Bering cut him off.

'I have every right, sir. And every intention of exercising that right.'

Suddenly, the wind seemed to go out of Steller's sails. He gestured vaguely with his hands and sat down on the edge of his bunk.

Bering was astonished to see that the German was on the verge of tears.

'Come, Herr Steller, let us talk as reasonable men.'

Steller mumbled a reply which Bering did not hear.

'I promised you your day in the field, Herr Steller, and I am a man of my word. You have had at best only a foretaste and, as God is my witness, your time *will* come. But there are other priorities, other responsibilities which I must respect.'

'Priorities? Responsibilities?' said Steller, his voice muted now. 'What priorities and responsibilities are there other than to respect your mandate?'

'Precisely. And my mandate is clear. I have supreme responsibility to my ship and to my men. As to the specifics of your own mission, I will say only this. The *St Peter* sails on the morning tide to track the mainland coast as far as weather and ice permit. Thereafter, we shall make sail for Kamchatka —'

Steller made to protest, but Bering raised a warning hand, cutting him off.

'— we shall make sail for Kamchatka and overwinter there, returning next spring to complete our task. What is more, we shall squander no more time in the search for Gama Land and other such nonsense, but shall sail from Petropavlovsk directly east and north. You shall have ample opportunity then to continue your work. In which, I hasten to reassure you, this Expedition takes great pride.'

Mollified, Steller looked up. He forced a smile.

'I know you as a man of your word, Captain-Commander. I shall take you at your word and I shall hold you to it.'

'Then let us say no more on this.'

'If you permit me, sir, I have one more thing to say.'

Bering nodded.

'Continue.'

'From what little I have seen and learnt today, I predict with certainty that the seas will narrow to the north. The evidence is there. Siberia and America were once joined, sir, and now lie only a few miles apart. The evidence is all around. God knows — and I grant you this, Captain-Commander – that I am unversed in the ways of the sea and unskilled in the arts of navigation. Yet, I say to you, these two continents are separated now only by a narrow stretch of water. You will find your Northeast Passage, Captain-Commander. And, when you do, I shall count it an honour to be at your side.'

'The honour, Herr Steller, will be mine.'

The two men stood. Bering extended a hand and Steller took it. They looked at each other for a time, then Steller turned and left.

Steller was not to know that this had been the last coherent conversation he would ever have with the Captain-Commander of the *St Peter*.

Aboard the St Peter
Latitude 56° North, southwest of Cape St Elias
August 10, 1741
The squat spider dipped its pairs of legs into the black ink and scurried this way and that across the virgin parchment, tracing an increasingly erratic pattern that finally smudged and merged into a single blot. It paused at last, its beady eyes fixed on some invisible prey, its sensory bristles quivering, its lethal forward appendages poised to crush and kill.

An open hand swept down, crushing cephalo-thorax and abdomen, pulping the arachnid's innards and spreading a scarlet mush flecked with white across the chart.

'Drink this, father,' said Laurentij Waxell, reaching a calloused hand behind the First Officer's head and pulling him gently up into a sitting position.

The infusion was sweet and strong and Sven Waxell drank it down at one gulp. He was awake now. There was no spider.

Waxell shook his head to clear it. Pain shot through him as he swung his legs over the side of the bunk and stood up. He spoke through swollen lips and gums.

'How long have I slept?'

'Not long,' answered Laurentij.

Waxell looked at his son, deeply ashamed of that quick surge of jealous rage that the weak often experience in the presence of the strong. Laurentij's features were wind-burnt and drawn, but his eyes were blue and clear and his touch decisive and oddly reassuring.

Waxell braced himself with both hands against the table. He looked down at the neat charts so painstakingly drawn by distant mapmakers. Useless. Worse than useless. And, as the Captain-Commander had so often counselled, they were dangerous. They showed land where there was none and no land where land should be.

The spider had gone, but its spindly tracks were etched on the parchment.

On Bering's orders, Waxell had steered the *St Peter* to the west, hugging the mainland coast and looking always to edge northwards. But the prevailing winds and the tentacular promontories reaching far out into the ocean drove the vessel inexorably to the southwest.

Waxell had long since abandoned any hope of charting a course to the north and west and holding to it. That was where the Northeast Passage must lie, but they could find no way through to the sea which fed into the Bering Strait. Their days and nights were dictated by the vagaries of the wind and the unpredictable contours of the land. The weather had been tolerably good, but intermittent storms proved a major hazard. Out of seemingly nowhere an island would loom out of the driving rain ahead of the *St Peter*, forcing them to change tack abruptly and seek the safety of the open sea. Steering between these islands and the mainland beyond was not an option. Who could guess what dangers lurked close below the surface?

How far to the south they would be forced to voyage before they could finally round the islands offshore of the American mainland and set a firm course for Kamchatka and the safe haven of Petropavlosk was a matter of conjecture.

A vessel under sail is a helpless hostage to the elements, thought Waxell, staring ruefully at the loops and meanders on his chart. Here, he saw, they had steered east to travel west; there, they had tacked briefly north to progress south. Only yesterday, they had tracked back along their previous course to extricate themselves from a web of islands from which no other safe exit could be found.

The crew were cold, hungry, weary, ill and afraid, but they stuck to their tasks. He was proud of them. Yet there were times when Waxell imagined they cast sidelong glances at their First Officer. Never more so, than when the *St Peter* was forced to put about once again and steer back towards a landmark they had passed only a day or so previously. That these furtive glances signalled their anxiety at his own visibly deteriorating health never crossed Waxell's mind. They were anxious and afraid, that much he could tell. He failed to understand that what fuelled their anxiety more than anything else was the prospect of day-to-day command of the *St Peter* passing to someone they had long since ceased to trust.

Valery Khitrov.

Waxell could articulate no specific complaint against the Fleetmaster Lieutenant, but the hours spent at Khitrov's shoulder weighed heavily. The Russian responded promptly to every order, but his arrogance and overbearing self-assurance were undiminished.

Waxell fingered the sketch Khitrov had made of Cape St Elias. It was typical of the man. Neatly and authoritatively drawn, with bold and decisive spokes radiating out from the island hub towards the mainland, where Khitrov had studiously shaded the contours of steep mountains falling sharply to the foreshore.

Neat, authoritative, bold, decisive. Drawn and signed with a flourish. All show and little substance. The College of Cartographers in St Petersburg would no doubt approve.

Waxell made his way aft to Bering's cabin. He knocked and waited. There was no sound from the other side of the door.

Waxell pushed the door open cautiously and peered round it. Bering lay waxen on his bunk, snoring lightly. Steller sat at the table, writing. The German raised a finger to his lips, motioning Waxell to be quiet.

Waxell closed the door gently and climbed the steep steps to the afterdeck. Assistant Navigator Khotenshev was at the helm. The seas were moderate and the sky clear. Shading his eyes against the sun, First Officer Waxell looked towards the mainland, seeking out a safe anchorage.

It was time to go ashore again in search of fresh water.

Aboard the St Paul
Latitude 54° 14' North
August 10, 1741
Since that day in late June when he had finally given up hope of sighting the *St Peter* ever again, Aleksey Chirikov had held course due east for some seventeen days before veering northeast on a favourable southwester that drove the *St Paul* swiftly towards the Americas, to a point a full ten degrees of longitude beyond Bering's landfall at Cape St Elias.

The *St Paul* had approached the Alaskan mainland in mid-July and had promptly turned west by northwest along the irregular ribbon of archipelago whose criss-cross of deep but treacherously narrow channels shielded the mainland. His new heading had taken him within a hundred miles of Kayak Island, crossing Bering's outward route no more than a week after the crew of the *St Peter* had sighted Mt Elias. Chirikov had no way of knowing that he would bisect the *St Peter's* subsequent heading on at least three further occasions as he voyaged south in open seas before turning sharply east again – any day now, he told himself – on course for Petropavlovsk.

Chirikov turned to Fleetmaster Dementiev and asked the question they had asked each other repeatedly over the past weeks.

'I wonder where Bering is?'

'Like as not, he'll be at the bottom of the sea by now.'

Chirikov thought otherwise. But where Vitus Bering was and what had happened to him was no longer Chirikov's concern.

Aleksey Chirikov and the *St Paul* were going home.

Aboard the St Peter
August 28, 1741
Steller sat at the tiny writing table, attempting to impose some semblance of order on his notes and observations.

He looked over at the bunk where Bering slept. Some time before dawn, Bering had taken a massive dose of laudanum. He would lie in this cataleptic state for several hours at least. The Captain-Commander lay so quietly these days that Steller felt obliged to check periodically whether he was still breathing.

Steller could scarcely contain his frustration at the injustice of it all. He deeply resented that the Imperial Great Northern Expedition had taken the better part of ten *years* to come this far, whereas he had been allotted a meagre ten *hours* to explore this new continent. Worse, he had not set foot on mainland America but had to be content with having seen the merest fraction of some island or other which lay immediately offshore.

Despite a firm assurance from Bering that they would return to the Americas the following spring, Steller felt cheated.

The notes he had taken and the crude sketches he had made seemed an altogether too meagre return when one considered the hardships and humiliations he had endured, not to mention the time and effort he had expended in order to secure accreditation to the Expedition in the first place.

Stashed in the cargo bay – safely, he hoped – were the specimens he had gathered on Cape St Elias, together with some inconsequential odds and ends that Valery Khitrov had seen fit to bring back with him that day on the yawl.

All in all, it didn't add up to much. True, he had a cache of plant specimens stored under lock and key at a fellow scientist's quarters back in Petropavlovsk, but those items had been gathered along the way from St Petersburg to Kamchatka. For my contribution to the Expedition to be *meaningful*, thought Steller, I must collect evidence from beyond Siberia itself. From the Americas.

He thumbed through his notes and sighed. Much of what he had confided to his journal was general rather than specific. All he had to show for his trouble was intelligent extrapolation rather than hard fact. He had *speculated* on differences which appeared to exist between the climate in Siberia and that of the Americas. He had *surmised* that climatic conditions in Siberia and in the Americas greatly influenced the type and distribution of plant life. He had *assumed* that plants came into bloom earlier here than at comparable latitudes in Siberia. And he had *conjectured* that new species of animals and birds populated the American mainland.

His growing conviction that Russia and the Americas had once, a very long time ago, been connected by a land bridge was, perhaps, the wildest speculation of all. So much so, that he hesitated to commit this outrageous theory to paper, fearful that the scientific community would hold him up to ridicule.

Steller's Pietist background and scientific training had conditioned him to observe, record, collate and compare before jumping to any premature conclusions. He was nothing if not honest, and he despised those facile permutations of fact and fantasy, of reality and myth, from which even the most celebrated ethnographers of the age – including, sadly, the illustrious Conrad Gessner – had not been immune.

Speculation.

Extrapolation.

Guesswork.

He set down his quill. He crumpled the sheet he had been working on into a tight ball and hurled it across the cabin in disgust.

Steller felt precious little inclination to go on deck these days. For one thing, each time he went topside, some wag or other would inevitably imitate a trumpet and blow a short fanfare. Steller hated that, hated being reminded he was *persona non grata* and a figure of fun. What he hated even more, however, was the sight of land lying so tantalisingly close yet so exasperatingly out of reach. It was all too plain that the officers and crew of the *St Peter* had only one thing on their minds – to head for home. That he could understand, but he could not forgive their unremitting indifference to this mysterious land they had travelled so far to discover.

He looked up as Waxell entered.

'Herr Steller,' whispered Waxell, glancing over at Bering as if any noise could conceivably disturb the Captain-Commander.

'First Officer?'

'You should be informed that we are heading north by northeast towards land.'

Steller was immediately alert.

'Does that mean –?'

'Yes, Herr Steller. We shall be putting boats ashore some time tomorrow morning. I thought you should know. That is, if you wish to accompany us.'

'Most definitely. Thank you for your consideration, First Officer.'

Waxell made to leave but paused in the doorway, glancing across at Bering.

'The Captain-Commander is well?'

'The Captain-Commander has been in some pain and requires sleep. Do you wish me to wake him?'

Waxell hesitated.

'No. That will not be necessary.'

'May I presume to inquire, First Officer, what has occasioned this change of heart?'

'It is quite simple, Herr Steller. We must take on water.'

'I see. Well, I must say, that *is* welcome news. So the Expedition will not be returning empty-handed after all. Although I would suggest that we have travelled an inordinate distance simply to fetch water from the Americas.'

Steller immediately regretted the remark. The First Officer was doing his best in extremely adverse circumstances. To his relief, Waxell appeared in no way offended.

'Water is water, Herr Steller.'

Steller smiled.

'If only that were true, First Officer.'

The Bay of Islands
August 30, 1741

The longboats left the *St Peter* early that morning, with Valery Khitrov in charge of the yawl and Steller relegated to his now familiar position in the water boat.

Steller watched as the yawl preceded them to the beach. Valery Khitrov jumped off as the boat crunched through the shingle. He waded the last few steps to the shore. Steller knew what was coming next. He had witnessed the Fleetmaster's histrionics once before, on their arrival at Kayak Island.

'I claim this land in the name of the Empress of All the Russias and the Motherland,' shouted Khitrov.

Word perfect, thought Steller.

The water boat eased against the beach and Steller climbed out, Lepekhin by his side. There were twenty or so empty barrels to be filled and Steller knew he had ample time to explore the island, one of perhaps a dozen or so that ringed the pleasantly sheltered bay.

He had mixed feelings on that score. Steller had felt all along that, if the water barrels had all been properly filled before the *St Peter* had so hurriedly left Cape St Elias, then this frantic search for fresh water would now be totally unnecessary. On the other hand, he was honest enough to admit that, if fresh water supplies had not started to run low, there would have been no need to put ashore – and this opportunity to continue his research would have been lost.

Their first priority was to locate a spring and Steller was delighted when, after walking no more than a hundred paces from the beach, he came across a small stream. He traced its source to a spring nearby and tasted the water. It was fresh and deliciously cool. He hurried back to the beach to inform the others of his discovery, confident that they would be pleased. And impressed by his resourcefulness.

When he reached the shore again, he could scarcely believe his eyes. One of the three barrels they had transported in the water boat had already been filled and the men were in the process of filling a second from a stagnant pool of water that had gathered at the top end of the narrow beach.

'Stop!' shouted Steller.

They did.

Khitrov, who was squatting on a large chunk of driftwood and supervising operations, immediately stood up.

'There is a problem, Herr Steller?'

'Yes, Fleetmaster Khitrov, there is a problem. What on earth do you think you're doing?'

'I should have thought that obvious,' said Khitrov, grinning broadly. 'We are taking water from this pool *here*,' he said, pointing to the brackish water in the pool, 'and we are putting it in that barrel *there* so that we can carry it to that little boat *over there* and take it to –'

'You are a fool, sir,' said Steller, cutting him short.

Khitrov scowled. The men around him fell silent, watching.

'What *is* obvious,' continued Steller, 'is that you don't know what you are doing. This water is foul and tainted with seawater. It is unhealthy. It is unsafe. Have your men come with me. I have located a freshwater spring no more than two hundred paces from where we stand.'

In his anxiety to prevent the crew loading the contaminated water, Steller had spoken without thinking. He knew immediately that this challenge to Khitrov's authority would not go unanswered.

Khitrov turned to the men.

'Carry on, lads, and pay no heed to this delicate flower who calls himself a *scientist*.'

The men laughed and set to filling the second barrel.

Steller was beside himself with rage.

'You pigheaded idiot! What you are doing is as dangerous as it is unnecessary. Have the men come with me this instant. We need *fresh* water, why can't you understand that? Fresh water, not this tainted muck.'

The men hesitated. Steller's outburst was persuasive. Their hesitation angered Khitrov. He stepped closer to Steller, so close that the young German could smell the stench of cheap vodka and stale chewing tobacco on his breath.

'No man calls me an idiot,' snarled Khitrov. 'But then, Herr Steller, you're not much of a man, are you?'

Steller took a pace backwards. One of the men behind him imitated the sound of a trumpet.

Ta-ra, ta-ra.

'I seek no quarrel with you, Lieutenant.'

'Then, sir, you are best advised to curb your tongue. Be off with you, Mr Scientist, and go about your own business.'

Khitrov bent down, cupped a hand, and scooped up a mouthful of water.

'A trace of salt, no more. Excellent for cooking with.'

The men laughed again.

Ta-ra, ta-ra.

Steller shook his head and turned dejectedly away. There was nothing more he could do. He had best be about his own business. He called out to Lepekhin and they set off across the island.

The water incident was soon forgotten. They were on one of the larger islands in the group – if not the largest – and Steller felt that, on balance, things might even have changed for the better.

Of animal life there was little trace other than the occasional Arctic fox, but the moss and lichen-covered sandstone and slate rocks played host to a great variety of sea birds which perched on outcrops or circled overhead: gulls, guillemots, cormorants, auks and puffins. Save for the occasional scrawny shrub, however, the island seemed virtually barren. Steller attributed this to the island's exposure to strong winds which gusted from northeast and southwest across the rocky surface, stripping it of fertile topsoil.

From his research on the Kamchatka Peninsula, Steller was nevertheless able to identify several antiscorbutic plant and grass varieties lodged in crevices between the rocks. He picked as many of these as he could carry back to the *St Peter*. It was growing more evident every day that these plants and grasses would prove invaluable.

Steller improvised a crude shelter – no more than a strip of canvas secured by several loose rocks – and resolved to spend the night on the island. As the wind freshened and the sun dropped lower on the horizon, however, he thought better of it and returned to the shore.

Steller approached the officers immediately on his return to the *St Peter* and again tried to persuade them that the water Khitrov had taken on board was unsanitary. Waxell seemed open to persuasion but the others merely laughed.

Bering slept.

The Bay of Islands
August 31, 1741

They went ashore again early that morning. Steller was relieved to note – but was careful not to comment on the fact – that the First Officer had ordered two of the full water barrels brought on board the previous day to be emptied and transported back to the island to take on water from the spring Steller had found. Valery Khitrov was charged with this mission and accepted it with his customary poor grace. All this extra work was because of that lily-livered German scientist, he said, loudly enough for Steller to hear.

The day started badly.

Able-bodied seaman Yevgeny Shumagin was a thickset individual with a shock of red hair. He was extremely popular with the crew because of his cheery disposition and his liking for practical jokes.

Shumagin and another of the hands jumped out of the yawl to pull it up the beach. Shumagin doubled over and fell forward on his face. The others in the yawl laughed. Shumagin was up to his tricks again. Steller looked on from the water boat as Valery Khitrov aimed a playful kick at Shumagin's backside.

'Get up, you clown. We have work to do.'

Shumagin did not move. Khitrov looked for a moment as if he was about to kick Shumagin a second time, but the seaman groaned and rolled over on his back, his face purple and his eyes bulging.

Steller sprang from the water boat and waded as quickly as he could up the beach to where Shumagin lay.

The man had swallowed his tongue. Steller forced the jaw open and reached into Shumagin's mouth, desperately trying to pull the tongue forward.

Too late. Shumagin convulsed and died.

They stood around helplessly, looking at the body. Shumagin's gums were so raw and ulcerated that only the tips of his loosened teeth were visible. Sores covered his upper chest. Steller took a clasp knife and slit open the seaman's breeches, feeling for the knee joints. They were swollen to twice their normal size, the skin around them distended and almost translucent.

'What's wrong with him?' asked Khitrov. He watched as Steller reached up and drew a hand over Shumagin's face, closing his eyes.

Steller looked up.

'Wrong with him, Fleetmaster? Why, there's nothing wrong with him. Now. He is dead. He has passed on. As many others will do if you do not follow my advice.'

It was a sad moment but Steller had difficulty in suppressing a smile as he watched the expression on Khitrov's face swiftly change from wild-eyed incomprehension to animal-like self-preservation.

'Unload the water boat and return immediately to the *St Peter* for the barrels we loaded yesterday,' rapped out Khitrov. 'Bring all of them to shore and refill them at Herr Steller's orders. And prepare a burial detail.'

It was too much to expect Fleetmaster Khitrov to apologise. But Steller felt vindicated. And that was probably enough.

They buried Shumagin with great difficulty, wedging the body into a hollow between two boulders, shovelling sand on top and covering the mound with heavy rocks. Someone fashioned a crude driftwood cross and Steller said a short prayer.

Valery Khitrov looked on. His pride and his authority had been seriously dented. It now looked as if there was some truth in what the lily-livered German scientist had predicted. In an effort to reassert himself, Khitrov had the final word.

'From this day, this island shall be known as Shumagin Island in memory of our dear departed able seaman colleague and friend.'

The others nodded and crossed themselves one more time.

Khitrov led his party along the beach to the spring Steller had found the day before. They started filling the barrels as the water boat made its way back towards the *St Peter*.

Steller's appetite for further exploration had gone. There were others sick on board the *St Peter* and he knew that his place was by their side. Perhaps they would all listen to him now.

The water boat returned more than an hour later with four more empty barrels.

'It blows a storm out in the bay,' reported First Mate Hesselberg, 'and the *St Peter* strains at anchor. You'd best be returning next time with us, Herr Steller.'

Steller was surprised. Here, on the lee of the island, the air was almost still and the sun was distinctly warm on his face. He looked out into the bay and saw that, as the First Mate had said, the sea was choppy.

The short crossing back to the *St Peter* reminded Steller of his first taste of the sea aboard the *Konstantin* on the voyage from Kiel to St Petersburg. The wind had come up with a vengeance, driving spray over the prow. The small boat rose and dipped alarmingly, making little headway. From the stern, Steller watched the muscles on boatswain Jansen's broad back and thick forearms strain and knot as he struggled with the oars. Steller gagged and threw up violently. He inched forward towards the boatswain and grasped one of the oars. Jansen grunted a reply that was lost in the wind. He moved to one side, leaving Steller room to sit abreast of him on the cramped wooden spar. Together, they heaved on the oars as the water boat gradually edged closer to the waiting *St Peter*.

At long last, George Wilhelm Steller felt he belonged with the Imperial Great Northern Expedition.

Shumagin Island
September 3, 1741
Valery Khitrov huddled closer to the fire and prayed that the wind would drop. In his heart, he knew he should have braved the short crossing to the *St Peter* three long days and nights ago. Instead, he had insisted that each barrel be filled to the brim with fresh water. The storm had caught him off guard.

They crouched under a rock overhang, eleven of them in all besides himself. Their faces were pinched and haggard and they were hungry. They had eaten only some berries they knew for certain to be safe. Some had chewed on dried seaweed, a poor substitute for tobacco. Others, their teeth slack and their gums suppurating, could eat nothing.

They were afraid.

Afraid not of the elements but of what the Captain-Commander might do. The unspoken thought in every mind was that Bering – or First Officer Waxell, who now seemed in command – would think them lost and weigh anchor for the onward journey home, leaving them to rot here on this God-forsaken stretch of rock.

Khitrov saw that most of the men were ill. Two could hardly stand, let alone walk. Another moaned incessantly and was on the point of death. Those who could walk stumbled along the beach, dragging stumps of driftwood back along the shore to keep the fire piled high.

The fire was sporadically visible from where Waxell stood on the deck of the *St Peter*. Thank God, thought Waxell, Khitrov and his party – or at least some of them – were still alive. He had decided to wait out the storm which, mercifully, had now veered to blow from the northwest, so that the vessel was partly sheltered by a large island to the north.

The mood on board was ugly. Steller had reported Shumagin's death and the men were saddened and angry. Their anger was directed primarily at Fleetmaster Khitrov, who seemed to have a knack for getting things wrong. With a wind such as this behind them, they could have travelled many miles to the east on the home-ward leg. Instead, they stood exhausted and dispirited on the deck, craning their necks for any sign of Khitrov and the others.

Waxell had reported their situation to the Captain-Commander but, inevitably, Bering was comatose. Each time he emerged from Bering's cabin the men would look at him expectantly. What were the Captain-Commander's intentions? Were there new orders? Were they going home? And, each time, First Officer Waxell maintained the fiction that he had spoken with Bering. The Captain-Commander's intentions were to wait for Khitrov, he announced. There were no further orders. But, yes, they would be going home. Soon.

Late that afternoon the wind dropped sufficiently for a long-boat to be launched. First Mate Hesselberg helmed the craft to the shore and sent men ahead to find Khitrov. They returned within the hour, with eight men walking slowly behind them and a further two carried on makeshift litters. Second Mate Iushinov had died during the night. The men climbed wearily into the longboat and Hesselberg gave the order to make for the *St Peter*.

In their haste to leave the island, the yawl was left behind.

Together with seventeen barrels of fresh water.

Aboard the St Peter
September 1741

From the journal of Lieutenant-at-Sea Sven Waxell

September 4, 1741

The conduct of Fleetmaster Lieutenant Khitrov again gives cause for concern. I reproach less his poor judgment on remaining onshore when clearly ordered to return, and more his dereliction of duty in leaving the yawl and the water barrels ashore.

In his haste to save his own skin, Fleetmaster Khitrov has made our position untenable. I sail now in command of a surly and ailing crew, with the warning words of Herr Steller ringing in my ears. Now that Khitrov and the remains of his party have been secured aboard, I have ordered – for surely this must be the Captain-Commander's intention – that the St. Peter make all speed for Petropavlovsk. We shall sail to latitude 53 degrees north then turn east on a bearing for Kamchatka.

In faith, I lose all patience with Fleetmaster Khitrov and his careless ways. Upon weighing anchor to sail southeast out of the Bay of Islands, the Fleetmaster brashly took the sounding lead from Laurentij's hand and promptly let it fall to the ocean floor.

My impatience with him knows no bounds.

The Captain-Commander still lies below and only I and Herr Steller know that he has relinquished effective command. I have counselled the men to be of good cheer for we are sailing homewards, but they view each change of course with great suspicion.

As we emerged from the shelter of the bay we drove straight into a heavy wind from the west and, seeing no alternative, I have given the order to helm about and wait for a favourable wind. I have noted this in the ship's log and have stated my reasons plain for all to read.

God knows, I wish this venture were at an end and that I am soon absolved of the unwelcome responsibilities that have been thrust upon me. I draw consolation only from the continuing good health and spirits of my son, who seems largely unaffected by the illness that has befallen us.

Chapter Four

AMERICANS

Off Shumagin Island
September 4, 1741

The Aleuts watched from behind the rocks as the big black beast with the gull-grey wings slowly left the bay and moved into the open seas beyond. They watched as the beast came back again and settled on the water, waiting.

What creatures were these that came from the belly of the black beast? Were they men, these pale-faced beings with long hair? Or were they gods? If they were men, then where had they come from? Were they pelt-seekers who came each year from the far side of the big waters? And, if they were gods, what did they want?

The council of elders met and decided. They would go to these creatures and they would bring gifts.

Able Seaman Stronsky saw them first and sounded the alarm.

The crew of the *St Peter* stood at the rail and counted the canoes as they rounded the headland. There were at least thirty, most but not all with two men aboard. They paddled slowly but steadily towards the *St Peter*. As they came closer, the hands saw there were three men in the lead canoe – two seated and clutching squared-off double wooden paddles and a third, who stood upright in the curved prow.

First Officer Waxell ordered musketeers to stand to but to conceal their weapons. He sent Laurentij below to alert Steller.

To his surprise, Steller and Bering came on deck together.

The Captain-Commander was unsteady on his legs but seemed to have composed himself for this rare appearance topside. His shoulder-length hair was brushed and carefully parted and his face, although deathly pale, was clean shaven.

'We have guests, Captain-Commander.'

Bering simply nodded. He turned to look at Steller as if seeking confirmation that the scene before him was real.

'They come in peace and carry no arms,' said Steller. To no-one in particular.

'Then we shall greet them accordingly,' said Waxell, ordering the crew to be silent and to make no gesture that might be misconstrued. He called for the Koryak interpreter, whose professed knowledge of various Siberian tongues had often been put to the test and invariably found wanting.

Steller thrust himself between Waxell and Bering, taking in the scene and attempting to commit to memory as much detail as possible. This was finally the moment when West met East or, he reminded himself with a wry smile, when East met West. It depended on one's point of view.

The lead canoe was almost abreast of them. The others held a respectful distance.

The ramrod figure in the lead canoe was chanting now, alternating a high-pitched nasal whine with low, guttural sounds that were little more than grunts. He punctuated this salutation with a series of gestures, raising his head to the heavens then lowering his eyes as if in submission. His left arm extended to its full length, palm open, then his elbow crooked, bringing the open hand back across his chest to rest on his heart. The gesture was repeated several times. The incantation continued.

'Interpreter?' said Waxell.

The interpreter watched and listened intently. He shrugged his shoulders.

'Herr Steller?' said Waxell, clearly irritated by the Koryak's incompetence and seeming indifference.

Steller could not be certain, but he thought he identified a pattern to the strange sounds coming from the lead canoe. The gestures were matched time after time by the same syllables intoned with growing urgency.

'It is an incantation,' said Steller. 'A ritualistic incantation. I cannot say for certain whether we are being welcomed or threatened.'

'For Christ's sake, man, which?'

Steller watched as the figure in the lead canoe suddenly stopped chanting and flung both arms out wide. The silence was total. The lead figure – a chieftain probably, or a shaman – snatched up a long stick with feathers attached to it. He shook the stick and, immediately, the other canoes started forward again, paddling towards the *St Peter*.

The crew tensed. Steller hissed a warning as the musketeers fingered their weapons.

'Wait!'

As the canoes drew closer, Steller saw that they differed greatly from the kayaks used by the Chukchis on the Siberian Peninsula. These craft had split bows and wide sterns and were made of wooden slats covered in seal pelt and cunningly jointed bone that flexed and undulated with the swell.

The figure in the prow of the lead canoe was surprisingly short, little more than five feet tall. His shoulders were immensely broad and powerful, his legs stumpy and bowed. He wore a tunic of animal hide and a headdress decorated with what appeared to be eagle feathers. His face was daubed bright ochre and deep red. A thin tapered animal bone pierced his nostrils.

Steller called out first in Russian, then in German, there being no reason to suppose that the figure would understand either language. The response was immediate. The chief raised his feather-tipped staff and threw it towards the *St Peter*. It landed well short of the vessel and floated this way and that on the water.

Was this a gesture of submission? An act of defiance? Of aggression? Or merely a traditional welcome? Steller had no way of knowing.

From his tunic, he took a piece of mirror and held it to the sun, flexing his wrist so that the rays reflected on the water and, with some adjustment, on the canoe and its occupants. They were startled by this but seemed impressed rather than afraid.

Steller hurled the mirror towards the canoe. Predictably, his aim was off. The mirror fell short, but one of the seated figures at once dived from the canoe into the freezing water. He disappeared below

the surface for a full half minute, then reappeared, clutching the
shard of mirror in his hand and waving it triumphantly.

The lead figure was chanting again, repeating a short phrase
over and over. Steller turned to the interpreter.

'You have *no* knowledge of this language?'

'None, sir.'

'Then can you at least imitate the phrase he chants?'

The interpreter thought for a second or two, then nodded.
Stepping forward, he raised his arms in salutation and chanted along
with the figure in the canoe.

Ah-LOO-shin-ah. Ah-LOO-shin-ah.

They chanted in unison as the canoe drew even closer. The figure
in the prow broke off suddenly and reached down to his feet. He
picked up what looked like a bundle of feathers attached to a long
pole. He thrust the pole towards the *St Peter.* The men on deck
recoiled.

'Take it!' commanded Waxell.

One of the crew leant out from the side and retrieved the offering.
A large bird of some sort, an eagle perhaps, or a Siberian falcon.
A bird of prey certainly, judging by its cruelly-hooked beak and
talons.

The figure in the canoe stooped again and picked up another
pole. He held out a magnificent shimmering-black sea otter pelt.
Then another pole, and another pelt.

'We must reciprocate,' whispered Steller, stripping off his thin
shirt and handing it to the crewman. Steller stood shivering, his
pale body bristling with goose flesh as the crewman tied the shirt
to the end of the pole and motioned for it to be withdrawn. The
figure retrieved the shirt and held it aloft. It flapped in the breeze.
He seemed uncertain what to do next.

'*Ah-LOO-shin-ah*,' intoned the interpreter, anxious to demonstrate his value to the proceedings.

The figure raised the eagle-staff high above his head and waved
it slowly from side to side.

'*Ah-LOO-shin-ah*,' shouted the occupants of the other boats.
'*Ah-LOO-shin-ah*.'

The canoes turned and made for the shore. All except the lead canoe. The figure motioned with his staff and pointed first to the *St Peter*, then to the shore. Once. Twice. A third time. The gesture was unmistakable.

'They welcome us. He wishes us to go ashore,' said Steller.

As if to confirm this, the lone figure stooped over the prow and scooped up a handful of seawater which he brought to his lips but was careful not to drink. He stooped again and repeated the movement. He shook his right hand as if to dry it, then motioned to his mouth and rubbed his ample stomach in a circular motion.

Food.

Food and drink.

'They wish to prepare a feast for us,' concluded Steller.

'They wish to make a feast of us more like,' put in Valery Khitrov.

Waxell turned to Bering.

'What are your orders, Captain-Commander?'

'I believe they mean us no harm,' said Bering. 'But the decision is yours, First Officer.'

With that, Bering went below.

Steller was insistent that they put ashore. Khitrov was adamant they should not. Waxell was in two minds. The crew were indifferent: they had enjoyed the spectacle but saw no good reason to waste any more precious time.

Waxell reluctantly decided that ten men, he, Steller and the interpreter included, should launch the longboat and head for the shore. The men were armed with muskets and sabres concealed under strips of sailcloth. They carried an assortment of trinkets, some dried biscuits and – although Steller had strongly advised against this – three small kegs of vodka and one of brandy.

They followed the lead canoe with difficulty. It seemed to glide effortlessly across the water, whereas the longboat pitched and tossed and made heavy going of it. Inshore, the sea was unexpectedly rough and it was only with great difficulty that boatswain Jansen contrived to bring the craft ashore.

The chieftain – as they now surmised the figure in the lead canoe to be – was waiting patiently for them on the beach.

'*Ah-LOO-shin-ah*,' said the Koryak interpreter tentatively. The chief looked at him blankly, then motioned Waxell's party to follow him along the beach.

They made their way to the headland and rounded it. Beyond was a fast-flowing river and a path which led along the near bank into the hinterland. Thin scrub and moss and lichen-coated rocks lay to their right. They were relieved to see ahead of them only some windswept shrubs and the very occasional tree. No dense undergrowth or forest that might conceal an attacker.

They had walked little more than half a mile along the river bank when they came to a sharp bend in the river. The path was dangerously close to the river's edge now and they had to watch their footing. Beyond the bend was a large clearing ringed by sharpened driftwood poles lashed together with seaweed and grasses.

Waxell swallowed nervously as he led his party through a narrow entrance that opened out into a broad expanse of compacted sand and river silt. On every side were crude but substantial huts fashioned from wooden saplings driven into the ground, bound at their apex, and covered by a patchwork of hide, skin and bark carefully stitched together to form taut, dome-shaped dwellings.

The womenfolk watched unsmiling as Waxell and the others moved through the compound to the largest dwelling. In front of it stood two stout poles from which several skulls were suspended.

'I don't like the look of this,' muttered Jansen, voicing what they all felt.

The chief sat on a ground covering of overlapping hides. Waxell and his men squatted cautiously, their weapons close at hand. Wide-eyed children peered out at them.

The chief moved his hand almost imperceptibly and several young girls appeared, each holding a bark bowl of fruit and berries or a bark tray piled high with a coarse dough bread scorched at the edges. Behind them came two young men carrying between them a sturdy pole from which the carcass of a young deer had been slung.

The food was placed on the hide mats in front of them. Two gourds were brought. The chief drank first from one then from the other, before handing the first to Waxell and the second to Steller. They drank hesitatingly but were pleased to find that the liquid was no more than a strong and bitter concentrate of fermented fruit juice. They sipped and passed the gourd along to the men beside them.

The chief pulled a bone knife from inside his tunic and sliced a generous portion of meat from the carcass, spearing it with the point of the knife and biting a chunk from one end. He chewed thoughtfully, then smiled, passing the meat to Waxell. Waxell bit off a piece and nodded to the chief. The meat was remarkably tender and tasted not unlike the salted beef he had enjoyed as a child.

'Good,' he said, smiling at the chief and patting his belly.

The others followed suit. The young girls who had brought the food were crouching behind them now, their dark eyes fixed on these strange visitors. They were dressed similarly to their menfolk and wore almost no ornaments. Their skin was a deep olive accentuated by the dark areolas of pubescent breasts.

Steller ate little and drank sparingly. He was relieved to see that Waxell was doing likewise, although he continued to pat his belly from time to time and mutter ingratiating words of appreciation.

This was going nowhere, Steller concluded.

'It is time to offer gifts, First Officer.'

Waxell turned to the man beside him who had already reacted to Steller's suggestion and was loosening the cord which fastened the muslin bundle they had brought with them. With studied care, Waxell brought out the trinkets they had assembled. Beads. Mirrors. A seaman's knife. A sailmaker's awl. Some yards of silk cloth.

The chief bent forward, taking each item in hand as it was presented for his inspection and approval. He seemed pleased. He took the awl in his right hand and stabbed it into a slice of the coarse bread. One or two of the crew laughed at this but a dark look from Waxell discouraged them.

The chief stood up and Waxell got to his feet also. The chief weighed the awl in his left hand and clasped his own bone knife in his right. He looked long and hard at both implements, then presented the bone knife to Waxell.

'*Ah-LOO-shin-ah.*'

'*Ah-LOO-shin-ah,*' echoed Waxell self-consciously, knowing full well that the phrase obviously meant something other than 'thank you', but at a loss for some more accurate way of showing his gratitude at the exchange.

The chief sat down again and clapped his hands.

From behind the hut came four men carrying a square wooden frame which they rested against the two upright poles decorated with skulls. Spreadeagled naked across the frame, his hands and feet bound to each corner, was a tall, dark-skinned man whose features, to Steller's utter amazement, were of a decidedly negroid cast. The man's eyes rolled in his head and he was trembling violently.

The chief rose slowly to his feet again and eyed his captive, who was whimpering now. Waxell and Steller exchanged glances. Imperceptibly, Waxell shook his head. Do nothing, his look said.

Waxell and his party were in no doubt that they were about to witness a ceremonial sacrifice. They also suspected that it had been arranged for their entertainment and edification.

The chief took the awl in his right hand and started to make tiny pricks and cuts in the man's upper body. Droplets of blood oozed from the incisions and trickled down the negro's chest, gathering into rivulets of blood and sweat. The chief's attention moved to the man's upper thighs, where he continued to jab the awl with studied concentration, as if decorating an animal hide.

The man moaned continuously, screaming only occasionally as the awl probed deeper than perhaps intended. The chief was behind him now, moving the awl across his shoulders, then down his back. He stabbed fiercely into the buttocks and was rewarded with another bout of screaming.

Steller looked at the young girls. They sat motionless, their tongues flicking out from time to time to moisten parched lips. Suddenly, as if by a pre-arranged signal, one of them stood up, reached for the gourd of fruit juice, and walked over to the frame. She lifted the gourd high above her head and poured the liquid

slowly over the man's head and shoulders. His scream of pain intensified as the acid juice flowed down over and into the myriad cuts
that covered his body.

Out of the corner of his eye, Waxell saw a hand stretch slowly
towards the sailcloth where the muskets lay concealed.

'Belay that,' he snapped, conscious that the whole tribe had
come out of their huts to witness this degrading spectacle. Upwards
of sixty men now stood in a semi-circle behind his party, grunting
their approval at each new thrust of the awl.

The chief was working on the head now, carefully probing and
stabbing with the awl around the victim's hair line. With a sudden
jerk of his hand, he yanked the tight black curls backwards. There
was a tearing noise like a sail shearing in the wind as the hair came
away. And, with it, most of the scalp.

The figure on the wooden frame was still. He had fainted.

They threw water on him until he came round. Then the chief
started again.

He was holding a thin-bladed bone knife which had been honed
razor-sharp. He applied the knife to the victim's right ear, then
brought his hand down quickly, slicing the ear off close to the skull.
The chief stood back, admiring his handiwork. As if disappointed
at the lack of symmetry that had resulted, he repeated the process,
this time with the left ear.

Steller felt the man next to him try to rise in long overdue protest.
Swiftly, he clamped his hand over the man's leg and forced him
back into a squatting position. Someone in Waxell's command had
vomited. The stench was overpowering and Steller felt bile flooding
his own mouth.

The chief had not finished. Cupping the victim's flaccid and fear-
shrunken genitalia in his right hand, he slowly excised one testicle,
then the other. The men standing behind Steller roared their appreciation, laughing and pointing at the folds of skin that hung loose
like a turkey's gizzard. With a final flourish, the chief grasped the
penis and sliced it through cleanly at its root, throwing the member
casually over his shoulder in the direction of the onlookers. One
of the young girls caught it and squealed in delight.

It was still not over.

The chief swept his hand across and down the man's belly and upper abdomen, splitting the skin as neatly as one might slice an apple. The innards tumbled out, trailing on the ground.

Waxell had seen more than enough. He reached into the roll of sailcloth behind him and drew out his pistol. Stepping smartly up to the wooden frame, he cocked his piece, pressed the barrel against the negro's temple, and pulled the trigger. The mutilated body convulsed. The man died instantly.

The crowd shrank back, one or two of them flinging themselves face down on the ground. Waxell's men scrambled for their weapons.

'Single volley! Fire!' yelled Waxell and a flurry of shots rang out. The crowd dispersed immediately. As the men quickly reloaded, Waxell stepped forward and rammed his empty pistol hard under the chieftain's chin. Steller had snatched up a sabre.

'Kill him! Kill the bastard now!' shouted Waxell.

He is a human being, thought Steller. An ignorant savage but a human being with an immortal soul. Thou shalt not kill, he thought, as he plunged his sabre deep into the chief's chest.

They ran back along the river bank, rounding the spit of land that separated the estuary from the beach where they had come ashore. The longboat was still there. Undamaged.

They pushed the craft through the shallow surf and climbed aboard, looking anxiously back towards the beach. A group of savages had rounded the headland and were closing on them. Waxell called out to those with muskets.

'Above their heads. Now!'

They fired. The men on the beach stopped in their tracks and watched as the longboat rowed out to the *St Peter* and the gods with firesticks mounted the big black beast with the gull-grey wings.

Aboard the St Peter
September 5, 1741
The *St Peter* lay at anchor in the bay at the mercy of the tides and prevailing winds.

Those who had been ashore with Waxell had brought back lurid tales of their experiences. Their accounts, inevitably exaggerated and embellished, had sent a ripple of fear through the remainder of the crew. The night watch had been doubled and the hands were visibly relieved when the sky finally lightened towards mid-morning with no further sign of the hostiles.

Sven Waxell was as relieved as the next man. The Captain-Commander had shown little interest in their short expedition on land. Waxell offered him only a truncated report, conscious that Bering seemed concerned only to ascertain whether any hands had been lost.

'The men are our most precious resource, First Officer, and we must tend to their welfare. The sole duty that remains to us now is to bring them safely to port. Make all speed for Kamchatka. Winter is setting in and the days are shorter.'

Waxell was impressed. It had been many weeks since he had heard the Captain-Commander speak at any length or articulate his thoughts so clearly. There was a lightness in Waxell's step as he went topside. The Captain-Commander was almost his old self again. The eyes were clearer, the hands no longer trembling. Waxell found Steller hunched at the afterdeck rail. He eyed the German with new-found respect.

'The Captain-Commander seems much restored, Herr Steller. I can only conclude your ministrations have been to great effect.'

'The Captain-Commander is far from well, First Officer. But the scurvy has retreated and, for that, we must give thanks. My ministrations, as you call them, have helped, but I would remind you we are all in the hands of a higher power.'

Waxell saw that Steller was in no mood for talk. He thought he understood why.

'My compliments, Herr Steller. You acquitted yourself most admirably yesterday.'

Steller looked up. His eyes had sunk deep in his head and there were dark rings around them. The stubble grew patchily on his cheeks.

'Taking a human life constitutes no grounds for admiration, First Officer. I am deeply ashamed of what I have done.'

'Your shame is mitigated by the service rendered to us all.'

'I rendered no service to myself, First Officer, nor to my own conscience.'

'Forgive me, Herr Steller, but you have led a most sheltered life that ill prepares you for a voyage such as this. The sea is not your element.'

'In that you are right, First Officer. The sea is not my element and I care little for it. But you should understand that, for me, the sea is merely a means to an end. My utility lies elsewhere. And my mission is to understand and advance the world we live in, not destroy it. I neither seek nor take credit for what transpired.'

'Then hear this, Herr Steller. You have earned my respect and that of the men at my command.'

'If that is so, I have earned it at great cost to myself.'

Waxell turned away. He had given credit where credit was due. If Steller chose to wallow in self-pity, then that was his affair. Waxell had no time for self-righteous soul-searching. The *St Peter* was rigged for departure and Waxell would not be sorry to leave.

It was Laurentij who saw them first. He shouted a warning as the canoes – half a dozen at most – appeared in single file out of the grey sea mist. Waxell brought the musketeers to readiness as the canoes paddled towards the *St Peter*. The lookouts craned their necks, straining to see if other canoes were heading in their direction. They reported that, for the moment, there were none.

The six canoes seemed to pose no great threat, thought Waxell. A dozen or so hostiles armed only with crude lances were no match for men armed with muskets and sabres. He glanced at Steller, who had seen them also.

'What say you, Herr Steller? Are you game for a battle at sea?'

Steller did not reply. His gaze was fixed on the approaching canoes and the men in them. He saw that their faces were again daubed in red and ochre paint. Most wore colourful headdresses of feathers and grass. What fascinated him most, however, was that one or two hostiles wore hats apparently fashioned from tree bark. He had seen similar hats before – in the northern Kamchatka Peninsula – and this was further confirmation of his supposition that these natives and those of the Siberian coast were of the same stock.

The canoes had taken up station to the lee of the *St Peter*. The occupants were waving to the crew. They seemed friendly enough. One of the crew took off his serge sea cap and waved it above his head. He put it on again, then took it off, then put it back on once more. The occupants of the canoes quickly caught his drift. First one, then another took off his own bark hat and waved. Laurentij Waxell seized the initiative. He grabbed a boathook and tethered his own cap to it, then held it at arm's length over the side. The lead canoe came closer and the man in front reached up to retrieve Laurentij's gift, solemnly exchanging it for his own hat, which he carefully attached to the boathook. Laurentij immediately set the feathered bark on his head, much to the crew's merriment. The native in the canoe did likewise with Laurentij's cap. His companions shouted their delighted approval.

Sven Waxell turned to Steller, who was sketching furiously.

'And what say you *now*, Herr Steller? It seems they bear us no grudge after all. Perhaps they are even grateful to you for ridding them of their chief?'

'That does not absolve me of my guilt, First Officer.'

But, in some strange way, it did.

Petropavlovsk
October 14, 1741

The *St Paul* anchored in the bay just before noon. A longboat ferried Aleksey Chirikov to the wooden pier. The dock was deserted. No-one was there to greet him. All things considered, Chirikov preferred it that way.

'What news of the *St Peter*?' was the first question he asked of the garrison commander later that day.

'None.'

Chirikov nodded. The news was unwelcome but did not distress him greatly.

After all, he thought to himself, the *St Peter* is in capable hands and there is no cause for concern.

* * *

Aboard the St Peter
October 1741

From the journal of Lieutenant-at-Sea Sven Waxell

October 10, 1741

The elements conspire against us since leaving the waters off the American coast. Most days, the St Peter beats against unforgiving headwinds and violent storms. Yet on days of clear weather our vessel is becalmed, with next to no wind to fill her sails.

I confer each day with Khitrov and the junior officers, yet confess I am in two minds whether to hold course for Kamchatka or make sail back towards the Americas to sit out the winter. It has been advocated that we bear due south to seek more clement weather and the safety of the Kurile Islands. I do not favour this.

October 18, 1741

After a day of calm and a weak sun, the wind has veered to blow strongly from the northeast. We make better progress, albeit under shortened sail.

My resolve is final: we shall endeavour to reach Awatska Bay before the onset of winter. Accordingly, I have instructed that we tack to 52 degrees north, then hold as steady a westerly course as the Almighty in His wisdom shall grant us.

My great concern is for the men, for many are no longer up to their tasks. All are weak and most are sick, complaining incessantly of ulcerating sores and a heaviness of the limbs. I am myself no stranger to these maladies and confess I am assailed by a general lassitude which, I pray, will not be adverse to my judgment.

I report daily to the Captain-Commander and seek his counsel. He acknowledges each report but gives little by way of advice, being himself most unwell. Herr Steller informs me that the Captain-Commander is weakened by the scurvy and needs rest if he is to survive. God help us, we all need rest.

October 20, 1741

It is my sad duty to record that Guard Corporal Kishlev died last night and that two others of the ship's complement are at death's door. Our would-be surgeon professes no remedy for the general condition of the crew. I have no respect for the sawbones and lean increasingly on the advice and counsel of Herr Steller, who is himself weary yet in extraordinary good health.

The winds change by the hour and we are at their mercy. There is little water left – no more than a dozen barrels at the last count – and much of that tainted. I have ordered drinking water to be secured under lock and key and apportioned only at the discretion of First Mate Hesselberg.

The air is bitter cold now and the fogs plague us. More than once Fleetmaster Khitrov has helmed us close to islands which threaten to tear the bottom out of the St Peter. He deserves no reproach on this account for he helms without charts.

Laurentij is well and vigilant.

October 27, 1741

We have been driven northwest on strong winds and lie by the best reckoning at most 100 sea miles east of Awatska Bay. We shall continue some two degrees to the north to gain the Kamchatka coast, then follow the coastline back southwest until we reach port.

The men are exhausted and two more of their number have passed on. Yet they are spurred by the certainty that, God willing, we shall soon be at our destination.

Chapter Five

LANDFALL

Commander Islands
November 5, 1741

Seaweed drifted by the hull and sea birds screeched a welcome.

The sea shelved to sixty fathoms, then fifty-five, then fifty. The *St Peter* crept forward in the half-light of morning. Those among the crew who could still stand and walk carried their sick shipmates topside.

They could smell the land.

The sky gradually lightened and the day broke fresh and clear. A gangrenous winter sun cast long shadows across the deck. The crew raised a weak cheer as the grey silhouette of land appeared on the distant horizon to the northwest.

First Officer Sven Waxell thumped Fleetmaster Khitrov resoundingly on the back, rivalries and personal animosities for the moment forgotten.

'Take her in, Fleetmaster,' said Waxell.

As the contours of the land became clearer, the crew gleefully pointed to familiar landmarks: here, the distant tip of a peninsula, there, a towering headland and the bold indent of a bay.

Kamchatka.

Waxell ignored Khitrov's smugly premature boast that he had helmed the *St Peter* successfully to her final destination. The First Officer was delighted they were within sight of land – and, by extension, of civilisation – but he was nobody's fool. By his reckoning, the *St Peter* was at least a full two degrees north of Awatska Bay. No matter, he was confident they could now bear southwest in sight of the coast until they reached Petropavlovsk. And, if need be, they could put ashore at any point along the way.

The worst is over, thought Waxell.

Once the general euphoria had died down, Waxell drew Valery Khitrov to one side.

'We lie a full two degrees north of Awatska, Fleetmaster Khitrov.'

Khitrov would have none of it

'If that isn't Awatska Bay, I'll eat my hat – and yours too,' he retorted.

Waxell did not answer. He had already resolved to bring the *St Peter* as close inshore as he could. Once their real position was confirmed, he would take great pleasure in watching Khitrov eat both his words *and* his hat.

Neither had reckoned on the storm that gathered behind them with such sudden fury, driving the *St Peter* towards the land. The wind was on them without warning, tearing at mains and topsails before a weakened crew could furl them. Within minutes, the shrouds were in tatters and the mainmast denuded. The storm abated as suddenly as it had struck, leaving the *St Peter* floundering in a placid sea.

They took stock of the situation. The vessel was now close enough to shore for them to see that this was not Awatska Bay. The familiar landmarks they had been so eager to identify were the product of wishful thinking.

'It makes no odds,' pronounced Khitrov, his hat firmly on his head. 'The mainland is close. We should anchor in that small bay up ahead to effect repairs and take on fresh water.'

Waxell marvelled at Khitrov's ability to gloss over his short-comings both as a navigator and as a man. But Khitrov was probably right, he thought. We need water and there is nothing for it but to repair the shrouds. He went below to inform Bering of his decision.

The Captain-Commander roused himself with obvious difficulty and splashed cold water on his face.

'How many water barrels are still full, First Officer?'

'At the last count, no more than six, Captain-Commander.'

'And how many men are indisposed?'

'About half the ship's complement, sir.'

'Awatska lies how far to the east by your reckoning?'

'Ninety miles, sir.'

'Then my counsel would be to proceed to Awatska without further delay.'

'We are without mainsail, Captain-Commander.'

'That is of little consequence now we are so close. We can reef in and sail short, can we not?'

'That is possible.'

'You have sought my counsel, First Officer, and I have given it.'

'Aye-aye, sir.'

It did not escape Waxell that Bering had given counsel rather than a direct order. To ignore a direct order would constitute a serious breach of discipline which carried the severest of penalties. Disregarding the Captain-Commander's opinion, on the other hand, would merely be discourteous.

Sven Waxell had taken a decision and saw little justification to revoke it. The circumstances were far from normal, he told himself, and there was little doubt in his own mind that Bering was so distanced from the facts that his judgment could be deemed questionable.

Waxell gave the order to anchor the *St Peter* at nine fathoms and to put a boat ashore. He reasoned that the damage to the vessel might prove impossible to repair, in which event he would send runners to the nearest settlement on the Kamchatka Peninsula to secure transport for the crew.

The plan was sound but destined to fail.

The inshore surf whipped up without warning, sending the *St Peter* into a spin. Angry waves dashed the vessel, which broke free of its mooring and careened headlong towards the outer reef. Fresh anchor ropes were dropped but found no purchase. At the helm, an ashen Khitrov fought to check the *St Peter* as she plunged towards the reef. A petrified crew watched as the vessel was swept across the rocks, banging and scraping her keel on the rocks below.

They knew they were going to die.

Once across the outer reef, however, the *St Peter* slewed to a standstill in calm water. The immediate danger was past. Some of the men fell to their knees and crossed themselves. Others, too ill to do even that, simply wept.

Waxell knew at once that there was no going back. That they had crossed the reef without ripping the insides out of the *St Peter* was nothing short of a miracle. From his vantage point on the afterdeck he could see the waters heaving and churning beyond the reef, breaking on the rocks and sending great spirals of spray high into the late afternoon sky.

'Shit,' said Khitrov.

Steller emerged from below. He had long since decided that his life lay in the hands of a Greater Power. When danger threatened at sea, his usual practice was to stay below, close his eyes, grit his teeth, and hope for the best.

'What has happened?' he asked.

'We are inside the reef,' said Waxell.

'I can see that, First Officer,' said Steller, looking back towards the open sea. 'But how do we get out to sea again?'

'Am I to understand you take no pleasure in the prospect of *terra firma*, Herr Steller?'

'On the contrary. Yet I would be pleased to learn *which* land lies before us.'

'The mainland, Herr Steller. Kamchatka,' replied Waxell, with distinctly more confidence than he felt.

Steller could tell by the position of the late afternoon sun that the land before them ran roughly northwest by southeast. The Kamchatka Peninsula ran almost directly northeast by southwest. He was about to point this out to the First Officer but thought better of it.

He assumed the same thought must have occurred to Waxell.

Commander Islands
November 7, 1741

The *St Peter* lay securely at anchor in the calm waters of the lagoon, but neither its officers nor crew doubted that the next squall could rip the vessel from its moorings and dash it against the inshore rocks. Frantic preparations to go ashore were made.

Scurvy had ravaged the vessel's complement. Several hands had already died and been accorded summary burial at sea. Other dead were to be brought ashore and consigned to a shallow grave.

Steller had plied the Captain-Commander with infusions of antiscorbutic plants which temporarily staved off the worst symptoms of scurvy, but Bering had since sedated himself to the point of coma to dull the stabbing pains that tore at his abdomen. First Officer Waxell who, for some inexplicable reason, had repeatedly declined Steller's ministrations, was now seriously ill, as were his two junior officers. Even Valery Khitrov, who had always appeared to have the constitution of an ox, had been forced to take to his bunk to relieve the pain in his bloated joints that had been aggravated by many hours at the helm. More than half of the remainder of the crew had been struck down and were unable to perform even the lightest of tasks.

Steller concluded that the chain of command was effectively inverted the moment they went ashore. He drew no satisfaction from this. On the contrary, he felt a nagging sense of guilt at the instinct for self-preservation that had sustained him throughout the voyage. This irrational guilt was compounded by the fact that he had insisted that the two companions on whom he most depended – his Cossack bodyguard Lepekhin and the surveyor Plenister – had followed his prescriptions. Both had lost weight and complained of fatigue, but both were in radiant health by comparison with the rest of the crew.

Steller was at a loss to explain why Laurentij Waxell remained so robust. The youngster had also lost weight, but he continued to do the work of two men. Steller resolved that, time permitting, he would establish why the First Officer's son was not afflicted to the same degree as the others.

Time was a vital resource which Steller knew he could not afford to squander on idle speculation. At the first opportunity, he went ashore with Lepekhin and Plenister to test the lie of the land. Waxell, despite his condition, accompanied them. Steller saw that the First Officer was in no shape to reconnoitre the terrain but understood Waxell's reluctance to relinquish effective command. A skeleton crew remained on board the *St Peter*, together with Bering and Khitrov.

Optimism had never been Steller's strongest suit, but several hours spent exploring the foreshore and the land immediately beyond convinced him that their situation was by no means as hopeless as it might at first have seemed. He scribbled feverishly in his notebook, recording an abundance of birds and animals, among the latter seals, sea otters and white foxes. Vegetation was sparse, but Steller identified a number of useful plants that he had previously seen on the Kamchatka Peninsula, including watercress nasturtiums and blue and white-flowered speedwell which he knew would combine to a nutritious salad.

There was a decided lightness in Steller's step as he returned to the foreshore where they had left Waxell. He had brought back a wealth of information and a handful of plants and grasses. He was embarrassed to find the results of his foraging yielded little more than a canister of herbal tea. Plenister, in the meantime, had adopted a distinctly more pragmatic approach. He had shot several brace of ptarmigan and instructed a couple of Cossacks to kill and skin a seal. Lepekhin had also been busy and had erected a crude tent to shelter them against the long night.

Waxell had rested most of the day and was in better spirits. He roused himself on Steller's return and seemed in rare good humour.

'What cheer, then, Mr Scientist?'

'I have discovered much that will sustain us, First Officer. The men can rest here until their strength returns. There is food, there is water, and there are natural medicines.'

Waxell tore a strip of seal meat from the primitive spit and sucked on it, his grotesquely swollen gums unable to cope with the rubbery flesh.

'Then, by God sir, we shall be on our way again before the week is out.'

'God willing, First Officer. And if the weather holds.'

Aboard the St Peter
November 11, 1741
The wind freshened from the east and blew fiercely across the lagoon, rocking the *St Peter* at her berth and sending flurries of

snow across her bows. The shortened foresail flapped loudly in a
strengthening wind and the few men left on board looked at each
other nervously, comforting themselves that the vessel was tightly
secured by no fewer than five anchor lines.

Almost everyone was ashore now, including the Captain-
Commander who had been carried there on the broad shoulders
of Laurentij Waxell. Steller and Plenister had found a small cove
further along the foreshore which afforded a degree of natural shelter
from the wind and snow. The Captain-Commander had been made
as comfortable as possible under a strip of sailcloth suspended from
driftwood branches. He had said nothing since leaving the *St Peter*
and Steller was concerned.

Bering sat in a half-upright position, his eyes closed. From time
to time, he grimaced as the pain came again, lancing through his
abdomen. Towards late afternoon, however, Steller was able to ease
him into a sitting position and persuade him to drink some speedwell tea sweetened with the last of the honey.

The wind was blowing more strongly now and the snow was
drifting into shallow banks that clung to the rocks behind them.

Out in the bay, the first anchor line snapped.

Then another.

Sven Waxell had spent the day shuttling between the shore and
the *St Peter*, retrieving such supplies as were needed to weather the
approaching storm. With each delivery to the shore, he reported to
Bering. The Captain-Commander said nothing, but merely nodded
to confirm that he had understood and, Waxell could only assume,
approved.

A third anchor line snapped with a deafening crack and Bering's
eyes opened wide.

'First Officer!' he croaked.

As luck would have it, Waxell was on the point of embarking
in the longboat for a final crossing that day to the *St Peter*. Waxell
whirled round, astonished to hear the familiar voice of command
for the first time in many days.

'Sir?'

'Beach her!'

Waxell crouched down, his ear close to Bering's cracked lips.

'Beach her, I say!' whispered Bering. 'Beach her *now*!'

Waxell returned to the longboat and gave the command to row once more out into the bay. Each crossing had proved more hazardous than the last and this time was no exception. The men heaved at the oars, fighting the foaming surf and the heavy swell. They came abreast of the *St Peter* as the fourth anchor line gave way, sending the vessel into an uncontrollable spin.

'Beach her, Fleetmaster!' shouted Waxell above the growl of the sea which churned white around the hull. The deafening wind threw his words back at him. He waved both arms and pointed repeatedly towards the shore.

'Beach her!'

The forward lookout cupped his hand to his ear, straining to understand the command.

The fifth and final anchor cable frayed and separated. The *St Peter* broke loose.

At the helm above, Valery Khitrov felt the vessel surge forward. He spun the wheel this way and that, edging the vessel momentarily away from the rocks, then losing all purchase as the *St Peter* slewed round and drove shorewards.

In the longboat, Waxell heaved a sigh of relief. Khitrov had understood the order and was helming the *St Peter* directly towards the shore. There was nothing more for Waxell to do. He ordered the longboat to come about and return to land.

Khitrov had heard nothing.

God only knew what Waxell had shouted. Khitrov had lost every vestige of control. He was powerless to bring the *St Peter* to bear on the safer shingle shore to starboard. The vessel reacted erratically to each spin of the helm, responding at first, then obeying the whim of the sea. Khitrov's arms and shoulders screamed in agony as he clung desperately to the wheel, fighting each yard of the way.

The *St Peter* broke to port again. Out of the corner of his eye, Khitrov saw two of the hands leap the rail and plunge into the sea. They were swept away and disappeared from sight. The vessel had spun to starboard once again and Khitrov felt a rush of elation as the shore drew closer. He had no thought now as to what Waxell might or might not have shouted. His only concern was to exercise the only option left to him: run the *St Peter* up on the beach.

The helm was wrenched from his grasp as the vessel veered sharply to port once more and impacted on the rocks. The unmistakable sound of timbers splintering reached his ears as the *St Peter* heeled over. The sea rushed in over the bows as the mainmast snapped and crashed through the deck of the disembowelled vessel.

Khitrov was back at the helm, spinning it one way and another, searching in vain for a response. The *St Peter* was pinioned at the bows and at the mercy of the sea that pounded against her stern. Khitrov watched in horror as the vessel seemed to lurch further to port. He saw its deck planks bend and snap like the wishbone of a chicken.

The *St Peter*'s back was broken and Khitrov knew there was no saving her now. He looked towards the rocks, gauging the distance and steeling himself to jump to safety.

He was too late. The afterdeck tilted towards the sea and a wall of water crashed in over him. He felt himself carried high above the water then dashed down into the pounding surf. He could hear himself screaming as his body was tossed towards the jagged rocks.

And then there was nothing.

Waxell watched, helpless, from the comparative safety of the longboat. He had silently applauded Khitrov's efforts to follow his order to beach the *St Peter*. The Fleetmaster had done everything that could be reasonably expected of him and more.

The *St Peter* held a minute more on the surface, her timbers fractured and her masts gone, then she slipped below into the mercifully shallow water. Tears streaked Waxell's face as she broke up and sank.

She had served them well and now she was no more. There was no telling how many hands had been lost with her. But Waxell knew that an arrogant but ultimately brave man had perished in a vain bid to save her.

The longboat drew up on the beach and Waxell walked slowly along the shore to break the news to the Captain-Commander.

Commander Islands
November 1741

From the journal of Lieutenant-at-Sea Sven Waxell

November 11, 1741

The sad state of my health and the rigours of command have caused me to neglect this journal and I chastise myself for my failure to record more faithfully the many events that have transpired since we left the coast of the Americas. I break silence only to record the tragic demise of Fleetmaster Lieutenant Sophron Valery Khitrov whose courage and dedication to duty command my every respect.

It is true that Fleetmaster Khitrov failed in his brave attempt to helm the St Peter to safety on the Kamchatka Peninsula, yet no reproach attaches to his conduct or to his seamanship. That the men do not mourn him is of little concern to me for I know full well they are fearful of what next lies in store for us. I trust that this journal will one day fall into safe hands and that his selfless act of courage will be known to posterity.

As to the St. Peter, our vessel now lies broken some four fathoms deep yet a scant hundred paces from our place of refuge onshore. For myself, I know the despair that fills the heart of every mariner who has lost his command. I say this in no disrespect to the Captain-Commander, whose indisposition has forced upon my own self a heavy responsibility. I attribute no blame to myself for the loss of the St. Peter but feel only a great sadness that we shall not sail in glory into Petropavlovsk but must of necessity complete our journey overland.

To that end, I have resolved to seek out among the crew some that are not stricken with scurvy. I shall order them ahead to secure transport for our return. I am most concerned for the life of the Captain-Commander. It may be of little consolation, but I have named after him and in his honour the islands which lie directly offshore of our position.

This entry must conclude by acknowledging the sound counsel of Herr Steller, whose value to our cause has recently proved beyond estimation. Had we heeded his advice more promptly, many lives might have not been lost. Almost alone among us, he is in sound health and works without thought to his own welfare to provide for ours. In this endeavour he is most ably assisted by my son Laurentij, who gladdens this father's heart in a period of hardship and trial.

God knows I am weary of this and long to regain my beloved wife. I grieve for her in that she has no news of us these many months and I pray that we are soon reunited.

Commander Islands
November 12, 1741

He lay face down and motionless, his blue-cold fingers crooked into the shingle, his sea boots bobbing up and down in the gentle surf at his feet.

Suddenly, he coughed violently and vomited seawater, voiding his lungs. He gasped for breath, sucking in the cold air. He choked and vomited again, conscious now of the searing pain in his ribcage and the sting of salt water on his forehead and cheeks.

Summoning up the last of his strength, he pressed both palms down on the shingle and pushed himself half upright. He opened his eyes and looked around. Sand, shingle, driftwood. The effort proved too much for him. He slumped forward on his face again, pillowing his head against his forearms.

He lay there for some time until the water inched up around his waist. He felt his legs go numb and his testicles contract. Reaching out with both hands, he nudged himself up the slope of the beach, then rolled over onto his back.

There was no warmth in the sun. He drew his legs up and forced himself into a sitting position. He was looking out to sea now, watching the waves break over the reef. He looked to his right and saw nothing, only the seemingly unending stretch of foreshore. He turned his head to the right and saw nothing.

He was alive, but he was alone.

It was all coming back to him now. With a supreme effort of will, he hauled himself to his feet. He had to decide. Left or right? He chose left.

Tears streaming down his face, Fleetmaster Valery Khitrov tottered along the beach in search of what was left of the *St Peter* and its crew.

Bering Island in the Commander Islands
November 13, 1741

They gathered sad and silent on the foreshore, watching the waves wash unremittingly over the rump of the *St Peter*'s afterdeck which still angled above the surface, swept clean by the waters which drove across it from the open sea beyond. Broken spars floated off into the surrounding surf and barrels and biscuit tins bobbed tantalisingly close.

A head count had established that seven of the crew had gone down with the *St Peter*. Three men – one Cossack guard and two deckhands – had been thrown up half-dead on the shore. Among those who had perished was First Mate Hesselberg. Of Fleetmaster Khitrov there was no trace.

Mercifully, most of the sick had been brought ashore before the *St Peter* foundered. Some had not survived the short journey, others lay close to death, their gums suppurating, their joints inflamed and bloated.

Sven Waxell paced up and down the beach, his mind still tormented by the loss of the *St Peter*. He had ordered an inventory taken and, to his surprise, had established that sufficient provisions had already been brought ashore to sustain the remaining crew for two or even three weeks, providing they husbanded their meagre resources. Most weapons had been saved, together with a large quantity of musket shot. Some precious tools had also been salvaged. As soon as the sea settled, he decided, they would venture out in the longboat to recover what they could from the *St Peter* and the water that swirled around her. He could not risk using the longboat until the seas had calmed.

Waxell concluded that their situation was serious but far from hopeless. He needed to know how far the peninsula on which they were stranded jutted out from the main coastline. A dozen or so of the crew were still comparatively healthy, together with Steller, Laurentij and the surveyor, Plenister. Steller's Cossack guard, Lepekhin, had developed a high fever and was delirious.

Waxell had already resolved to assemble an advance party to move inland and make contact with the nearest settlement. It seemed logical to entrust this mission to Plenister and four others. Laurentij and the remainder of those who could still walk would stay with the main party where they were sorely needed to rig shelter and collect driftwood to build campfires. A small detail of no more than four men would be despatched inland to forage.

The driving rain had stopped, but it was bitterly cold. The men found shelter where they could, cowering against low outcrops of rock and stringing strips of sail from driftwood poles. Fires were lit and tea was brewed. Hollow-eyed and racked with pain, they peered out from their makeshift huts as Plenister and his party assembled their gear and left.

'God go with you,' shouted one man, but his words were lost on the wind.

Steller looked on as Waxell pushed himself to the limit, moving from one small group to the next to ensure they had followed his instructions to the letter. Steller knew what the First Officer seemingly did not, namely that Waxell himself was seriously ill. He listened as the First Officer's commands became progressively incoherent.

'You must rest, First Officer.'

'I must see to the men, Herr Steller.'

'You are of little value to them without rest,' countered Steller. He seized Waxell by the arm and, half-coaxing, half-bullying, forced the First Officer to seek shelter and sleep. He bedded Waxell down on a mound of blankets and furs. The First Officer continued to protest but gradually fell silent. He slept.

Steller turned his attentions to the Captain-Commander, who had been made as comfortable as possible under a sailcloth canopy.

He had no illusions: Bering was dying. Steller could only marvel at his resilience, at his refusal to give up. Bering's hands were a mass of sores, the fingernails an alarming blue-black. His eyes were sunk deep into his skull. His hair was falling out in great fistfuls, and his arm and knee joints were so inflamed they could not be bent. The stench that came from him was unbearable as he repeatedly soiled himself where he lay. He moaned intermittently and turned his head away each time he was offered food.

Steller clamped the Captain-Commander's head firmly against his body and forced a coarse gruel between his lips. Bering gagged. A watery slime dribbled from the corner of his mouth. His eyes flickered open and he groaned gently. Steller put an ear to his mouth.

'No more. *No more.*'

Steller ignored him and tried again to force the gruel into Bering's mouth. The Captain-Commander gritted such teeth as were left to him, stubbornly refusing to accept the viscous liquid. Steller reached inside the Captain-Commander's coat and took out the phial of laudanum, which he held to Bering's lips. Forcing Bering's mouth open, he poured a few drops onto the tongue. He cradled Bering in his arms until the Captain-Commander grew still.

Bering Island
November 14, 1741

Laurentij saw them first. He called out to Steller and pointed.

Six figures plodded along the shore, shrouded in a slate-grey morning mist. As they drew closer, Steller recognised Plenister and the advance party. His heart sank. They had left along the shore to the northwest, but they were returning from the northeast.

What Steller had long suspected had proved to be true.

Plenister threw down his musket and slumped into a crouch. The others sat or lay, exhausted.

'What news, Master Surveyor?' asked Steller, knowing only too well what the answer would be.

'This is not Kamchatka,' said Plenister. 'The Kamchatka Peninsula lies further to the west. This is an island. The mainland

lies to the west, I tell you, Christ knows how far. We saw no mainland shore.'

Steller looked at the sky. Snow clouds were gathering to the north
and east. He glanced along the foreshore, taking in the assortment
of hastily-improvised shelters. Inquisitive faces poked out from
several of them. What news had Plenister brought? God have mercy
on us, thought Steller.

Plenister said something that Steller did not catch. The surveyor
was pointing to one of his men.

'He is alive,' said Plenister again. 'We found him.'

Steller suddenly understood. Plenister had left with four companions. He had returned with five. The extra man, his head swathed
in a crude bandage, eased himself up gingerly onto one elbow and
grinned at them.

Fleetmaster Lieutenant Sophron Valery Khitrov had come back
from the dead.

Chapter Six

THE LAST WINTER

Bering Island
November 16, 1741

The wind gusted against the shore, shredding their flimsy shelters. Flurries of snow coated hair and beards, compacting them to ice. Campfires were doused and precious cooking pots scattered across the shingle.

This is the beginning of the end, thought Steller. We will not last out the winter.

Waxell's condition had neither improved nor deteriorated. Khitrov was still largely incapacitated by the injuries to his head and ribs. One junior officer was dead, the other ravaged by scurvy. Plenister had recovered from his ordeal but was weak and listless.

Bering was still dying.

Steller knew he had to act now, before it was too late.

He had no reason to expect that the men would rally to his command, but no other course was open to him.

'Assemble the able-bodied,' he said to Laurentij. 'Have them bring picks and shovels and anything that can break ground.'

They stood in a group – seven of them – while Steller issued his instructions. They knew instinctively that the burden of command had passed to this frail German whose eyes, unlike their own, still betrayed a manic intensity.

'You, you and you,' said Steller, pointing to three of the strongest. 'Collect the poles from the huts and gather as much driftwood as you can find. As many long branches as possible. You others come with me.'

He led them to an area far enough above the high-water line.

Steller thought back to what he had seen on Cape St Elias. He marked off a small rectangle some ten feet long by seven feet wide and instructed the men to dig down a full five feet. Their arms ached and they complained bitterly. More importantly, however, they stuck to their task. The soil was a mixture of earth, sand and shingle, hardened to an icy crust on top but still unexpectedly soft and loose underneath.

'Dig!' he commanded.

They dug.

It took more than two hours for the first shelter to be excavated. Steller ordered deep grooves to be chiselled into the longer sides of the rectangle. The three men detailed to collect driftwood had returned with a first batch. Steller hauled hut poles into place, settling them across the pit and anchoring them in the grooves. Strips of sailcloth were placed over the poles and coated with sand. Stones and smaller pieces of wood were carefully placed on top. Drifting snow would gradually cover this primitive roof and seal in some of whatever heat was left. After all, thought Steller, the Aleuts and other tribes live in snow huts.

Steller ordered Laurentij to scavenge for blankets and pelts to line the inner walls of the trench. A small opening was left on the island side to afford access. The worst of the sick men were carried up from the beach and lowered into the pit. Eight of them, laid out side by side, some conscious, others oblivious to their new surroundings.

'In all faith, Herr Steller,' said one of the work detail, 'this is a bonny grave we have dug.'

'Better that than leave them to the white foxes,' retorted Steller.

To his surprise, the men laughed.

Their unexpected good humour wilted when Steller chose another site and ordered them to dig a further pit. Then another. Six in all, to house the remaining officers and crew, and a seventh to serve as a rudimentary kitchen.

By noon next day, the pits had been dug and filled. Bering, Waxell and three others shared one pit, with between six and eight men housed in each of the others. When it was done, Steller sat wearily on a log and surveyed the scene.

The pits had been dug in a semi-circle and were no more than a couple of metres from one another. The 'kitchen' was located in the curve of the semi-circle and, when he eased himself down into it, Steller was delighted to find that the wind fell away almost completely.

He allocated one able-bodied man to each pit, detailing their responsibilities: to feed the men in their charge, to keep them as warm as possible, to tend as best they could to any injuries, and to remove and bury the dead as and when necessary. Meanwhile, Steller, Laurentij and the assistant surgeon were to man the kitchen, preparing food and ensuring a continuity of supplies.

He gave a firm instruction that snow was on no account to be eaten directly. The body used precious energy eating snow, he had concluded. Instead, it should be melted down and flavoured with herbs and grasses.

Steller knew it was essential to establish order and routine. He ordered Laurentij to relieve each man of whatever implements he had in his possession – awls, axes, knives, cups and bowls. The men were unwilling to part with these prized possessions but, eventually, these were collected and stored in the kitchen. The same went for any rations that had been jealously hoarded. The men were even more unwilling to contribute these but saw the sense of it and complied.

Survival was a communal effort.

They refused to hand over some of the weapons in their possession. This worried Steller but there was little he could do about it.

Devising and adhering to a daily routine proved easier than Steller had expected. Carefully-rationed food supplies were portioned out four times a day. The six men detailed to take charge of the shelters took it in turn to hunt for game and to deliver their booty to the central kitchen, where Steller and Laurentij worked round the clock to excise heart, kidneys, liver and lights.

The staple diet was a glutinous stew of seal or sea otter, its monotony leavened only by the occasional ptarmigan. Seal blubber was boiled down to make it more palatable and precious tallow extracted to make candles.

By the end of the first week, Steller saw that the men had settled into the new routine. Some were better off than others. The most ill had difficulty eating the food provided them and, invariably, vomited it up some hours later. Those who kept the solid food down fared much better. Steller saw, to his satisfaction, that some of the worst cases of scurvy were retreating.

The men were by no means healthy, but they were alive.

Steller continued to tend to the Captain-Commander. He did so more out of a sense of duty than out of conviction, fully aware that Bering's days were numbered. Of more practical concern was the need to keep Waxell alive and restore him to some semblance of health. Should Waxell fail to survive, command would in principle pass to Fleetmaster Khitrov, who was now recovering rapidly.

This was a prospect which Steller faced with the greatest trepidation. The men hated Khitrov and, irrationally or not, appeared to blame the Fleetmaster for much if not all that had happened to them. They felt that Khitrov had failed them by losing the *St Peter* and they recalled with increasing bitterness instances where Khitrov had mistreated them or contributed in some way or other to their plight. Oddly enough, the men placed no blame on the Captain-Commander, whom they continued to hold in unqualified respect and admiration. The question on everyone's lips as each new day dawned was how the Captain-Commander was faring. Was he still alive? Was he growing stronger? When would he come to see them?

Steller knew the answer to these and similar questions, but he knew also that Bering was some sort of talisman whose continued well-being was an essential component of morale. Accordingly, he answered each question as positively as he could. Yes, *of course* the Captain-Commander was still alive. Yes, he did appear to be getting stronger. Yes, he would be coming to see them any day now.

In some situations it was better to lie than surrender to the inevitability of truth.

Bering Island
November 22, 1741

The inchoate desire to cling to life diminishes over time as a strange lassitude sets in. The body slowly shuts down, the mind retreats into itself. Reactions become dulled and responses automatic as routine dilutes danger and physical discomfort is replaced by the gentle euphoria of passivity.

Steller detected the unmistakable symptoms of this euphoria and cast about for some means to counteract them. He identified a fundamental paradox. The majority of the crew were gradually recovering from the worst effects of scurvy. Some would die, that much was certain, but many would survive only if they overcame the inertia in which they had slowly acquiesced.

He knew that, while routine was essential to their longer-term survival, the men needed physical and emotional outlets if they were to survive the winter. He was relieved when some of them began to shake off their lethargy, at least to a degree. First one, then another ventured out during the day. They retrieved muskets and sabres from the kitchen-*cum*-armoury and set off in search of seals and sea otters which they proceeded to kill indiscriminately, slaughtering many hundreds more of these hapless creatures than could conceivably be needed for food.

Animal carcasses littered the area around the settlement, the meat stripped from their bones by the foxes which clustered around the camp, seemingly oblivious to the hunters in their midst.

Steller was revolted by the mindless slaughter but saw merit in it. Disgusted as he was by the sight of rotting carcasses and the scavenging foxes, he accepted that the frenzied killing provided a cruel but valuable focus. It gave the men something to do. Better that, he reasoned, than to hibernate their lives away or, worse still, vent their anger and frustration on each other.

He was surprised that the men appeared to have no interest in the pelts of the animals they had killed. These were discarded carelessly, strewn about the perimeter and left to rot.

Few emotions are stronger than outright cupidity. Steller resolved to build on this, pointing out repeatedly to anyone who would listen that they were neglecting an unprecedented opportunity. These pelts were more valuable than gold, he insisted, and should be cured carefully and stored.

Most of the men disregarded his advice at first – no doubt on the grounds that they did not expect to survive. Besides, of what real value to them could these sea otter pelts be? They were stranded on an island thousands of miles from home. As their bodies healed, however, and with the knowledge that survival was a distinct if remote possibility, some of the men started collecting pelts, conscientiously scraping them clean, washing them and hanging them out to cure on tall racks erected beyond the reach of the predatory foxes.

To Steller's relief, First Officer Waxell was gradually recovering his strength. His son Laurentij had tended to him religiously, hand-feeding his father at first, then encouraging him to fend for himself. Steller knew that Waxell in no way felt he had relinquished command. This was welcome news, since Steller had long since decided that his own authority would diminish over time.

As others took their share of kitchen duties, Steller had more time on his hands to compose his thoughts. He concluded that the men required nourishment of a different kind.

Most were distracted at best by the daily round of the hunt. In quieter moments – of which there were many – their thoughts often turned to the lives they had led and the prospect of death. Some prayed incessantly, asking for forgiveness and absolution.

This was Steller's territory and he resolved to do something about it.

As a German, Steller's own brand of faith was largely sculpted by what he liked to think of as 'Lutheran' objectivism. As a Pietist, on the other hand, Steller embraced the notion of 'world wisdom' and the desirability of keeping an open mind to other cultures and forms of religious observance.

To the best of Steller's knowledge, not only had the samples he had collected during the Expedition been lost but also the precious books he had zealously guarded among his possessions ever since leaving St Petersburg. He had nothing, not even a bible, with which he could console the men. Other than his own resilient faith.

He did his best, convening the men in small groups and speaking to them earnestly about life and death and the destiny of the human soul. To his astonishment, he found the teachings of the German mystic Meister Eckehart to be of the greatest relevance to their situation.

Day after day, Steller struggled manfully to help them understand what this disciple of St Augustine had preached in his *Book of Divine Consolation*. He explained as far as he could in layman terms how the spiritual union between Man and God passed through four stages – dissimilarity, similarity, identity and detachment. At the outset, said Steller, God is all; at the ultimate stage, the stage of detachment or *Gelassenheit*, the soul is above God.

To those still willing to listen, Steller expounded Meister Eckehart's then revolutionary concept, that Man must abandon all things, even God, if he is to pass beyond God, effectively to another plane. The fires of Hell would burn away all earthly attachments and the devils would emerge as angels.

He was careful not to point out that, in spite of a beautifully reasoned defence, Meister Eckehart was branded a heretic by Pope John XII in 1329. 'I may err,' Eckehart had written then, 'but I am not a heretic. The first error is that of the mind, the second that of the will.'

The men listened dutifully. Some understood, most did not. Gradually, they drifted away. They had better things to do with their time.

Uncertain whether he could hear or not, Steller spent hours sitting beside Bering, holding the Captain-Commander's hand and speaking softly to him of faith and Man's immortal soul. Late one evening, Bering stirred and opened his eyes.

He spoke faintly but clearly.

'I am no Eckehart. My errors are of the mind, not of the will.'

It saddened Steller to think he would never understand the last words he ever heard Bering utter.

Bering Island
December 4, 1741
'You stinking horse's turd,' shouted the Cossack, whipping a blade from his tunic and striking it deep into the belly of the man kneeling across from him. The man's eyes opened wide in surprise as he looked down and saw the rivulet of blood tinge the edges of the knife.

The Cossack leaned forward, grasping the wounded man behind the neck and pulling him forward, forcing the knife even deeper. He jerked it upwards and turned it sharply before wrenching it free. Blood oozed from the wound, spreading over the other man's lice-infested tunic, then congealing swiftly in the cold air.

The wounded man clasped his stomach. He tried to protest, but no words came. Slowly, he toppled forward onto his face, his back-side sticking up in the air. He died within seconds.

The Cossack carefully wiped the blade clean on the man's tunic and returned the knife to its sheath. He reached out and retrieved a pile of sea otter skins which lay beside the dead man, dragging them across to his own side of the pit and adding them to the growing stack behind him.

'He was cheating,' announced the Cossack.

The other players gave no indication whether they agreed or not. In any case, it was too late.

The rudimentary playing cards were cut from thin slabs of wood, their face values burned into them with a hot iron. There were seventy-eight cards in the deck, fifty-six of them numerals and twenty-two others – *tarots* – identified by the traditional features of hearts, bells, leaves and acorns. Every effort had been made to cut each wooden card to identical size and to etch the numerals and suits with care, but regular usage had stained the deck to such a degree that the more watchful players among the crew could identify virtually each and every card by the markings on the reverse.

The Cossack looked around at the others. The game was a bastardised version of *écart*, the aim being to discard in sets of three or more cards of the same value or lay down a 'street' of cards of different values running in sequence. The first player to lay down all his cards would win.

He fanned through the dead man's discards until he found the offending sequence. Instead of a street running four-five-six, the man had laid down four-four-six. An illegal play.

The others muttered their approval. The Cossack was right. Whether the man had actually cheated or had simply misread the values marked on the offending card was a moot point. They remembered the knife nestling inside the Cossack's tunic and said nothing.

This was the second man the Cossack had killed that week.

Money had no meaning here. In any case, they had long since gambled away the small amount of roubles in their possession, losing most of them to none other than the Cossack. Sea otter pelts, on the other hand, were now the currency of choice. For some, collecting pelts was simply a means to an immediate end – securing access to The Game itself, the only real distraction available to them. For others, who still clung to the forlorn hope they would one day make their escape from the island, accumulating the prized pelts was an all-consuming passion.

One day, they told themselves, these skins will make us rich.

Waxell knew that the gambling fever which infected the camp was a cancer that would ultimately eat away whatever remained of the healthy tissue of comradeship and shared hardship. He had cast about for some effective way to stamp it out or, at worst, mitigate its effects. The chain of command was fragile now, however, and he feared his authority over the men would be lost if he outlawed this simple yet dangerous pastime.

When he learned that yet another man had been killed – the second that week and the fourth in all – he understood that it was time to act. There were options open to him, the most obvious being to clap the Cossack in chains and convene a formal court martial. It was an option he was not anxious to take. That would set a precedent that could drive a wedge between the crew and himself.

Much to Steller's surprise, Waxell sought him out and asked his advice.

The timing was unfortunate.

Steller and Assistant Surgeon Betge were in the process of amputating the gangrene-ravaged leg of Able Seaman Khristov. The procedure was simple. Snow was packed tightly around the offending limb until it was completely numb. The surgeon's saw was heated over a flame and wiped clean with rubbing alcohol. A wooden gag was clamped across the patient's mouth and two of his comrades held him down.

Betge worked as quickly as possible, whipping the saw to and fro across the bone, severing it just below the knee. This was the fifth amputation he had performed since they landed on Bering Island.

Waxell bent down and poked his head into the dark kitchen which temporarily doubled as an operating theatre. He was just in time to hear a dull thud as the lower part of Khristov's leg separated and dropped off the table. He turned his head away as Steller tied off the arteries with fish gut and Betge retrieved a white-hot cauterising iron fashioned from a soup ladle that had been beaten flat. He heard the hiss as the iron was applied to the jagged wound and smelt the nauseating stench of burnt flesh.

For Able Seaman Khristov, the real pain would come later. Like his predecessors on the table, he had fainted early on in the proceedings. He would awake to find himself bandaged with strips of linen torn from a filthy shirt and bound with cord.

'How is he?' asked Waxell. 'Will he survive?'

'A week, perhaps a little longer,' answered Steller, climbing out of the kitchen pit and filling his lungs with great draughts of fresh air. Steller's tunic was flecked with dark blood and glistening fragments of bone. He looked at Waxell and shrugged his shoulders.

'I am no surgeon and I regret to say that young Betge has even less knowledge of the craft than myself. The leg should have been severed much higher up, well above the knee. But then we would have lost the patient at once.'

Waxell nodded. Another man lost, he thought to himself.

'I must ask something of you, Herr Steller.'

'Ask.'

'How many more men must die on this God-forsaken island?'

Steller wiped his hand across his face.

'You know full well, First Officer, that I have no ready answer. The men eat well now and the scurvy has in the main been arrested. In some cases, sadly, it progressed beyond medication. More will die, of that I'm certain, but as to how many –.'

'And what of the Captain-Commander?'

'By rights, the Captain-Commander should have died many weeks ago. His scurvy has abated but other – greater – pains remain. I can do no more for him. His legs and crotch are ulcerated and he passes dark fluids from his anus.'

'Can he resume command?'

Steller was silent for a moment.

'No.'

'How long?'

'How long will the Captain-Commander live? That is difficult to say. A day, a week. Less than a month, most certainly. He remains alive only by a supreme effort of will.'

Waxell paced up and down.

'Then I am in command?'

'As you have been these many months, First Officer.'

Waxell waited for Steller to say more, to volunteer advice. To *ask* advice of a civilian went against the grain.

'Herr Steller, I must ask your advice,' said Waxell finally. 'In my position, what would you do?'

'Do?'

Steller was a compassionate man yet not above pettiness. Ever since the start of the voyage, he had offered advice only to have it rejected out of hand. His recommendations had consistently fallen on deaf ears. Even Waxell, courteous as he generally had been, had disregarded Steller's counsel – especially regarding the crew's health.

Although he was ashamed of it, Steller could not help savouring this moment.

'Yes, dammit, what would you do in my position?'

'As I see it, First Officer, we shall all perish if we remain here. Most will survive the winter, but what then? Another short summer and another winter of pain and suffering?'

'The men have given up, Herr Steller.'

'No, First Officer. It is *you* who have given up.'

The remark caused offence, precisely as Steller had intended.

'I? I have given up, you say? How dare you, sir!'

'By your leave, how can I say otherwise? You are *in* command but you have not *taken* command. I am poorly versed in such matters, but I believe it is your duty to exercise your authority. To exercise that authority before it is too late.'

Waxell thought back to the Cossack. To the perceptible disintegration of the chain of command. To the general lassitude that pervaded the camp. To the winter ahead.

'And exactly *how* would you advise me to exercise that authority?'

'You must build another vessel,' said Steller smoothly.

Waxell stood and stared. With a snort of derision he turned on his heel and walked away.

The man is a fool, he muttered to himself. A naïve *civilian* fool.

Bering Island
December 19, 1741

Captain-Commander Vitus Jonassen Bering lay alone and in semi-darkness, his head resting against the wall of the pit, his decimated body contorted in agony. The last of the laudanum had been administered during the night.

He was unaware that anyone had entered the shelter until First Officer Waxell spoke the words Bering had waited so long to hear.

'Captain-Commander Bering, with respect, sir, I formally relieve you of your command.'

Bering opened his eyes. He could perceive only the silhouette of the First Officer standing between him and the faint pre-dawn light from above. His tongue was swollen in his mouth. He swallowed and made a supreme effort to enunciate clearly.

'My respects, First Officer Waxell. I commend you. You have done your duty well.'

Bering's eyes closed.

There was nothing more to be said.

Waxell saluted. He left without a backward glance.

Bering gave thanks to God that his reason and powers of speech had not failed him as his body had. How would posterity judge him? He had done his best in an impossible situation, but had he been too cautious? Too lenient? Had he served his men well? Had they respected him? Understood him? Even loved him?

Questions. Questions he had asked himself time and again. He had found no answers.

He thought of Osa, conjuring up her image one last time.

He turned his face against the pit wall and died.

There were six in the burial detail. Sven and Laurentij Waxell, Steller, Khitrov, Plenister and Assistant Surgeon Betge acted as pall-bearers. Every man who could walk attended the short service held beside the shallow grave carved out of the gentle slope above the foreshore.

Steller and Betge had stripped off his soiled clothing and washed him as best they could. They wrapped him in layers of sailcloth and set his cap upon his chest, together with his sabre and a small Danish flag they had found in his sea trunk. Thick wooden planks were laid on top of the body and a layer of stones piled on them to keep scavengers at bay.

A simple driftwood cross had been carved with the inscription:

CAPTAIN-COMMANDER VITUS J. BERING
b. Horsens, Denmark 1680 ~ d. Bering Island, December 19, 1741
Requiescat in pace

Acting Captain Sven Waxell's voice broke as he delivered a short funeral oration.

'He was our Captain-Commander in good times and in bad. A righteous and God-fearing man, slow to anger, temperate in judgment and loyal to his rank and mission. Those who would judge him harshly do so in ignorance and self-interest. We who have known him bear him every respect.'

As the earth was quickly shovelled over the grave, Waxell looked round at the assembled crew. This was the first time he had seen them all together since the day they had stood on the foreshore watching the sad remnants of the *St Peter* founder on the rocks in the bay.

It was too good an opportunity to miss.

'We pay our respects this day to a master mariner and to a man of courage, vision, and great tolerance and perseverance. We would do him the gravest injustice of all if we do not complete the mission that was placed in his trust. Let us then say a brief farewell and be about our duties.'

Waxell looked across the grave at Steller.

'We have work to do. I tire of this land and long for home.'

Bering Island
December 25, 1741

The death of the Captain-Commander had acted as a catalyst for change. The gambling continued, but no further deaths were reported as a consequence of it.

There were grounds for optimism now. One detail routinely foraged for sea otter and seal, another drove further and further inland in search of firewood. A third detail, among them several amputees, assumed responsibility for general maintenance and the preparation of food.

At Waxell's orders, the accumulated pelts were cured and stored at a central point, on the strict understanding that they would be taken back for sale in Kamchatka in the spring and the proceeds divided equally among officers and men. If they would ever reach Kamchatka – and by what means – rarely came up for discussion.

Steller had ample time to spend days in the field, observing and recording the habits of the animal life, less plentiful now, but still abundant. His preoccupation with the flora and fauna of the region was matched by his growing interest in the behaviour of the men, both individually and collectively. It was he who suggested to Waxell that they institute a regular working roster, with rest days on Sundays, hours set aside for physical exercise, and strict observance of holy days and other festive occasions.

Steller noted that, while the chain of command was still respected, there was a new sense of sharing and cooperation. Even the surliest members of the crew had come to recognise that it was in everybody's interest to sustain morale and build some semblance of *esprit de corps*.

As ever, there was one notable exception to the general rule: Fleetmaster Valery Khitrov remained his usual uncooperative self, his surly attitude compounded no doubt by the low esteem in which he was held.

Christmas Day 1741 had been earmarked for special celebration. Preparations began several days in advance. The cooking detail made a special effort to present their standard fare in the best possible light. Additional tallow candles were moulded. Those who could sing prepared a medley of songs to reflect the diverse national and regional origins of the crew. Waxell wrote a speech calling for peace on earth and goodwill towards all men. He read the first version through, found it unbearably pompous, tore it up and started again.

With the utmost reluctance, the First Officer agreed that four of the crew be allowed to launch the longboat and row out at low tide and through broken ice to the remains of the *St Peter*. They returned triumphantly with three barrels that had somehow remained intact. To their disappointment, two contained only foul-smelling water. The third, the smallest of the three, contained vodka.

The crew were elated. Today *would* be a day to remember.

For Georg Wilhelm Steller, it certainly was.

Just before noon, Steller and Laurentij Waxell had busied themselves in the kitchen, attempting without any great success to prepare an enormous pudding of flour, ptarmigan eggs and handfuls of salmonberries they had secreted underneath the snow for just such an occasion. Steller looked on as Laurentij spat out a stream of tobacco juice, drank a mouthful of water and dipped a spoon to taste the unappetising-looking concoction.

'I didn't know you chewed tobacco, Laurentij.'

Laurentij blushed.

'I don't, Herr Steller. I hate the taste.'

'But –,' said Steller, gesturing to the dark brown wad that stained the snow at their feet.

'Tree bark,' said Laurentij. 'I chew it all the time. But, please, Herr Steller, don't tell the others.'

Steller laughed out loud. After all this time, he had at last discovered why young Waxell had remained so resiliently healthy when everyone around him had succumbed to scurvy.

'May I have a specimen for my collection?' asked Steller.

'Of course,' said Laurentij, still blushing. 'You won't say anything, will you? Please?'

'No, of course not,' answered Steller, inwardly regretting that he had uncovered Laurentij's secret so late in the day.

The discovery was the first of two Steller was to make that day. All his life, Steller had avoided alcohol. He had observed its effect on others and vowed he would never touch the demon drink. Paradoxically, if the longboat had recovered *more* vodka, he would have kept that vow. Unfortunately, the crew had quickly grasped the fact that the small keg would not last long unless it was adulterated. They brewed a quantity of tea and allowed it to cool before adding the alcohol to it, storing the mixture in one of the large water barrels that had been scrupulously scrubbed out for that purpose.

And so it came to pass that Georg Wilhelm Steller drank alcohol for the first time in his life. He immediately felt lightheaded but strangely happy as they ladled out cup after cup of the mixture.

'How is this flavoured?' he asked.

'With potato,' came the explanation.

'Whatever it is, it is quite delicious,' said Steller, treating himself to another cupful. The men around him laughed. The German was certainly enjoying himself. He deserved to. After all, if it hadn't been for him . . .

As the afternoon wore on and the light started to fail, the tallow candles were lit. There was singing, some robust dancing and a bout of joke-telling, each story more ribald and coarse than its predecessor. Steller was puzzled to find that he was unoffended by the vulgar humour. It was vulgar, certainly, but not without wit, he decided.

Valery Khitrov decided otherwise. He stood up suddenly, brandishing his wooden cup. The man was clearly drunk.

'You laugh now, fools. But you will laugh out of the other side of your miserable faces before this winter is over.'

The excited conversation dried. All eyes were on Khitrov. He had their attention at last.

'And as you go to meet your Maker, remember why we are shipwrecked in this armpit of an island. A toast, then, to the man who left us stranded here. I give you Captain-Commander Bering, God rot his soul.'

There was a shocked silence.

Steller rose from his place on unsteady legs and walked over to where Khitrov was standing. He had never before experienced such blind rage. His tiny fist drew back and swung in a wide arc, connecting with Khitrov's nose. There was a crunch as bone and cartilage shattered. Khitrov reeled back, struggling to find purchase on the soft snow. His arms flailed wildly as he fought to keep his balance. He fell heavily on his back and lay there, his nose pulped beyond recognition.

Steller came out of his trance as loud spontaneous applause broke out. The men were all around him now, pumping his hand and pounding him on the back. Khitrov lay where he had fallen, blood gushing from his nose and mouth. He had had enough.

Steller accepted the congratulations, dazed by what he had just done. He had betrayed his better nature. He had struck a fellow human being.

And, by Christ, it felt good.

Bering Island
February 1, 1742

It is often said that miracles, like beauty, are in the eye of the beholder.

A hefty storm lashed the encampment that night and the men cowered in their shelters. They knew that, if the storm persisted, no details would be sent out the next day. As day dawned, however, they saw that the storm had run its course. The sky was clear and the wind had dropped.

Slowly and wearily, the men crawled into the daylight. They looked out towards a calm sea and the sight of the *St Peter* beached on the foreshore, driven off the rocks by the storm and an unusually high tide. The vessel was a sorry sight, its timbers buckled and its masts hanging loose, but the men cheered wildly. The *St Peter* had been their home. Now, it might be the instrument of their homecoming.

The driftwood detail was excused from duty that day and ordered to make the *St Peter* fast on the beach. First expectations were soon dashed. The vessel was beyond repair.

'But not beyond use,' said Waxell cheerily, turning to Steller. 'You shall have your new vessel after all, Herr Steller.'

'God willing, First Officer.'

Bering Island
February 1742

From the journal of Acting Captain-Commander Sven Waxell

February 4, 1742

Our most devout prayers have been answered by the elements. A bountiful Providence has delivered the St. Peter into our hands these three days ago. We give thanks that the vessel lies securely on the beach below our shelter. I report to my great sadness that she is beyond all repair, but her salvation may yet prove the salvation of us all.

I have ordered the St. Peter stripped of all that is useful and undamaged – timbers, ropes, sailcloth, materials, implements and stores. Much harm has been done to a once proud vessel, but she holds items of great value if we are to ready a new craft and sail her to Kamchatka.

I have commanded scouts to reconnoitre the coast to seek out a more suitable place from which to launch my new command.

The men rejoice at the prospect of home and I rejoice with them. Yet much is still to be done and I fear it will be many weeks ere we commence rebuilding. The St. Peter's timbers are staved in and her iron rusted. We will salvage what we can and pray that it is sufficient to build a new vessel that is truly seaworthy.

My own experience in Okhotsk and that of some of the crew benefits our enterprise greatly. I take consolation that we have readied a vessel for sea before, albeit with great difficulty and after many setbacks. Our most precious asset in this important undertaking is none other than Laurentij, whose fascination with all things nautical has now borne fruit. He recalls with great precision – and who am I to gainsay his memory? – how vessels are best proportioned and rigged. He sits each day by my side and draws with bold strokes the lines and tolerances we must respect.

My great fear is that the men accept all too readily our imminent release from the bondage of the island. I know, however, that Kamchatka lies to our west. How far we must sail and in what weather and seas, I cannot say. As to this, I report with no little satisfaction that our scouts have found vestiges of other craft washed ashore a few bays distant from where we camp. This fills me with hope that Kamchatka lies close at hand and that our voyage, once undertaken, will be short.

I estimate that the St. Peter will be shorn of its fittings by no later than the early spring. The weather continues inclement and the days are short. The men work willingly but the elements which so generously yielded up the St. Peter now conspire against us.

Bering Island
August 9, 1742

One by one the restraining chocks were knocked away. Willing hands seized the ropes, taking up the slack. They heaved until the ropes grew taut and the blubber-greased pulleys squeaked and groaned in protest. Wood screeched on wood as the hull slowly came alive. The *St Peter* shuddered into motion, inching off its platform and angling down the shallow incline of the fragile wooden slipway.

A high tide lapped the lower sections of the ramp, caressing the vessel's narrow beam as it dipped tentatively into the waters of the bay. The men heaved again, muscles screaming, hands chafed and bleeding. And again and again, until the *St Peter* was coaxed the final few feet. The launch ropes slackened as the vessel embraced the water and floated off.

They held their breath, watching the *St Peter* wallow ungainly and complacent on the light swell.

Acting Captain-Commander Sven Waxell clapped his son on the back.

'By all that's holy, she's an ugly bitch.'

'Aye, she's that all right,' said Laurentij Waxell. 'But she's *our* ugly bitch. And I, for one, love her dearly.'

Bering Island
August 13, 1742

The masts had been set and the rigging secured. Crew and stores were boarded, prayers said, and the anchor weighed.

The patchwork sails unfurled and caught the wind. The crew stood shoulder-to-shoulder on the cramped deck as the new *St Peter* crept out to sea in calm weather and on a favourable breeze, tracking parallel to the coast of the island they had come to know only too well. They waved an excited farewell to familiar landmarks – the narrow indents of Sea Otter Creek and Whale Creek, the looming presence of Mount Steller, the crenellated cliffs of Southeast Point. They fell silent as the land receded and the rebuilt *St Peter* set an uncertain course for Awatska Bay.

On the island shore, Arctic foxes swarmed over the abandoned camp, snapping and snarling as they scavenged for scraps.

A lone male, larger than the rest, scratched and scrabbled at the base of the wooden cross that marked the final resting place of Captain-Commander Vitus Jonassen Bering.

EPILOGUE

The new *St Peter*, with a complement of forty-six officers and crew, reached Kamchatka safely and anchored in the port of Petropavlovsk on the evening on August 27, 1742. They had been declared missing and presumed dead eight months before. Their safe return and the memory of the thirty-two men who died during the final voyage are commemorated by a silver plaque in the church of Petropavlovsk.

Martin Petrovich Spanberg returned to St Petersburg and Osa Bering. Vessels under Captain Spanberg's command were the first to sail from Kamchatka to the northeastern ports of Japan in 1738.

Lieutenant Sven Waxell was promoted to Captain First Rank. He died in 1762.

Laurentij Waxell followed in his father's footsteps. His proposal of marriage to Benthe Bering was rejected in 1744.
Aleksey Chirikov retired to St Petersburg in 1743 with the rank of Captain-Commander and was popularly hailed as the discoverer of Alaska.

Lieutenant Sophron Valery Khitrov remained in service. He was eventually promoted to the rank of Admiral in 1753.

Imperial Grand Council members Ernst Johann Reichsgraf von Biron, Andrey Ivanovich Graf Ostermann and Burkhard Christoph Graf von Münnich were exiled at various times to Siberia. Von Biron was granted amnesty in 1762 and returned from exile to the Russian Court where, in 1763, Catherine the Great ordered him restored to the ducal throne of Courtland in Latvia. He died three years later. Ostermann quarrelled with von Münnich and was banished to Siberia, where he died in 1747. Von Münnich was exiled by the Empress Elizabeth but granted leave to return to St Petersburg in 1762. Until his death in 1767, he served as director-general of the Baltic ports under Catherine the Great.

Grigor Pisarov was stabbed to death in a St Petersburg brothel in 1752.

The Empress Elizabeth died in 1761. Her reign saw consolidation of Russian interests in the Ukraine and her coalition with Austria, France, Sweden and Saxony against Prussia, England and the House of Hanover sparked Russian involvement in the Seven Years' War. She is better remembered, however, as the 'frivolous Empress', whose wardrobe reputedly ran to 15,000 dresses. Her legendary and androgynous beauty was offset by her spendthrift ways and her predilection for cross-dressing.

Professor Stepan Krasheninnikov published his *Description of Kamchatka Land* in 1755, the year of his death. His work appears to rely heavily on observations and findings recorded by Georg Wilhelm Steller.

The crew of the *St Peter* are said to have gifted Steller over 300 prime sea otter pelts in recognition of his role in saving their lives on Bering Island. The subsequent sale of these made Steller a comparatively rich man. Steller's *Tagebuch einer Reise mit Bering* (*Journal of a Voyage with Bering*) chronicles his involvement in the final two years of the Imperial Great Northern Expedition, and his posthumously-published works *De bestiis marinis* (*On Marine Beasts*, 1751) and *Beschreibung von dem Lande Kamchatka* (*Description of Kamchatka*, 1781) are widely acknowledged as benchmark contributions to natural history. His name is most famously appended to Steller's Jay; Steller's Sea Eagle; and to *hydrodamalis gigas*, Steller's Sea Cow, a large aquatic animal, now long extinct, of the order *sirenia* (which includes the manatee and the dugong). Steller's conclusions on scurvy anticipated those of the celebrated English naval surgeon James Lind, whose *Treatise of the*

Scurvy was published in 1753. It was not until 1795 that the British Admiralty put Lind's antiscorbutic prescriptions into practice. Steller died prematurely in St Petersburg in 1746.

In 1778, the English sea-captain James Cook sailed from Petropavlovsk north through the Bering Strait to Icy Cape in Alaska and North Cape, now Cape Schmidt, in Siberia.

Vitus Bering's grandson joined the Northeastern Secret Geographical and Astronomical Expedition of 1785 to 1793 which explored northeastern Russia and the northwestern American coast. The first to be credited with navigating the Northeast Passage ocean route connecting the Arctic and Pacific Ocean, however, was the Swedish navigator Nils Adolf Erik Nordenskjöld, who achieved this feat during a voyage in 1878 and 1879.

In 1991, 250 years after Bering's death, a Danish-Russian expedition visited the Commander Islands to ascertain where the crew of the *St Peter* had overwintered. On Bering Island, they exhumed a body presumed to have been that of the Captain-Commander. The crude 'coffin' contained only a skeleton; no objects of any kind were found along with the body. Forensic examination in Petropavlovsk suggested that Bering – if it was indeed he – had died from peritonitis. The skeleton was returned to Bering island and reburied there in 1992. The wooden cross that marked the grave has been replaced by a metal one.

Russia held effective sovereignty over Alaska until 1867, when the territory was sold for the sum of US$7,200,000 to the United States of America under the terms of the Alaskan Purchase negotiated by US Secretary of State William H. Seward. Alaska was admitted as the 49th State of the Union on January 3, 1959.

The Imperial Great Northern Expedition of 1733 to 1742 has gone down in history as one of the most ambitious and most significant voyages of scientific discovery in the history of the world.

Ah-loo-shin-ah is a corruption of the Aleut Eskimo word for 'the land that is not an island': Alaska.

APOLOGIA AND ACKNOWLEDGEMENTS

As a work of 'faction' rather than a contribution to academic research, the present narrative unashamedly arrogates every licence which attaches to that genre.

Although the novel is anchored in historical fact and, one dares to hope, intelligent speculation, it makes free with dates, places, persons and events. Where it seemed appropriate (or convenient), the exact sequence of events has been adapted. Some of the *dramatis personae* have doubtless been shortchanged, not least the oft-maligned Ernst Johann Reichsgraf von Biron, whose reputation has recently been revised in a more positive light. The land route followed by the Imperial Great Northern Expedition has been altered, some might say arbitrarily. The diaries of Lieutenant-at-Sea Sven Waxell are a construct; the machinations attributed to the fictional Imperial Grand Council are perhaps overstated; and, not least, the role of Georg Wilhelm Steller as saviour of the expedition has been inflated to a degree which is perhaps unwarranted but arguably commensurate with his own high opinion of himself.

Anna Christina (Osa) Bering's record of the overland journey to Siberia is a figment of the author's imagination, as are indeed the romantic interludes *en route* between her and Martin Spanberg, the baser motives attributed on occasion to Aleksey Chirikov, and the overtly hostile comportment of indigenous populations.

For these and other shortcomings of an academic nature the author offers only token apology, trusting instead that the immense undertaking that was the Imperial Great Northern Expedition is, at worst, hinted at by this narrative.

The original impetus for this account was given several years ago by a colleague and friend of long standing, Noel Fox, who commissioned an outline treatment with a view to chronicling on film Bering's role in the 'discovery' of Alaska. The outline notes he made available back then were invaluable as a point of departure. Steller's *Tagebuch einer Reise mit Bering 1741–1742* was a valuable background source for the later phases of the expedition.

Over a period of years, by far the most substantive contribution came from the authoritative pages of the historical writer's most-prized source, *The New Encyclopaedia Britannica*, and from the astonishing wealth of information mined from what promises to be the richest lode of all, the Internet. Much of the latter material was demonstrably inaccurate or riddled with inconsistencies; without it, however, this novel would never have been completed.

It is invidious to single out specific sources, but mention must be made here of data available from the Flensburgs Enkebolig Historical Museum in Horsens, Denmark; the historical research assembled by Stephen K. Batalden in his *Siberia and the Far East*; sections on Siberia in the *Catholic Encyclopaedia*; the index to Sutherland's 1717 *Treatise on Nautical Terms*; the East India Company *Journals of Captain William Keeling and Master Thomas Bonner*; Bond's *Plain and Easie Rule to Rigge any Ship*, published in 1664; *the Red Book of the Peoples of the Russian Empire*; the introduction to *Journey to Other Worlds* co-written by Bonnie W. Styles and Terence J. Martin of the Illinois State Museum; James Lind's 1753 *Treatise of the Scurvy*; the *Duties of Officers and Men* and *The Sea-Man's Vademecum*, drawn from the Maritime History Virtual Archives and updated by Lars Bruzelius; James Love's *The Mariner's Jewel* of 1733; Albert Hastings Markham's *Arctic Exploration* published in 1992; an unattributed article on *World Exploration and Geography* in the World Almanac and Book of Facts 2000; and Leonid Sverdlov's *Russian Naval Officers and Geographic Exploration in Northern Russia*, published in the November 1996 issue of the journal *Arctic Voice*.

Bering: The Russian Discovery of America, an impeccable piece of scholarship authored by Professor Orcutt Frost, was published only in November 2003; had it been available earlier, the present author's own task would have been considerably easier.

That these and a multitude of other sources often proved contradictory is of little consequence by comparison with the inspiration they provided.

I wish to express my gratitude to several persons without whose encouragement and input this faction would not have been written. To the aforesaid Noel Fox, for his initiative; to Alan Hope, who advised me on a first treatment for the screen; to my friend Harald Hotze, who never failed to counsel and encourage; to Maire O'Reilly, whose loyalty to the cause was unstinting; and, not least, to Graham Booth and Tony Glover, who badgered and browbeat me over the years into completing the manuscript.

Sincerest thanks must also go to my publisher Hugh Andrew at Birlinn/Polygon and to his staff, particularly Neville Moir; and to Nicky Wood, who dotted so many 'i's and crossed so many 't's. Lastly, I thank Sheila Taylor, a constant and loyal partner and friend whose support and patience were often tried but never found wanting.

Eddie Crockett
La Roche-Bernard
France
July 2004